Ivy in Stills

Ivy in Stills

a novel

Ka Hancock

This book is a work of fiction. Names, characters, places and incidents either are products of the author's imagination or are used fictitiously. Any resemblance to actual events, specific locales or persons, living or dead is entirely coincidental.

Copyright © 2024 by Ka Hancock

All rights reserved. No part of this book may be reproduced or transmitted in any form or by any means without written permission from the author.

Manufactured in the United States of America

kahancock.com

ISBN 979-8-3507-1667-2

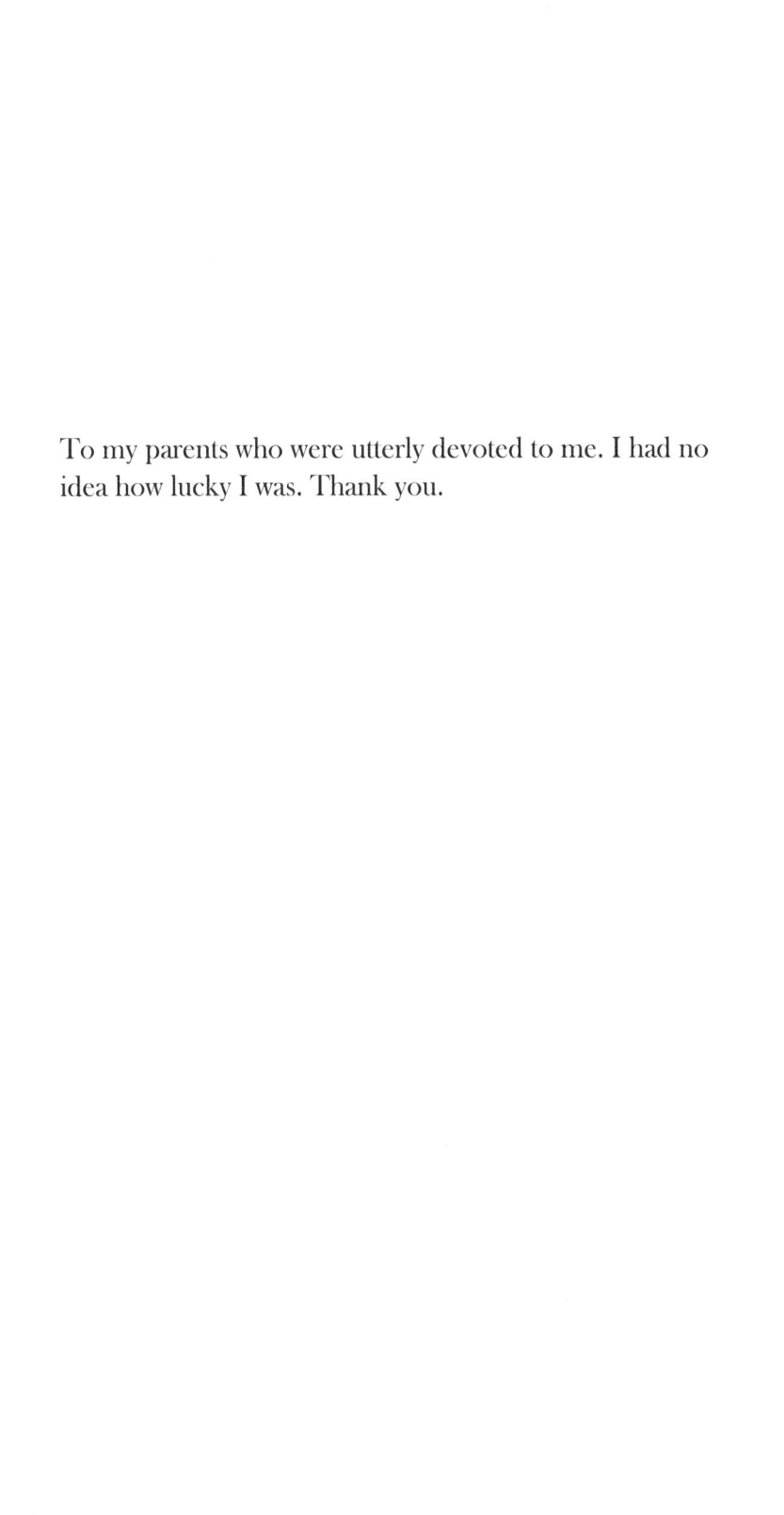

To my parents who were utterly devoted to me. I had no idea how lucky I was. Thank you.

One—Mia

Lullaby warned me that he'd be late, and he was. Lawyers. So, I asked for another Pepsi and watched the lunch crowd at Mo's dwindle. Then I pulled my camera from my backpack and busied myself scanning the digital images I'd taken last night at the cemetery. They were for a project I was working on. My uncle Giff died in Vietnam, and I'd wanted some pictures of his headstone. Colonel Gifford Leland Sutton had been my father's only brother—and Dad had been a sport when I'd asked him to come along. He'd even brought the flowers.

Some of my pictures were completely stellar, if I did say so myself—just Dad's long, Levi-clad legs, a fifty-year-old granite marker in the foreground sporting a tattered flag, and gerbera daisies hanging from my father's old veined hand—all captured in black and white, of course. I was pleased with almost all of them. Those that didn't make the cut, I deleted from my SIM card.

As I was admiring my work, a raised voice outside the window—the streaked window—next to me, caught my attention. It was a woman, agitated, pacing up and down the sidewalk and dragging a little boy in her wake. She was wearing heels, a full skirt and she was arguing loudly with someone on her cell phone. What fascinated me was the child at her side, who had a fist full of that skirt in his hand. He was a tad grubby compared to the woman. There was a story there, and I couldn't help it; I pulled the blinds up just high enough to get the shot. Then I focused my lens, zoomed, and clicked off what I knew would eventually pare down to just that little hand grasping that wad of skirt. What did it mean? Don't leave me? Stop yelling? Please don't fight with Dad again? It didn't really matter, I guess. Whatever it was made for a great photo, especially from behind dirty glass.

When she finally hung up, she was crying, and thankfully she bent down and picked up the little boy. He was still clinging to her skirt and brought it with him up to her shoulder, so for a moment before she walked away, she was skirt-tugging and child-hugging and defeat-weeping in equal measure. *That* might have been the money shot...but taking it, without her permission, suddenly felt exploitive, so I didn't. A little hand buried in his mom's dress was one thing. Capturing someone at their worst moment without their knowledge was something else entirely. I watched her, neck craned, as she turned the corner. Then I stowed my camera.

When the waitress asked me if I wanted a refill, I realized another twenty minutes had passed, and I started to get annoyed. I ordered a grilled cheese and large fries—to go. As I waited and thought about the rest of my afternoon, my phone pinged. It took me a minute to find it in the massive bag in which I haul around my life. If it was him canceling, I was going to scream.

But it wasn't the attorney. It was a text from Sophie.

My three best friends were backpacking across Europe this summer, and I was living vicariously through them—and their cruel texts and even crueler pictures. Today they were at the Roman Coliseum. 'Wish you were here,' Soph texted.

'Beware of adorable Roma kids! One robbed my dad blind, exactly where you're standing,' I texted back.

I'd wanted desperately to go with them, but I was stuck in Monterey completing my final semester in advanced photography before I graduated in August. So, Bryn, Sophie, and Liz left me, ever so rudely, and were off experiencing cheap food, intercontinental men, and hostel life while I responsibly wrapped up my degree, missed and obsessed about one Derek Lehman, and housesat with my brother, Bo. By the end of the summer, we'd all have stories to tell, and I was absolutely certain mine would win. My girls would have their exploits through the canals of Venice, the streets of Madrid, the halls of Versailles. But I'd have Bo. And adventures with my brother's OCD would surely trump anything they could experience. It usually did.

I sighed, feeling a little sorry for myself, and looked up to find my probable lunch date looming over me. "Miss Sutton?" said a rather good-looking, older-ish man trying to look young.

A bit surprised, I sized him up and wondered how long he'd been standing there waiting for me to acknowledge him. He had short, mostly silver hair, a dark beard, was crisply dressed and reeked of wealth...and arrogance. He also looked like he worked hard to look that good. I almost asked him for a cheeseburger just to be funny. Instead, I smiled. "It's Mia. Are you Mr. Proctor?"

"Daniel Proctor," he said. "Thank you for meeting me. I hope I haven't kept you waiting too long," he said. "I had a bail hearing that ran a little over. My apologies."

Yes, you kept me too long! I head-screamed. *Forty-five minutes is a yoga class!* But I just fake-smiled and said, "My aunt warned me that you'd be late."

He eyed me with no amusement as he sat down across from me.

"That sounds like Lullaby. How is the old gal these days?"

"Deliriously happy, I'm sure," I said. "She got married last month and is on her honeymoon."

He lifted a brow. "Really? I guess that explains why I've been relegated to meeting with *you.*" He said this looking the tiniest bit irked. "Lullaby owns my building. We've been friends for years—though not good enough friends to justify an invitation to her wedding it seems."

I shrugged, not sure what he wanted me to say to that brilliant observation, so I just said, "I guess not."

He continued to look perturbed.

"My aunt's email said you were interested in renting her pool house for a few days," I said. I didn't tell him that Lullaby had

Ivy in Stills - 3

warned me not to be bullied by this man. I also didn't mention that my aunt had in no way indicated that she considered Daniel Proctor to be a friend, which led me to believe he was working me.

He regrouped. "Probably more like a few weeks, although I hope not that long. I'm sure I mentioned that to her. She helped me out once before with an out-of-town client. I was hoping she'd be willing to do it again. But apparently, that's up to"—he spread his hands—"*you*."

Now he just looked condescending. I didn't like Daniel Proctor.

Thankfully, the waitress showed up, so I didn't have to be rude in return. She set down my to-go order and my bill. The attorney eyed me icily, then ordered a cup of coffee and a chef's salad. When she walked away, he said, "You can't stay?"

"Sorry."

When I offered no explanation, he cleared his throat. "So, about the pool house..."

I grimaced a bit to make my refusal look heartfelt and said, "Mr. Proctor, I really don't think I can help you. Like I said, Lullaby is traveling for the foreseeable future, and my brother and I are just housesitting. I'm not sure we're what you're looking for, my brother is kind of a...*handful*, and I'm at school most of the day. I'm not a maid or anything."

The man stopped me with his lifted hand. "That would not be the expectation, Miss Sutton. I'd be renting the pool house for a young woman who is very self-sufficient. It's for my daughter, Ivy, actually. She's visiting from Georgia. She's had a rather traumatic experience. She's here...*recuperating*."

"How traumatic?" I blurted. "Sorry. I mean...how traumatic? Did she witness a triple homicide, or did her cat just die?" I lifted a brow and didn't let go of his eyes. "I mean, you're asking if she can live with me. I think I have a right to know what I'm looking at."

He studied me, seemed curious, maybe a bit surprised. Then he nodded. "I'll paint you a picture. Her wedding day. Back yard full of people. Vows being spoken. Officiator says, 'anyone object to this union, speak now *blah blah blah*.' Not-so-ex-girlfriend—apparently—stands up and announces to the world that she's pregnant with the groom's baby. You can imagine the rest."

I stared at him, felt my shoulders sag. "Oh. My. Gosh."

"Exactly. That was May 3rd—five weeks ago. And I'm at a loss. Ivy came home with me from the wedding, and now she says she's never going back to Savannah, and I'm growing very concerned for her. Her mother is there and misses her terribly. Ivy needs to go home. And sooner rather than later. I know she's depressed. I got her a therapist, but that doesn't seem to be helping. I think she'd probably feel better if she lost some weight, but we can't really talk about *that* without her crying," he said with annoyance.

His words made me cringe, and I'm sure my face said so.

The attorney looked pointedly at me. "I'll be honest—I think she'd feel a lot better if she looked a little like you."

Again, the cringe. But I didn't have to look down at myself to know what he was seeing: Thin girl, nicely proportioned in a black tank top, blond hair pulled back in a messy bun, earrings bigger than my head. Decidedly bohemian style. Daniel Proctor didn't offer details about his daughter's size, but I could imagine the dad of the year had been unkind in his remarks if not his attitude and I was suddenly sad for Ivy. On so many levels.

Oblivious to where my mind had wandered, the attorney rambled on. "I don't know what else to do, Miss Sutton. I'm traveling next week, and I need to get Ivy out of the company condo. We have a client coming to town to testify in a trial and I *need that condo*."

"Where will she go? I mean, since the pool house probably won't work out?"

He sighed, looked again perturbed. "I guess a hotel, which isn't ideal. She'd be infinitely more comfortable at Lullaby's."

"Why hasn't she been staying with you?" Again, the blurt I'm rather famous for.

Daniel Proctor narrowed his eyes at me. "It's... it's complicated." He held my gaze for a cold beat, then unnarrowed his eyes and softened his expression. Actually, he suddenly looked incredibly tired as the waitress set down his food. When she walked away, he sighed and attempted to regain neutral ground with a smile that seemed forced. "So, you're a student?" he said, I suppose in an effort to keep me seated.

I nodded.

"Where?"

"MPC."

"Monterey Peninsula. Good school. What's your major?"

"Art Photography. I'm done in August, but I'll graduate in the spring."

"Really? Then what? Photography sounds very competitive," he said. "Do you have an emphasis?"

"I do everything, but I love imperfection. Black and white, mostly."

"Interesting," he said, looking less than impressed.

"I think so. I think it's fascinating, actually. Perfection isn't real, you know. It's a big lie, and yet the world worships it." I took in this aging man trying to stop time by dying his beard. "But that leaves the raw stuff, the honesty of imperfection wide open. For me." I lifted a shoulder and gave him an exaggerated smile.

He looked skeptical as he bit a carrot. "And you think there's a market for that, huh?"

"I do. I think there will always be a market for honesty, Mr. Proctor."

He fought a smile as the waitress refilled his coffee. "Touché, Miss Sutton."

"You'd be amazed how beautiful flaws can be," I said, refusing to be put off by him.

He filled his mouth with salad and shrugged. "You'd have to convince me of that."

I scooted to the end of the booth. "Well, some of my best work will be on display Monday night at the campus library. Maybe you could bring Ivy by to meet me. I think it should be up to her if she wants to live in my aunt's pool house." What I didn't say was I suddenly thought I'd do just about anything to help that poor girl.

The attorney cocked his head. "So...are you saying we have a deal?"

"No. I'm saying *maybe* we have a deal. I think it should be up to Ivy. And if she decides she wants to, I'll have to warn her about Bo—my brother is a bit *persnickety*. He's not dangerous or anything, he's just extraordinarily high maintenance. But that shouldn't affect your daughter. And you'll have to work out all the money details with Lullaby—I won't be doing any of that. But...other than that, let's just let Ivy decide what she wants to do."

Daniel Proctor studied me for a moment. He didn't say anything, but finally he lifted his coffee mug in a bit of a toast, which I took to mean we'd come to an agreement. I stood. "Good," I said picking up my lunch. Then I slid my bill across the table to him with a forced smile. He had kept me waiting for forty-five minutes, after all. And he was a bit of a jerk.

Two—Bo

Seven minutes to three. Plenty of time. Pliers arranged in alphabetical order: bail forming, bent nose, chain nose, crimping, round nose, and split ring. Files lined neatly on the other side of my work area. Top center is where I keep my chasing hammer and anvil. Other essentials for this afternoon's project: spool of bronze wire, container of glass beads, tumbled and hand-polished yesterday. I stand back to take in all this precision, instruments as sterile as any surgeon's. It's a glorious sight. Four minutes to three. My glass has been chilling since two, filled with water filtered by my Royal Berkey. No ice. Three o'clock. I sit down and get to work.

I made my first bracelet when I was seven years old and found the perfect vehicle for my tortured creativity. That my mother loved it proved to be my baptism into a world I would never leave. I make jewelry. I am a creator, curator, and connoisseur of wearable art. My goal is to create a piece a week that can be replicated with slight deviations. However, a personalized commission can sometimes take longer. I work four hours a day hands-on, plus another two or three for sketching—I draw my ideas out in elaborate detail and experiment with shapes and colors long before the project ever reaches my worktable. I also devote four hours a week to journaling and bookkeeping. There are beads to order, findings to keep stocked, precious gems to track down, and found objects to study for inspiration. In addition, I do my own fulfillment, so packing and shipping must be attended to every morning. I keep meticulous notes on every piece, from concept, to sketch, to its unique supply list—a lineage of sorts. Then once I bring the piece to fruition, my sister takes a series of studio-quality photographs of the finished product for my website. I get between 500-600 hits a day on *Sutton*—a name I obsessed about for well over a year, which is my nature. I actually liked the shortened, more visually appealing version of Benjamin Oliver Sutton Signatory. I'm Ben Oliver Sutton, owner of said website. Signatory was where I had to sign—which resulted in a label I could live with—BOSS—until my sister pointed out that I'd have to share it with a brand of underwear. So, I opted for the rather unimpressive *Sutton*. I don't know if my sister really loved it or if she just got tired after about—not about, but exactly—forty-seven lesser possibilities. Mia gets like that—tired. But she's a good sport.

What I really wanted to name my company was *Precious Bane*, after the 1924 novel by Mary Webb. The book has layered meaning for me. I love the story, of course. I love the idea of ill-defined beauty which is the premise, and I love finding wonder in ordinary things. Plus, the name represents the bane that *is* me, which demands perfection of every piece I excruciate into existence. I'm proud or possibly ashamed to say that some of me bleeds into each of my creations. To bring it all full circle, I even wanted to include a passage from the book with each of my designs, some unintentional wisdom from Prudence Sarn or Kester Woodseaves. I thought it would have made for a highly personal piece. But Mia didn't think the average jewelry consumer would appreciate my attention to such details. I'm pretty sure what she really meant is she didn't think most people would know who the hare-lipped heroine of that remarkable novel was, or the weaver who adored her, which I find terribly disturbing. So, I settled for *Sutton*.

But, it *did* take a bit of Xanax to do so.

Three—Ivy

I shouldn't have come here. I don't belong. I'm a fish out of water in California, and that's just a fact. But I was not functioning particularly well, and by the time I got on that plane nobody had really asked my opinion anyway—not that I could have answered coherently. Maybe they did. I don't know, I was not myself. I'm still not. Somehow when you have a southern accent people can take you for an illiterate hillbilly, and when you look like you been run over by a tractor trailer it's hard to convince them otherwise, and when you just don't care one way or the other, it's doubly hard.

The truth is I wake up every morning, and I still can't seem to find *me*. I look for that girl, but the me I was before what happened, happened is nowhere to be found. And since what happened, happened, I couldn't stay in Savannah. I'm never going back there again. But I'm not sure I can stay here either. I do not fit in my dad's world.

I think I knew—even as messed up as I was—that me being here was too far outside of Daniel's comfort zone to do me any good. He's not that kind of father. Mom made him bring me, I do know that, and because of the terrible shape I was in he couldn't really say no.

Daniel isn't cruel, exactly. He just doesn't know what to do with me. His expertise is problem-solving, but if it's not a problem that can be solved by throwing money at it, he's lost. That's why he does things like order me a salad in his kindest meanness when I want a pork chop, or offer to pay for a Planet Fitness membership because there's one here and one near where I live in Georgia, or fix me up with eight sessions with a life-coach—because eight sessions ought to do it—and then grill me after each one on my emotional progress and then get frustrated with me when talking about getting dumped at the altar thirty-one days ago still makes me cry. I just started my third round of eight sessions. My dad is very frustrated.

I think he means well. But somehow his way of showing it always makes me feel bad.

Pembroke says Daniel just doesn't understand trauma. That is completely, 100% true. But then what happened to me probably doesn't strike him as trauma. Even I am ashamed of the caliber of my trauma compared to what others have gone through. So, it's probably not really Daniel's fault.

A man in our process group was car-jacked at a red light. A monster pulled Terrance out of his brand-new SUV, hopped in, and took off. When he realized that Terrance's wife was in the passenger seat, the goon opened her door and shoved her out while he was speeding away. She was hit by an oncoming pickup and is now a paraplegic. Terrance relives three things every day: the feel of his wife's hand in his the moment before it happened, the shocked helplessness of being yanked out of his car, and the sight of his wife bouncing off the pickup. That's what PTSD is, a loop of agony on constant replay.

I have no business being included in a group like this. No one was maimed in my trauma, not really. Even though I relive every detail every day, just like Terrance does, just like all of them. Details like the way my wedding dress felt against my legs when I walked down the path. The backyard crowded with friends and happiness. The look on Tim's face when a very pregnant Angela Doyle stood up and announced to the world that she was having his baby. His choked-up "I'm sorry, Ivy. I'm sorry, I'm so sorry..." Those words echo in my head all day long and wake me up at night.

I feel so stupid and so pathetic, and I hate myself for it. Fortunately, according to my life coach, Adam Pembroke, patheticism is not in and of itself a mental illness. That is quite reassuring to all of us—Terrance, Shelly Alawalla who was raped, John Pratt whose house burned down, and Delilah Jones who ran over her German Shepherd. That's my posse of devastated but non-mentally ill cohorts who meet twice a week, and struggle, like me, to conquer our trauma. And if not conquer it, exactly, then at least figure out how *not* to be swallowed up by it.

The thing is, everyone in my posse has someone to kind of help them through the dark swamp of their pain. I have Daniel, which means I'm pretty much on my own.

Four—Mia

One of my favorite things to do—because I'm just that full of myself—is to take photographs of people checking out my work. That way I can get a sense of the impact I've had. I'm pretty sneaky about it, but if I'm caught, I just smile and strike up a conversation. My dad says I'd be a great stalker except for my personal style, which tends to be a little too *identifiable*. I like loud jewelry and turban wraps and long skirts, and I wouldn't wear shoes anywhere if I could get away with it—a trait I share with my mother. I looked a little like that tonight. But I was wearing sandals.

They were here somewhere, my ever-so-supportive parents. The last time I'd seen them they were chatting it up with my instructor, who, I was pretty sure, had told them nice things about me. He was an 'A for sex' type instructor, so, though he liked me, I was probably getting a B.

At the moment, I was focused and zoomed-in on two old men who were intent on my collection, which I'd entitled simply *U'rban*. All black-and-white 16 x 20s and 20 x 20s. Currently, they were discussing an image I'd captured of a none-too-clean bearded collie parked next to a rusted fire hydrant. I'd captioned it *No Tags*. The picture had been taken just before sunset, down in Carmel, and the dog was so forlorn, I'd almost brought him home, which would have literally killed my brother. But I did feed him. He had the most beautiful sad eyes.

My lens was still trained on the old men when they moved out of my shot to make room for another apparent admirer of sad dogs, and I didn't miss a beat as I focused in on the familiar face. Super-dad, Daniel Proctor, found my name on the collection and proceeded to size up my aptitude—photo by photo—with a critical gaze. I watched him assess my work for a moment then shifted my lens to the girl standing next to him. She was short with an amazing shock of thick dark hair that fell in loose curls past her shoulders. *Was that natural? It couldn't be!* I zoomed in more. She had flawless skin and was wearing not a drop of make-up. Mirrored aviators were pushed back in her great hair to reveal wounded eyes, blue. She was swallowed up in a long black sleeveless dress, and she was wearing red Chuck Taylors on what looked like very small feet. I couldn't help it, I took the shot. This girl was gorgeous in a sad, I-have-a-butt-for-a-dad-and-had-a-tragedy-at-the-altar kind of way.

I moved my lens back to Daniel Proctor, who seemed reluctantly impressed with my work. Then I stowed my camera in my bag beneath the refreshment table and walked over to the attorney and his daughter.

"Hello," I said on approach. He looked at me, then back at a photograph I'd titled *Battu at Sunset.* The subject was a deserted pier on the end of which sat a pair of well-worn ballet slippers, the ribbons suspended on a breeze. It was an accidental shot of the restless Pacific against a second-coming sunset. And it had won me an honorable mention last spring.

"My wife would love this," he said, still taking in my work. "Is it for sale?"

I laughed. "Everything's for sale."

He looked over at me, but he did not smile. "You're very good."

"Shocking, right?" I said, holding his gaze for a beat, then glancing at his daughter. Daniel Proctor straightened as though he suddenly remembered why he was there. "Ivy," he said. "This is the girl I was telling you about."

I flashed him a mock-glare. "That sounds weirdly...*ominous*, and like he forgot my name," I said to the girl. "I'm Mia."

"Ivy Talbot." The girl smiled, almost involuntarily, it seemed. "My dad said nice things about you. Good to meet you."

"I don't believe *that*," I chuckled, loving her decidedly southern accent. "But he did tell me that you're looking for a place to stay."

"I am," she said, pushing a strand of that great hair behind her ear. "But just 'til I get settled some place permanent, so it shouldn't be too long."

At this, Super-dad made a noise that was a cross between a groan and a sigh. He attempted to cover it with, "I especially like this one," while glancing at another of my photographs, *Tilda and Rosalee*. "Friends of yours?" he said, eyeing his daughter with annoyance.

I took a step toward him. "Not then, but we're good friends, now."

He looked at me like he'd forgotten what he'd asked me.

"They're 91-year-old identical twins," I said. From my periphery, I could see Ivy, who seemed upset. Suddenly preoccupied with her, I rambled. "I saw them on Venice Beach and loved that they were dressed like movie stars. They let me snap them, but only if I promised to post the pics to their Facebook page. So I did." I shrugged, again glancing over at Ivy. "Except for that one." I indicated my exhibition piece. "Are you all right, Ivy?"

"I'm good. Just not great company, I'm afraid. But I sure like your pictures. These ladies remind me of my grandmother."

I smiled, worried about her. "They thought I'd finished, so they'd stopped posing. That's always when the good stuff happens," I said conspiratorially in a silly attempt to lift her mood. The shot had been taken from behind, and the ladies were as close as their two wheelchairs would allow. I pointed to Tilda, who was reaching as high as she could from her sitting position to retrieve a payphone. Rosalee was assisting by holding up her sister's arm. They were both laughing. The phone was a non-working relic.

Ivy nodded and took a step to the right. "And this one? Tell me about the Marine."

I smiled at the photo I'd taken last summer. "That's my boyfriend and his niece," I said wistfully. "He's in Syria, and it is seriously killing me."

"I bet..." She sniffed.

"Ivy, please!" Daniel Proctor said, none too kindly. I wanted to kick him.

"Sweetheart, we're leaving." My mother thankfully interrupted. She looked like Blythe Danner wearing round-tinted glasses. She leaned in for a kiss, and my dad nodded. "Another great exhibit, Meez," he said. "Well worth cutting short my golf game." He was a head taller than my mom, and his silver hair was still thick and a bit unruly.

I laughed at his quip about his golf game because he was a terrible golfer. I turned to Super-dad. "These are my parents, Jack and Eileen Sutton. Mom, Dad, this is Daniel Proctor," I told them. "And this is Ivy. She might rent Lullaby's pool house for a little while this summer."

"Well, how lovely," my mother said, extending her hand. "And how nice to meet you. Look at this beautiful hair!" she said touching it.

"Thank you, ma'am," Ivy said. "I'm just glad it's behavin' tonight."

Mom laughed. "I love your accent. Alabama?"

"Georgia, ma'am."

"Even better." Mom winked.

"Dad, Lullaby owns Mr. Proctor's building."

"Which one?" Dad said. "That sister of mine owns half the commercial real estate in Monterey."

The attorney scratched his temple and looked annoyed. "My practice is Willis, Proctor, and Holmes."

"Oh, sure up on Telegraph, by Pacific Grove."

Daniel nodded, then rudely dismissed my dad and turned back to my work.

I rolled my eyes, and Dad winked at me. After my parents walked away, I wished Daniel Proctor would leave as well. "Sorry," I said to Ivy, "I have to mingle. It's twenty percent of my grade. Just let me know about the pool—"

"I'll take it," she interrupted.

"What?"

"I'd like to rent your pool house. If that's okay."

"Oh...absolutely," I told her. "But...don't you want to see it first?"

"I'm sure it will be fine." She looked at her father, then back at me. "It will be fine. When can I move in?"

"Ummm," I shrugged. "Day after tomorrow—Wednesday." I'd need at least a day to peel Bo off the ceiling after I told him. "Day after tomorrow should be fine," I said again.

The library closed at ten o'clock, and at 9:55 there were still a few die-hards we were herding toward the exit so we could clean up. Straighten, vacuum, and take out the trash—that was the library's price for hosting an event. A few minutes later, I had just lugged an industrial sized Hefty bag to the dumpster and was walking back when a dark car pulled up next to me. I flashed a look of aggravation in the driver's direction as down slid the window.

"I wonder if we could talk, Miss Sutton," said Super-dad.

"Where?"

"Well, here."

"As in, your car? In the dark? Do I look insane?"

He studied me, then nodded. "Fair point."

I let him squirm for a second. "There's a coffee shop up the street, on the east corner—Bruno's. I could meet you there. Ten minutes?"

"I'll be there," he said. Then he drove off without looking the least bit sheepish, which I really thought would have been the decent thing for him to do.

Fifteen minutes later, he was in a corner booth looking deep in thought and like he was there against his better judgment. There was a cup of coffee in front of him and a sweating glass of Coke on my side of the table. I slid in across from him and picked up the soft drink. After a much-needed gulp, I set it down. "Thanks," I said.

Daniel Proctor looked at me and did not smile, and again he looked very tired, very burdened. With no preamble, he pulled an envelope from his breast pocket and handed it to me.

"What's this?" I said peering inside. It was an American Express Platinum and a business card. I looked up at him. "I told you, you're going to have to work out the rent with Lullaby."

"I will," he said. "I've already emailed her. That's for Ivy...for incidentals."

"I don't understand. Why didn't you just give it to her?"

"I tried. She wouldn't take it."

I sat back and folded my arms, took in the self-important attorney who seemed so full of secrets. "You and your daughter don't like each other much, do you?"

"It's complicated," he said with utter non-reaction. He seemed to catch his callousness and tried to self-correct with, "Of course, we like each other...it's just...she was raised in Georgia, and we don't know each other as well as we should."

His words rang hollow, and he knew it. And he knew that I knew it.

I took another sip and eyed him over the rim.

He stared at me, and I think he was again trying to muster some kind of sneer to put me in my place, but he just couldn't seem to conjure it. "The American Express can be used for anything Ivy needs—or wants," he finally said to me. "But I receive notice each time it's used, so if charges begin to look suspicious, the card will be cancelled."

I deadpanned him. He was a peach.

"The business card has my cell number, as well as my answering service—they can reach me day or night, in case of an emergency." He cleared his throat. "My daughter knows not to just show up at my office. I'm far too busy for disruptions like that. But I can generally meet her anywhere with proper notice."

"Sounds like love to me."

Now he glared.

I didn't react.

"I'd appreciate the same consideration from you, Miss Sutton," he said with authority.

"I can't imagine that will ever be a problem," I said, stowing the envelope in my bag. I met his eyes and went for broke. "You mentioned that you have a wife—who presumably has excellent taste in black and white photography—but she doesn't seem to be part of all this..."

Daniel Proctor narrowed his gaze at me, tried once again to look intimidating. "As I said, it's complicated and really none of your business."

"Fair enough," I said homing in on my own gift for non-reaction. It was actually easy because Daniel Proctor suddenly struck me as the definition of pitiful dressed in a nice suit. "Fair enough," I said again.

"How can I reach you, Mia?"

I wrote my cell number on a napkin and slid it across the table.

He picked it up but said nothing.

I drained my Coke, stood up, and said, "Have a good night, Mr. Proctor." Then I walked out.

Five—Bo

I love my sister. I do. I wasn't sure about living with her, but I think it's going to work out just fine for the summer. Or at least I thought so. Mia respects my routine, my need for structure, space and privacy. And she's good at swatches. I've put down earnest money on a loft downtown, and it needs to be outfitted. I'm not very excited about it, but I need a studio because of my growing business. There are a million small decisions that have to be made, and Mia knows how overwhelmed I can get having to make them. She's patient. Much more so than Camille. Camille would be a nightmare who'd take over and everything would require a committee vote, which would be even more stressful. So, no, of my two sisters, Mia is the easiest to live with—and create a workspace with. She also gets me. She understands my need for order.

She knows I have a routine and a company to run and that I don't deal well with distractions or disruptions. She knows how those tend to paralyze me. This is why I do not understand what is happening. What is happening? Mia has just informed me that she has taken it upon herself to rent out the pool house. She has invited a complete stranger to live on the property with us. This stranger will roam about Lullaby's environs at will, disturbing the natural order of my life, invading my privacy, ruining my concentration. I sound like a baby, I know, and if I'd known guests were a possibility I would have made other arrangements for myself. But that's not an option now. And my sister has had the temerity to lob this information at me just as I was swallowing my toast, which caused my throat to seize as it does when I've been surprised, and I nearly choked. I coughed so hard that I sprayed masticated nine-grain repulsion all over the placemat, which now necessitates a load of kitchen laundry, which is a Friday task, not a Tuesday task. What is she thinking? We're not a commune! There will be extra noise to contend with, additional dishes to sterilize, the bathrooms will require more frequent scrub-downs. Having another person in my immediate proximity will require dedicated awareness of her presence, hyper-vigilance, and panic-prevention exercises. Of course, I expelled all of this rationale at my sister as I attacked the placemat with a paper towel, my appetite completely abandoned.

Mia looked at me with her enviable calm and said, "Breathe, Bo. I think you'll like her. She's very quiet, and she seems nice. Her name is Ivy, and she's recovering from a pretty bad break-up—the worst, in fact. The guy left her on their wedding day, in the middle of their vows. How can we say no? We can't." She stood up, gave me a look that said we were nice people who were going to help a fellow traveler through a rough patch. "Cheer up, Benjamin. We probably won't even know she's here."

Then she left. My sister just dropped her ostensibly compassion-riddled bombshell in my unsuspecting lap and walked out to live her day. And here I sit still frozen in my chair, perniciously obsessing about the death threat that's been leveled against my intractable need for order.

Six—Ivy

I zipped my suitcase and filled the pillow I was stealing with my underwear. I'd been staying in a studio apartment owned by my dad's firm, usually used to accommodate their out-of-town clients. They had a couple of these studios, and I'd been parked in this one for twenty-two days. And now, it seemed, much to Dad's disappointment, I was moving into yet another temporary living situation when what he really wanted was for me to go home. I think he finally figured out that wasn't happening any time soon.

I'd told him I'd only be infringing on Mia Sutton's hospitality for a short time—just until I figured myself out. Unfortunately, that was *provin' to be my undoin'*, as I was fond of saying to my support group. *Damn* Tim. Who knew his kick in my gut could have so completely transformed the girl I was into this sad, puffy little invalid? I'm so mad at who I've turned into, I could spit. And I'm just so tired. I don't know what's become of my dignity or my ability to resist peanut M&Ms. I just know the result is that I can no longer button my jeans, and I don't even know if I care.

I blew out a breath. I was never going home, but I could just walk out of here and drive... drive somewhere far, far away. The trouble was, wherever I went, I'd have to take *me* with me. I sat down on the bed and dialed the number my dad had given me. Mia Sutton was out of breath but seemed honestly pleased to hear my voice.

"Ivy, hey!"

"Hi, Mia. I was just letting you know I'm on my way. I wanted to make sure it was still okay."

"Oh...of course. But it might be easier if you meet me where I am, then we can go home together. Do you know the MPC campus?" she asked.

"I know where it is...from the other night."

"Great. I'm playing tennis across from the stadium. That's on the southeast corner. Meet me there, then you can follow me to Lullaby's. I'll watch for you. What are you driving?"

"A silver Honda Accord. You haven't changed your mind, have you? About me moving in there?"

"No! No, of course not. I...I'm just not sure anyone is home at the moment to let you in the back...where the pool house is."

"Oh. Gotcha. I'll be over in a few minutes."

I hung up feeling like a total loser. That girl should be easy to dislike: she was pretty, perky, talented, annoyingly overly-confident (per Daniel—which I didn't mind at all because it bugged him so much), and, oh yes, enviably thin. But she'd been so darn nice at her exhibit that I just couldn't not like her. I pressed #3 on my phone—speed dial for my grandmother—but I just got her machine, so I called Bree. It took her a long time to answer.

"Hey, baby."

"Hey, Mama."

"How are you, sweet cheeks?"

"I guess we're trying something new," I said.

"A new what? A medication?"

"No. A Mia..."

"Oh...your dad told me about her."

"It's just temporary until I find a place of my own. I need you to put some money in my account."

Mama sighed.

"You owe me two paychecks—and there's some cash in my top drawer."

She ignored me. "Ivy Lee, I told you, I'm coming out there in a couple of weeks—Your grandmother is coming with me—and we are bringing you home. Enough is enough."

"You can come if you want to, Mama, bring Geneva but I'm not going back with you. I told *you*, I'm never going back there again."

"Ivy, that's ridiculous. This is your home."

"Mama..."

"Okay, okay. We'll talk when I get there."

"Bree!"

She sighed again. "I just miss you, baby. I don't have to remind you what a nightmare the store is without you."

"I miss you, too," I said, pretending her missing me had nothing to do with the store.

"Ivy, if you hate this girl, you know you don't have to go through with this."

"I know that Mama. But I already don't hate her. And I think you should think about hiring some summer help. Transfer thirteen-hundred dollars into my account, please."

"Iveee..."

"And bring the cash from my drawer with you when you come. I'll need it."

"Ivy!"

"I mean it, Mama. I'm starting over."

Seven—Mia

I was sitting on the top bleachers panting when I saw her pull into the stadium parking lot. I'd just kicked Grady Pope's butt at tennis, and he wasn't super happy about that. I didn't care. Seemed to me playing with an ex that I sort of detested had seriously improved my game. Win! I thought, climbing down.

Ivy got out of her car looking a little tentative, like she was not sure she was in the right place. She was wearing jeans rolled up at the ankle and an elliptical hemmed white tee that hung below her hips. She was short, so she looked a little like an oompaloompa, but adorable. Her great hair hung in those wild curls, and she was wearing her aviator sunnies. I walked over to meet her.

When she saw me, she cocked her head. "Hey, Mia."

"Hey! You found it."

She smiled, shyly. "Good GPS."

I laughed. It was Wednesday in early June, and there was no one on the football field and just a few guys on the track. "Do you care if we walk?" I said. "I need to cool down a bit." I looked at her feet. "You're wearing flip-flops. Are those okay? Do you have any other shoes?"

"Not really. I mean, I have some, but they're too small. Daniel bought them for me."

"You call your dad Daniel? That's cool. Well, we're just walking, so not a big deal."

Ivy smiled. "I told him I needed some runnin' shoes. You should see what his secretary got me." Ivy sighed.

I laughed. "We can fix that. A girl has to have the right shoes. There are a lot of trails near my aunt's house. My brother runs every day, he can show you where they are if you're interested."

Ivy nodded. "That would be great. I have to do something."

We crossed the street, and I took a deep breath. "How are you feeling about all this?" I broached. "I wasn't sure the other night if you were totally down with the idea of moving into my aunt's pool house."

Ivy looked over at me. "I'm sorry about being so off-putting when I first met you. It wasn't you. It's just that Dad and me…we'd been arguing…" She waved the words away. "Long story, but no, I'm awful grateful to be moving in with y'all. But I should be able to find my own place soon…I just need a job first."

"That would probably help," I smiled. "What kind of work do you do?"

"I just barely got certified. I'm an X-ray tech. I was fixin' to get a job when Tim and I got back from our honeymoon. Aside from that, I've been helping Bree. My mama owns a shop in Savannah. I make paper for her."

"Really?"

"Mama's an artist. She paints on fancy paper that she makes and sells—that I make. It's fun. She's real talented."

"So, do you live in Savannah?" I asked.

"Yeah. We live above our shop on Montgomery Square—right in the heart of Savannah. I live there about half the time, and the other half, I stay with my grandmother, Geneva, a few miles away. I'm very fluid, and Mama and I do our best when we aren't always together, if you know what I mean."

I laughed. "I so do! I absolutely adore my m—" We were suddenly interrupted by the irritation of a wanna-be jock who was trying to get by us.

"To the left, Stick and Tubby," he muttered loud enough that we heard him. He was smallish and over-muscled, and my first reaction was to run after him and…I don't know what, kick his rather unimpressive bum. He loped ahead, and when he reached the bleachers, he stopped and grabbed a bottle of water from a blue gym bag. I looked over at Ivy. "What a little toad."

Ivy looked slightly wounded but tried to wave it off as mere annoyance.

"I think I hate him," I said.

Ivy chuckled, and I knew I was winning her over.

When we reached the bleachers, we stopped. "Let's sit for a minute," I said. Jogger boy was across the field, so I walked over to the blue gym bag he'd left unattended and unzipped it.

"What are you doing?" Ivy gasped.

"Gee," I said. "Someone has left a perfectly good bag here. We should investigate," I winked. There was a six-pack of Dasani with one missing, a pair of sweats, and a wallet, which I opened. It belonged to one Roger Wallace.

And on cue, Roger Wallace shouted from a quarter track away, "Hey! What are you doing?" I looked up and waved at him. "I'm parched. What about you, Ivy?" I checked the seal of a water bottle, and when it popped, I handed it to her.

"No!" she said, pushing it away.

I took a gulp just as Roger Wallace skidded to a breathless stop in front of us. "What the hell?" he panted.

"Hi, Rog." I smiled. "We just wanted to introduce ourselves. I'm Mia, and this is Ivy."

"What?"

"Mia, Ivy. You owe us an apology."

"What are you talking about?" he said grabbing his bag.

"Yeah. You called us Stick and Tubby back there. Are you twelve?"

"Seriously?" he said, clawing through his bag.

I took another sip, then opened the wallet Roger Wallace didn't know I had. "5'4" 168. No wonder you run."

"Give me that!" he seethed.

I pulled it to my chest. "The apology?"

Ivy in Stills - 27

"I'm sorry. I'm sorry. Now give me the damn wallet."

"Oh, you can do better than that, Rog," I said, still clutching his wallet.

He took a calming breath. "I'm sorry," he said from behind his teeth.

I cut my losses and held the wallet out to him with a smile but pulled it back. "For what it's worth, Roger, it seems to be working—the running. You look pretty good out there," I fibbed. "He looks good, right Ivy?"

"What?" she coughed.

I handed him back his wallet. "Friends, Rog?" I stuck out my hand, and he seemed confused but shook it. When he finally did, despite himself, it was with a bit of a grin. I elbowed Ivy and she stuck out her hand. Roger Wallace scratched his temple, then shook Ivy's hand. "I... I'm sorry about what I said back there."

"I just knew you were a decent guy, Rog," I told him. "Ivy said you were a jerk, but I didn't believe it for a minute."

"I did not!" Ivy yelped.

I drained the bottle of Dasani and handed it back to our new friend, and we all got back on the track. Roger Wallace took off at a dead run—he might have even been showing off a little. And Ivy and I continued on our stroll. After a minute, she said, "How did you do that?"

I looked over at her.

"I mean it. How—why did you do that?"

"Ivy, you *always* have to stand up to put downs. It's the first rule of being a girl. Didn't your dad ever teach you that?"

"Uhhh. No. Daniel's not really that kind of dad."

"Really? What kind is he?"

"He's more of a dad in name only."

"Oh," I said, thinking this was not hard to believe at all. I nodded. "Well, I guess I'll have to work fast to impart all of my dad's best stuff." I grinned. "You in?"

Ivy looked down and shook her head. There was a smile in her voice when she said, "You called him a toad."

"What? Who?"

"That guy."

"I did?"

"Geneva called Tim a toad."

"Geneva is..."

"My grandmother."

"And Tim is..." I asked even though I knew.

Ivy let go of a deep breath, and her blue eyes got watery.

Eight—Ivy

Tim.

I looked over at Mia in all her fit, long-legged, blond pony-tailed perfection and shook my suddenly heavy head.

"Sometimes unloading on a stranger can be a good way to vent," she invited as we walked.

"I'm too embarrassed," I whined. "That boy wrecked my life and turned me into the Pillsbury Dough Girl."

"You mean you weren't always this adorable?" Mia said—she actually said that, and I thought she was making fun of me, but she didn't seem like she was. I just smiled even though I was crying, and Mia Sutton put her arm around me like a mother hen and said, "He hurt you."

"He didn't just hurt me," I told her. "He ruined me."

"What happened?" Mia said, turning serious.

I felt the tears and the familiar humiliation overtake me, and I breathed deep and shut my eyes. That's all it took for the image of my most awful moment to bloom once again in fully pixelated detail. My wedding day. My friends. My love. My Tim...crying...walking away from me...with her...pregnant her. "I felt so small..." I said, a little surprised that I'd said the words out loud.

"Let's sit. Should we sit?" Mia said, and I followed her to the bleachers, mostly because she was dragging me.

"You don't have to tell me if you don't want to, but I'm a good listener."

I smiled. Mia Sutton really was so nice. "I've loved Tim Marsh since I was six, but in high school, he started falling in love with me...and out of love with me, too. So, it was a rollercoaster. But then last year, I guess it stuck because he asked me to marry him, which meant that I had finally won. It was always a competition between me and Angela—and I won...or I thought I'd won..."

"Was Angela...?"

I looked over at Mia. "Yep. The pregnant stealer of my husband-to-be."

"Oh. Right. Continue."

"It was supposed to be the perfect day. May 3rd in Savannah...you can't really go wrong, and Geneva's backyard is just huge with big old live oaks dripping with Spanish moss. Palmettos everywhere. Big ol' pots of spring flowers. Lots of lace, bouquets of camellias and azaleas. White balloons in the magnolia trees. It was all a bit over-the-top, but so, so pretty.

"My grandmother called it my stand-alone day," I told Mia. "And I was so happy that it eclipsed even my nerves at being the center of attention. I'm not particularly comfortable in the spotlight. There's always been a little too *much* of me, if you know what I mean—which you probably don't—and now there's a good ten pounds more of me. But Geneva said I should be proud and stick out what God gave me. So, in that fabulous dress, that's kind of what I did." I laughed a little, lost in the remembering.

"First of all, I'm *loving* your grandmother," Mia said. "Second, we'll talk about the *too much* later. Now, tell me about that dress."

I swallowed over the knot in my throat. "It was gorgeous. It was a ball gown that started out a little big but because I was so nervous about the wedding, I lost a few inches, and it had to be nipped and tucked a bit. I was beautiful." I shrugged at Mia. "Is that awful to say?"

"Absolutely not!" Mia said.

"My skin was great, and thanks to a bucket of toxic chemicals, my hair was shiny and straight, and I remember thinking that a stranger was looking back at me in the mirror. She was just beautifully... *engineered*: Spanxed and styled and highlighted into a polished version of the rather ordinary me." Again, I laughed at the memory. "Well, you don't live your life as Geneva Talbot's granddaughter and come out unscathed."

"She sounds completely and utterly amazing," Mia said.

"She is. She's the grand dame of Isle of Hope—that's where I live in Savannah—well, the other place besides my mama's. She fancies herself a bit of a mystic."

"No way."

I nodded. "She journals and maps the *interventions of the Universe,*" I said. "And she keeps meticulous track of her predictions. She's a big predictor. My mother, Bree—Aubrey—is more real-world; she's an artist, like I told you. My mama is her own beautiful planet, spinnin' to her own happiness, most of the time."

Mia laughed. "We will be having a long, long conversation about them, I can promise you that. But right now I want to hear about Tim."

I shook my head. "Like I said, we'd been best friends forever. All through high school, we were either in love, or I was nursing him through his break-ups, mostly with Angela Doyle—my villain. She left Savannah a couple of years ago—I thought—to make her way in the world as dancer—the naked kind." I sighed. "Tim really needed me then. Actually, he's always needed me. I soothed him when he lost the state championship for our high school team against Rowan Oaks. I let him climb in my window and cry all night when his parents split up and again when they got back together. I promised never to tell anyone that he flunked out of Georgia Tech after two semesters. I even cheered his promotion to assistant manager of Tire World over in Pooler. He promised one day he'd be regional director over radials."

"What are radials?"

"Radials. They're tires. He wants to be Director of Tires. That sounds so stupid, doesn't it?"

"I don't know, maybe," Mia said, and it made me smile.

"It does," I said. "I know it does. Anyway, we started dating for real after high school, and when he asked me to marry him, he said he wasn't good enough to ask me, but he was asking me anyway. And he said I was always his safe place, and I thought I'd never heard more beautiful words." I swallowed over my swollen throat and did my best to not cry in front of Mia. But when I turned to her, she'd teared up, too, and I lost the battle. "So, we got engaged at Christmastime and set the date for spring."

"Was the ring pretty, at least?" she asked me.

I chuckled through my tears. "Yes. It was two small diamonds set at an angle on a silver band. I loved it. I pawned it a few days after I got here. Got $270 for it."

Mia laughed and then tried to apologize, but I stopped her. "I know. I think it was the prize from a cereal box."

We laughed some more, and it actually felt good to be talking about my heartache with this girl who was feeling more and more like a friend. After we pulled ourselves together, I told her that my dad had made it just in time. "His flight was delayed," I said. "But he made it."

Mia nodded. "Oh, that's good. Is that good?"

"Well, it made Mama happy. I hadn't seen him for over a year. He lives here, in California, so our paths don't cross too often. My parents were never married, but we stay in touch because he's still madly in love with my mom."

"Really?"

"Totally. She's his forbidden fruit." I nodded at Mia, who was just kind of digesting my story. "I know, it's weird," I said. "Anyway, he walked into Geneva's bedroom that day and said to me, 'You belong on the cover of a magazine, Ivy Lee.' That was just so nice to hear."

"I'm sure it was," Mia said. "Because I'm sure you did. Is Tim going to enter this story anytime soon? I'm dying here."

I smiled. "So, Daniel is walking me down the aisle—my grandmother's backyard, rose-petaled aisle—and he whispers to me, 'This boy...he's good?' and I whispered yes. 'Is he worthy?' Daniel says, and I said 'Dad, it's Tim. It's always been Tim—' like Daniel had paid any attention to my life. And he says 'Oh, right. Well, I'll kill him if he ever hurts you.' And then... Tim *did*."

"What happened?" Mia asked.

For a minute I couldn't really speak because my throat had closed over. "She was there," I finally said.

"Who?"

"Angela."

"Oh."

"I wasn't absolutely sure it was her because I was so amazed that *everyone* was there. It was almost standing room only, and it made me so giddy, I thought I might faint. But I was okay because just ahead, there was my Tim standing in the gazebo. That's all I needed, Tim's eyes on mine, pulling me toward him and our life together—my life as Ivy Marsh. But he wasn't looking at me. And when I got to his side, he seemed a little surprised." I was quiet for a minute as the details pierced me all over again. Tim's sickly pallor, the way he wouldn't look up. I looked over at Mia. "I asked him if he was okay, and he said he was just nervous. Father Dominic welcomed everybody, and my dad did his thing and gave me away, then he sat down, and I slipped my hand into Tim's because he seemed to need it. My heart was pounding like it should have been, but I knew something wasn't right. Tim was staring at his shoes, and it looked like he might throw up on them. Then in the middle of Father Dom talking about the sanctity of marriage, Tim started shaking his head."

"Oh, Ivy..." Mia breathed.

"And when Father Dom said if anyone objects to this union, Angela stood up pregnant like no body's business, and Tim started crying, and he wouldn't look at me. He just kept saying, 'I'm sorry, Ivy, I'm so sorry, I'm so sorry.' And then he just walked off the gazebo."

"Ivy..."

"I just felt so small, like I was dissolving, almost. There was this big, collective gasp as everyone watched my almost-husband run away. He *ran* away. Then 100 faces turned back to me in...in total...and abject pity. And it only got worse when Angela Doyle—the naked dancer of his dreams—stood up and waddled out after him."

Mia stared at me. "I have no idea what to say to you right now."

I hung my head. "It was my very own *Carrie* moment. Pig's blood pouring down on me as the entire yard sat gobsmacked at my devastation. It was the worst moment of my life. And, no matter what I do, I can't seem to unlive it."

We were quiet for a long time, then Mia said, "What did you do? Did you scream? Throw things? Did you get mad?"

"Not then," I sniffed. "When I could feel my legs, I just went upstairs and crawled in my bed. I didn't even take off my wedding dress, just dove in and pulled the covers over my head. But I wished I could have just taken a long walk in the ocean. I was pretty messed up, so Mama begged Daniel to bring me back with him to California to *regroup*—that's what she called it. Regroup. It wasn't supposed to take this long, just a few days, so he agreed. He wasn't thrilled, but he did it for Bree. He put me in a hotel at first and gave me his credit card. He told me to go shopping, I'd feel better. He told me to get whatever I wanted. But there was nothing I wanted—except a pizza. So I ordered two. I figured if no one wanted me, I'd make the best of it with ice cream and pizza and Comedy Central." I shrugged. "Junk food, twenty-four-hour laughs, and no one to bug me. And no one did."

"Wow..."

"I think Daniel thought some miracle was gonna happen, that some divine intervention would heal me, and he could send me home. He left me alone for a few days, but he called a couple times to express his *heart-felt concern*. When he finally came by and saw the state I was in, he just started yelling. Yelling about the food everywhere and that I hadn't been out of bed. He said it was disgusting and he was planning to sue Tim for destroying my life. He called him worthless and other things—terrible things—but the way he yelled, it made it sound like I was the worthless one." I looked over at Mia. "That's when I got mad. After he left, I went crazy. I was stripping the bed and I got all tangled up and I just started screaming at the sheets because my foot was caught in the elastic corner. I was screaming and bawling and acting like a crazy person, completely out of control. And in the middle of this terrible tirade, I caught my reflection in the dresser mirror, and I couldn't believe it was me. My dad was right—I was a disgusting mess, and I hated myself and Tim for making me that way. It was the most awful I've ever felt. I started to sob, and I didn't stop till the next day. That's when I pawned my ring. That was a bad day. It's like I fell down and broke myself. And now I can't seem to find all the pieces, so I can't put myself back together."

Mia's mouth had dropped open, and she was shaking her head. "I'm so, so sorry that happened to you."

I shrugged. "Me, too."

"I don't know you, Ivy," she said. "But I don't believe you're ruined. I'm going to say something mean here—you will learn that about me, I can be blunt—but here goes: It takes an extraordinary man to actually ruin a woman, and Tim just doesn't sound that extraordinary."

I looked at her holding her breath and could not find fault with her reasoning.

She breathed. "You did get run over, though. Bad. You got hurt in the worst way. But I am one hundred percent sure that if you won the heart of a guy whose biggest aspiration is to become the tire director in a place called Pooler, there is someone with equal, if not better qualifications in your future. I'll bet my hair extensions on it."

I swallowed and started to laugh. Then I cried. Then I laughed some more. And Mia Sutton let me. Without platitudes or serious attempts to divert me, she simply let me feel her words. I'd spent the last month reliving the day: the images, the sounds, the pain, the brush of my dress against the heat of my embarrassment, and though I'd shared it all in my PTSD group, this was different. Mia wasn't advising me, challenging me, pointing out the misplacement of my flawed affection or telling me I was better off. She just listened. Finally, I looked over at her. "Thank you for letting me get all that out."

"Thank you for telling me," she said. "That couldn't have been easy."

I wiped my nose and took a breath. "Now, you, Mia. Tell me about the time *you* were dumped in front of a hundred Georgians and a California lawyer."

She smiled. "I like you, Ivy."

I liked her, too. "You said you have a boyfriend? Tell me about him," I said.

She pulled a thinking face. "Well, yes. Maybe I do. I think I do. I don't know. You know that place just past boyfriend but not all the way to the next place?"

"I am familiar with that general region, yes," I said.

She sighed. "His name is Derek Lehman." She nodded. "He's in Syria, with the Marines. He's been there for three months."

"How did you meet him?"

"I'm a photographer, you know that. Last year, one of my instructors asked me to help him with a family photo shoot. It was Derek's family." She looked at me. "They were all together for his grandfather's 93rd birthday, and it was cool because Derek had just graduated from Camp Pendleton and was in full uniform—he looked amazing. His dad was in the Navy, and he was in full uniform, and his ancient little grandpa had been a pilot in WWII, and he was in full uniform. It was awesome."

"Sounds awesome."

"Yeah, so my job was to arrange people and make sure their faces weren't in shadow and they were all looking where they were supposed to—nobody picking their nose. But instead, I was taking pictures. I couldn't help myself. I'm very into random shots where people are just being themselves, no pretense, no posing. Derek happened to be hunkered down in front of a little girl—his niece, I found out later. She's four, has Down syndrome—Lola, absolutely adorable—and that day she had little dark pigtails, and one of the ribbons had come loose. So, Derek—aka Mr. extremely sexy Marine boy—is trying to fix it. It's cuter than cute. She's laughing, he's laughing. She's barefoot and on her tiptoes, trying to reach his white hat, which is making his task impossible. He's in full pressed-pleat blues down as low as he can go trying to tie this little, tiny ribbon with his big man fingers." Mia shook her head. "It was the shot of a lifetime. Not to mention the perfect excuse to accost him." She laughed. "And I accosted the hell out of him."

I laughed, too. I had less than an hour of experience with Mia Sutton, but I could totally see her doing that.

She sighed. "He trained as a sniper. We've been together almost a year, and he's been gone three months. And now I think I might love him." She looked at me and got serious. "And I wish I didn't—did I mention he's a sniper? In Syria?" She shook her head and sighed. "I'm learning that it's a lot harder to worry about a sniper you might love than a sniper who you just like a lot."

Nine—Bo

I was perspiring, which I loathe, so I needed another shower. But I was too behind to take the time for one—my sister would be here any minute. So, in addition to being sweaty, there was a knot of conflict tangling in my gut—oh, the joys of anxiety. I had to focus. I'd already lost nearly an entire day of work scrambling to get ready for our *tenant*—a day that I could not afford. A normal person would prioritize. But my personality doesn't really *do* priorities; everything muscles its way into the number one position, which can be a little knot-producing and sweat-inducing.

Case in point: Katrina Gearhart, the producer of the airport soap opera *Winged Passion*, is a fan of my work. Last week she commissioned a choker in the shape of a snake that is to be found on a dead body in episode eleven of next season. It's a great opportunity for me, as the piece is to be featured repeatedly as a clue in the murder of the dead person on whom it will be found, and *Bo Sutton dba Sutton* will subsequently appear in the rolling credits at the end of the show. It's a thrilling prospect—achieving it should take precedence. And it does...and will. Eventually.

My problem is my sisters. Their lives intersect with mine, and their issues somehow become my issues because we share genetics and loyalty. Exhibit A: Mia and her dropped-bomb which effectively exploded all my business plans into oblivion—temporarily. And ten minutes after that bomb, elder sister, Camille dropped another in my lap when she informed me that she had miraculously managed to escape her tyrannical farce of a husband for a few hours. She will be convening her book club—where else

Ivy in Stills - 39

but right here on Lullaby's freshly mopped patio, *tonight*. Of course. And of course, she's begged me to whip up something for her friends to nosh on for the event. I'm very good at that sort of thing so because I love her and pity her, I will accommodate her. The knot feels made of barbed wire.

I'm not whining, just acknowledging the actual fact that there is just one of me to deep clean the pool house, super sanitize the bathrooms, vacuum, polish, and reorganize, put together Camille's food, complete the preliminary drawing of the killer snake, and order the materials, including the teardrop African emeralds that last week were still on backorder.

I groaned, audibly. I didn't have the time or the proper hygiene to adequately welcome a stranger into Aunt Lully's home. But none of that seemed to matter—she was on her way.

I had just finished vacuuming when I heard Mia pull into the garage. My hands went a little sweaty—a little more sweaty—but otherwise I refused to telegraph my anxiety—*deep breaths*. Deep. Breaths. Mia would see it, of course, but hopefully I would not alarm this poor girl with my skittishness. I don't do well with new people. Mia got all the social ease Camille used to have. I got the least, which I've always found to be monumentally unfair.

When I came back from shelving the Dyson, Mia and our new lodger were in the foyer, where the girl's blue-eyed prettiness disarmed me—I don't know why—and naturally ignited my demon angst. Inward sigh. Thankfully, she was busy being a little shell-shocked, so I don't think she noticed. Aunt Lully's house has that effect on people: 6500 square feet of Provence-inspired Mediterranean luxury replete with superior workmanship set in the bluffs high above Monterey Bay.

"Bo, there you are," Mia said. "I want you to meet Ivy Talbot. Ivy, this is my brother, Bo, which is short for Benjamin Oliver. You can call him Bo or Benjamin."

"Hi," I said, proudly betraying nothing of the circus going on inside me.

"So nice to meet you," the girl said with southern warmth and a timid smile. A smile that sort of amplified her prettiness which sort of amplified my anxiety.

"Hi," I repeated, and then I went mute. She smiled a bit wider, a bit nervously and my eye started to twitch. *Was it? Was my eye twitching?* Thank goodness Ivy Talbot kindly looked away seeming to lose interest in me as she resumed her perusal of Lully's home, giving me the chance to rub my belligerently dancing eyelid.

"It's beautiful here," she said in a soft drawl, hopefully none the wiser. "So quiet."

I nodded, blinking furiously.

Mia rolled her eyes at me. "We're taking Ivy's stuff out to the pool house, then we're headed to the Del Monte Center for some shoes. Do you want to come with us and hit Whole Foods?"

I was tempted—so tempted. I needed several things, but it was too soon to be shopping with a stranger. "I don't have time," I coughed, not fooling my sister. "I've got macaroons ready to go in the oven—for Camille. But maybe you could pick up some organic onions? Their fresh catch? Some baby reds?"

"Make me a list," Mia harrumphed, walking Ivy through the foyer to the kitchen where French doors lead to the courtyard and the pool house beyond.

"It's all so clean..." I heard Ivy say, as well as Mia's, "That's all Bo. My brother's a bit of a germaphobe."

I wilted. And Ivy Talbot caught my wilt as she turned back to me.

"It was nice to meet you," she said again smiling, and then hurried out the door.

"You, too." I muttered under my breath. "Thanks, Mia," I added. "For that succinct description of me. Germaphobe. Don't mention that I'm also very well-read, have a master's degree in literature, own a thriving company, am a gourmet cook, and run marathons... I'm just clean." I sighed, bothered, as my sister and our new renter laughingly made their way across the patio. Then I noticed the fingerprints Mia left on the glass and grabbed the Windex.

Ten—Ivy

The Del Monte Center was rocking, so Mia had to park a few blocks away, which, if I'm being honest, annoyed me a little. My feet hurt, and I was hungry. "So..." I sighed. "I think you're right about the shoes."

Mia smiled. "You won't be sorry. My mom's a huge runner. My whole life, she's gotten up at the crack of dawn to hit the trails behind our house. She says a good pair of shoes can change your life." She shrugged. "I don't really know about that since I don't run, but we ought to be able to find you something better than flip-flops."

"Is your whole family athletic?"

"Well, my dad golfs. He's not very good, so I don't think that really qualifies. Bo runs. He does marathons—he just ran the Avenue of the Giants a couple of weeks ago."

"What's that?"

"Oh, it's fun, it's a marathon through the redwoods. Mom did it with him this year."

"Well, my goodness!" I said, truly impressed.

Mia nodded. "Yep, I took pictures, lent moral support, ate doughnuts." She laughed, and I was finding her laugh to be very trustworthy and revealing about her—Mia Sutton did not seem to give a lick what people thought of her. I'd known her all of one day, which wasn't long to base an opinion on, but I knew I truly, madly envied that about her.

The light turned, and we joined a small throng in crossing over. "He seems nice, your brother. A little nervous. Is he not thrilled to have me staying with y'all?"

"Oh," Mia waved away my words. "That's just Bo... He's not thrilled that *I'm* there. He's..." she shook her head. "Bo's awesome, don't get me wrong. He's just...*finicky.*" She turned to me as we reached the other side. "That makes him interesting...if a bit odd. And sometimes exhausting."

"Oh," I said. "I thought it might be *me.*"

"Oh, heaven's no. He's just very uptight about everything. He likes order and struggles with disorder. That's why he cleans—which I love by-the-way. He cleans and cooks and reads and runs and makes fabulous jewelry. In his spare time, he cleans some more because he hates germs. And he drives a lot of people crazy in the process—his girlfriends last about a week." Mia shook her head. "But that's my obsessive-compulsive brother for you."

I looked at her and she smiled, so I did, too. "Well, we've all got somethin', I guesss. That's what makes us *us.*" I shook my head and whistled. "But he's *waaay* too pretty to have all that going on. I promise you I will do my plumb best not to make his life any harder."

Mia smiled bigger. "Ivy, you are adorable."

"Well, I don't know about that," I said, not sure what she meant. We'd reached the mall entrance, and a little old man was holding the door open for us. We walked in and I thanked him, then I turned back to Mia. "And what about your sister?" I said. "Did I hear you say you have a sister?"

Mia nodded, still smiling at me. "Camille. She's her own mess," she said, pulling a face. "She's married to the devil. Long story," she sighed. "She has two little girls who are pure cuteness—Scout and Olivia—who totally adore me, by the way."

"Well, of course they do!" I said.

"Camille doesn't run either—since we were talking about that. But she used to dance—she was an amazing dancer. Before she married Satan." She pointed. "That's where we're going.

I followed her gaze to the Neon *Carpe D Sports* sign and walked in behind her. "Anyway," she said, not skipping a beat. "I'm pretty sure my nieces are Camille's exercise these days."

"Oh, right," I said, catching up to her meaning. "And what about you?" I said as I took in the enormous store full of all things athletics.

"Me? I dabble," Mia said. "I like tennis and yoga. And Lully has a pool, so I'm kind of digging on morning laps these days. Do you swim?"

"Not really," I said. "I mean, I know how, I just...don't. Much."

Mia laughed. "Well, you're welcome to join me if you want. Bo's stingy with morning caffeine, so it's pretty much how I wake up. I'm usually in the water by 7:00. Ish. If you're interested."

"Hmmm. It's not my best look."

"What isn't?"

"This body. Wet. In swimming attire."

"Oh, my gosh, you are hilarious." Mia looped her arm through mine. "Ivy, nobody cares."

For some reason, I actually believed her. "I guess I'd better look for a swimsuit, then."

She squeezed my arm. "Fabulous! I mean you could borrow one of Lullaby's, but three of you could fit in one of her suits."

"What?"

"True story."

We wandered over to the shoe department, where Mia talked me into a pair of Altra Paradigms, which meant nothing to me, but they felt amazing on my feet. Much more so than the Saucony Triumphs from my dad. Those were nice, and way too small. But that's what happens, I guess, when you put your secretary in charge of doing a kindly deed, a secretary who has never once laid eyeballs on your daughter's feet.

After that, we hit Macy's for a swimsuit. I couldn't find one worth trying on in Carpe D—and even the one I shimmied myself into in the Macy's old-lady department was a truly traumatic experience. It was red, one piece, defied the laws of physics, and pushed everything up and out and over to the point that I vowed never to be seen in it and could not believe I had actually let Mia talk me into buying it. But it was over and done, and I was starving.

We ate in the food court, and I thought I was hungry enough to eat my own arm. But the strangest thing: nothing tasted good, and that rarely happens. I got pizza and breadsticks from Sbarro and an Orange Julius, just like Mia. But I only got through half my pizza. I kept seeing my marshmallow layer leaking over the red swimsuit, my dad wishing I'd go home—or worse, that I wasn't even here—Tim's sorry eyes...Tim walking off the gazebo...Tim not wanting me...

"Hey?" Mia said. "You okay?"

I smiled, because that's what I do when I'm about to get weepy. "It's just been a long day. I think I'll take this with me. Have it later, maybe," I said, wrapping my pizza in a napkin.

Mia narrowed her eyes at me. I had not fooled her, but she was kind enough not to pry her way into my personal hell, which I appreciated immeasurably and was another reason I knew I was destined to like this girl very much. I smiled again and excused myself to go to the restroom so poor Mia could finish her pizza without my drama.

When we got back *home*, Mia's sister, Camille, was there with about a dozen other ladies, and that fact seemed to surprise Mia. "I can't believe she's actually here," she said to me. Then, to her sister, "You made it."

Camille pulled a little face at Mia, then smiled at me. "You must be Ivy."

"I am," I said, a little startled that she knew who I was.

Camille was pretty like Mia but with darker, shorter hair. She was also wearing *a lot* of makeup. "Girls, we'd better get started," she sang out, reining in her friends who were admiring the house. It turned out this group of women was Camille's book club, and she graciously invited us to sit in for their discussion of *Dancing on Broken Glass*.

"I've got some photo editing to do," Mia said, apologetically. "But Ivy can, if she wants."

"Ummm, actually I think I'd better unpack," I said. "But I heard the book was good."

"So good!" Camille said, smiling at me and hugging her sister. "Maybe next time. It was nice to meet you, Ivy."

Mia walked me out to the pool house and made sure I didn't need anything. "I'm fine," I said, even though suddenly, despite my weird pizza experience at the mall, I would have killed for a cookie or four that Mia's brother had arranged on a big platter by the outside fireplace. I swallowed. "I think I'll take a shower," I said. "Then I need to call my mama."

Mia nodded. "Okay. I guess I'll see you in the morning."

"Yes, you will. And if I get very brave, or lose a little of my mind, it will be at 7:00. Poolside," I said, already hyperventilating in dread at the thought of me in that red spandex.

She laughed. "Totally up to you, Ivy. Goodnight."

Hours later, I couldn't sleep. Of course, I couldn't. It had been a strange day torn from the playbook of someone else's life, and I couldn't quite settle. I checked the clock at 1:25. I could hear crickets in the distance, and the night air pouring through my open window was just cool enough to need all the blankets on the bed. I'd told my PTSD group how the dark and the quiet were my enemies, and it turned out that we all struggled at night. We all felt a little re-victimized by it. Daytime was easier, with its cushion of noise and light and movement. The sweet distraction of television, traffic, weather, people arguing and breathing around you. At night, there were just memories, loud and vivid. Terrance had funnily suggested we change the time of group therapy to 2 a.m., any night of the week. There was resounding agreement.

I turned over and punched the pillow. I missed the me who could sleep. I missed the lightness of being that I had never once appreciated before I'd gotten so weighed down with sadness and disappointment and extra *me*. I missed Savannah. I missed Geneva and even my mom. And I missed Tim, and I was deadly afraid I always would.

I got up and pulled the extra blanket off my bed and walked out into the devil night. I couldn't see it from my window, but from the courtyard, the view of the bay and Cannery Row was spectacular and deliciously distracting, just what I needed. I sat down in a lawn chair nearest a stone fireplace where embers were still glowing from an earlier fire and pulled the blanket tighter around me.

I wondered what Tim was doing and if he might be thinking about me. I wondered if he regretted what he'd done and wanted me back. I knew he didn't. But I was just crippled enough to still fantasize that he did.

I was a little lost in my head when I heard the French doors open behind me, and I immediately cringed. I didn't want to see anyone, and I didn't want anyone to see me. Hadn't Mia gone to bed hours ago? I ventured a quick glance and saw Bo Sutton set down a bucket and some towels on a wicker side table, then he walked past me to the edge of the patio. He hadn't noticed me. I watched him stand there for several minutes, taking in the glimmering view. The moon was bright enough that I could see him pretty clearly. He was wearing jeans and flip-flops, and his untucked shirt hung beneath a dark sweatshirt. A slight breeze was pushing around his longish Josh Groban hair. It was dark, but I could still see that good looks ran deep in this family. He didn't know I was there, and any second now he would turn around, and the sight of me would startle him. I cleared my throat, and he jumped predictably. "I'm sorry." I grimaced when he quickly turned. "I so did not want to scare you, but that's exactly what I did. I'm sorry," I said again.

"Ivy?"

"Hi. I couldn't sleep so I...Is it all right that I'm sitting out here?"

He nodded, rallying "Of course," he said, walking toward me.

I pulled the quilt tighter around me in an insane effort to hide myself from him. Bo Sutton was maybe 5'10" and looked every bit the runner that he was, all sinewy and not overly muscled. Lean and precise, and pretty—like I said, *pretty* ran in this family, and it made me nervous. But then he seemed nervous, too. For a moment we just looked at each other in the moonlight. Then he nodded. "Ummm, can I get you anything?"

"I'm sorry?"

"Do you need anything? Is your room okay?"

"Oh, it's great. Thank you so much for letting me *invade* y'all's space like this."

The way he looked at me made me suddenly wonder if he'd had any say in the matter. He nodded and tried not to smile, it seemed. "Well, have a good night. I'm just going to wipe down the furniture, then I'll be out of your hair."

"What?"

"Oh, and if you're hungry, there are some macaroons on the counter—I made them for my sister's book club, at her insistence, and they probably ate three. So, you're welcome to them. There's fruit, yogurt, prosciutto. Please help yourself."

For a second, I thought he was toying with me, which I knew was ridiculous. "Thank you."

He cleared his throat. "I'm not sure Mia was supposed to tell me, but she said you were going through a tough time. Something about a ruined wedding?"

Tears suddenly stung my eyes as the Tim-sized knot in my stomach made itself known again. All I could do was nod.

Bo nodded, too. "I'm sorry some men are bastards."

A laugh pushed through the sadness, and I said, "Me, too."

Bo Sutton's smile was a bit uncertain. "I'm sorry that happened to you."

"Me too," I said again. I stood up, hoping he didn't see what was happening to me, what always happened to me when I thought of Tim and my *ruined wedding*. "I guess I'll go back to bed, now."

"Oh, I didn't mean to chase you off..."

"No... You...you didn't."

"Well, okay. Goodnight, Ivy."

From inside the dark pool house, I watched Mia's brother meticulously begin to wipe down and dry the first of eight wicker chairs. There was also a table and two ottomans. Mia had said he was odd—that was becoming evident—but he still seemed nice to me. And the fact that he was a germaphobe must be why he was cleaning the patio furniture at two in the morning. From the precise way he was going about it, I could see it would likely take all night if someone didn't help him. I threw on my jeans and went back outside.

"Can I help you?" I startled him, again. "I keep doing that, I'm sorry. Do you have another rag?"

He looked at me like I was speaking in tongues. "What?"

"I want to help you. It's late, and clearly it's important that this furniture gets cleaned, so let me help."

"Why?"

"Well, for one thing, I wouldn't feel right about drifting off to sleep while you're out here working your tail off in the middle of the night. That doesn't seem fair."

"Well...really, it's just how I like to do things. I'm kind of a one-man show."

I smiled. "Not tonight. So...do you have another rag?"

"Ummm... no. One man job only requires one rag."

"I see." I picked up the towel that he'd draped over the arm of the second chair. "Well, how 'bout I dry, then?" Bo Sutton seemed suddenly nervous, and I felt bad that I was making him uncomfortable. "You can show me exactly how you want it done," I said.

He slumped a little, like he'd been caught being silly. "You probably think I'm insane."

I knelt down and started drying the seat he'd just wiped down. "Why? Because you like clean furniture?"

"Because I like clean *lawn* furniture at two in the morning."

I shrugged. "Well, this way, it won't be waiting for you when you wake up. And when it's done, you won't have to think about it anymore tonight. Oh, my, I sound just like my grandmother. She used to say that to me when I didn't want to do my homework."

He relaxed a little. "Make sure you go in one direction, so you don't...you know"—he cleared his throat—"leave streaks."

It's wicker, I thought, but corrected my technique without stating the obvious.

For a while we worked in silence, which I didn't really mind, but it was a bit weird. "So...did you sit in on the book club?" I finally ventured.

"No," he said, definitively. "All that estrogen is a bit much for me."

I laughed.

"Which is kind of a shame because I have a great appreciation for good literature."

"Like what?" I said, moving with him to the next chair. "What's your all-time favorite book?"

Bo Sutton thought about this. "That's too hard. There are too many wonderful stories—ask me which one taught me the best lesson."

"Okay. Which one taught you the best lesson?"

We'd reached the next chair—a foot away—where Bo Sutton discarded the rubber gloves on his hands and replaced them with a new pair. I suppressed a nervous giggle because that was about the strangest thing I'd ever seen. Bo offered me a pair, but I declined—I was only toweling, for heaven's sake, no need to go crazy. He re-wet his rag and proceeded to wipe down the seat.

I cleared my throat and got back to it. "So, you were saying?"

"That would have to be *Precious Bane*. I wanted to name my company after that book. Do you know the story?"

"I don't"

"It's about discovering wonder in ordinary things and how love can sneak up on someone who can't imagine they deserve it."

"Really?"

"Plus, the name—*Bane*—represents...*me*. I drive me and everyone around me a little nuts with my need for perfection."

I looked at Bo Sutton, his hair deeply shading his face in the patio light. "I never heard of that book, but I think I'll be doing a little Amazon shopping as soon as I'm done here."

"Oh, don't do that. I've got an extra copy," he said, not looking at me. "You missed a spot," he pointed with his rubber-gloved finger.

We were quiet for another minute while I re-toweled what was surely evaporating in the breeze anyway but was clearly stressing my new landlord. In all my twenty-one years, I'd never met such a curious man. I liked him, but he was more than a bit peculiar.

"So..." I ventured again. "You're house-sitting? This isn't actually where you live?"

"No. I mean, yes, we're housesitting for my aunt Lullaby. She's in France with her new husband."

"Lullaby. I never knew a Lullaby. When will she be back?"

Bo Sutton was once again intent on his scouring of the wicker, but he managed to shrug one shoulder. "You never know with my aunt. She said the end of the summer, but that could mean next summer."

I laughed. "And where do y'all live when you're not here housesitting?"

He smiled, and I didn't know why. "Well, I had a townhouse," he said. "But I've outgrown it...my business has outgrown it, I should say—I work at home. So, I'm looking at a loft downtown with dedicated space for my studio." He shook his head and grimaced. "But I don't know if I'm really a loft person."

"Oh, I'm definitely not." I was quick to agree. "I need cozy, soft things, old things that hug me. My mama has an ancient, overstuffed sofa—kind of lumpy. It swallows you right up when you sit in it. That's very much my style."

"And where do you live?" he said.

"Georgia—Savannah, Georgia. Born and raised. But..." I shook my head. "I won't be going back there."

"Why is that?"

"Oh, it's a long story."

Now he stopped and looked at me. "It's not because of the ruined wedding?"

I nodded. "Yep. I am boycottin' an entire state because I was dumped. Now who sounds insane, Bo Sutton?"

That got me my first laugh from the nice-looking but very tightly-wired Mr. Wicker-scrubber.

Eleven—Bo

I'm not a good sleeper. Since I was small, I've always found far too many things to worry about to waste time sleeping. It used to upset my mom. She'd come into the kitchen at six a.m. for her chilled water before heading out on the two-mile run she'd taken every single morning of my life, and there I'd be, sitting at the table fully groomed, reading a book, just waiting for the day to start. And when she got home, I'd have breakfast ready. I was a good cook in the third grade, which is why I'm an excellent cook now. Which I suppose is why my worries this morning were incessantly culinary-related.

It's hard to know how best to please a renter-slash-houseguest, and I did not want to disappoint Ivy Talbot on her first official day here. Especially now that I knew her. Somewhat. I'd asked Mia if the girl had any food allergies, and my ridiculous sister said she had no idea. So, after an hour of pro and conning a full breakfast of egg-white omelets filled with imported feta and baby spinach, honeyed fruit, and nine-grain muffins versus homemade granola and Greek yogurt, same honeyed fruit, but with green tea, I gave my obsessing a break and went to look for my extra copy of *Precious Bane*. There was time. It wasn't yet seven.

I still couldn't quite believe what happened last night. Ivy Talbot had been so friendly and open, and I'm usually so repellent. But she seemed to have missed that. I'm not sure what happened to me, either: I don't usually warm so quickly to people, especially women—unless I'm medicated, which I wasn't. I'm usually far too busy emitting toxic waves of anxiety to invite anything but avoidance. Unless I'm medicated. But last night was different. Ivy was different than most women I'd met. She was either not aware of my anxiety or simply didn't care, which I found surprisingly *freeing*. But then I think she was just pretty self-involved herself. It looked like she'd been crying—or wanted to. There was something very fragile about her, almost bruised, and I was actually quite shocked at how it drew me in—I generally avoid other people's problems. But she was wounded, I guess that was the difference, and almost like she didn't think anyone would notice. And she had those pretty eyes. Sad, but pretty. All I could think to do was offer her food when all I really wanted to do was sit down, at a comfortable distance of course, and talk to her. And then when I had the chance, all I could do was say something absurd about her wedding, which sort of put to death any further conversation.

I groaned, reliving the awkward moment. This is why I work in isolation—really, it's a kindness to the rest of humanity. These were my thoughts as I surveyed the wall of boxes lining Lullaby's RV garage. Aunt Lully didn't have an RV, she just had space for one if she ever had a yen for a weekend home on wheels. Consequently, all my earthly belongings were crated and organized in rows the likes of which Costco would envy. And somewhere on the second row—B—was a pallet of boxes filled with books.

When Ivy had insisted on helping me scrub down the lawn furniture, I'd almost had a seizure, I swear. I'd steeled myself to feel ridiculous, and I had, a little. But that was all me, it was nothing she'd said or done. In fact, again, it almost seemed like she'd been oblivious to my oddity—well, again, maybe not oblivious, but certainly not bothered by it. And it had been... *nice* being with her. Easy, even. Surprisingly so. And we'd talked about books—and she'd seemed honestly interested in *Precious Bane*. I had to find it for her. I had to, or I would have nothing to say to her.

Where was that book?

I looked for thirty-eight minutes—to no avail—and had to stop, which forced the sensible breakfast choice of granola, yogurt, and fruit. At that point, it became a time management issue—granola didn't require any preparation, nor was it temperature dependent. It merely had to be on the table and look appetizing, which I could manage and still be downstairs on time. My goal was to make it to my workroom—a converted bedroom in Lully's basement—by 8:00.

But I'd left my phone on the washer last night when I'd put in a load of towels, which now necessitated my walk past the pool, which I was dreading because Mia and Ivy were doing laps.

Lullaby had designed her home to match her larger-than-life personality. And since Monterey was not weather-friendly enough to justify a showpiece in the backyard, my aunt had built her pool indoors. It was a marvel of engineering and indulgence, not to mention 30,000 gallons of untrustworthy chlorination. And wouldn't you know the 20x40 wonder of Italian marble resided in its own glass room directly across from the laundry suite—hence my angst.

And at the moment, my sister and our lodger were swimming in that untrustworthy chlorination almost certainly with their mouths open. Well, Mia was swimming, Ivy was sort of pretending. When she realized I'd caught her half-hearted effort, she looked a little sheepish. I waved so she wouldn't think I was rude—or gawking—at which point she disappeared beneath the water.

"Bo!" Mia shouted. "Some producer called a minute ago—I forgot her name, but she said she was sending someone over at noon to look at a snake?"

"Today?" I coughed.

"You left your phone in the laundry room, so I answered it. It's on the table."

"Today? As in *today*?"

"Yes, today," Mia laughed. "She said she was sorry to call so early—she said she thought she would get your voicemail."

I saw my sister's mouth moving, heard utter ridiculousness emanate, and could not believe what she was saying. Yesterday was supposed to be committed to sketching, material gathering, pricing, and the formation of a solid vision that naturally required time and devoted creativity. But yesterday had gotten away from me with the arrival of Ivy Talbot, so no sketching had taken place. No pricing. No devoted creative effort whatsoever. I had nothing to show my client.

And then it started. The pounding in my chest and in my ears, the breath I couldn't get in or out. The seizing of my throat. The certainty of impending death. Quickly and decidedly, I knew this time I was dying. I started to tremble, and then I staggered, trying to reach the closest chair. This wasn't happening. Not now! Please, not now!

"Bo!"

The familiar wail filled my ears, high-pitched, terrifying.

"Bo! Ivy! He's having a panic attack! I need your help," I heard Mia shout through a tunnel.

No! Don't help me. Just let me die this time! Then my legs abandoned me. Suddenly my sister was there, wet, and holding me up. Then her friend, also wet, draped my other arm around her. Together they maneuvered me to a teak lounge and lowered me onto it. Now I was not only dying but also mortified to be doing it in front of these sodden witnesses. And I was wet—with unclean water.

"Bo, you're breathing too fast," Mia barked. "Slow down. Concentrate! Ivy, watch him while I find a paper bag." Then my sister was gone, and Ivy Talbot calmly placed her cool hands on my face. "Bo. Open your eyes," she said. "Look at me."

I did, or I tried to, but I couldn't focus. She came closer. She smelled like chlorine. "Bo," she said, softly in her drawl. "Look at me. Listen to me. You're okay. You're fine. Just breathe with me. Just breathe."

Her thumbs were now gently stroking my cheekbones, and her face was inches from mine. She was so incredibly calm. "You're havin' a little panic attack. That's all. And the good news is it's not a heart attack. See, silver linin'."

I absorbed each word. She was crazy. There was no *silver linin'* in this moment. It *was* a heart attack! Could she not see my heart trying to pummel its way out of my chest? Was she blind? I was dying! *But don't let go of me. Please don't let go!*

"Keep breathing, Bo," Ivy crooned. "Slow down. You're doing great. You're doing great."

Then Mia was back and holding a paper bag against my face, but I was still locked on Ivy's eyes, as if to let go would hasten the stopping of my treacherous heart. It was a primal terror, void of reasoning.

"Bo, breathe," Mia said. "In, slow. Good. Now out, good. Nice and slow." I let go of Ivy's wrist, which I had been crushing, and took the bag from my sister. Slowly, and in a flood of humiliation, I came an inch back to myself, then another inch. Somewhere a phone rang and Ivy, holding her arm to her chest, left my side to answer it. Mia held out a glass and a small orange pill. "Take this."

I resisted because that's what I do, but Mia was right, I needed it, even if I hated that I needed it. I took the little Xanax from my sister and swallowed it down with a sip of water I could tell had not been filtered. Then I closed my eyes and willed myself through this episode. Xanax works fast, and because I rarely took it, my system responded quickly. Within just a few minutes, the edge was off, and my panic had distilled down to just my worse than usual anxiety—and, of course, monumental shame. How had I let this happen in front of Ivy Talbot, a stranger I would have to face all summer?

"Bo?"

Speak of the devil.

"That was a Miss Edmonds, your noon appointment about a snake? She said she had forgotten a conflict and wanted to come at eleven instead."

I groaned.

"I hope it's okay, but I told her your morning was booked and she would have to call you back tomorrow."

I looked at this girl shivering in her red swimming suit, nothing but concern—and quick thinking—in her blue eyes. "Thank you, Ivy," I said fairly gushing relief. "That's perfect."

"Good thinking, Ivy!" Mia piped. Then to me she said, "I'm calling Mom. I have a class shoot, and you can't stay alone."

"No." *Could my humiliation be more... humiliating?* "I'm fine," I insisted. "I'll be fine."

"I'm not leaving you alone, Benjamin. You know the rules."

"Mia!" I snapped.

"I could stay," Ivy said, and we both looked at her. She shrugged. "I know I said I was planning to start my job search today," she said to Mia. "But maybe that could start tomorrow, or I could just do a little Googling today."

Mia seemed torn. "That's nice of you, Ivy," she said. "But that's a lot to ask."

"Definitely too much to ask," I insisted, wishing I was anywhere but here. I got to my feet, which was a lot harder than I made it look. Panic is like a bullet that leaves you stunned and blood-drained, but still alive—in a manner of speaking. "See, I'm just fine," I said again.

But then my preposterous knees turned to noodles, and I fell face-first into Ivy Talbot's damp chest.

Twelve—Ivy

Oh, I do love me a good adrenaline rush! Who knew a crisis could so utterly and completely propel me outside of myself and into superhero status? But it did, and for a minute there, helping Bo Sutton felt like the reason I'd been born. His involuntary familiarity with my upper body, notwithstanding.

Of course, like any good high, the effects were short-lived, and when I walked back to the pool house after having participated in the saving of Bo's life, I met my reflection in the full-length mirror on the closet door, and *my* life came screaming back. I wanted to cry. Damp, limp hair, some plastered to the side of my face, a body, twenty percent of which was hideously encased in old-lady-shaped Lycra, the remainder too hard to look at without squinting. The depth of my self-loathing had never been so poignant. How could I have let this happen?

I sat down in a sodden heap and called Geneva.

"My dearest girl!" she sang out. "How did you know I needed an Ivy fix?" And with that endearment, I was immediately rendered mute. "Oh, sugar plum…Come home, and let me love you. Come today."

"I can't do that," I croaked.

"What's happened, sweetie?"

"Gran, I'm a whale."

"You're not a whale."

"I'm a baby whale."

"Ivy Lee, that is simply not true, but if it were, you would still be lovely, because you are you."

"I hate myself. I don't know what's happening to me."

My grandmother sighed. "It's temporary, my sweet."

"Being a whale?"

"Most likely. But I'm talking more about the upheaval in your little life. Being this unhappy..."

"I hate it!"

"I know. It's very painful. But your life has suffered a chaotic eruption, and you are buried in the ashes. It's not pretty, and it's not easy. But as I've told you a million times: every life worth living includes at least one year of ashes, my love. It's a refining process."

"That's what you tell me."

"Well, you should listen to me, because I am very, *very* wise."

"You are..." I tried to smile.

"You won't always feel this way, my sweet girl," she promised—again. "And when you stop, you will be even more extraordinary than you were before. It will just take time. Now, tell me what has prompted these tears today."

So, I did. I started with Daniel making the arrangements for me to live with Mia and Bo Sutton, and how disappointed he was that I wasn't going home. Geneva huffed, predictably—my grandmother did not like my father. I told her about how much I liked Mia—how down-to-earth and confident she was. Gran laughed when I told her about the guy calling us *stick and tubby* at the football track and how Mia had handled him. I told her about Bo's panic attack this morning and how scared I was for him and how nice he was, and something in my voice betrayed me.

"He's nice?" Geneva said.

"Yes. He's a little strange, but I can tell he has a good heart."

"Well, how lovely is that? People with good hearts make for good karma—even the strange ones. Sounds like he's had a rough go today. Perhaps he could use some nice in return."

I looked down at myself. "Well...I may have blinded him with my centerfold-caliber magnificence, I probably *should* go check on him."

Ivy in Stills - 61

"That's my girl," Geneva said. "Sounds like you've landed in a good nest, for the time-being. You just breathe deep and let the Universe restore you."

I sighed. "Okay...because, you know, me and the Universe...we're tight..."

Geneva chuckle-sighed. "I love you, Ivy Lee."

"I know you do. I love you, too." I hung up and felt a smidge better, which was why I called my grandmother in the first place. No matter what I was, or who I became, what I did or what happened to me, Geneva Talbot would still thoroughly love me. And it was amazing to me, the lifesaving power of knowing that. If I was back home, I'd tell Mama I was spending the weekend with Geneva and head on over to Isle of Hope and sit on Gran's porch—no, wait, the wedding had been over there...never mind. I hung my head and gouged my hands through my tangled hair. Sigh.

Well, at least I'd gone for a swim this morning. I hadn't done that in...*ever*. Four laps—nothing to write home about, but still. And it was almost 9:00, and all I'd had was a glass of juice...and a hearty helping of adrenaline. That was a good start.

I took a shower, dried my hair, put on my least repulsive pair of jeans and some lip-gloss, then went to the main house to make some tea for Bo Sutton. While it steeped—four minutes exactly—I wandered around the massive living room. It was an elegant splash of style—Mama would say eclectic. Oversized furniture, lots of fancy throw pillows, I mean *lots*—some tasseled, some beaded, works of art each and every one. Huge windows let the sun in. There was a big fireplace and on the mantle were lots of pictures of Bo and Mia and Camille and two little girls who had to belong to Camille. The soft color on the walls made everything very soothing, except for a big ol' garish painting above the fireplace. I'd seen it when I first got here, and I still didn't know what the heck it was, even upon closer inspection. It was Picasso-esque, not really my wheelhouse, but interesting. I moved closer until I could make out a head, eyes—three, I think, a body(ish) shape—or maybe just a big red balloon, a hand—a four-fingered hand, very odd arrangement. The timer went off in the kitchen, which thankfully meant I didn't have to think about this *masterpiece* anymore—which, more sadly still, I had no real appreciation for in the first place.

I made the tea according to Mia's written directions, which she'd asked me to follow exactly, and found Bo downstairs, right where she'd said he'd be. I'd been given strict instructions to check on him, which Mia had warned me he would hate but tolerate if accompanied by tea. "Knock, knock," I said stupidly.

He was standing at the window, seemingly deep in thought. He turned with the tiniest scowl, which he quickly strove to retract. "Ivy. Hello. I told you, I'm...I'm fine."

"Oh, I knew you would be. I just brought you some tea."

"You shouldn't have bothered. I'm..."

"Very particular?" I finished for him. "I know. Lemon balm with a teaspoon and a half of organic honey, steeped exactly four minutes, in twice-filtered water. Of course." I smiled as I handed him the mug encased in a paper towel. *If he asks, you haven't touched the mug,* Mia had warned.

An infusion of pink colored Bo's face. "Thank you. That was...*very* kind." He looked at me, compelling me to look anywhere but back at him. I cleared my throat nervously and took in the room, which was its own world. Shelves and shelves of small plastic containers, each clearly marked, lined the walls. Two very bright lamps illuminated a compact worktable. On another table sat a laptop and an open sketchbook and a stack of small black boxes inscribed with Bo's logo in calligraphy—*Sutton*. I wanted to pick one up for a closer look, but I didn't dare touch anything. Finally, I again met Bo's eyes. "How are you feeling, really?"

He dropped his gaze. "Exhausted. And very embarrassed."

"Why?" I smiled. "It's not cause you fell into my *private property*, is it?"

He groaned, and colored deeper. And smiled. "Sorry about that."

I waved away his concern. "I was just teasin'."

"I really am sorry," he said. "That was quite a production you were forced to endure. That hasn't happened for months."

I shrugged. "Well, you were forced to witness the rather hideous situation going on in my backyard. If that didn't stop your heart—and not in a good way—then I think we should call it even."

Bo Sutton looked perplexed. "I don't know what you're talking about."

"My butt," I grimaced. "I'm talking about my butt."

Bo blew into his tea. "You're funny."

"I am?"

"Ivy, I'm sorry to report that I can't remember your butt. I thought I was dying. All I saw were your eyes, which are beautiful, by the way. And I think I broke your hand while you were trying to calm me down." He took a sip of his tea, hummed appreciatively, and studied me over the rim. "How did you know what to do?"

He thinks I have beautiful eyes? "What?" I said.

"Talk to me like that. You talked me down like a professional," Bo said. "Are you? A professional?"

"Oh, no. I just...I've seen my life coach do it. I have a life coach—which should tell you everything you need to know about me, Bo Sutton." I pulled a face, but when Mia's brother didn't react to this disclosure, I said, "I've seen him do it for Terrance—a guy in my posse."

Bo looked intrigued as he took another sip of tea. "You have a posse?"

"My PTSD posse. And our fearless leader-slash-life coach is Adam Pembroke. We sit around on Tuesdays and Thursdays and talk about our trauma, and sometimes dredging it all up makes us anxious. But Terrance—his wife was hurt real bad—sometimes he has terrible panic attacks when he talks about her."

"Panic on top of trauma. That's not fair," Bo said.

"No. It's not. It's awful."

"And Adam Pembroke? He's a therapist?"

"I don't really know what he is," I said. "He's probably not a real therapist. My dad was very concerned that I not be *psychiatrically* labeled, so he hooked me up with a life coach, which is apparently more acceptable in his world."

Bo nodded. "Well, labels can be hard to transcend."

I looked at him, and when he didn't expound, I couldn't help myself. "You sound like you know," I said. "Do you have one? A label?" My hand found my mouth too late. "Oh, I'm so sorry, Bo. I probably need a license for this hole in my face."

Bo Sutton chuckled, his eyes half hidden behind his wavy bangs. "It's okay. I have an anxiety disorder, which is a label I can live with."

I moved my hand. "That doesn't sound so bad."

"Well... anxiety is a big umbrella that other conditions live under—or hide under." He shrugged a shoulder. "I take irrational pride in not being officially diagnosed with OCD—obsessive compulsive disorder—which I could very well have. I've just never stuck with a therapist long enough for them to make that unequivocal determination." He shook his head. "I probably have it. I don't like germs. I don't like the idea of germs. I like order." He looked around his very ordered workspace. "I like lists and everything checked off those lists before I go to bed at night."

"The lawn furniture..." I said.

He nodded. "I don't do disruption very well. I'm not particularly flexible. I don't always have a panic attack in response to disruption like I did today, but I'm pretty compulsive, and sometimes I do." He took another sip of his tea. "So, I probably have it, or maybe I'm just..."

"A very interesting man?" I finished for him.

His mouth bent in a lopsided grin. "Well, I like that better than mentally deranged."

"Oh, me too." I smiled. Then the silence got a little awkward, and it seemed like a good time to leave. I was about to say so when he said, "So, is he helping? Your life coach?"

Ivy in Stills - 65

I shrugged. "I don't know. I still wake up every morning sad and humiliated and betrayed and feeling bad about myself. So, if he's helping, he's taking his sweet time."

Bo smiled, but looked sorry and like he didn't know what to say, and it felt uncomfortable. I sighed and tried to smile, too. "Well, I'll leave you to your creating. Can I get you anything else?"

"No. This is just right." He indicated his cup. "Thank you."

I turned to leave, and as I did, he called after me. "Ivy?"

"Yes?" I said, turning back.

"For what it's worth, your backyard looks fine to me."

Now it was my turn to color, and I imagined a deep magenta. But there was no malice, no teasing insincerity in Bo's face, and it caught me off guard. I smiled again, this time self-consciously. "Well, now I know that in addition to the other noteworthy elements of your personality, you are, in fact, also a very nice man who may or may not be hard of seeing."

He was laughing when I walked out.

Truth be told, so was I.

Thirteen—Mia

The next week, we were on our way to my parents' house for Sunday dinner. It's tradition. It's Mom's way of taking a peek inside our lives so she can offer us unsolicited advice and make sure we start a new week with a fresh dose of motherly support. We're adults, she knows we have lives, she understands if we can't make it, but I usually make the effort. Mostly it's for Bo, who never misses—she worries about him. And it's for Camille, who rarely comes anymore. But the timeslot never changes, and the front door is always open if my sister can manage to stand up to the scumbag she's married to. Of course, it's for me, too, because having a daughter in love with a soldier serving in hell is always a concern. Happily, today I could report my Derek was alive and well and, according to the pic attached to the email I'd gotten in the middle of the night, winning a bundle playing cards with his buddies. Before he was deployed in March, Derek had become a regular at Sunday dinner. My parents adored him.

I'd invited Ivy Talbot again today, not really expecting that she'd be interested in joining us. She'd declined last week, but this morning she'd surprised me and accepted. Of course, I'd assured her that she could leave anytime she wanted—she could drive my car home if it came to that, and Dad could drive Bo and me back to Lullaby's.

"There won't be any fireworks, Ivy," Bo promised from the backseat. "Camille won't be there."

Ivy looked perplexed. "Is she not invited?"

"Oh, that's not it," I chimed. "Peter—her stellar hubs—just won't allow it. It's Sunday, after all, and Sundays are reserved for family—read: *him*." I looked over at Ivy and rolled my eyes. "We're not fans of *Pete*. He hates it when I call him that."

"It goes both ways," said Bo. "He can't stand us either."

"Shocking, I know," I chuckled. "He's a creep," I said. "The only good Peter Diamond has managed to contribute to the world at large would be his adorable daughters."

"So, is it a bad marriage or *real* bad marriage?" Ivy asked.

I glanced at Bo through the rearview mirror, then over at Ivy. "He's awful, and my sister has never been the same since she married him," I said.

"Oh, I'm so sorry," said Ivy.

"And the girls have become small pawns in their parents' domestic nightmare," Bo added.

"Yep," I nodded. "And it's killing my mom and dad."

"Oh, my goodness! I'm so sorry," Ivy said again. "Are you sure I should be coming? This sounds like serious family stuff. I feel like I might be intruding."

I looked at her. I'd known Ivy Talbot less than two weeks, and every day she was just such a nice surprise. "It won't be serious unless Camille shows up, which she won't," I said again. "And my parents are thrilled that you're coming—you met them at my exhibition, remember?" I said, turning onto their street.

"I do. They were nice."

My dad was watering the hibiscus in the front yard when we pulled up, and he greeted us with a wave and a smile. He was the older version of Bo—same height and build, wiry with the same untamed hair but shorter than Bo's, and lots of silver. When we got out of the car, Dad pulled Bo close with gusto, and my brother embraced him the same way. Bo was my dad's pride and heartache. "You look good, Benjamin. I hope you brought your sketches."

"Of course. We'll look at them later, Dad," my brother assured.

After my father hugged me and teased that I looked fresh from a Grateful Dead concert—high praise for a girl like me—he turned to Ivy. "Dad," I said. "You remember my friend, Ivy Talbot—from my exhibition? Ivy, this is my dad, Jack Sutton."

"Hello, sir," Ivy said stiffly, extending her hand. Of course, Dad pushed it away. "We're huggers around here," he laughed. "So, brace yourself, Miss Ivy." Then he swallowed her up. When Ivy didn't seem to mind, it struck me that she could probably use a few more hugs in her life. When my dad released her, she was smiling.

Mom was in the backyard setting the picnic table, and she too got smiley when she saw us. She was wearing a linen dress, no shoes, and a big straw hat. "Well, hello there, strangers," she sang out. She too pulled Bo into her arms, which evidenced her ever-present concern for him. I'd given her a blow-by-blow of his recent panic attack and suffered a minor scolding for not calling her sooner. She eyed me now for an update. My smile said he was fine. She took hold of his face—a feat only she could get away with—and tugged it close to hers. "You look good, sweetheart. Are you?"

"I'm good, Mom. I am," Bo said.

She hugged him again and looked at me over his shoulder. I nodded, reiterating that he was fine. My brother wasn't as fragile as my parents feared. Yes, he was seriously obsessive. Yes, he was mildly agoraphobic. Yes, the meds he refused to take regularly would help, but he knew his limits. Yes, his germaphobia could be a pain in the butt. But there were worse things than being a human Mr. Clean. And all things considered, him spending the summer with me at Lully's house was working out better than I'd hoped.

"Mom, you remember Ivy?"

"I do! How could I forget that hair?" my mother said, taking Ivy's hands. "Welcome to our home." She pulled her close, and I heard her say into Ivy's ear. "I understand you were phenomenal with my son last week. I can't thank you enough."

"Oh, well...I was happy to help," Ivy said.

My mother patted her face—Mom was very touchy-feely where faces were concerned—and hair, apparently. "You're a doll," she said. "I'm so glad you're here."

Dinner was salmon grilled on cedar planks, except for Bo's which was double-washed, sprinkled with extra virgin olive oil, and hermetically sealed in foil. *Wood? Do you know what wood is exposed to? It's nature's petri dish!* There was also Parmesan risotto, fresh baked rolls, summer salad, and fresh-squeezed lemonade.

We had just settled around the table when my nieces came screaming through the backyard. Camille, looking harried, showed up right behind them, wearing the biggest sunglasses known to man. I was so surprised to see her that I dropped my roll.

Fourteen—Ivy

The first thing I noticed was that the little girls were adorable. Tiny, both with dark curly hair, one short, the other long, and they didn't seem to know where to run. The second thing I noticed was how everyone seemed to freeze from shock. Mia even dropped her roll. But she was sitting closest to the patio door and seemed to recover the quickest, so she grabbed the little girls, singing, "It's my movie stars! My sparkly diamonds. My partners in crime!" She kissed their laughing faces until they each broke away and bee-lined for a grandparent. Those grandparents then pulled them hungrily into their respective laps and continued the snuggling. Of course, Mia pulled out her camera—that girl always had her camera. Bo looked shell-shocked.

While Mia snapped pictures of the littles, she kind of laughed nervously and said to her sister, "Has hell frozen over?"

I thought Camille's giggle was forced and had an artificial quality to it, and I wasn't the only one. When Mia took a good look at her sister, she set down her camera and narrowed her eyes with suspicion. Camille was wearing these enormous dark glasses that did not hide the fact that she'd been crying.

"Oh, Lord," said Mia, suddenly very serious. "What's happened?"

"Honey?" Mia's mom said, noticing as well.

Camille sighed shakily. "Nothing! It's nothing," she insisted. "Can't I just come to Sunday dinner? Did I need to call first?" she asked, clearly peeved. "Can I have some salad, please?"

"Of course you can, sweetheart," Eileen Sutton said. "Sit down. I'll get you a plate."

It looked to me like Camille's glance traveled around the table but never landed on anyone, almost like she was challenging anyone to dare say something. I might be wrong about that—you couldn't really tell what was going on behind those goggles.

Eileen stood up, still clutching the littlest of the two girls who said to her, "Daddy hitted Mommy." But besides Mia's mother, who gasped, I think I was the only one who heard it. The others were listening to Camille fib badly about being 'just fine'.

"Who's dat?" the older child asked her grandfather. She was pointing at me.

"Scout, this is our friend, Ivy. Can you say 'hi'?"

"Hi. Ivy is a funny name."

I smiled. "I think so, too. How old are you, Miss Scout?"

She held up four fingers.

A second later, Olivia came running out of the kitchen in front of Mia's mom, who carried out extra plates, cups, and utensils. Eileen set them down, then reached across the table and took her oldest daughter's hand. "What did he do?"

Camille pulled her hand away. "Nothing, Mom. We just argued a little. People argue."

"Did he hurt you?" Mia's dad said.

"Has he been hitting you?" Bo finally joined in.

"No! Stop it! All of you!" She glanced my way. "You're embarrassing Ivy. Hi, Ivy."

"Hi. I like your glasses," I said, lamely.

"Thanks." Then she shouted at Olivia, who'd run into the yard. "C'mon, Liv. You need to come eat something." She scooped some risotto onto a plate. "You, too, Scouters."

"I'm not hungry," Scout said, nuzzling closer to her grandfather.

"I know, sweetie. But you still need to eat."

"Camille? *Sweetheart?*" said a man suddenly standing in the patio doorway holding a biker's helmet. And with the seemingly innocent arrival of who had to be Camille's husband, the already tense mood froze as decisively as if a gun had been fired. "Get the girls, *honey*. It's time to go." The hard set of his jaw made the gentle tone of his words ring hollow. Camille did not look up, but the plate she was scooping risotto onto started to tremble. I reached out and took it from her.

No one said a word. It was like Lucifer himself had shown up.

The man was darkly complected with deep-set eyes. His black hair was short, straight, and combed off his brick of a forehead. He took in the faces of those gathered, stopping briefly at mine before moving on to Eileen, who was sitting next to me. "Camille, get the girls. We're leaving," he said calmly, but with an edge.

"No," she said, but it was drowned out by his shout for his younger daughter, who did not know he was there. When Olivia saw her father, she started to cry.

Mia scooted closer to Bo. "Pete, they just got here. We're eating. Sit down, and I'll share my salmon with you. You can eat salmon, it's heart-healthy." Mia looked over at me. "Pete here is *very* protective of his vital organs and is rather picky about what he eats."

He glared at her, but Mia was unaffected. I, myself, did not dare react.

"Camille...*Now!*" he seethed, not taking his eyes off Mia.

Camille looked up at her husband. "I'll be home later," she said shakily.

"I don't think so, *sweetheart*," Peter said.

"Let's just calm down," Jack Sutton said.

I was suddenly tense and looked at Bo because I didn't want to look at what was unraveling here. We stared at each other for a few seconds, then Bo stood up and walked over to his brother-in-law. "You heard her," Bo said. "She'll be there later. Why don't you go home and cool off?"

"Why don't you shut up, Bo? This has nothing to do with you. And for your information, I don't need to cool off. I've just come for my wife, who's not feeling very well."

Bo didn't back down. "Is that what we're calling it now?" he said with heat. "*Not feeling well?* If my sister took off those ridiculous sunglasses, would we see your handiwork? And what about the other night when she was buried under an inch of make-up? What about then?"

"Bo! Pleeease stop talking!" Camille whined.

"What other night?" Peter said to his wife. "What's he talking about?"

"Bo, sit down," his mother said shakily.

"Are you hitting my sister now?" Bo demanded.

Camille's husband pressed his face close to Bo's, and though Bo flinched, he did not back away. "Your sister is a class-A clutz," said Peter. "If she's bruised, it's her own doing. I'd never hit my wife. Now step away, Benji, you're starting to irritate me." With that, the man shoved Bo away with a single pointed finger.

"That's enough!" said Jack Sutton as he slowly stood.

"Peter, *stop it!*" Camille said from behind clenched teeth.

"Camille, get the damn kids in the car! Now!"

"I will not!"

"I'd like you to leave my property, Peter," Jack said. "Right now. Go on."

"I'm not going anywhere without my family, old man!" Peter said icily.

That's when chaos ensued. Mia started shouting at Peter, and Camille started crying. And when behind me Olivia's crying got louder and Scout, who'd been roughly set aside by her grandfather, who was now insisting he would call the police, covered her ears, it broke my heart. I didn't know what to do, but I had to do something. So, I stood up and beckoned the little one with my finger, and amazingly, she scrambled to my side. I scooped her up, and she clung to me like she was drowning. Olivia, too, was suddenly next to me, and I took her hand as well. "I hate yellin', don't you?" I said gently, turning them away from the dramatics.

"Me too," Scout said into my neck.

We made our way across the backyard and around the corner to where there was a giant volleyball pit. "Wow," I enthused. "That's the biggest sand pile I have ever seen."

"It's for bollyball," the little one informed me. "We can dig?"

"I think we should. I love me a good dig."

Scout looked up at me and smiled shyly. "You talk funny."

"I do? I thought it was y'all who was talkin' funny," I said, drawlin' thick and purposeful.

Both girls giggled, momentarily distracted from the ugliness going on several yards away. Naturally, I seized upon this, and for the next few minutes, as the yelling got more intense and the expletives got more graphic, we dug great big holes and sang silly songs. And they were none the wiser when the police arrived. In fact, I made sure that Scout and Olivia had their backs turned to the patio and were belly laughing over my amazed discovery of their buried toes in the sand when Peter Diamond was escorted out of the backyard between two of Monterey's finest.

Fifteen—Bo

As soon as the police left with my brother-in-law, I had to lock myself in the bathroom and hyperventilate for twenty minutes. It was a combination of things: my sister's awful marriage—her letting herself be in that awful marriage, and my parents worry over her awful marriage, the way that piece of human garbage talked to them, to us, to me—calling me Benji, his finger in my chest, Ivy Talbot seeing his finger in my chest. That was probably the worst. All of these factors were colliding, fomenting, and effervescing inside me with no outlet but to explode into anxiety. That's what was happening. All because of my sister.

Thank goodness Mom had slid a paper bag under the door. And right after that Mia slid an envelope with a single Xanax under there, too. But I didn't need it; I didn't want to need it. Instead, I sat on the edge of the tub and hung my head between my knees and kept a washcloth of questionable cleanliness on the back of my neck while I breathed into the bag and waited for the tingling in my hands to go away.

As I hung there, I thought of Ivy, and how I'd promised her there would be no fireworks today. And then it had turned into the freaking Fourth of July. But she was…*amazing*. As long as I lived, I didn't think I would forget the way she'd rescued my nieces from their parents' unholy tantrum. And she probably had no idea that it was her nervous smile from across the table that emboldened me to confront Peter Diamond—a definite first for me.

I stood up from the tub and took some deep, slow breaths as I paced the small bathroom. I should have been exhausted—that was the usual curtain call to something like this. But, instead, I felt slightly exhilarated. I'd done something I hadn't known I could do. I'd acted with raw, unthinking instinct that had pole-vaulted me past my usual crippled self. It was primal and innate and dare I say manly. But that monster was hurting my sister, and I couldn't let that happen sitting down and silent. And I didn't even know that I couldn't let that happen until today.

The rub was that before the night was over, Camille would bail him out of jail. I knew she would. She'd changed drastically since she'd married Peter. Once a lot like Mia, Camille had become small and timid and unsure of herself. It had been like watching her die. And it was killing my parents.

"Bo? You okay, son?"

"I'm fine, Dad," I said through the door. "I'll be out in a minute."

Twenty minutes was the grace period, and I'd reached it. But I really was fine. If I knew how fresh Mom's towels were, I would have taken a shower. I really needed a shower. I settled for washing my hands and face. Twice.

"Uncle Bo! Uncle Bo!" my youngest niece shrilled through the locked door. "I needa go potty. Now!"

"Go in Grandma's bathroom, Livvy," I said, needing a couple more minutes.

"Mommy's in there crying. Let me in. Hurreee!"

I opened the door and found my almost-three-year-old niece with her pants down around her ankles and already leaking. I swept her up and plopped her onto the toilet. I may have been screaming a little. Or maybe that came after I realized my shoe had been doused with her pee.

Shaking again ensued. As did a pounding heart and light-headedness.

I don't do well with urine.

***

It was a while later when I finally came out of the bathroom in my stocking feet and Xanax coursing through my bloodstream. If

I'd been home, I simply would have trashed the shoes and socks and probably the jeans I was wearing—who knew how much of my niece's biological material might have splashed upward? Then I would have showered, of course, and scoured my feet and followed up with a good soak in rubbing alcohol. No Xanax. But away from my own world, I had to make do with a foot-slosh in Mom's tub and a pair of dad's socks. I was coping but barely. And of course, the little pill was helping.

Dad had finally been able to coax Camille out of the other bathroom, and now they were all sitting around the dining room table. Camille looked like hell. She'd taken off her sunglasses so her bruised cheekbone and puffy eye were clearly visible. Mia was taking her picture, and Camille was being very belligerent about it, insisting we all just mind our own business. Mom was crying because, big surprise, Camille was planning to bail Peter out of jail. I couldn't stand it, so I didn't sit down. I hated my sister at the moment for what she was doing to herself, her kids, and my parents. And of course, she was blaming me.

"What were you thinking, Bo? Why on earth did you bring up the other night? This whole thing is your fault!"

I glared at her as I walked by. "Go to hell, Camille," I said. Then I went to find Ivy.

I found her in the kitchen washing the dishes. "What are you doing?" I said.

"Just trying my best to be invisible. What are you doing?"

"The same, I guess."

Ivy smiled timidly.

"What a nightmare," I sighed. "I'm so sorry, Ivy. And I'm embarrassed for my family, and I'm sorry you had to see us all acting so unhinged. Especially when I promised that you wouldn't have to deal with any of this—I'm so sorry. If I say it ten more times, will you believe me?"

Ivy shook her head, dismissing my words. "Oh, stop. Camille doesn't know how lucky she is to have ya'll in her corner. She's in a bad situation." She looked at me and nodded. "You have a nice family, Bo, don't apologize for them. Your parents are wonderful. And, despite everything that happened today, it was nice to be in the middle of a real family. Even one in crisis. I never really had that, so I didn't mind at all." She handed me a wet plate, and I was a bit appalled. "There's a dishtowel in the drawer over there," she said, jutting her chin. "That's what your mom said."

I stared at her.

"You do know how to dry a dish don't you, Bo?"

"Well...I do. But I'm more of a dishwasher guy. You know, heat boost on the double rinse setting."

"That's nice, but as you can see, we're doing these by hand. So, suck it up, buttercup, and get to work."

My mouth fell open, and she grinned. And when I couldn't come up with an adequate objection, I found a presumably clean dishtowel in the drawer by the sink and set to the task of drying the presumably clean plate—all against my better judgment, and rather surprised at myself. It must have been the Xanax.

Ivy Talbot watched me with a bemused expression. "What?" I said. "Am I doing it wrong?"

"No. It's just that I don't think I've ever seen anybody be so *thorough* in their dish-drying before. In fact, you are so thorough you just might rub a hole in that plate."

"Oh, sorry," I said, putting the dish in the cupboard. "Like I said, I'm a dishwasher guy."

She laughed and went back to her washing.

"Ivy, can I ask you a question?"

"As long as it's not the size of my underwear."

I rolled my eyes at her. "You worry too much about that stuff."

"Says you and my grandmother." She grinned without looking at me.

"Well, that's kind of my question. Mia told me your parents were never married, and you just said you never really had a family...so...Ivy, who raised you? Was it your grandmother?"

She handed me another plate. "She would say the Universe did, but yes, Geneva raised me. Geneva Talbot, that's my grandmother. But my mom helped some too, of course, so I guess you could say I was raised by committee."

"Right..." I noised.

"I know that probably sounds strange, but my mama was kind of busy growing herself up when I came along. She loved me, don't get me wrong, but all my deep raising, my *intentional* raising, was done by Geneva. She took care of me—and my mom."

"What about your dad?"

"He paid the bills. But he's always lived here in Monterey. With his wife and family." Ivy glanced over at me then back to the sink.

"Oh...so..."

She grimaced. "It's a tiny bit complicated. I'm a secret that was supposed to stay put in Savannah," she said. "My dad's none too happy that I'm here."

"What are you talking about?"

She shrugged a shoulder and sighed. "My parents had a little fling twenty-two years ago...and I am the product of that fling," she said, finally meeting my eyes.

"What?"

She nodded. "My dad was a 32-year-old lawyer in town for a conference. Mama was a 19-year-old waitress going to art school. They fell into raptures that weekend. I came along right around the time Mama found out he was married."

I stopped drying to stare at her, and I'm not sure, but my mouth may have been hanging open again.

"My parents have been carrying on my whole life, and someday, *someday*, Daniel will leave his wife and marry my mama—she swears to it." Ivy smiled wearily. "She swears to it the way some people swear the earth is flat—which of course doesn't make it one bit true."

I stared at her, a bit stunned.

"Not the fanciest pedigree," Ivy chuckled. "But it makes for a good story, right?"

"I...I don't know what to say."

"I know...it's kind of a crap story, so maybe just say, 'Ivy, that must explain why you are such a complex and fascinating bundle of issues,' and we'll call it a day. How 'bout that, Bo Sutton?" she said resuming her task in the sink.

"You are..." I pushed out.

"I beg your pardon?"

"You are a pretty fascinating bundle of issues."

Ivy met my eyes. "Oh, you have no idea," she smiled, teasingly.

Her smile was insanely calming given the insanely un-calm story she'd just told me.

"Anyway," she said. "I'm sure that's why today—despite the drama—has actually been so nice for me. You're a real family. Flawed. Problematic. Wildly interesting." She winked at me. "Like I said, I like the whole idea of family, Bo. Even the messy ones." Then with a wry chuckle, she added, "And yours is pretty darn messy."

Sixteen—Ivy

A few days after that terrible afternoon, Eileen Sutton dropped by to check on Bo. She'd been to Costco and had brought a big box of cleaning supplies with her that I knew would bring a Christmas-morning smile to his pretty face. But Bo was out running when she got there, so I invited her to keep me company. I'd been on the patio Googling more jobs on the laptop my dad had loaned me. I had a new list of six rather promising possibilities and a busy afternoon in the making. I was ready for a break. I offered to make her some tea, but she said she'd just polished off a latte from Starbucks.

She was wearing a white flowy skirt and a turquoise tee, with bangles around her thin wrist, and she said she was actually happy to have caught me alone for a minute. I shut my computer and gave her my full attention because that was just so nice to hear.

"I wanted to thank you, Ivy, for what you did the other night," she started.

"For doing your dishes? That was nothing," I said, waving away her sweetness.

Eileen Sutton smiled but looked like she could cry. "Not the dishes—although, that was lovely. I meant rescuing my granddaughters. That was..."

"Oh..." I touched my heart. "That was my pleasure. They were little gumdrops. I could have swallowed them whole...Are you crying?"

She slumped slightly. "I'm just so sorry about all that..."

82 - Ka Hancock

I scooted an inch closer to her. "Oh, Mrs. Sutton. Don't be sorry on my account. I feel terrible for *you*. It must be so hard watching your little girl go through something like that."

"Oh, Ivy, you have no idea! And there's just nothing we can do about it. *Nothing!*"

"I'm so sorry," I said again. "I wish I had magic..."

"Oh, you are so sweet! Magic would be nice."

I smiled. "My grandmother does happen to have some superpowers," I told her. "She's coming next weekend. Maybe she can conjure up a spell for ol' Pete. Something along the lines of terminal droolin' or a nice incontinence curse—a little dribblin' at inopportune moments might be just the ticket. Or maybe just a classic Vienna sausage-sized penis curse."

Mrs. Sutton's eyes widened, and for a split second I thought I'd stepped in it. I did not know this woman well enough to say the word penis in her presence. What on earth was I thinking? But then a laugh coughed out of her. And it was a good laugh, honest, a cackle, even.

"I'm so sorry," I said. "I did not mean to be that familiar with you. Or make light of your family's tragic situation. Please forgive me."

Eileen Sutton patted my hand as she caught her breath. "I will not! That is exactly what I needed this morning. And just so you know, I'd pay good money for those curses."

I smiled, immeasurably relieved.

She sighed and dabbed at one eye. "It is hell, though," she said. "I guess you know Camille bailed him out of jail."

"I heard."

She shook her head and gazed absently over my shoulder. "At least he's not hurting the girls."

"That's good...I guess..."

"I can't believe I think that's worth merit," she said. "But of course, it is."

I nodded, not sure what she needed from me.

"She promised if that ever happened, she'd leave," Mrs. Sutton said anxiously. "Mia made her swear that if Peter hurt either one of those babies, she would bring them here. Peter has never been here." Bo's mama breathed shakily, and I could see she wasn't really doing as well as she pretended. "I guess that's the line in the sand, Ivy; apparently the emotional trauma those little girls face every day doesn't meet the criteria. But if that monster ever hurts them physically...then that's when my ridiculous daughter will do something..." She looked at me like she'd just realized I was there. "Oh! I shouldn't have said that about Camille. I shouldn't be burdening you with this at all...I'm so sorry."

"Don't you worry. They say talking is the best thing for processing a crisis." *Thank you very much, Adam Pembroke.*

"I like your curses better." She gave me a sad smile.

A door slammed in the house, and a moment later, Bo appeared on the patio, damp from his run, his unruly hair pulled back with a gray sweatband, his calf muscles bulging. He didn't look like Bo—he looked *better* than Bo, and if I'm honest, it was a little shocking.

"Hey," he said a bit breathlessly. "Hey, Mom what are you doing here?"

"Hello, darling. I just did a Costco run, so I dropped some things off for you. How are you doing?"

"Clorox wipes?" he said with brows lifted hopefully.

"Back in stock." Eileen smiled with exaggerated triumph.

Fist pump. "Yes! Finally. Hey, Ivy."

"Hey, Bo," I said, gathering my paraphernalia, nearly dropping the laptop. "Good run?"

"Yeah, it was great. What are you doing? You don't...You don't have to leave."

I said, "I do. Someone out there is just dying to hire me, they just don't know it yet." But what I was thinking was: *I so do. Because I literally cannot stop staring at you Bo Sutton.*

Eileen Sutton stood. "Well, thank you, you darling girl, for letting me unload—that was more than you signed up for."

"It was my pleasure, Mrs. Sutton. Really. You can bend my ear anytime."

"Only if you call me Eileen." She gave me a quick hug. "Deal?"

"Okay. Absolutely. Eileen."

"That sounds so lovely the way you say it." She winked.

Over her shoulder, sexy Mr. Sweaty smiled. "What job are you applying for?" he asked.

"Oh, gosh. I found openings at the art store, Wallpaper World, the Poodle Groomery..." I laughed and it sounded chirpy and ridiculous to my ears. Settling down, I said, "I am bound to be employed by the end of the week." For some weird reason, I did not mention that I had also filled out the lengthy application for X-ray tech at CHOMP—Community Hospital of the Monterey Peninsula. Maybe because that seemed a bit too committed, too permanent. Or maybe it was the fact that CHOMP was not hiring X-ray techs at the moment but would keep my application on file. I smiled and proceeded to back away from my overly attractive audience—nearly tripping on my own feet—and by some miracle made it into the pool house. "I'll catch y'all later. Wish me luck," I yelled.

What in the good Lord's name was the matter with me?

Seventeen—Bo

It's been almost three weeks since Ivy Talbot moved into Lully's pool house. And I'm quite proud to say that my routine is in process of successfully molding itself around her life. In all honesty, she makes it easy. She is not messy. Or needy. Or annoying in any way. In fact, I'm quite comfortable around her—and even more astonishing, she seems to be comfortable around me. She goes to her therapy appointments on Tuesdays and Thursdays, and I don't really see her those days. In fact, I've come to plan dinner around things that can be safely left on a tray outside her door. Mia thinks her life coach is a quack because Ivy seems to feel so bad whenever she comes home from seeing him. I don't know because Ivy doesn't really talk about it. She's actively looking for a job, which would indicate she plans to stay for a while. Surprisingly, this is fine with me.

This morning, she and Mia were still in the pool. I had homemade blueberry yogurt, which I'd left waiting for them in the fridge, and flax seed muffins were keeping warm in the oven. The table was set, and on Ivy's plate—wrapped in cellophane, of course—sat the copy of Precious Bane I had finally located exactly where I'd put it—in the bottom box at the bottom of a stack of boxes full of alphabetized novels on a crate in Lully's garage. I'd known it was there. It had just taken some reorganization to get to it, and now that I had, I so hoped she'd read it—talking books was one of my very favorite pastimes.

It was three minutes to eight. I filled my chilled glass with twice-filtered water and headed downstairs to start my workday.

Nearly an hour later, I was about halfway through a preliminary sketch of a poison ring I'd been thinking about when Mia barged in and completely destroyed my tenuous creative effort.

I glared up at her from my worktable.

"Sorry." She mock-grimaced. "But this is important. I brought tea," she said, handing me my mug sheathed in a paper towel.

I softened my glare to a sneer and took it. My sister looked her usual brand of free spirit: long skirt, tight, white tee shirt, hair piled to one side, held loosely in place with what looked like bejeweled chopsticks, gigantic hoop earrings she'd pilfered from me. I took a sip, eyeing her over the rim. "Five minutes."

She pulled a face at me. "Ivy's mom and grandmother are coming to town, and I think we should have them over for dinner. And I think you should cook. Thoughts?"

I swallowed. "No. NO."

"Yes," she said, nonplussed. "We should do this for Ivy. Let's do it on Sunday. And we'll invite Mom and Dad. It will be nice. It will be perfect." Mia stared at me.

"No. In what world would it be perfect? I can't do that."

"Yes, you can. I'll help you. We can eat on the patio. Let's have those great kabobs you barbeque with the chicken and the shrimp...and I'll make a salad."

I stared at her, my mind screaming, *no, no, no way!* But out of my mouth came, "I'm not sure about kabobs...and you *can't* make a salad."

My sister smiled in annoying triumph and headed for the door. "I'll leave the details to you. And...I haven't mentioned it to Ivy yet. I leave that to you, too. You're the best, Bo. I don't care what anyone says." She checked her watch. "That only took two minutes." Then she grinned and was gone.

It was like a microburst—a two-minute microburst—had come out of nowhere and leveled my unsuspecting morning. *I cannot entertain for strangers. I can't...not with kabobs...not on a Sunday...THIS Sunday!* What was Mia thinking? I set down my tea, but I needed both hands to do it without spilling, and I still sloshed a little onto my drawing. Then I dropped my head into my suddenly sweating palms. The wave was rising, rising. The breathless, fear-soaked crescendo of prickled emotion would soon overtake me unless I could breathe it back down, crush it back into its hole with my concentration. In...two, three, four. Out...two, three, four. In...breeeeeathe. Out...blooooow. I rubbed circles into my moist temples for a long time counting my breaths. *You can do this. You can get past this moment. You can even tell Mia no if you really want to.* Breathe. Just breathe. When I finally felt stability lift its weak head, I nearly wept with relief. That was a close one. Panic averted. Good job, Bo.

But now I needed a shower.

I pride myself on handling things like this without the aid of pharmaceuticals. The tradeoff, however, is time spent on unscheduled grooming, a disrupted creative process, and the apparently inevitable obsessive thoughts that have spring-boarded from this turn of events: Ivy's family is coming, and my ridiculous sister has left it to me to inform her of our earthshattering plan.

Forty minutes later, I was still so annoyed with Mia that I was overly rough in my flossing—a task not technically necessary after this impromptu shower, but such an integral part of my grooming routine that a departure from it now would have left me at odds with myself.

When I finished, I wiped down the mirror, the sink, the fixtures and gathered the laundry. At 10:36, the bathroom was put back together, I was put back together and feeling at emotional status quo as well. Give or take a pause.

I *could* tell Mia no. But the truth was her idea was a good one. I sighed and went to find Ivy...by way of the laundry room.

Eighteen—Ivy

I wolfed down the *snack* Mia called my breakfast and jumped in the shower so I could be ready if my phone rang. I was waiting for word on two jobs: cashier at Wallpaper World and sales associate at the art store. Of course the call came while I was in there soaked to the gills and all lathered up, and I missed it. So, I was dripping and anxious when I listened to the message from the wallpaper store: *Thank you so much, Miss Talbot, for your interest. We have filled the position but will keep your application on file. Feel free to check back with us in the next few weeks. It was a pleasure to meet you.*

I slumped onto the toilet in a sodden heap and pulled the towel around me. I really wanted to be able to tell Mama and Geneva that I was gainfully employed so they could stop nagging me about going home with them. I sighed, fighting discouragement. Oh, well, there was still the Monterey Arteria, which was my first choice anyway. I wrapped my hair in the towel and checked my skin in the fogged-up mirror, where of course the rest of my nakedness was on full display. But shockingly, there seemed to be a bit less of me. I thought it was the steam, some kind of optical illusion through the condensation, so I rubbed a wide swath in the glass with vigor. Nope, that wasn't it. Evidently, I had actually shed some of my midnight stuffed-crust pizza indulgence. Damn. Early morning swims and Bo's terribly stingy good-for-you cuisine looked kinda good on me, in a creeping-back-to-normal sorta way. But then I made the mistake of turning around to check out my naked backyard, where there was still ample evidence of my deadly nocturnal meat-lover's noshing, and just like that, I was back to my short, round, big-bummed girl reality. Sigh.

There was a sudden pounding on the door, and I kinda screamed for being so startled—and naked. Just a sec!" I yelped, grabbing underwear and jeans. "Be right there!" But my words were drowned out by more loud knocking.

When I swung open the door a minute later, I expected Mia, so I was a little surprised to find Bo standing there, hand poised, ready to thump again. He, like me, was freshly showered, although he was the only one of the two of us who smelled medicinal. "Hey, Bo," I said. "Is everything okay?"

He eyed me with curiosity. "Yes. Why?"

"Well, the way you were beating on my door, I thought the house was on fire and you were attempting to save my life."

It took him a moment to process this, but then he smiled. "Oh, sorry. No. I...I just wanted to talk to you. You look nice, by the way."

"I do? Well, thank you, Bo. I think we can blame your organic...*everything*. Nobody has ever cared what I ate before. Including me," I laughed. "So, if I'm shrinking, it's your fault."

Again, he seemed the slightest bit lost. But then he took me in in my entirety, landing once more on my face. "I actually meant your hair—pulled back like that, it makes your eyes look really...*blue*."

"Oh...right." I cleared my throat. "What did you want to talk to me about, Bo?"

He stepped farther into the room. "Well, I've been thinking."

"Okay."

"Your family is coming this weekend."

"Sunday," I said.

He swallowed. "Right. I...I knew that. And, well...Mia had this idea and...I think it's a good one...and..."

"What is it?" I said, growing tense.

"Well..." he breathed, looked anxious.

I gulped, slapped my chest. "Oh, my goodness...you guys want me to leave. You want them to take me back with them."

"What? No. No, that's not it! We want to invite your family to dinner."

I stared at him. "I'm sorry— *What?*"

"Would that be okay with you?"

I kept staring, not sure I'd heard him right.

"Ivy, it's just dinner..."

"Really?" I breathed. "Are you kidding?"

"My parents will be there, too. It's Sunday, so..."

"Really, Bo?" I said again. "You'd do that for me?"

He nodded. "Yes."

I was so relieved that he wasn't there to help me pack that I wanted to cry. I brought my hands to my face and felt the sting of tears. But then what he was offering hit me. Since I'd been here, I'd watched this prisoner of perfection carefully navigate his world, knowing how crucial routine and non-deviations were to his sanity. I could only imagine what this kindness was costing him, probably tantamount to donating a kidney if I'm honest. But all that was buried just under the surface of this nice guy dressed like any other nice guy, albeit a bit more crisply in pressed jeans, starched blue oxford—tucked in, of course—his wavy hair still damp from his shower, the whole kit 'n kaboodle smelling slightly antiseptic. He was as beautiful as his gesture. "Bo Sutton, I could kiss you."

His eyes widened in probable terror, and he tried to laugh. I put my hands up to show him I was totally kidding. But then I lowered them. "I know it's hard for you to have people in your personal space, but...could I hug you?"

Another laugh, but a less nervous one.

"Just a little one?" I moved closer, slowly like I was approaching a wary animal. And then I was there, my hands resting gently on his shoulders, his softly on my hips, which I found utterly amazing. And that was it. It was a lovely, awkward, delicate, almost hug that involved no trace of actual embracing whatsoever. But it was perfect.

"Thank you, Bo," I said looking right in his eyes. "I think that is the nicest thing anyone not related to me has ever done."

"Really?" he said shakily.

"Yes, really."

"You're welcome, Ivy," he said kind of whispery.

It made me smile...and almost cry, if I'm being honest.

Nineteen—Mia

It had been a hairy week. I broke a camera lens, Bo's African emeralds got lost in the mail, and Camille was not returning anyone's calls, which made us all tense. Ivy was also tense because she had not found a job, which she was desperately hoping to have in place before her mom got here tomorrow. She'd also had a particularly rough time in her group therapy this week, but she wasn't really talking about it. Needless to say, it was not shaping up to be a great weekend for entertaining.

But, of course, Sunday didn't care—it showed up anyway.

Ivy and I had planned to pick her mom and grandmother up from the airport at 3:15, but at the last minute, it turned out that Super-dad was on it. And since he was coming here anyway, I invited him to stay for dinner. He accepted so fast that I figured he'd had advance intel, probably from the butterfly that was Ivy's mom. But it was cool, and Ivy was fine with it. This was apparently how she'd been raised—her parents together on random occasions, playing the happy couple and by extension the happy family. And that's what we'd be today, evidently, just one big happy family made up of Talbot women, a sleazy little Ken-doll lawyer, and a bunch of Suttons. I'd even invited Camille, but she hadn't responded to my texts or calls. Mom hadn't heard from her either, and she was a mixture of anxious, scared, and frustrated. I didn't know who to be madder at, Camille or her armpit of a husband.

The good news was Bo seemed to be on his game despite his missing gemstones. But time would tell, it always did. Just to be on the safe side, he and I had decided on a simple menu that I could complete if he was overtaken by a sudden impulse to wash his hair. We were having grilled chicken breasts stuffed with seafood and breadcrumbs. Those were in the fridge and ready to throw on the barbeque. There was also a fresh fruit salad, boiled baby reds drizzled with olive oil and herbs, crunchy artisan bread, and for dessert, raspberry tarts he'd made last night. A too simple meal by Bo's standards, but a foolproof one by mine.

My parents arrived at 4:30 looking fresh and falsely buoyant over their barely concealed angst for my sister. Of course, Mom tried to jump in to assist with the last minute everything, and with coaxing, Bo allowed her to set the table. We were eating on the patio under the pergola, where the temperature was 75 and a bit balmy—but Bo still insisted on Lullaby's good china. He was starting to climb beyond his usual intensity, so I suggested he show Dad the snake choker he'd soon be famous for. He agreed but launched into a frustration-laden commentary about the US Postal Service. Dad almost followed him downstairs without permission but thought better of it. He winked at me, and I nodded my understanding.

From the kitchen window, I saw Ivy come out of the pool house and immediately get to work helping my mom. She was wearing a flowy wrap dress and platform sandals that gave her some height, and her hair was messily piled on her head. She looked very California.

"This is a nice thing you and Bo are doing today, Meez," Dad said, seeing what I was seeing.

"It's just dinner."

"Hmm-hmm," he noised as he kissed my head.

As I folded citrus dressing into my fruit salad, I heard the chimes. "Showtime."

"I'll go," Dad said.

I finished with the salad as polite commotion rang out in the front foyer. Then I ran my hands over my long skirt and scooped my hair (and abundant extensions) over one shoulder, making sure my bra strap hadn't escaped my tank, and walked out to meet our guests. In the entry, everyone was talking at once, so I just took them in. Ivy's grandmother, the legendary Geneva Talbot, was lovely—tall, thin, ancient, with mile-long white hair. She looked slightly formidable in a long turquoise caftan and red silk shawl. She was holding both my father's hands and thanking him. Ivy's mom was shorter, with an amazingly young face for someone with a child Ivy's age, and a gorgeous shock of incongruous platinum-colored hair that hung in loose curls to her shoulders. She had on a completely fabulous white sleeveless dress, short and snug in all the right places. She also wore a massive necklace of contrasting metals that made me drool.

These were stunning women who filled the space with energy. Ivy's dad, again, struck me as trying too hard, with his seemingly store-bought tan, bleach-white teeth, and dyed beard. He was wearing khakis, a pink shirt with a navy-blue sweater he wore over his shoulders like a cape. When he saw me, he smiled. I flashed him the peace sign and walked over and introduced myself to the ladies.

Geneva instantly took my hands. "Oh, goodness, aren't you just the loveliest girl! My dear, dear Mia...I'm so happy to finally meet you, again."

"Have we met?" I asked, knowing we hadn't.

"As soon as my Ivy told me about you, I had no doubt in my mind that we'd known each other in a prior life." She studied my face and gave me a genuine smile that made me sort of believe her.

"Really?" I said. "I wish I remembered, because that sounds extremely cool."

Her smiled broadened. "And this is your brother? Benjamin?"

I glanced behind me to see that Bo had made his way up from the basement. I tugged on him because he seemed a bit planted, and of course his eye was twitching. "Yes. This is Bo."

"Hello," he managed.

The white-haired woman clasped her hands at her chest. "Hello to you. It is truly lovely to make your acquaintance. I have heard *nothing* but niceness about you from my Ivy."

"Thank you," he managed. Then a big, fat, awkward *nothing*.

"I'm Ivy's mom," said a smiling—knowing—Bree Talbot, rescuing him. "Thank you so much for having us. This home is incredible."

Bo nodded, mutely.

"It belongs to our aunt Lullaby," I said. "We're just house-sitting for the summer.

Bree looked around appreciatively. "I love her taste. Is that her?" She pointed to the bizarre self-portrait of Lully hanging over the fireplace.

"Yep. That's our aunt."

"I love it! I wish I could meet—"

"Mom!" Ivy shouted bounding into the foyer. "Geneva! You're here!" And just that fast, Bo and I were forgotten and Dad faded away as Ivy was swept into a four-armed embrace that went on and on and left them all a little weepy. I was a mama's girl myself, so I could imagine the weight of this reunion. I'd never let go either.

Bo retreated before I did, but soon enough everyone was heading out to the patio, where Dad picked up the introductions and filled the glasses. Daniel Proctor rather purposely hung back with me in the kitchen, offering moral support as I sliced the loaf of French bread and arranged it in a basket. "My daughter looks very good, Mia. How is she doing?"

"I think she's doing okay," I said absently. "She has her moments and doesn't really like to talk about Tim. And when she comes home from her therapy group, she's a little quiet. But she'll get there."

He seemed annoyed. "I think it might be time for a chat with Pembroke. This is just dragging on too long."

I glanced at him, appalled.

"What?" he said.

"You can't do that—*chat* with her counselor." I met his raised brow with one of my own.

He chuckled. "I think I can. I'm the one paying him."

That Super-dad had access to what Ivy undoubtedly thought was private struck me as unethical, and it must have shown on my face.

"What?" he said again.

"That's just *wrong*," I said, handing him the basket of bread. "Ivy would be hurt. She trusts that guy to keep her confidences. She might even trust you." When Super-dad had no snappy comeback, I cleared my throat. "She's better than when she got here. She's applied for some jobs, you know."

Daniel Proctor's jaw lost a bit of its tone, and hard disappointment flashed in his eyes. In an effort to hide it, I suppose, he looked out at everyone gathered on the patio. I followed his gaze. Ivy was at the barbeque with Bo, their heads bent together. He sighed. "Well, we'll see about that..."

A few heartbeats later, he looked back at me, his jaw reconstituted, his eyes the picture of goodwill. "She does seem better, though. Thank you for whatever you're doing, Mia."

"I'm not really doing anything. I like Ivy. A lot. It's nice having her here." I grabbed my camera—because I'd promised to take pictures—and stepped through the French doors to the patio.

"Has she lost weight?" Super-dad said, following me out.

"I don't know. But doesn't she look great?"

Twenty—Bo

"Bo, thank you again for doing this," Ivy said to me as I filled the platter she was holding with grilled chicken. I did not want her to see the depth of my anxiety, so I didn't immediately make eye contact. "You're welcome," I said into the barbeque.

Everyone was filing out of the house, and I took a deep breath. In less than thirty minutes, this would be over—at least, the meal. After that, it was anyone's guess how long these people would linger, but I had an escape plan. I'd simply clear the dishes and retreat to the kitchen—and I'd make it a point, this time, to be sure that everyone was finished eating before I did.

Mia walked out of the house with Ivy's dad, and as he sat down next to Ivy's mom, my sister gave our table the once over and said, "Everything looks fabulous. Let's eat."

Because I'm me, I spent just a moment too long scraping chicken remains off the grill, so the only seat left was between Mia and my dad, which may have been by design. I sat down as Dad stood up with his glass. He'd asked me ahead of time if he could start things off, and I'd laughed because the implied alternative was me doing it, which we both knew I'd sweat my way through.

"I want to extend a warm welcome to Ivy's family," he said. "It is wonderful to have you here with us."

"Here, here," said Mia.

"And I want you to know that it has been a rare treat getting to know your Ivy. She's a lovely girl, and we just might have to adopt her!" He chuckled and lifted his glass. "To Ivy and her family."

Ivy was clearly touched, and she met my dad's eyes with soft emotion. But her father looked rather perplexed, as though he was just hearing the news that his daughter was special for the first time. It bothered me. Geneva lifted her glass the highest. "You can't have her, but we understand completely." She laughed. "And thank you for having us!" She then turned and covered Ivy's hand with her bejeweled one.

"Yes. Thank you, so much," Bree echoed. "This is just lovely." She reached past Daniel and touched her daughter's arm, and when Ivy looked over, they too exchanged a smile. It was easy to see that Ivy was very, very loved by these women.

After Dad's toast, we got down to the business of passing the food. I watched with keen interest what everyone helped themselves to and was concerned when Geneva passed on the potatoes. What was wrong with my potatoes? Did I need to offer her an alternative? Maybe rice? Did we have rice? How long would it take to make rice? Maybe couscous?

"Down, boy," Mia whispered, sensing my angst. "Mom, can you pass the salad?" she said, effectively diverting my attention.

The salad had stalled between my mother and Bree because they were deep in an easy conversation that had started with Mom's compliment of Bree's hair. I listened as it evolved into what Bree did in Georgia, which turned out to be teaching an art course at the college and owning a shop in the historic district of Savannah. My mother fingered Bree's massive necklace, which led the conversation to what I did, which prompted Dad to brag about my snake choker that would be guest-starring on *Winged Passion*. Bree was duly impressed—she knew the soap.

She was pretty, Bree Talbot, but trying too hard to be sexy, in my opinion, with those bare shoulders and no bra and all that makeup. But that was all for Daniel Proctor. Clearly. The two of them were intensely into each other, much more than they were into their daughter. I was bothered by that and disgusted when, after the conversation with my mom wrapped up, Bree again reached past

Daniel to get Ivy's attention. She asked her if she'd ever been to Carmel-by-the-Sea, and Ivy said she hadn't, to which Bree grinned and said, "Well, we just might have to change that." She placed her hand on Ivy's and squeezed, but on its way back, Bree's hand made a brief pit stop in Daniel's lap. This distressed me on numerous levels—she was eating with that hand, passing food with that hand. I must have reacted, I might have groaned, done a little fidgeting, because Mia discreetly placed a tiny pill in my teaspoon. I think she'd seen what I'd seen, which was in poor taste and disgusting but not pill-worthy. I handed it back to her.

"Bo," said Geneva.

"Yes?" I responded smoothly, betraying nothing.

"I hear you are building a loft. Tell me about it?"

"Well, yes. It's a big open space. Lots of natural light. I'll either sell it or move into it, I haven't quite decided. It's not far from here, just over by the college. Maybe ten minutes away."

"How lovely. And this will be your workspace?"

"Yes—in theory. It has great light, great feng shui, but it's noisy over there...so I'm conflicted."

"Creative people are so very interesting." She smiled. "I would love to see what you do. Would that be possible?"

I swallowed. This request hung far outside the parameters of the designated plan for today, and I wasn't sure how to react. Especially knowing I hadn't vacuumed my workroom since yesterday.

"He'd love to show you, Geneva," Mia said, jabbing the pill back into my hand, which was clenched in my lap. "He makes beautiful things. I want him to make me an exact replica of the necklace Bree is wearing."

Geneva laughed. "If you ask her, Bree will probably give you that one. She has hundreds."

"Good to know." Mia grinned. Bree was obliviously tuned into Daniel Proctor and unaware of what her mother had offered.

"Now tell me about this house," Geneva continued. "It has such a lovely *soul*. It undoubtedly belongs to someone very special. Your aunt, did you say?"

Mia nodded. "Lullaby."

"Lullaby! That's superb!" Geneva gushed.

"She's on her fifth honeymoon," I announced.

"How extraordinary," Geneva said. "This home is a reflection of her, am I correct?"

"Completely," Mia said.

"My sister is a very free spirit," laughed my dad, entering the conversation.

Geneva looked around. "You know, I can tell. I'd love to meet her."

Mia nodded. "She's very outspoken. Last year she heard Biden was golfing down at Pebble Beach, so she marched herself down there to chat with him." Mia laughed. "Of course, she couldn't get near the place, so she gave a note to someone, to give to someone else, to give to someone in the secret service to give to Joe. And she was arrested."

"Detained," Dad corrected.

"Oh, for heaven's sake," Geneva said. "What did it say?"

Mom piped up, laughing, "She would never tell us. She said it was between her and the President, and it had to be said."

"Mercy!" said Geneva. "She sounds remarkable. It's not one bit surprising that she's part of this divine family." She turned to Ivy. "It's no wonder you're thriving here, sweet pea. Maybe we'll let you stay a while longer." She winked.

Ivy lifted a brow and kept it lighthearted. "I told you, Gran, I'm never going home. You'll just have to keep coming here if you want to see me."

Naturally, this news bothered Daniel Proctor. He put his arm around the back of Ivy's chair. "Don't be ridiculous, *honey*. Of course, you're going home." He laughed, but his words rang a bit desperate.

"It's not ridiculous, Dad. I'm sorry. But I'm not. Ever."

Bree leaned in. "Sweetie, we've talked about this..."

I was staring at Ivy, feeling suddenly protective of her. But she held her own. "California is growing on me," she said. "I'm sure they need X-ray techs here, too."

"Hell, yes we do!" I heard myself blurt. "I mean, we have terrible, terrible accidents here which is great...you know, for the broken bone business...which employs X-ray people."

Mia rolled her eyes at me.

Geneva smiled and took Ivy's hand. "You will live wherever you live, dear girl, that's completely up to you. But there will come a day when Savannah calls you home, even if only for a short time."

"Savannah can call all it wants, Gran. I'm never answering—"

Just then, something strange happened over by Bree and Daniel, and Bree's wine was knocked over, which filled Daniel's plate and some of his lap. The glass teetered and then almost in slow motion fell off the edge of the table, shattering. Bree's face turned as crimson as the wine staining the Belgian linen tablecloth. It was too much. I started to hyperventilate. Dad patted my knee and slipped a Xanax onto my plate, making sure I'd seen it, then handed Ivy's mother his napkin. Ivy stood up and gathered hers and Daniel's plates, then stacked Geneva's on top of those and hurried toward the kitchen. She seemed grateful for a reason to escape. I gathered the glasses and followed her in while wine-dabbing and apologies sang out behind us.

"Are you okay, Ivy?"

"I'm fine. I'm sorry." She deposited her dishes in the sink, then shook her head. "No! No, I'm not fine! I'm not fine at all! When are they going to stop deciding my life for me." She met my eyes as hers filled with tears. "Where's your broom?"

I was torn between needing to sweep glass and offer words of comfort. I froze. But Ivy barely took a breath.

"I mean, in what scenario do they think I would show my face in Savannah *ever* again?" She slumped. "This was a mistake. I'm so sorry, for dragging y'all into my drama. And to think I was starting to feel not pathetic. I'm so pathetic!"

"Ivy...No. You're not pathetic."

She waved away my platitude. "Does my dad really think I don't know I'm being ridiculous? I know I'm being ridiculous!" she shouted. "I freaking know! But I am never going back there."

I nodded repeatedly, like a possessed bobblehead. "Good. Good. I don't want you to go."

She shut her mouth. "What?" she said.

The world, like a giant computer screen, froze. "What?" I said back.

"What did you say, Bo?"

"Nothing." I said, willing the words back down my throat, even though they were words I thought I meant. "The broom is over there." I pointed. "In that closet."

She looked at me. I looked at her.

Then I sighed and watched Ivy retrieve the broom and then—probably filled with even more emotion than when she'd walked in—walk back out to sweep up the murdered wine glass. All this took place while I inwardly lamented my hopeless ineptitude. What was wrong with me? I groaned—loudly. Again, this is why I rarely venture outside of the careful construct of *me*. It's really better for *everyone* if I stay within the walls of my own life.

I pulled on a new set of rubber gloves and set about rinsing the plates. From the window over the sink, I watched as my father took the broom from Ivy and hugged her with his free arm. He was good at easy affection without forethought, and I hated that he'd never taught me how to do that. As they stood there, Dad mouthing words I was certain were designed to comfort and reassure, Mom joined in, and soon Ivy was smiling. They liked her. But what wasn't to like?

Bree and Daniel had relocated near the fireplace and were in deep discussion. It looked to me like a parental intervention—possibly a bullying—was in the works. I wished I had the courage to walk out there. Puff out my chest, saunter over, and just invite myself to sit down, languidly, like I owned the place, and simply eyeball them in a 'leave your daughter alone' kind of way. But of course, I didn't—I'm not a saunterer. I'm not a chest-puffer-outer. I'm a dishwasher loader. So, that's what I did.

But, strangely, I managed to break two more wine glasses in the process. One pretty seriously.

Twenty-One—Mia

As my father took the broom from Ivy, who'd started to sweep up the mess her parents had made, my mom buried her in a hug. I sighed, hurting for her, and muttered under my breath, "Well, that went well."

Geneva Talbot, who was still sitting next to me at the table working on a raspberry tart, patted my hand with her gnarled one. "Nothing like a little southern melodrama for your Sunday entertainment. I do apologize, Miss Mia."

"For Ivy? Don't you dare!"

"Oh, heavens no. I apologize for my daughter and that little Svengali she calls a boyfriend."

I lifted my brows and stifled a grin, rather enjoying that I was apparently not the only *un*-fan of Daniel Proctor. Instead, I followed her gaze to where the Svengali in question and his butterfly had wandered to the lounge chairs near the patio fireplace. He looked pouty and she looked penitent, still trying to dab at the wine in his crotch with a linen napkin.

Geneva sighed, and I looked over at her.

"I've picked up on the fact that Ivy and her dad don't get along very well," I said. "But, even still, she doesn't seem ready to leave here."

"Yes. She's made that very clear," Geneva said. "Much to Daniel's chagrin. Obviously. Which does tickle me." The old woman met my eyes and grinned.

I laughed, again loving our mutual disdain for Super-dad.

With dinner more or less wrapped up, Mom picked up a pile of sodden napkins and asked Geneva if she could bring her anything when she came back out.

"Oh, my goodness, I am stuffed to the gills with deliciousness. Except I might just eat this last tart, if no one else claims it."

Mom laughed. "Bo would love that! There is no better compliment for that son of mine than an empty dessert plate."

"I will second that," Ivy added, holding the dustbin as my father swept the last of the glass into it.

Just then, Bree walked up to her. "Honey," she said to Ivy. "C'mon over by the fireplace."

"Mama..."

"C'mon, sug, your dad and I just want to talk to you."

"I will not argue with you about this," Ivy insisted.

"I know. I know. It's just a little chat."

"I mean it, Mama," Ivy said, following reluctantly. She glanced back at us, and I felt sorry for her.

We all felt for her. Mom watched her, then sighed and headed into the kitchen. Dad watched her as he started scraping the barbeque. And Geneva and I watched her like she was a girl headed to the gallows.

When Ivy sat down with her parents, I turned to Geneva. She smiled. "Miss Mia, I cannot thank you enough for being such a lovely friend to my little raincloud. You, your family, this place...it all seems like exactly what my sweet girl needed to put herself back together."

I chuckled. "Raincloud. I don't see her that way. Not really. She's just going through something. That's all. We've had some long talks, and she seems to be getting better every day. She has a life coach-slash-counselor. I think he's really helping her."

Geneva nodded and ran a bony hand down a snowy white plait of her hair. "She's told me about him," she said. "And I think you're right, which is wonderful. It was agony to see her so hurt, and it's such a relief to see her healing now. Bree wants her to come home, obviously, but I think she should take the time she needs. I do. I really do. She'll come home when she's ready. And she'll be stronger and wiser and kinder when she does—although, I don't actually know if that last one's possible." She winked.

I smiled. "Well, she's welcome to stay as long as she wants. But I have a feeling she's getting some pretty good pressure over there." I gazed again at the intense discussion taking place by the fireplace, where Ivy was flanked by her parents. Bree was rather pleading, Daniel had leaned in, looking lawyerly, stiff-jawed and unyielding.

"Oh dear," Geneva sighed. "That little Svengali thinks he's Tony Soprano..."

I laughed. "He really does seem kind of awful."

She shook her head, staring. "Oh, Miss Mia...you have no idea. But if the devil gives you a present that makes you happy every day of your life, do you think he's still the devil?"

I looked at her. Hard. "Oh...that's a good one. I don't know."

"Me neither," she said wearily. "Me neither." Geneva dabbed at her thin lips and stood up. "Come with me, my dear. It's time for us to rescue our girl."

I followed her across the patio and into the center of a very brittle family conversation. I felt awkward but only a bit since I was blanketed in the warmth of Geneva's billowy shadow, the breeze rippling through her gossamer dress making her appear a bit like a windblown goddess.

"So..." the old woman sang out. "Did you tell Ivy here about our surprise?"

"Mama! No, not yet! We're a little busy here." Bree seemed flustered, which was clearly her mother's intent. Super-dad just seemed instantly annoyed, but if Geneva noticed him at all, she didn't show it. Bree quickly regrouped and was about to spring forth with something apparently amazing when Geneva stopped her.

"I just had a thought," Ivy's grandmother said with mock spontaneity. "I think Mia should join us—if she wants to, of course."

Bree's mouth formed an O. Then she said it. "Oh, wouldn't that be fuuuun!" she squealed. She jumped up and took my hand.

Of course, I had no idea what they were talking about and neither did Ivy, from the look on her face.

"Sugar," Bree said, like a drum roll, then laughed. "We are stealing you away for a couple of days in Carmel—Carmel by the Sea. How does that sound? Heavenly, right? Am I right?" She laughed some more.

"Mama...What?"

"I know you're not working, so we made reservations. And Mia, you'll come show us all the best places to eat and shop and play and shop and shop and shop. You have to!" She giggled. "We'll have a spa day. Say you'll come with us," she said, tugging on my hand.

I stared at her, thinking of all the reasons I shouldn't or couldn't possibly miss class. But then I thought of all the great images I could capture in Carmel, which was a bona fide shutterbug's mecca. "Maybe..." I said.

Ivy was suddenly relaxed, having eluded the heaviness of whatever they'd been discussing before Geneva and I had walked up. Now she slid over and patted the lounge chair to make room for me, and I happily escaped Bree's grip.

Geneva laughed. "I'll leave you gals to the details. Now, I must go beg Benjamin for the recipe for those sinfully scrumptious tartlets." She eyeballed Super-dad, who was clearly bugged. "Daniel," she said, sweetly. "I believe Mr. Sutton could use some help with the barbeque, if you're finished here."

Ivy's Ken-doll-clad, wine-stain-crotched daddy bristled, and I coughed to hide a giggle. Geneva smiled, then winked at me.

Geneva Talbot was a big winker, and I liked her. I liked her a lot.

Twenty-Two—Bo

I was just scooping the last of tiny wine-glass shards into the trash can when Geneva Talbot made her way in from the patio. She was carrying what was left of the bread and an empty tray that had held raspberry tarts. I quickly dried my gloved hands and took them from her. She smiled.

"If I were in a restaurant, I would ask for a couple of those heavenly tartlets to go. I understand you're responsible for those, dear boy."

I felt myself blush a little as I lifted my brow in the affirmative. Then I peeled off my gloves and reached for the aluminum foil, "I have another half a tray in the fridge; you're welcome to them."

"Oh, Benjamin, you are too, too kind." She looked around Lully's kitchen appreciatively, and I followed her gaze. Here, the colors were soft but rich, the style slightly southwestern with clay tiles and turquoise accent pieces. Lully loved to cook. She loved to have parties and serve up international cuisine that she prepared herself. She had cookbooks from all over the world, and her collection was housed in a custom-built bookshelf that spanned the far wall next to a massive table that seated twelve. She had a formal dining room, but her kitchen was her heart. That's what I told Geneva.

"I feel like I know her," the old woman said. "You can tell a lot about a person by the *feel* of their home. Your aunt is happy, I think."

I nodded. "She is."

"And good..." Ivy's enigmatic grandmother said, taking in the kitchen again. "Goodness inhabits these walls, this home." Her eyes came to rest on me. "Present company included, Benjamin."

I chuckled nervously as I wrapped the tarts.

Geneva Talbot smiled, eyeing me. "Oh, pay no attention to me, dear boy. I did not mean to embarrass you. I just...I just sense things sometimes, and then I can't help but acknowledge them. Out loud."

She was still smiling when my curiosity broke free. "Soooo...What else do you sense about me? I mean, if you don't mind my asking."

"Not at all, Benjamin." She walked back toward me, and I was suddenly tense. And when she took my hand in both of hers, my impulse was to recoil because I'm me, and I'm definitely not a hand-holder. But Geneva Talbot was a force that I could almost feel flowing into me. Her hands were very warm, her eyes very intense. "I think you are an utterly fascinating man, Benjamin Sutton. And, if I were to guess, I would say perhaps tortured with far too much self-doubt."

"Who told you that?" I said, and then caught myself. "I mean, why do you say that?"

She squeezed my palm. "Just a sense. I also sense that you are a profound gift to the few you let into your very eccentric world, which I would wager is small, because I have a feeling you don't trust easily."

I eyed her with suspicion. "My mom told you to say that."

"No," she chuckled. "It's written in your aura."

"I have an aura? That can't be good."

Geneva laughed.

"So... my problem is I don't trust anyone?"

"Benjamin, your *problem*—if you want to call it that—might be that you simply don't trust *yourself*."

I stared at her. "Really?"

"And *that* has been known to interfere with one's capacity to experience joy. Which is a shame."

"Yes," I said.

"You know that joy is your birthright, don't you?" She winked.

"I didn't. No." Ivy's grandmother was a little out there, but my pathetic self drank in her words. I laughed nervously. "It's like you've known me for years."

"Not me..." she said. "The Universe..."

"Hmm." I thought she was finished, so when she wouldn't let go of my hand, it alarmed me a little.

"There is a worry in your family," she declared. "Can I ask?"

I looked at her, confused.

"Forgive me, but I felt it at dinner undeniably, just a glimpse. But it seemed imprudent to mention it in the midst of all the loveliness."

I was taken aback by her insight. "Oh. Well...um."

"My apologies. I didn't mean to pry, dear boy—though it is my particular gift: prying."

I stared at her staring at me. It was as though she could see what I wasn't saying. "It's...it's my sister."

"Mia?"

"No, no. Camille. She's my older sister. She's...she's in a bad situation, and we're all just...we're all worried about her. That's probably what you felt."

"She's married?"

I nodded. "To a jerk."

"Oh my. Is he...unkind to her?"

"He's awful."

"Goodness." Geneva let go of my hand to touch her throat. "Are there children?"

I nodded again. "Two little girls. Right in the middle of it."

"Oh, that is a worry. And they fight? Your sister and her husband?"

"About *everything*." I grimaced. "He's very controlling. He's obsessed about his health, and insanely critical that Camille's not.

He harps on her about what she eats, what she feeds the kids, where she goes, who she talks to. He's a nightmare, an absolute nightmare."

"Oh..." Geneva moaned. "That is no way to live. I'm so very sorry. I wish I had more time to help."

"What? What do you mean? Why would you do that?"

"Because I'm here, of course."

To my continued confusion, I suppose, she said: "Benjamin, the Universe often answers life's injustice by placing those in need in the path of those in a position to help. Surely this makes sense to you." She shook her head, distracted. "But we're here for such a short time, I'm just not—"

We were interrupted then by *everyone* stepping back into the kitchen at that moment. Ivy and her Mom walked in, arms linked, grinning, and whatever worries I'd had about Ivy's conversation with her parents seemed suddenly quite overblown—the annoyance on Daniel's face notwithstanding. Mom was chattering about a candy shop not to be missed on Ocean Avenue, and Mia seemed to know just the one she was referring to. So did Dad.

"What's going on?" I said feeling decidedly left out.

"Oh, nothing, Bo," Mia said with teasing in her eyes. "The girls are just headed to Carmel for a for a couple of days, so you finally get the house to yourself."

Twenty-Three—Ivy

Early the next morning, Mama and Geneva picked us up in their rental car, which we loaded up with the necessities for a two-day getaway. Mia and my mother had become fast friends, which did not surprise me, because, well, Mia was Mia and the same thing had happened to me. Mia was a people magnet, genuinely nice, and any weirdness that had brought us together a month ago had only been weird until I moved into the pool house. One day. From then on, we'd simply become friends. But that was Mia. She was one of those people you couldn't help but be attracted to: confident, funny, easy to trust. And she did not abuse those gifts. She came from hearty stock, so my experience had been the same with her family.

Even Bo, who was his own unique experience. A bit more work, but equally special.

But if it was true that I was becoming an honorary Sutton, it was just as true that Mia was fast becoming an honorary Talbot. In fact, because Mia had so admired the massive metal necklace my mother had worn to dinner, Bree had given it to her—which sort of baptized Mia into my family.

Mia made the trip fabulous. She knew all the lesser-known art galleries, the quiet restaurants, the off-the-path boutiques, and she even got us into a great day spa called *Under Currents*. Her friend, Joslyn Wu, worked there, and she was able to schedule us all at the same time. Massages, shampoos, manicures, pedicures. New extensions for Mia, and a haircut for me—albeit after much prodding from everyone. But I bit the bullet when Joslyn said, "Cutting your hair off is like starting your life over." It was a good metaphor for me. I think I lost a good two pounds, but afterwards I wondered why I'd waited so long. I loved it! My shorter, tamed curls made my neck seem longer and framed my face in a way that made my eyes pop. This, of course, made it hard to resist the other thing Mama had been bugging me about my whole life—my eyebrows. Joslyn Wu completely transformed my look that afternoon, and when I walked out to meet the girls, Geneva started to cry, Mama's mouth fell open, and Mia took a bunch of pictures. I giggled like a little girl and couldn't remember the last time I'd done that.

After that we shopped, and something rather amazing happened. Either the measurements in California were different than the rest of the nation, or I had simply shrunk. I called Mia into the dressing room where I was trying on a handkerchief skirt with a funky hem.

"What? What's the matter?" she said, alarmed when I pulled her into the little room.

"Is that me?" I said to her, our eyes meeting in the mirror.

"I *love* that skirt!" she said.

"It's too big."

"Okaaaay. And?"

I lifted my shirt and showed her the way the skirt hung loose around my waist.

"Oooohhhh...looks like I'd better see if they have a smaller one." She walked out but stuck her head back in. "You're hilarious," she laughed.

When Mia came back a few minutes later, she had an armload of dresses and jeans in sizes I hadn't seen since junior high. One blouse was even a *Medium*. When I walked out of that store with my new clothes and my new hair and a smile that was real down to my toes, I felt like I'd been christened by those folks on *What Not to Wear*.

Later, while Geneva took a nap, and Mia caught up with her friends who'd called from Europe to taunt her, Mama and I decided to walk to the beach. Mia said to stay on Ocean Avenue and she'd find us, so we set out on our own.

"Oh, I do love it here," Bree said as we strolled.

"Me, too. Thanks, Mama. This was perfect."

She squeezed my arm. "I've always loved Carmel," she said. "But my very favorite time to be here is Christmas. You should see this town all dolled up for the holidays."

I laughed. "When were you ever here at Christmastime?"

My mother looked at me coyly. "Sweetie, I meet your father here a few times a year. And more than once it's been during the holidays."

"What?" I stopped, feeling like I'd been punched. "*What?*"

"Oh, Ivy. Don't look like that."

"You've been here? At Christmas? And you never brought me?"

"Well..." Mama stammered. "It was time set aside just for your dad and me. You know we don't get to see each other very often."

"And before my wedding debacle, I saw him even less than that," I said, suddenly more hurt and annoyed than I was prepared for.

"Hey!" she said, seeming surprised by my tone.

"Hey, what?"

"What is wrong with you, Ivy?"

"Nothing," I said, staring straight ahead. "I don't know. That just seems..."

"Now, you just hold on! You're actually upset because I spent private time with your dad?"

"I don't know," I snapped. "I guess I am, Mama." I looked at her. "Did you ever think, even once, that maybe I might have liked to come to a place like this with you?"

She chuckled. "Well, I'm sorry, Ivy; it just didn't work out that way for us."

"*Me*, you mean. It didn't work out that way for *me*. You seem to have done just fine." I was upset, and again it surprised

Ivy in Stills - 115

me *how* upset, and I couldn't really explain it except to realize that when I was home in Georgia the idea of my parents had seldom crossed my mind. Daniel was *here*, and me and Mama...our life was *there*, and except for the occasional surprise—or wedding—that was our life. Except I guess it really wasn't the same for my mother. Well, of course it wasn't."

"What is the matter with you, Ivy?"

"I don't know. Nothing, I guess."

Bree took hold of my arm and stepped in front of me. "Ivy Lee Talbot, you do not get to judge me. You haven't lived my life."

I stared at her. "Have you lived your life, Mama? Really? Hooking up with Daniel on, what? A quarterly basis? That's your life? Please." I turned away from her, but just as fast I turned back. "And by the way, if there is anyone who has earned the right to judge you, that would be me! Who do you think I am? Have you met me? I'm the girl you gave this life to. I'm the girl you decided didn't need a decent dad—at least not as much as you needed your cross-country booty calls."

My mother's jaw hardened. "Don't you dare talk to me like that!"

I shook my head. "I just don't get you, Mama."

"It's complicated, Ivy. And it's none of your business."

"Well, that's not true! You are my business, Mama! Your life touches mine. You and Daniel are my *parents*."

"Keep your voice down! You're causing a scene!"

"Do I look like I care, Mama? And it's not that complicated. What exactly is complicated, Mama? That Dad is married to someone else? Has kids and a home and a life here? What's complicated about that? Aside from you two sneaking around for my entire life."

"I do not have to listen to this, Ivy Lee. I love your father."

"So what, Mama?"

"And he loves me! We *will* be together. *Soon.*"

"Mama! How long are you gonna keep believing that fairytale?"

"Stop it! *Stop it right now!*" She fingered away the sudden tears that had pugnaciously appeared in her eyes. "I can't believe you're treating me this way," she said. "And I came all this way to do something nice for you."

"Oh, please! You came all this way to see *him*."

"That is not true, Ivy. That's just mean."

"Then where were you all night?"

Her mouth dropped open, and she was caught. Then she was upset. "That is none of your business. I don't answer to you, young lady." She stared at me until her lip started to quiver. "I think we need a break, Ivy. I'll see you later at the hotel." And with that, Mama left me where I stood and crossed the street.

Twenty-Four—Mia

I caught up to Ivy and her Mom just before they crossed Ocean Avenue at fifth, an area active with sidewalk commerce. But when I realized they were in the midst of a rather intense conversation, I held back and busied myself snapping pics. I tried to be discrete as I shot a haggle going on between a barefoot watercolorist and an overdressed woman undervaluing his product. But even as I captured the sideshow in my lens, my true attention was on Ivy and Bree, and they were animated enough for me to catch the gist of their argument. It made me a bit queasy. I'd already seen the peeled back version of Super-dad and knew he was a dud of a parent, but right there in the middle of tourist central, Bree Talbot became a caricature of one, too.

Apparently, she'd been meeting up with Daniel for years to soak up his undivided attention and shallow promises—at times at Christmas, right here in Carmel—sans Ivy. I could see the sad impact of this revelation on my new friend, and I ached for her. The disbelief on her face shimmered with a pain so raw, so completely unprotected, it was almost exquisite in its bruised humanity. It would surely be a puncture wound in any half-decent mother's heart, which *was* my cruel motive for capturing it. So, I aimed, focused, zoomed and clicked. I wanted to hurt Bree. I wanted her to recall this incident in its entirety. Especially since despite the damage she'd done, she behaved like any bratty, petulant, self-absorbed woman and defended herself at the expense of the one she'd hurt. Then she proceeded to huff away, the victim.

I captured that, too, and mocked her under my breath.

The barefoot artist eyed me crouched rather near his turf. "What are you doing?" he said. He had not been successful with his sale to the *Real Housewives of Carmel* wannabe, so he was a titch snippy with me. I fake smiled to ease his pain. "I'm a photography major over at MPC. I'm working on my final portfolio."

He narrowed his eyes suspiciously.

"I really like your stuff," I added, pouring it on. Then I snapped a picture of his booth and hurried over to Ivy.

I came up from behind and slipped my hand in hers. "You okay?"

If I startled her, she didn't show it. She just shook her head, clearly not okay. "Did you hear all that?"

"Yes," I said. "And you were phenomenal."

"I hurt her."

I squeezed her hand. "My mean self would say she deserved it, Ivy," I told her. "But my smart self is going to tell you honestly that your mother hurt herself. You just held up the mirror."

Ivy looked over at me with tears in her eyes. "I don't know. Just when I think I'm finally crawling out of this hole…What do I do now?"

I linked my arm through hers and led her gently across the street. "You want to scream at the ocean? You want to be alone? You want to cry? Eat? What are you thinking?"

"I think I'm mad," she whimpered. "I think I'm really, really mad."

"Mad's good," I said. "Mad is very cleansing. Don't be afraid of it. Especially when you're so entitled to it."

Ivy looked at me. "Really?"

"Absolutely!"

"Mia Sutton, I do not think there are enough people like you in this world," she said to me. "No one has ever given me permission to be mad. About anything."

I laughed. "Girl, you don't need permission."

"I do...because *mad* just does not come natural to me. I do *hurt* pretty good—I've got *hurt* down, but I just don't seem to do mad well at all. It feels wrong."

"What are you afraid of?"

"I don't know. Maybe...maybe feeling it too deep. Getting lost somewhere that I can't come back from. Hating, maybe." She shook her head. "I never want to hate anybody, Mia. I never want to hate Mama. Or Tim. Not even Daniel...and I think that one might be a short trip." She tried to laugh. "I guess I think anger and hate are kinda twins. I don't know. I think I'm a little bit crazy."

"Nah. You're a little bit too nice. But not crazy. Should we grab a Coke?"

"That would probably be good. Caffeine usually levels me out."

We'd crossed to a little bistro that had outdoor tables and no apparent waiting. When the waitress seated us, we ordered Cokes and an order of onion rings to share without looking at a menu. Ivy glanced around, sighed, and found my eyes. "Thank you, Mia."

"For what?"

"Not judging me. Or if you are, hiding it so nicely."

I smiled and was about to say that it wasn't her I was judging when she added, "And please, *please* don't think less of Mama."

"Oh...Ivy..." I winced and made a show of the tiny space between my thumb and forefinger. "Maybe just a little," I said. "But I promise not to hate her."

The waitress set down our drinks, and I proceeded to peel the paper from my straw. To Ivy's sad demeanor, I said "Okay, allow me to impart another of my dad's annoying pearls of wisdom."

"I'm listening.'"

"He says we only get one life to truly ruin. *Our own.* Yours is yours. Your mom's is hers. Daniel's is his. Doesn't take a genius to see they're both doing a stellar job of destroying themselves. *But that's not your fault, and you can't fix it."*

Ivy got a little teary, and I felt a little bad but couldn't think what to take back.

She nodded, although it seemed a painful admission. "You know, I think he really loves her," she said. "Daniel. And I know Mama loves him. It's twisted, I know, but it's probably still love. It's just that for my whole life, it's been one pathetic promise after another. And she just keeps believing him."

"I'm sorry."

"And I don't know why. It's not like she hasn't had other opportunities. There's been a parade of nice men traipsing around in her life. But then just when I think she's moved on, Daniel resurfaces, and something happens and she's back in love with him." Ivy rubbed her forehead with the heels of both hands. "He's like a drug, I swear, and no matter how long she's sober, Mama always relapses on Daniel." Ivy sighed. "There was one summer when I was ten, turning eleven—that was the only birthday he was ever there for—he'd been gone a long time. But he came back and stayed that whole summer. We went to Disneyworld and the Everglades." She almost smiled. "He even taught me to fish that summer. We were like a real family. But then just after I went back to school, he up and left." She wiped her nose on a napkin. "I came home one day, and he was gone. And Mama curled up in a ball and died a little. *Again.* She's died a little *a lot* over the years. If you know what I mean."

I grimaced but said nothing.

Ivy looked tired, overly burdened. "I used to blame Daniel," she said, heavily. "I used to think Mama hurting was all his fault. But..." She shook her head and met my eyes with weary wisdom. "Mia, I just bet you have never once seen your mama for a fool."

I looked at her and had no words. It was true enough. I had never known my mother to diminish herself in any significant way—not that I was privy to, anyway. But I certainly wasn't going to say that to Ivy.

She nodded, understanding my silence regardless. "That's good because something awful happens to a daughter when her mama...*loses her shine.* You still love her, of course you do. But it's pitied-up love, worried-up love." Ivy shrugged but didn't break eye contact. "I only have a few women in my life of any real importance. Hardly seems fair for the one I need the most to do her best by me to have the nerve to be a mere mortal. Right? How dare she?" Ivy cry-smiled. "I try not to judge her, Mia, I truly do. But sometimes she makes it very, very hard."

I almost couldn't swallow over the knot in my throat. "I think you're amazing, Ivy. I think you're an amazing daughter and an amazing person. And I'm just so sorry that we can't pick our parents."

Ivy sniffed back emotion. "Well, I'd still pick Mama. Her only problem is that she hasn't been loved properly. If she had, she'd be a great Mom. So needless to say, I wouldn't pick Daniel." She tried to laugh. "He's not a good man. And I sure don't think he's a good dad...to me, anyway." Ivy brushed a tear off her cheek, regrouped, and picked up her sweaty Coke. "But at least we can pick our friends." She announced, chin lifted. "And I am sorry, but that is my superpower." She grinned weakly and tapped my glass. "To you, my friend, who got a truckload more than you bargained for when you agreed to meet my daddy-in-name-only for lunch."

"True, that." I smiled. "But, may I just say, totally worth it."

Twenty-Five—Bo

As a general rule, I live for isolation. I'm good with my own company, and I get easily lost in my work. But I have to admit that the house seemed a little too quiet without Ivy and, of course, Mia who typically wandered in and out all day. I missed them, and it bothered me a little. Few knew that my most earnest fear was that my particular weirdness would someday completely overtake me and leave me unable to function on my own. But this wasn't that. This was something else.

Ivy and her family had gone down to Carmel for a couple of days of exploring and reconnecting. It had been a surprise for Ivy, but for some reason that didn't make sense to me, they'd taken Mia. I hadn't been invited. Not that I would have gone, but it bothered me that I wasn't invited. It also bothered me that I was being ridiculous about it. I was a mess.

No. No I wasn't. This was good. It was good to have this time to myself; I needed to deep clean the dining room anyway. Especially since I'd seen a thin layer of dust on the wainscoting as I'd shown Ivy's grandmother around the house. I was mortified, of course, but Geneva Talbot was a class act and pretended not to notice. She'd simply said flowery things like: *The spirit of Lully's sanctuary is so vibrant.* And: *Everything exudes loveliness...*As if dust could exude anything but dust. It had made me blush, and she'd scolded me. "Now Benjamin," she'd said, "none of that," like she had read my mind. And that upset me for obvious reasons—I didn't like people reading my mind. I was already haunted by her prognostication that if I could just learn to trust, I too could be a happy human.

Now, I tried to dismiss her antics, nice as they were, as just the ramblings of an equally nice old woman. But they rang a little too authentic for that. And with Geneva's bull-horned declarations now added to the near-constant rumination of Ivy's terrible parents, my brain was tired. I was worried about Ivy. And then there was that hug last week—half-hug—in the pool house that was so unexpected, so genuine, so non-anxiety-producing that my obsession over it had been nearly incessant. All I had done was inform Ivy that Mia and I were planning the little get-together with her family. But her reaction had been...raw and real gratitude. And she'd hugged me. Sort of. And only after asking my permission, which I don't recall giving, but it happened anyway. And it was...*nice*.

I blew out a breath, and looked down at the chain I was beading where the price of my preoccupation became damningly clear. I groaned. I'd added in an errant amethyst to the long line of onyx beads. It looked absurd and I had no choice but to start over, which would put me a full—I checked the clock—thirty-six minutes behind schedule for the day. And to make matters worse, I thought I'd heard the chimes, which I couldn't ignore since that sound was immediately followed by loud and insistent pounding on the front door. A delivery? That didn't sound like a delivery knock.

Again, the chimes, followed by the knock. Something was wrong—something was terribly wrong. And though I almost took the time to obsess over the possibilities, instead I flew up the stairs.

On the porch stood Camille, with Scout close at her side sucking her thumb. My sister was holding a sleeping Olivia, whose arm was in a cast. I almost couldn't take it in, the scene was so foreign. "Good Lord, Camille. What's..."

She hurried past me and into the living room, where she laid Olivia down on the sofa. "The doctor gave her a sedative..." My sister looked up at me. "We need to stay here for a little while until I figure out what to do. And I need to pull my car into the garage just in case Peter knows more than I think he does."

"What? *What?*"

"Bo!"

"Okay," I nodded.

"Scouty, I'll be right back. Stay with Uncle Bo."

I started to tingle. What was happening? I looked at my niece. "C'mere, Scouters," I beckoned. Scout hesitated only an instant, and then she was in my arms. "Wh—what happened to Livvy?" I said.

Scout pulled her thumb out of her mouth. "She falled down the stairs."

"What? Where was mommy?"

"Her was fighting with Daddy." She started to whimper.

"Did daddy hit anyone?"

"He pushed Mama and Mama banged right into Livia. And Livia falled."

I swallowed, pulled myself together. "I bet that was so scary, little one."

My niece burrowed into me and started to cry.

"I'm so glad you're here, Peanut," I crooned, rubbing her back, feeling shell-shocked. "Nothing bad is going to happen to you here," I heard myself say. "And not to Mommy, either. And not to Livvy. Everything will be okay. Okay?"

"Okay."

I heard the garage door lower, and then Camille came back into the room. She looked like she'd slept in her clothes and her hair hadn't been combed. "What happened?"

She bit her bottom lip. "Did you lock that door?" She said, moving past me. She checked the front door, then turned the deadbolt.

"Camille, did you call the police?"

"No."

"Why?"

"Because it wouldn't matter. They'd arrest him, maybe, but he'd get out. I'm so terrified of him; I'd probably bail him out myself so he wouldn't be mad. That worked out great the last time. Right?"

"What about a restraining order?"

"Bo, he wouldn't care!" Camille started to cry, then. "How the hell did I get here? This isn't my life. What has happened to my life?"

I stared at my sister, thinking. You married a dog...You're still married to a dog...

Scout shimmied out of my arms and over to her mom, where Camille picked her up. "It's okay, Mommy. Don't cry," she said, patting Camille's chin.

I swallowed, my heart a giant ache in my chest at the sight. "Of course it is!" I said with more confidence than I felt. "You're here and we have ice cream, and everything is going to be fine."

Scout's eyes lit up a degree when I reached for her again. "Go take a shower, Camille," I said to my sister. "You'll feel better. Raid Mia's closet." With my spare hand, I slid the chenille throw over the still sleeping Olivia, then turned back to Camille. "Do it," I glared. Then to my niece, I said, "C'mon, Scouters, I think we might even have sprinkles."

Twenty-Six—Ivy

When we got back to our hotel Mama was resting—or pretending to—so I left Mia to fiddle with her camera and went to find my grandmother. She was in the gift shop buying trinkets, and she eyed me knowingly so I knew Mama had brought her up to speed on our tiff. I wandered around the shop until she was ready to pay, and then I added some chewing gum to her hefty pile of merchandise. While the cashier cashiered, I leaned my head against her shoulder, and she stroked my cheek. This told me that despite Mama being her beloved daughter, Geneva was not mad at me, which filled me with immeasurable relief. I could not bear being at odds with my grandmother.

We walked out of the gift shop and down to the quiet lobby where Geneva steered me to a sofa. She was wearing a flowy dress the color of a burnt orange and her long white hair was braided down one shoulder. When she sat down, she looked like she was holding court. She patted the cushion next to her, and I sat obediently.

"I'm not going home with y'all, Gran," I said, anticipating a lecture.

"I know that, sugar plum."

"I'm sorry. I'm still not ready to see Tim. And now I just plain don't want to deal with Mama."

She cocked her head, and I steeled myself for a talking-to. "You know," she said, "some things just can't be fixed, Ivy Lee."

"I know."

"You can sling all that venom at your mama if you want to. But to what end? She can't go back in time and un-have you. Not that she would ever do that."

"I know."

"Now your father, of course, was another story..." She sighed, making her silly face that broadcast the contempt for Daniel she kept buried just beneath her southern manners.

Daniel *was* another story. And though nobody had ever said the actual word *abortion* out loud—in my presence—I'm sure that would have been my father's preference. He *had been* rather married with children at the time of my parents' untimely coupling, after all. But of course, nothing screams happily-ever-after like a married big city lawyer in town for the weekend crossing paths with a cute-as-a-button waitress in the mood to party. It was surely a match made in heaven. Or at least a bar named Heaven's Detour, which was close enough to Bonaventure Cemetery to cast the spell that produced me. I looked at my grandmother. "Why are we talking about this?"

She leaned in. "Because I know that you know that it's 100% true that you got a bum deal," Geneva said. "That is just a fact. But another one is this: the Universe, or God, or whomever you give credit to these days, missy, gave you me to help pick up the slack. And I happen to love you very much, as I have told you about twenty-two billion times."

I smiled.

"And that might not be everything you deserve; it might not even be enough. But it is a lot more than some folks ever get."

I picked up her hand and kissed it. "I love you, too, Gran. And it's plenty."

"Well, whether you believe it or not, your dreadfully flawed mama loves you as well."

"I know that."

"Do you? Do you, really, Ivy?"

"I do. I'm just..."

"I know, sweet girl." My grandmother slipped her arm around me, and I settled into the place that was mine alone. There was no one around, but it would not have mattered. We were having a moment. Finally, she breathed deep. "Ivy, you may not believe this, but your mother is teaching you every day how to be better than she is, how to choose better." Geneva pulled me closer. "And I promise you this: If you are lucky enough to get to my age and can look back at your journey with any pride, or success, or wisdom...you will have her to thank for much of it. Don't forget that. Our mama's examples—good or bad—shape us as women." She lifted my chin with her gnarled finger until I made eye contact. "Our Bree is messy, that's a fact. And Lord knows how my best hanky stays soggy with her tears—not to mention how my trigger finger itches whenever I see, hear, or think of your father."

I nodded. I knew.

"But you, my darling girl, so overshadow all the nonsense those two have inflicted. You are the lovely gift that two foolish people gave each other. And gave to me. And gave to you. And that's most important."

I couldn't see her anymore for the blur of my tears. But I could hear every word.

"Of course, you're not coming home," she said. "But you're also not going to wallow in the outrageous love story of your silly parents. You..." she squeezed my chin. "You with your brand-new hair and pretty clothes, your creeping-back self-confidence, your never-gone kindness. You are going to live your life. Your very own life. Do you understand me, Ivy Lee Talbot? You are going to live how and where and whatever manner of life you want! Tell me you hear the words coming out of my mouth, granddaughter."

I swallowed. "I do, ma'am"

"That's my girl." She squeezed my hand. "So, do you have a plan?"

"I haven't really thought much past just *not* going home. But I have applied at the hospital here. As an X-ray tech. There's no openings, right now, but..."

"So...you really think you want to stay...here?"

I leaned my head back and sighed. "I don't know. I like it here. But it's awful spendy. And I'm just not sure if California is really big enough for me *and* Daniel."

Geneva leaned back, too, looked at the ceiling. "Well, if it's not, then maybe Daniel will just need to consider practicing law elsewhere, won't he?"

I laughed and cried at the same time. Reason 9,012 why I love this woman so much.

For the remainder of our trip, my mother was predictably cool to me but in a way that she thought only I could discern. She was wrong. Mia is excellent at picking up vibes. And of course, Geneva saw right through her meanness. Mama's limited eye contact, not so subtle effort at keeping her distance, and talking *around* me, not to me, was absolutely not lost on anyone, least of all my savvy friend. On the way to dinner, Mama even started the car before I had fully closed my door, which Geneva lit into her for. She tried to cover by finding me in the rearview mirror and feigning contrition. I ignored her. I was settling somewhat comfortably into my *mad*, which surprised me, and the sillier Mama acted, the easier she made it.

In the midst of all these theatrics, she was extra friendly to Mia. But Mia, bless her soul, deflected Mama's pandering by pulling Geneva and me into the conversation, or even better, starting a new one altogether. It seemed Mama had met her match in my friend, and Mia's subtle display of loyalty meant the world to me. And if I'm being completely honest, it seemed to hurt Mama more than it peeved her. I knew this because my mother, for all her faults, is actually quite proficient at reading a room. It was a little heartbreaking, and it somehow started to tame my irritation with her.

So, later while we were packing up to head home, I made the first conciliatory step by offering Mama some gum. She didn't take it, but she was surprised that I'd offered—it meant she didn't have to apologize—and she smiled at my olive branch. And just like that, we were on our way back to being fine. This is how we make up: one of us tests the waters—usually me—with a small signal that indicates I'm done being upset. Mama's either ready, or she's not. This time she smiled with full eye contact, so I knew we were off to the races. I have no idea how another girl and a mom with a Daniel all tangled up around the edges of their relationship would do it. But this is how me and Mama have always managed our turmoil—and we haven't killed each other yet.

We got home that night to find two cars in the circular driveway—a Jeep Cherokee and a Prius, which meant nothing to me but seemed to alarm Mia. "Oh, no..." she muttered from the back seat.

"What's wrong?" I said.

"It's Peter. What's he doing here?"

"Camille's Peter? That can't be good," I said under my breath.

Bree, oblivious, wanted to thank Mia's family once again for their hospitality, which seemed somehow trivial at the moment, but a necessary courtesy. Geneva seemed very preoccupied but agreed. She looked at me. "This Peter...He's the brother-in-law?"

I nodded as I dug around in the trunk for my bags. "He's bad, Gran. It's a mess."

We emptied the car of our spoils and headed toward the house. But as we stepped onto the front porch, my grandmother stiffened.

"Everything okay, Mom?" Bree asked.

Geneva looked at Mia, then at me, her brow deeply bent in worry. "No, I don't think it is." She looked at Bree, then at the house, then back at us. "Something feels very, very wrong."

Twenty-Seven—Bo

We were a family on the edge. Tension had morphed into bald ugliness between my father and brother-in-law, and the veins in Peter's neck bulged as he demanded that we produce his wife.

"She's. Not. Here," my mother shouted, cowering behind my dad.

"And if she was," Dad yelled over her, "I would never let you near her!"

"She's my wife, old man! Where is she? You know something!"

Peter looked like a respectable monster—he even smelled good. He was turned out in a blue suit and tie, and not a hair on his head was out of place—something I could truly appreciate. But his eyes were venomous, and he was scaring my mom. I stepped in front of him, shaking a little but I didn't think it was obvious. "You can't just barge in here and scream for answers that we don't have, Peter," I said, as forcefully as I could muster. "What have you done that you don't even know where your family is? What happened? Did you have another fight? Did you hurt Camille?" I said rather proud of my ruse.

Peter stepped closer and barked down at me. "Shut up! I don't answer to you, freak-boy!"

"That's enough!" my dad said, stepping between me and the towering Peter. It was a David and Goliath moment—my dad in golf shorts, his skinny legs probably trembling as he shouted, "You need to leave, or I'm calling the police," he said.

"Good idea, Jack. Call them! My wife is missing, and you know where she is!" Peter boomed. "I think they'll be very interested in that!" As he snarled, his chest expanded, and spit flew—which was particularly disgusting. It was easy to imagine Camille's utter helplessness when confronted with this rage.

"Peter, c'mon," I said, sounding small—and mad that I sounded small. "We're just as worried as you are. But think about it: Why would she come here if she wanted to hide from you? I mean, isn't this the first place you came to look for her? So, think. Where else would she go? Have you checked with her friends?"

Mom piped up, following my lead. "What about Bex? Or Darla?"

He eyed us for a moment, seeming to consider this. "Those bitches wouldn't dare..." He started pacing.

We were startled then by a loud knock on the front door that stopped everything for a beat. Peter looked hopeful and suspicious all at once. I moved past him to the door and opened it just as Mia was fumbling with her keys. She rushed into the house, Ivy and her family following behind. *Ivy?*

"What's going on?" Mia said breathlessly taking in the scene. "What's happened? Where's Camille?"

"Good question, Mia!" Peter bit, barreling toward her. "How 'bout you tell me? Where the hell have you been?"

"None of your business!" she sneered with her enviable overconfidence as she moved past him to my parents.

His nostrils flared. "I'm *done* playing games with you people!" he seethed, fists balled at his sides. "Where is my wife?" He looked at everyone else who had walked in. "Who are you?" he said to Ivy's mom. As Bree stammered to explain, Geneva shut the door and stepped out from behind her. She was wearing what looked like an orange nightgown, and her white hair hung like a snake down one shoulder. The look on her massively lined face was a cross between concern and alarm, but somehow, I found it unimaginably calming. She stared at Peter, brought her bony hand to her chest.

"Goodness," she breathed, looking right at him. "Has something happened to your wife? You look absolutely terrified."

Her words seemed to disarm him. They also gentled the tangible crackle in the room.

"What?" Peter said with a weakening sneer. "I...I don't know. I don't even know where she is."

Geneva nodded. "Well, no wonder you're worried." Without breaking eye contact with Peter, Geneva Talbot said softly, "Bo, do you know anything about this?"

Before I could answer, Mom blurted, "We don't know where Camille is either. We haven't seen her. We haven't heard from her. We're all worried sick!"

"Oh, my..." Still, Geneva didn't let go of Peter's eyes. "I'm so sorry. I don't know you, but I can see you're very frightened—and obviously with good reason. And clearly all that fear is fueling the fear that everyone else is feeling as well."

Peter's glare tried to take on rage. "I'm not afraid! Who are you?"

"I'm Ivy's grandmother, Geneva Talbot, and I'm so sorry for what you're going through," she said softly, her voice steady, soothing. She'd taken control of the room, and it was a thing of beauty.

Peter looked at her suspiciously.

"I don't know you," she continued. "But I'm very concerned about you."

I watched Peter swallow. "What are you talking about? Why?"

"I can't help but notice your heartbeat. It's throbbing in your neck. It's...it's beating far too fast, dangerously fast. You should sit down."

His eyes widened, and his hand immediately found his collar. "What are you talking about? Stop it, you old witch! I'm fine."

"I don't think so. Surely you can feel how hard it's working. The exertion. I'm afraid you're compromising yourself," Geneva said, kindly. "Please, you should sit," she said, again. "Can I get you some water?"

I swallowed, amazed. Had I mentioned that Peter was obsessed with his health? I must have. Either way, I knew what Peter was feeling because I'd felt that power flood through me when Geneva held my hands: An uncanny, and frankly unwelcome, but undeniable energy that flowed from her to me, and now from her to Peter. And he felt it, you could see it in his slackened features. It scared him. She was good.

"You're whacked," he said somewhat shakily. "I feel fine!"

She shook her head as she bore her eyes into his. "Please be careful...for your family. My dear husband died of a burst heart."

Peter seemed momentarily lost in her warning. Then he caught himself and sneered at Geneva—or tried to. He tried to sneer at all of us, but he'd lost his edge. So, instead he lifted his weak chin at my dad. "I think I will go to the police, Jack. You people are something else." Then, pierced again by Geneva's unrelenting gaze, he backed into the foyer and hurried out the door. "You people are crazy!" were his parting words.

No one said anything until Peter had screeched out of the driveway. Then Geneva looked at my parents, then me. "There's not much time, Benjamin. Where is your sister?"

Twenty-Eight—Ivy

The power of suggestion: my grandmother had made it an art form. But she would tell you that the secret to her mysticism is no secret at all—it's grounded in predictable human response. Bullies live to bully, and they cannot handle being outsmarted, especially when they don't even know it's happening. Geneva has always told me never to underestimate the power of intense eye contact, or the intimidation you can impose by stepping uninvited into someone's personal space. She insists these tools are available to everyone, even if few utilize them with her proficiency. My grandmother was able to get close to Peter Diamond because she posed no perceived threat to him, and, of course, she wore the presumed irrelevance of an old woman, which she always said was her secret weapon. Naturally, it didn't hurt that her roadmap of a face and the crag in her ancient voice had spell-casting powers of their own. Nope. Geneva Talbot was her own perfect storm that had left Peter Diamond almost certain that cardiac arrest was an imminent threat. And goodness, it would have been so much simpler had it been true! Sadly, my granny's actual abilities are quite limited, convincing though they may be.

"Bo, is your sister here?" Geneva asked again.

"Ummm, yeah." Bo, said, seeming unsure.

"I'll get her," Eileen said, looking like she was on the cusp of breaking down.

Mia stepped up to her father and wrapped him in a hug. "You, okay, Dad?"

Jack was looking at my grandmother with his mouth slightly agape. "I'm fine, honey. Geneva, what just happened? I don't know how to thank you. That was about to get very ugly," he said.

"Yes, it was," Gran agreed. "He's clearly a very dangerous man."

I felt Bo's eyes on me and walked over to him. "Are you okay?"

He nodded and continued to stare at me. "I think so. Never a dull moment around here," he said. "I like your hair."

I'd forgotten about my hair. "Do you?" I said touching it. "It's a bit drastic."

"No, it looks good. You look good. You look...*really good*."

I was about to be ridiculously self-conscious when Camille and her mother walked into the room. They were each holding a little girl who'd been crying. The littlest one was in a cast, and I swallowed my surprise. "Where have they been?" I asked Bo under my breath.

"In their car, in the dark garage. This day's been hell."

"Maybe we should leave," said Mama to my grandmother—she looked uncomfortable. I wasn't sure I agreed, but that may have been just because *I* felt better with them right where they were. Geneva nodded but seemed reluctant. Camille set Scout on the sofa and walked over to my family. She looked tired and unkempt and undone, and I wanted to cry for her. I wanted to cry for everyone. She put her arms around Geneva like she'd known her forever.

"Thank you so much," she said. "Sounds like you said all the right things to make Peter leave. I can't tell you how grateful I am."

Geneva leaned in and studied Camille. "What will you do now?"

"I don't know. He'll be back. Probably not tonight, but he'll be back, and I can't be here." She looked over at her mother, who was snuggling a little one. When she again saw the cast on her daughter's arm, Camille's breath got jagged, and my heart broke for her.

My grandmother looked around, and I followed the trail of her gaze. There was Jack, looking older and smaller than he had two nights ago—helpless anger etched in lines around his eyes. Eileen looking beat up, like the day had pushed her down the stairs. She never took her eyes off Camille. And Camille, whose prettiness had been stripped away along with the meat of what I could only assume was her *Suttonness*, having seen it in everyone else in her family. She now stood there reduced to a woman I'm sure she never intended to be.

"I'm very sorry for what has happened to you," my grandmother said to her. "To all of you," she then said to everyone. "This is an untenable situation."

Camille nodded and started to cry.

Geneva took her hands. "This might sound completely crazy, but have you ever been to Savannah, my dear?"

Camille sniffed. "What? Georgia? No, why?"

"I'm just going to throw this out there as an option. I live in a lovely area called Isle of Hope—it's just southeast of Savannah. I have a small home on my property—a guest cottage that I keep for friends. You're welcome to use it until you decide what to do."

Eileen let go of a little sob.

"I don't understand," Camille said. "Come to Georgia?"

My grandmother looked hard at her. "You don't know me; it probably sounds like the strangest offer in the world. But you and your girls will be safe there. I'll see to it."

Camille swallowed and then broke down.

"Oh, Mrs. Talbot..." Eileen breathed.

"It would be perfect," Bree added, nodding her head. "There are less than three thousand people on the island. If your husband is not familiar with Georgia, he'd probably never find you, because he'd never find *it*."

"That's true," I said. "It's very quiet. Very pretty. And my grandmother would take good care of you. That's what she does." I nodded at Mia's mama, who suddenly looked very overcome. "And your little sugar plums would love it there."

Camille's mouth had fallen open. "Why? Why would you do that for me?"

Geneva eyed her. "Because you've been placed in my path, and you're wounded. What kind of woman would I be if I didn't offer to help you?"

"I don't...Who does that? Who just opens their life and lets a stranger walk in?"

"Mia," I blurted. "In case you didn't notice, she did the same thing for me."

"I did?" Mia said. "Oh, I guess I did."

"Y'all did," I said, shrugging, meeting Jack's eyes.

Geneva smiled. "And we can't thank you enough. So, let us repay your kindness. The Universe always knows what needs to happen, and then she just hopes someone is paying attention. I guess we're just paying attention."

"Oh, my goodness," rasped Eileen, holding her throat. "I don't know what to say." Then to Camille. "Honey, what do you think?" Camille broke down then, and Eileen took my grandmother's hand. "We've been at a loss all day trying to come up with some way to keep her safe."

"Well, the offer is there," Geneva said. "Bree, what time is our flight?"

"11:40 in morning," Mama said. "I'll text Ivy the flight number when I get back to the hotel."

"11:40." Geneva nodded. "Why don't you just discuss it and let us know what you decide," she said to Camille. Then she made the rounds, first hugging Jack, who was very emotional in his appreciation. Eileen seemed to melt inside my grandmother's embrace. Geneva cupped her chin. "If they come, I'll take good care of them. And you are more than welcome to join them. Now or later. Whatever you think is best."

Eileen couldn't speak, but she nodded, tears rolling down her face.

When she got to Bo, she smiled and gently touched his arm. "Well, sir, it seems clear to me that you did everything just right today. Well done."

"Thanks, Geneva," he said shakily. "I appreciate that." They shared a smile that held a touch of conspiracy. Then my grandmother turned to my mom. "Ready, Bree?"

"I think so." Mama looked at me with soft eyes. "I guess this is it, Ivy," she said. She hugged me hard, and when she pulled back, I could see we were almost, but not quite, back to *us*—if we'd had just a bit more time, all the harsh words would have been erased and forgotten. But her smile was the tiniest bit stiff as she pressed an envelope into my hand. "I love you, Ivy," she whispered. "You know I do..."

"I love you, too, Mama." Assuming it was money, I stuffed the gift into my pocket.

Then Geneva was there enfolding me, squeezing the breath out of me, kissing my face. "Oh, my sweet girl!" she sang. "It was so lovely to spend time with you. Take care of yourself."

"I will, Gran."

"You are my heart."

"I love you too, Gran."

Twenty-Nine—Mia

We were up all night discussing it, but I think we all knew Camille would go. It was the best—and in the end, the only—immediate solution, given the stalking prowess of her insane husband. Her friends were terrified of Peter, so they were out, and there was no hiding her at Mom's or here. He would find her. We thought of moving her down the coast for a while, but Peter worked for SunTrust, so he knew how to trace credit card activity, and she had no income. If she charged anything, he'd know it, and Dad couldn't support her indefinitely, though there was talk of him taking out a second mortgage on his house. Camille shut that down.

"I don't think I have a choice," she said, tearing up. "At least until I can figure out what I'm going to do."

Ivy—who'd tried to go to bed thinking this was a family deal, but who I'd dragged back into our drama—leaned over and took my sister's hand. "Camille, I know you don't know her—and you don't know me—but I promise you that Geneva is exactly the person you saw tonight. Mama's a bit of a flake, but just in matters of love and men. You can trust them. And my grandmother will take excellent care of you and your little girls. She lives to nurture. She might actually nurture you to death."

Camille smiled weakly. "I have to get them away from here."

Dad agreed. "You do."

By nine the next morning, we were at the Target in Seaside, which was sort of on the way to the airport. We figured we only had about twenty minutes, so we split up. Ivy looked for backpacks, I took the girls for pjs, underwear, and summer dresses, Camille grabbed everything else. Mom and Dad were paying Peter an early visit to see if the night had produced my sister. It was vital that they continue to be frantic and engaged. Anything less would raise red flags.

Camille paid with her credit card, but it would be the last time she did. Dad had charged her airline tickets on his Visa and given her just under 500.00 in cash. Later this week, we would take turns using her debit card to withdraw cash in different counties, then we'd send it to her in a cashier's check. If Peter was monitoring the withdrawals—which he would be—he'd be running all over central California looking for his wife, never suspecting that she was nicely tucked away in Georgia. Camille said we probably had a week before he'd close the accounts, hoping to smoke her out. Dad also took her phone, which I thought was a little CSI, but he insisted and told my sister he would overnight her a new one tomorrow.

At the airport, I hugged Camille and didn't want to let go. "This is really happening," I whimpered. "I already miss you."

"Me, too, Meez. I don't know what I would have done without you and Ivy." She then pulled Ivy into our hug. "Thank you. Thank you so much, for everything," she told her.

"You'll be fine," Ivy said. "And don't be scared when my gran starts talking about your *year of ashes*. It's a Geneva thing."

Camille looked puzzled, but the ticket agent had handed her their boarding passes. "Gate 3, ma'am. You'd better hurry."

I hugged my nieces, knowing I would miss them almost more than I would miss my sister. For them this was being hyped as an adventure, and Ivy kept telling them *one more thing* they would love about staying with Geneva. "She has a room full of books," she said. "You can fish off her dock. Tell her to tell you about the limpkins in the birdbath. Oh, and there's a hidden fort in the Magnolia tree. I know, because I built it."

Camille smiled at Ivy as she hoisted two of the backpacks. She then arranged the lightest one onto Scout's shoulders and picked up Olivia. "We have to go. I love you!"

We watched them weave through security and through the doors to the gates, and then they were gone. I didn't think I'd cry, but the enormity of what was happening—my sister and her daughters running away from the worst excuse of a human on the planet—suddenly overwhelmed me. *How had this happened? To my sister? To my family?*

"Gran," I heard Ivy say into her phone. "It's me. Yep. We just dropped them off. They should be coming your way. Oh, you see them? Good." She gave me the thumbs up. "Okay, then. Thanks so much, Gran. Have a safe trip. I love you! We'll call you tomorrow. Tell Mama...tell her I love her, too."

"Successful transfer of custody?" I said as Ivy put her phone in her pocket.

"Geneva has them," Ivy said.

I looped my arm through hers for the walk back to the parking lot. "I have to tell you, I've never met anyone like your grandmother."

Ivy chuckled. "Yep. They broke the mold with her, it's true."

"Can I ask you something?"

"Of course."

"And I want the truth. Do you really believe in all that universe stuff?"

Ivy lifted a shoulder. "I believe in Geneva, so...I don't know."

I narrowed my eyes to a slit. "Tell me about her," I said.

Ivy shook her head. "You know that will take about a year," she laughed.

"Well, you'd better get started, then."

"What exactly do you want to know?"

"I don't know," I said. "Everything. Does she have a big family? Hundreds of friends? What about your grandfather?"

Ivy cocked her head. "She does have a lot of friends...But she'd trade them all for a big family. All my grandmother ever really wanted was to grow old with someone she loved and have lots of babies. But she didn't marry my grandpa until she was thirty-nine, and he died less than ten years later. She miscarried three times before my mama stuck and two times after. So, she only got Bree—that's kinda relevant to her life's journey. And then Bree was only—I don't know, six or seven when her daddy died, and she was mad and lost and hard to handle, according to Gran, and my grandmother was too heartbroken to rein her in. So, Mama was a wild child who took her time growing up, and I think if she had raised me on her own, I'd probably have been the same." Ivy looked over at me and arched a brow. "But Geneva saved me. She saved me and Mama. Gran used to tell me I was the bridge back to her lost daughter, and Mama told me once I was the highway back to her mama. So...allow me to introduce myself, Mia—Ivy Bridge and Highway." She laughed. "Are you bored yet?"

"Not even a little."

Ivy shook her head. "Geneva credits the Universe with my existence. She's never been a fan of my dad, but she's quick to point out that there was no other route from me to her than the Universe throwing her daughter into his path, so she can't bring herself to hate him. And if you really think about it, she's right. She says there are no real accidents."

"Hmmm. When you look at it that way, I guess she's right," I agreed.

"Yep. So, where Gran's concerned, there is no such thing as random. The word doesn't even belong in the dictionary. It's all the Universe being purposeful, bringing people together for a reason that might not be immediately evident." Ivy looked over at me. "I'm the first to admit my grandmother is a little bit out there, but it's hard to argue with her logic. Where people are concerned, anyway."

I thought about this. "She might be onto something. How else would you and I ever have become friends?"

"Exactly!" Ivy said.

"It's a little freaky," I said, unlocking the car door. "Hey, by the way, did you and your mom make up? It looked like things were better between you two last night."

"I think we did. She gave me some money. It's in my other pants."

"Oh good. You can buy lunch," I grinned. "And then you can tell me all about what a *year of ashes* is supposed to mean."

Ivy laughed.

"On second thought, I'll buy lunch," I said.

"Why?"

"Remember the other day when you said I got more than I bargained for when I met your dad?"

"Uh-huh."

"Well, look around, girl. I think we might actually be even."

Thirty—Bo

I had been feeling pretty good about myself for the last couple of days, but I wasn't particularly proud of that. I mean, my family was still more or less embroiled in a crisis—or the aftermath of a crisis—and I should have felt more subdued. That seemed more appropriate, even though Camille and the girls were now safely in Savannah, and by all reports adjusting well. That was a veritable triumph, and I wanted to give myself permission to relish it a bit. But no. I was obsessing about if that was really appropriate. And the very fact that I was engaging in this internal debate was proof of my enduring weirdness and then I started obsessing about that.

It's exhausting to be me.

The truth is, I am rarely the one to shine and seldom the one to save the proverbial day. But when Geneva Talbot pointed out that I had done everything right, I felt like I'd won the freaking lottery—and the feeling had stuck. In a very obsessive way.

That day, I'd been alone with my traumatized sister for several hours before I could track down my parents. And when they'd finally shown up, Camille had been brittle with anxiety, which of course had made me brittle with anxiety. She'd been like a caged animal. I'd offered her some Xanax—several times—but she'd refused. My mom had been able to calm her down to a degree, and they had made a plan to leave her car in Lully's garage and bring her and the kids home with my parents. But then Peter showed up. He'd never been to Lully's house, and Camille was floored that a resourceful man like her husband, desperate to track down his family, had figured out where Lullaby Sutton, a genuine who's-who of Monterey society, lived. I'd never seen Camille like that. When she heard his car, she absolutely lost control. Shaking, unable to breathe, couldn't talk. Raw, visceral panic. My parents didn't react much better. But suddenly—and shockingly—I knew exactly what to do. *Me.* I grabbed Scout, a flashlight, a package of cookies, and some cans of juice and told Camille to focus—*focus*—and follow me with Olivia. As Peter pounded on the door, I got them all in the garage and into Camille's car. "I'll get rid of him," I promised. "Just stay here and be quiet!" Six completely terrified eyes stared back at me with tenuous trust. Me. They had placed their trust in *me.*

With my parents looking completely petrified as well, I knew we didn't stand a chance of fooling Peter. I ran downstairs for the snake choker that Katrina Gearhart had commissioned and brought it up to the living room. "We have to convince him that your being here has nothing to do with Camille," I said, sounding unbelievably in charge. "You've come here to admire this. It's not done, but just please *admire it.*"

Peter pounded again and began shouting at the front door. "I know you're in there!" I took a breath and opened the door. I was shaking and my mouth had gone dry, but when I let him in, I was Oscar-worthy.

"Where are they!" he'd bellowed.

"Who?" I said, quick on my feet.

Peter barreled past me, screaming for Camille. If the absence of her car in the driveway was not convincing evidence that she was not there, then we were in trouble. But my brilliant mom used her overwhelming emotions to our absolute advantage. She looked suddenly terrified, dropped the snake choker. "What are you talking about? Where is she? What have you done?"

My dad made similar noises and threatened to call the police. When Peter lunged at him, I knew the whole thing was unraveling, and I had no answer for that. But then Mia and Ivy got back from Carmel, and it all changed. I would never forget how Geneva did her thing and looked inside my slimy, putrid brother-in-law. Peter, like me, had been unable to resist Geneva. It was like being hypnotized. It was like being helpless. Peter folded under her spell, and it seemed he couldn't get away fast enough.

I couldn't believe it. None of us could. It was as though Geneva had charmed my entire family. And when she looked at my sister and said: *You've been placed in my path,* it made all the sense in the world. To me, anyway. And if that was true—which strangely I didn't doubt—then the old woman had been placed in my path as well. And if I believed that premise, then I had to believe that Ivy Talbot had been placed there, too.

But superstition and supernatural forces were truly unexplored terrain for me. I dwelt in the company of hard facts, finite, explainable truths revolving around cleanliness and germs and the small but myriad dangers of ingesting anything not purified. I lived devoted to schedules and time spent carefully with a trusted few. My mind rarely had the wherewithal to climb another story to the unexplained. Which I suppose was why all of this was so hard to process, and why it was so hard for me to find an explanation for Ivy. My growing *awareness* of Ivy. My growing preoccupation with her.

I shook my head in frustration. I didn't have time for preoccupation—but here I was. *Fixated.* I'd never considered her unattractive for a moment—and I never understood why she did. But when she walked in that night, I momentarily lost my place in what was happening in my family's crisis. Ivy looked so different, so... *put together.* Her hair was shorter, and it made something rather magic happen to her eyes; they got bigger somehow. I'd never considered her imperfect in size—even though she did—but I could see there was *less* of her that night. She looked amazing, and it threw me, because her looking amazing had not been a factor in my liking her, had not really been a factor in my awareness of her at all. I liked Ivy because I felt comfortable with her, and I felt comfortable with her because I liked her. The people in my life who actually fit that stringent criterion could be counted on one-and-a-half hands. And it would be a vast understatement to say I'd been unprepared to find that there was room for Ivy Talbot on that small committee. I was too odd. I was too *me*. Women who ventured near me usually came to their senses about the same time I did. I was a loner not necessarily by choice but out of a certain wish to be considerate of the rest of humanity. That didn't mean I didn't long for things, like friends, relationships, meaningful conversations—just awkwardness-free conversations, actually. It just meant most of those things seemed more and more unattainable, so I did my longing from a comfortable distance.

But today the distance was not comfortable. Today Ivy wasn't feeling well, and I was worried about her. And *that* was definitely new terrain for me.

Today and yesterday, she had stayed in bed and refused to eat or be seen. And I couldn't believe how that had affected me. I was worried and I was sad, which was in direct conflict with my feelings of triumph over life, and I was helpless—of course I was helpless—which fueled my anxiety. Ivy wasn't talking to anyone. She could be dead, for all anyone knew. I'd made her breakfast, but when she hadn't answered the door to the pool house, I'd just left it there outside on the mat. That was two hours and sixteen minutes ago, and it was still sitting exactly where I'd left it, undoubtedly now teeming with microbes. Should we call the doctor? Should we call her dad? 911?

Mia said not to worry. Mia's dumb. Even so, it seemed the best I could manage would be, if Ivy hadn't moved by lunch, to replace the nine-grain muffins and fruit that I'd left this morning with soup and cucumber salad and another knock at her door.

I groaned. Agitated with my sister, who'd just left for class, leaving me with the enormous responsibility of a sick person on the property. I groaned again, this time loudly. Why did I care? People get sick. Most of them don't die. Not in pool houses. Why should I care? Why? I was too busy to care! I was too busy with a complex and time-sensitive order I'd received for three Renaissance poison rings. There wasn't room for Ivy feeling under-the-weather in my thoughts today. I had things to do, important things. I filled my chilled water glass, intent on my tasks.

But my thoughts rebelled, and as I headed downstairs, I simply could not get the girl with the new haircut and the self-proclaimed worrisome *backyard*, the girl who would not eat or talk to me today, the girl who could be dying in the pool house, but probably wasn't, out of my mind.

Thirty-One—Mia

When Ivy wouldn't get out of bed for the third day in a row, I threatened to call her dad. Then she did, and I did anyway. I had to; she looked like hell when she left for her group therapy. Something had happened to her, and she wasn't talking to me or Bo, and frankly it was scaring us. Mostly Bo, but his anxiety was contagious, so I called Daniel Proctor. I tried his cell, left two messages, and when I hadn't heard anything for two hours, I called his office. A young woman answered the phone: *Willis, Proctor and Holmes, how can I help you?* I figured Ivy's dad was a bigwig, I just didn't realize he was the number-two bigwig. I was transferred a few times, but when they couldn't find him, I ended up with the same cheery sounding girl, who offered to take a message. Beyond frustrated by now, I curtly said, "Tell him Mia Sutton called and that Ivy is sick. I'm very worried about her. Please tell him to call me back as soon as he can. He has my number."

"Who's Ivy?" the girl said.

"What?" I said, annoyed. "He'll know! Just have him call me, please! Mia Sutton, write it down." Then I pressed *End Call* before she could say another word, my patience officially spent.

"What?" said Bo, as I tossed my phone onto the couch.

I blew out a breath. "Nothing. We'll see if he even gets the message."

"What should we do in the meantime?" said my brother, who'd emerged from the basement for the second time in less than an hour for the 'Ivy Update'—oh the joys of living with an obsessive.

"I guess we just wait for her to get home and see if she's in the mood to talk."

"Did you actually see her leave?"

I sighed, my mood just getting better by the minute. "Bo, she took my car because hers has a flat. I handed her the keys. Pretty sure it was her. Why are you being so weird?"

"I'm not. I'm just...I'm worried about her."

I narrowed my gaze at my annoying brother and looked closely at him for the first time in a while. He was in a white polo and jeans, and his dark hair was just a bit longer than he usually wore it, which looked great on him. Bo got all the natural curl in the family, so Camille and I kind of hated him. But there was something else. "You really are worried," I said, surprised.

"Don't act so shocked," Bo scoffed.

"Okay," I said thinking for the first time there might be something more to his concern. He didn't look away from me as I stared, suspicion burning in my eyes. I could have given him a hard time. I didn't because he seemed so vulnerable—but steadfast at the same time. I leaned over and kissed his cheek—at which he naturally stiffened. "Be careful, Bo," I said.

"Why? What does that mean?"

"Ivy's our friend. Don't forget why she's here... Getting over the worst kind of breakup? Ring a bell?"

"What? I know that! Why are you telling me that?" His cheeks reddened half a shade as he checked his watch. "11:46! I don't have time for this!" he said, heading for the stairs, but then he turned back. "If you hear anything..."

"I'll come down and tell you," I promised, thinking about Bo and Ivy as *Bo and Ivy,* for the very first time. It was...strange.

To be honest, it felt *weird*. But I had to admit there was something about Ivy that made her feel ingrained in *me*—like we'd been friends long before I'd met her—just like Geneva had said. But I never imagined that she might have had that same effect on my brother. Bo was a super good-looking misfit who walked around the world insanely guarded. He was afraid of flying germs and bird poop and people who sneezed anywhere within a ten-foot radius of his person. He couldn't abide the thought that someone had handled his tomatoes or apples, or toilet paper for that matter, before he bought them. I just couldn't imagine him ever exchanging bodily fluids with...*anyone*. Hence, his fleeting relationships.

My brother would be a lot for a woman to take on, and to be honest, I couldn't quite see anyone—read: Ivy—volunteering for the job once they actually knew what the job was.

But what did I know? I'm just his sister.

Thirty-Two—Ivy

The posse was gathered in Adam Pembroke's small group room, and everyone had shared but me. I had to admit that I hadn't really been listening to the woes of my group, but I nodded and looked sorrowful when everyone else did, so I didn't think anyone had really noticed. The truth was, I didn't want to be here. I didn't want to be anywhere. I'd missed Tuesday because that's when I read the letter, and the only reason I was here today was because Mia had threatened to call my dad if I didn't get out of bed. She'd said she wouldn't have a choice; Bo was going bonkers with worry. So, I was here going through the motions, and now my life skills community was waiting for me to say something scintillating.

I sighed, looked mournful, which wasn't much of a stretch. "It's just Mama," I said, speaking a half-truth. Then I took my group of fellow wounded weepers on a little trip through my weekend to Carmel. I gave them a blow by blow of the argument we'd had and made it sound like the time I'd spent with Mama was the primary source of my current ennui. I satisfied everyone but Adam. But then, I guess that's to be expected since he is the paraprofessional.

A few minutes later, everyone was saying their goodbyes when he eyeballed me, and I knew I was caught. "Could I have a moment, Ivy?" he asked, and I wanted to cry.

"Sure," I said, lowering my eyes.

We sat next to each other on folding chairs. Adam Pembroke smiled. I tried to, but it came out tears.

"Talk to me...if you want," he said. "I know there's more to the story."

Adam Pembroke, AP, was a fortyish, lanky, balding, Black man who had an open face that said, *I'm interested and I have the time*, which is what made him such a good life coach, in my opinion. And as I was making this assessment, he leaned onto his elbows, "Ivy, are you all right? I'm worried about you." And I thought that was another excellent reason to like him so much.

I sniffed. "I thought my mom had given me some money," I finally said. "She gave me an envelope just before she left to go home, and I thought she was making up with me for our little tiff. But instead, it was a note with some news from home. Some devastating news." I pulled the envelope from my pocket and unfolded a sheet of fancy hotel stationery. I didn't really need to read it to know what it said, I'd read it so many times and crushed it so many times that I saw every word even in my sleep. But I cleared my throat anyway and shared what Mama had written with my kind, interested, open-faced, paraprofessional therapist.

Ivy,

Let me just start by saying I think it's time you got over Tim. All you're really doing now is hiding, and both your dad and I agree it's time you just came home. Besides, you've imposed on your father long enough, and lord knows I could use some help in the shop. The thing is: Tim is not worth it, and it's not the end of the world that he loves Angela and not you. It hurts, but it's not the end of the world. Now, I found out something last week that I didn't plan to tell you in a note. But after you picked that fight with me in Carmel and things kind of fell apart, well, you really left me no choice. So, anyway here goes...Tim and Angela got married on the 4th of July. They had a baby boy sometime in June, and now they're married. I know this will make you cry, and I'm sorry. But honestly, Ivy, it looks to me like you dodged a bullet, so please don't waste too *many more tears on him. You've cried enough. You'll find someone better. I know you will. If you're lucky, he'll be someone wonderful who will cherish you the way your dad cherishes me. I love him, Ivy, and I will not apologize to you for that. Love is a funny thing, a fickle thing. It can break your heart or someone else's. Sometimes it costs everything we have. But there's no shame in that. So, I'd appreciate it if you would mind your own business where my love-life is concerned.*

Call me if you want to talk. But seriously, put all of this behind you now and come home.

Mama

I looked up from my letter and met the sad eyes of my life coach—the man my father had hired to patch me up after I'd fallen off my wedding. He didn't say anything. Not for a minute. Then he reached over and squeezed my hand.
"That's some letter."
"Yep."
"No wonder you're hurt."
"I'm so hurt," I cried, my voice a thin flat line. I felt run over, and I knew I was hard to look at. But I didn't care. I had managed to shower and brush my teeth, and that seemed monumental after three days. My new hair just sort of did its own thing, which unless they were just being nice, my group had said they liked. I didn't care about that either. The floor was still mine, so I said, "I guess I only thought I'd been destroyed by Tim when he ran away from me as we were about to pledge our lives to each other. But turns out, he's the gift that keeps on giving." I laughed sadly. "And I just keep falling and falling down this never-ending sinkhole of mad and sad and not wanted and what the hell. And I sound so pitiful that I can't stand myself, and I can't stand that I can't stand myself because I can't stand being my own enemy." I swallowed a sob. "I

need *me* too bad! Not sure you've noticed, but I don't have much in the way of excess emotional support—I have me! That's it. And Geneva, who is conveniently not here—so just me!" I sniffed. "I have got to get a grip on this sad little life of mine, or I will drown in snot and tears, and that will make for a very woeful obituary."

"It will indeed," AP nodded in agreement. He crossed his legs and folded his arms, then looked hard at me. "Ivy, I'm going to give you this moment of self-pity because you've earned it and you're having a rough time. But then I'm going to remind you that you have me, and you have this group, you have new friends who are worried about you, and I know you, so I know you have old friends. But for now, you sing it, sister." He nodded again. "Sing it loud and proud. Get it out of your system. And when you're done, we'll do a little work."

I was confused but suddenly overcome, so I did; I sang it. I let the tears spill. I doubled over, and AP patted my back while emotion gushed out of me. At one point, he handed me a box of tissues, and I blew my nose. I carried on and on about the paper dolls my parents were in this situation—completely and utterly useless to me and how Mama's letter was just a big saltshaker with a loose lid that dumped harshness directly into my barely healing cuts—figuratively speaking, of course. When I came up for breath, AP gave me a bottle of water. When I finally stopped shuddering, he asked me if I felt better, and I told him I thought I did. A smidge.

He eyeballed me. "Good. Let's get to work, then."

"What you mean?"

"How about we dissect that letter?" he said, holding out his hand.

I don't know why I hesitated, but I did—it's not like I hadn't just read the whole darn thing to him. I handed it over, the demon correspondence from my mama bent and messy, mightily abused, very well-read, and much wept over. Sitting there in his big palm, it didn't look near powerful enough to produce all the drama that it had, but somehow it was and did. As I stared at it, my eyes started stinging and my nose started running...again.

We spent the next few minutes *dissecting* my reaction to my mother's news, and Adam dragged me kicking and bawling up close to the uncomfortable truth of my life. Tim and Angela had made a baby. This I had to face, which I thought I had—but it was deeper than just the baby. Tim, Angela, and I had been in a very strange triangle for many years. I had known this, too, for many years—it was a truth I was familiar with, had lived with for a long time. But at Christmastime, when Tim had chosen me and sealed the deal with a ring and date, I'd pretended there was no more Angela. This had been very foolish of me, AP pointed out in a kind but firm tone. He also pointed out that it was very much like Mama pretending there was no one else in Daniel's life. When he said that, my stomach turned, and I wanted to throw up. "No, it's not!" I insisted.

Adam just looked at me with a big ol' *Yes* all over his face, and it burned my eyes.

Then he went on to tell me that as harsh as it seemed, with a baby on board, it was not inconceivable—pun intended he said—that a relationship would follow—Tim's and Angela's, not Tim's and mine. "Another difficult truth, my friend," he said.

I felt defeated. It had felt like falling, just like I'd told him. Falling and knowing I would hit concrete, because concrete was coming up fast, but pushing the idea away, denying it was happening because I didn't want to deal with it. Kinda like running away to Monterey so whatever was going on with Tim and Angela in Georgia wasn't really real—until splat, I hit the concrete. I hit the concrete when I read Mama's letter. That's what I told AP.

"Was that really it?" he asked. "Was that really when you hit concrete?"

"What?" I said through the fog.

"Be honest, Ivy," my life coach said, looking hard at me. "Are you sure there isn't a part of you that was not surprised by this Angela and Tim thing—I mean, given your history?"

I didn't answer him, but I think he probably saw the stupidity shining in my eyes. He handed me another tissue, and I blew my nose. Again. "*But he chose me,*" I said pitifully.

Adam Pembroke bent his head, and his eyes got soft. "Sometimes, Ivy, the hardest truth to bear is the one we always knew and chose not to see. We can blame everything and everyone...but this one is on us. Right?"

I swallowed, unable to look away.

"The good news," he said, still soft, still kind. "I don't think you will ever let it happen again."

I sniffed, let a tear roll out of my eye. "I hope you're right. I don't think I could survive myself a second time."

He smiled. "You would. But you won't have to. You're stronger than you give yourself credit for, Ivy."

I wiped my nose, thinking I was being therapized by a big fat liar.

He shifted in his chair, draped his long arm over the back and looked at me. "So, that's the content of the letter," he said. "Now let's talk about the delivery."

"I don't know what you mean."

He cleared his throat and looked down at Mama's note. Reading from it, he said: "Ivy—not *Dear Ivy*. Not: *Hey, sweetie*, no particular kindness to prepare you for what she was about to tell you. I think that's...*interesting*. Just Ivy. Is that typical?"

I shrugged. "I don't know. She was still mad at me...so, yeah, I guess."

Adam eyed me as he sucked on his lower lip, then went back to the letter. "It's time you got over Tim. All you're doing now is hiding...you've imposed—imposed." He shook his head at the word—"on your father for long enough. And I need help in the shop. We've been patient." He dropped the letter to his lap with a sigh. "Can you hear the unkindness, Ivy? The patronizing tone in these words?"

"I can now," I said, a bit whimpery.

AP nodded. "How old are you?"

Ivy in Stills - 159

"Twenty-one."

"How does it feel, as a grown woman, to be told it's time to get over the man who turned your world upside down?"

"Not good."

"Or that you're just hiding here in Monterey and imposing on your dad while you do it? Or that everyone has been so patient with you, but you really need to go home now and get back to work?"

I swallowed—or tried to.

Adam looked at me, then back at the letter, and read from it again: *"Tim's not worth it?* It's not the end of the world that the man you love, the man you were minutes from marrying, loves someone else? Ivy, these are cruel words."

I looked at the floor and let the tears come. Again. "I know. They're terrible."

"And the kicker," he said. "I had something terrible to tell you—something I knew would hurt you, but after you picked that fight with me..." He shook his head. "...I decided you deserved no compassion from me so I put it all in a note and used a snotty tone and to make it extra painful, I added a ridiculous reference to the way your father adores me as a measuring stick for the kind of relationship you could only hope to aspire to." When he looked up from the letter, his expression was part disgust, part disbelief. "That's mighty rich, my friend."

All I could do was look at my shoes.

"Ivy," AP said. "What would motivate your mother to write this letter? *This* letter?"

For a long time, I didn't say anything.

"This is important, Ivy," he said. "What message do you think is behind this letter?"

I looked up at this man to whom I had clearly *not* given enough credit. "I don't know. We had a fight, and I guess she wanted to get back at me a little. I made her mad when I...I said something snotty about cross-country booty calls. Like I told the group, she'd been to Carmel before—without me, to meet up with my dad, and I didn't know that. It made me mad, and that made her mad." To AP's questioning brow, I nut-shelled my rather unseemly paternity and the twenty-two year on-again, off-again love affair that defined my parents' relationship.

He nodded, then looked back at the letter. "So, is it possible she thought she was justified in hurting you? I mean, you called her on her behavior, right? And she obviously didn't handle that well. Maybe she was hurt, or maybe she was embarrassed, or maybe she just got a glimpse of a woman she was not proud of—a woman who left her child at Christmastime and crossed the country for a booty call, and it suddenly felt as cheap and wrong to her as it did to her grown daughter." My lanky therapist blew out a breath as he stared at me. "I don't know your mom, Ivy," Adam said. "But based on what little I do know, it kind of fits, don't you think?"

I couldn't really find my voice, but I managed a tiny nod.

AP nodded too. "Yeah. But the thing is, that spotlight is hard to stand in for long—especially when it's your life on display. So it seems your mom shifted that spotlight onto you—*Stop crying and come home, Tim got married, he has a baby now, get over it, you'll find someone better if you're lucky like me...And this painful information is brought to you with all the gentleness of a dagger to the heart because you crossed me. Let that be a lesson to you, Missy...*" He folded the letter, handed it back to me. "Ivy, I want you to get very clear on the actual source of your pain. You received some harsh news, some painful news. News that would have hurt anyone. And in the moment when it counted most—when your mom could have softened that for you—she chose to take care of herself over you. Can you see that?"

"Maybe."

"No maybe." AP said.

I swallowed. "I love my Mama."

"I know you do. Of course, you do."

"I love her, but she's..." *What was she?* How could I answer my own question when I knew Bree was even better at this than AP?

Ivy in Stills - 161

He thought she was being all self-serving and manipulative to hurt me. But it was so much deeper than that. She was being self-serving and manipulative out of sheer desperation. I was just the sacrifice. I knew as long as I was here, in Daniel's backyard—close enough to his real family to turn him into a human ulcer—he would never leave. No more quick trips to Savannah for a steamy weekend with Mama, no meeting up in New York, or Dallas, or Phoenix or Denver. It was safe to assume that aside from Carmel last weekend, my mother's appetite for my father's affections had gone severely unfulfilled—apparently because of me.

I shook my head and finally answered AP's question. "I love my Mama," I said again. "But her loving my dad has made her...not a great mother, and only part of the woman she might have been if she'd never met him."

AP lowered his chin and lifted his brow. "So, it would seem. And that must be a very hard truth to live with, Ivy."

"It is," I said, feeling seen in my entirety for the first time in...*ever*. It was overwhelming, and the feeling brought new tears. "It truly is," I whispered. "But I actually think it's a harder truth—a crueler truth—for my mama."

My very gifted therapist nodded like I had finally figured out the winning combination to life's biggest mystery. He looked sadly pleased with me. Or maybe himself. "Bingo," he said.

I smiled half-heartedly; I had such a headache, and it was all I could manage.

"Now, the big question," he said. "What are you going to do?"

I looked past him and shook my head. "I'm not sure," I said, mulling. "I don't know for sure if I'm staying here in Monterey. But I do know that I'm not going home."

Thirty-Three—Mia

It was early afternoon, and I was separating 4X6 proofs into subcategories—faces, serendipity, nature, and incongruity. I'd chosen these themes which each reflected my broader theme of imperfection, and I was fairly pleased with the overall collection.

But not ecstatic.

I sighed as I took in the landscape of proofs scattered on Lullaby's massive living room floor, the gems not nearly as plentiful as I had hoped. I wanted to be excited; this was my senior project, after all. I blew out a discouraged breath, pulled my hair into a knot behind my ear, and started weeding again. I'd made some headway, adding a new subcategory—emotion—when Ivy walked in the front door. From my vantage point on my knees, two things immediately registered—the depth of her sadness and the looseness of her jeans.

"Hey," I said.

"Hey. What are you doing?" she said, dropping my keys on the coffee table.

"Nothing. Just going *cray* on my own work," I groaned. "How are you?"

"Oh... Fine."

"Don't lie," I said. "What's going on—she asks like it's any of her business."

Ivy didn't smile, not even a considerate grin. She just looked so very tired. I stood up. "Whatever it is, I'm so sorry. What can I do?"

Her eyes watered, and she shook her head. "You're so sweet. But it's...*my life*. I just have to weather it."

"You know you're scaring me, right?"

She looked through me for a long heartbeat, and her shoulders sagged. "Tim got married," she finally said on a sigh.

I felt my breath catch. "Oh...Ivy...What?"

"Yeah." She handed me a crumpled letter from her back pocket, and as I read it, she tiptoed around my proofs. The words were like pins in my chest. "June?" I said. "So, that girl was *really* pregnant at your wedding?"

Ivy didn't say anything.

I read the note again, this time through tears. "Ivy... I'm so sorry. Your mom's a piece of work," I said.

"That is the consensus."

I looked at her and grimaced. "I guess she doesn't get the irony."

"Oh, I think she does," Ivy said. "I just don't think she thinks I do."

"Oh. I guess that makes sense. Have you talked to her?"

"No. She's called a couple times, but I haven't picked up."

"What about your grandmother? Have you talked to her?" I asked.

Ivy shook her head. "No. Not about this. She called to say she's in love with your nieces, and Camille seems to be settling in. But I don't think she knows about this. If she did, she'd be talking to me real gentle about it. Checking on me—that's her way. *And* Tim would probably be in debilitating pain somewhere. Probably missing limbs...or testicles."

I tried to smile. "Ivy, are you okay?"

"I don't know. I have a real bad headache, but I think, generally speaking, I'm a little better than I was this morning. Is that me?"

I looked at the photo Ivy was pointing to and picked it up. It was a random shot I'd taken the night of the barbeque when her family was here. Now that I looked at it more closely, it did kind of have a *Bo and Ivy* vibe. "Look at that smile," I said, handing it to her. "I couldn't resist."

"I'm not smiling," she said. "I'm not doing anything."

"I know. You're just the glowing, completely unaware center of the shot. It's Bo who's smiling."

"That is nice," Ivy said, studying the photo. "And that he's smiling is unusual?"

"*That* smile is." I told her.

She looked up at me. "Can I have this?"

"Sure. I can make another copy."

She stared at it for another moment, then palmed her forehead. "Mia. Do you have any aspirin?"

"I'm sure we do. But Bo's the keeper of the drugs around here. His room is down the hall to the left. It's the one that looks like a surgical suite. They're in his bathroom."

"Thanks. I think I'll take some and just go lie down for a little while."

"Okay. He's probably got something stronger than aspirin, if you're interested," I said as she disappeared down the hall.

"Don't tempt me," she shouted back.

Thirty-Four—Mia

Just as Ivy was walking out to the patio, Bo emerged from the basement. I was headed to the fridge to grab a Pepsi, and when I looked up, I was met with his almost comical expression, which was a marriage of hurt and betrayal.

"What?" I said, popping the top of my soda.

"I told you to tell me when she came home! You said you'd tell me when she came home!"

I looked at my brother as I poured Pepsi over ice. "Bo, Ivy came home."

"Very funny," he said, watching her cross to the pool house. "When? How is she?"

"About five minutes ago," I said, taking a sip of my drink. "She has a headache. I sent her to your bathroom for an aspirin, and now she's going to lie down. End of story. Oh, except her horrible almost-husband got married and has a baby."

Bo had stopped breathing, and his face lost a shade of its color, and I immediately felt bad for being so glib. That is, until he erupted: "You let her into my room! How could you, Mia?"

"What?" I said, shocked. "She has a headache! Don't yell at me."

"I haven't vacuumed in there!"

I groaned. Then I walked away from my infuriatingly tormented brother. Of course, he followed me. "What? What?" he said, oblivious.

"Go away, Bo. Leave me alone. I have work to do."

"Well, how is she?"

I looked at him. Hard. "Really? She's a mess, Bo. She's very hurt. Tim, the man she almost married, married someone else. She's a little bit devastated. That's why she's been in bed for three days. That's why she has a headache. And I promise you—I absolutely promise you—Ivy could not care less that your room has not been vacuumed. Do you get that?"

He got it. I could see it in the way he looked as though I'd punched him in the stomach. I shook my head, *I'm sorry* on the tip of my tongue. But a loud pounding on the door saved me from— or robbed me of—the opportunity to say it. The sound startled my brother and me out of our moment, and we both moved toward the door.

I'd forgotten that I'd called Super-dad until I found him on the front porch, looking extremely agitated and revving up for another exuberant knock. My first thought was that this display of tension was worry over Ivy. But he quickly set me straight.

"How *dare* you leave a message like that at my place of business, Mia?" he seethed. "What were you thinking?"

"What are you talking about?"

"What was so urgent that you couldn't have used my cell?" he demanded.

"You didn't answer your cell. Or respond to my text message. What's the big deal?"

He breathed deep through his gritted teeth. "I was in court!" he said, taking a step inside.

I pulled the door open wider with reservation. Bo stepped aside.

The living room floor was still covered with my photos—although arranged in fewer piles—so I didn't invite Ivy's father past the foyer. He turned to me, still mad. "So? What was so important?" he glared.

I was suddenly defensive and not in the mood to share, so I just stared at him until I was back in charge. "Well," I finally said, "Bo and I are very worried about Ivy. She got some bad news a few days ago and has hardly been out of bed since. She's not eating or talking to anyone. I didn't know what to do, but I figured her father might. So, I called you." I checked my watch. "Four hours ago," I said pointedly. "I guess it's a good thing she wasn't clinging to life under the wheel of a semi."

Daniel Proctor narrowed his eyes as though he didn't believe me, and I really quite hated him then. "What bad news?"

I lifted my chin and met his eyes. "You should ask Ivy."

"I'm asking you, Mia. And I don't have a lot of time, so quit wasting it."

It seemed odd that Super-dad's wrath should be aimed at me, so I knew it wasn't. And though I love a good confrontation when I'm in the right, I cut my losses. I glanced over at Bo, who was doing his own share of glaring. "Tim got married," I said. "And he has a brand-new baby. And…Ivy's not taking it well."

Daniel Proctor's expression did not change. "Who?"

"Tim. *Tim.* Ivy's almost…*husband.*"

His exasperation was loud and decisive. "This is about *him*?" he carped. "I don't have time for this nonsense. It's beyond ridiculous at this point!"

"Not to Ivy," I said, frankly shocked.

"Well, that girl just needs to grow up and go home!" he said. "I can't deal with this. Not now. Not today."

I looked at Bo—who was staring a hole through the horrible attorney—wondering if we were really hearing this tantrum. At the same instant, Daniel seemed to catch himself and made a weak attempt to rein in his awfulness. With poorly affected concern, he forced out, "Is…is she all right?"

"No," I said. "That's why we called you."

Super-dad seemed surprised at my curtness and quickly tried to channel more *sorry* into his expression. "What would you like me to do, Mia?" he said with weary, disingenuous contrition.

I was about to respond when Bo moved to the door and opened it. "Just leave," he said to Daniel Proctor. "We've got it covered.

I'm sorry Mia called you. Clearly that was a mistake…and the last thing our friend needs right now."

Super-dad looked surprised that Bo had spoken. But for all my brother's failings, they were not betrayed in his square-shouldered, steely-eyed, firm-toned imperative, which he repeated as he opened the door wider. "Just leave."

"I came to see my daughter," Daniel said, eyeing Bo with what appeared to be an attempt to dominate.

"No, you didn't," my brother said, evenly. "You came to throw your weight around." Bo glared at the lawyer. "She's not here anyway. We talked her into going to her life skills group, and she's not back yet." He lied without flinching.

Daniel didn't move for a moment, but his smug superiority faltered, and we all knew the snotty little man was out of options. But it didn't stop him staring, biding his time, trying to intimidate. Bo didn't react. It was wonderful to watch.

"Tell her I was here, and to call me," Daniel demanded.

Bo didn't say anything. I didn't either. But I folded my arms and silently cheered when the boob finally walked out. On the porch, Ivy's dad turned, apparently having come up with more parting words. Sadly, we would never know what they were since Bo shut the door in his face, which I have to say made me smile.

"Well done," I said.

He looked at me, locked the door, and breathed. "I think I channeled Dad there for a minute."

"Of course you did! Nice job." I stared at my brother and could almost watch his heart slow down. "He's awful. Poor Ivy."

Bo nodded, chewing his lip.

"Hey, I'm sorry about earlier," I said. "The crack about you vacuuming and Ivy not caring."

He met my eyes. "One of these days, Mia…" he said. "One of these days, I swear I'm going to get on top of that stuff."

"I know you will."

"I'm going to take Ivy some lunch."

I followed him into the kitchen again, where he opened the fridge. "Bo..." I sighed. "Leave her alone. She has a headache."

He ignored me as he arranged grapes and cheese on a plate. When he was pleased with the presentation, he looked up. "You gave her access to my drug supply. She's depressed, devastated, I think you said. I'm checking on her." He walked past me, and I watched him make his way through the French doors and across the patio. Ivy had no idea the friend she had in my brother, who'd not only channeled my dad to protect her from hers but was now on a quest to sleuth out her possible suicidal tendencies. I sighed. Damn Daniel Proctor. Some kids get a crappy parent, some get a *really* crappy parent, and some get two.

I could not relate.

Back in junior high, Kyle Crandall broke my heart. I had loved him with the indomitable soul of a passionate thirteen-year-old. So, when he asked Tanna St. Clair to the afterschool dance and not me, I thought I would die. Mom was on her way to run a 5K, so she called my dad to rescue me from the depths of my bottomless, barely pubescent pain. I'm sure he said soothing dad things—that was his M.O.—but what I remember most was that he took me to the mall and bought me shoes: my first heels. They were red. He said they were my walking away shoes. That day, he told me life would hand me many disappointments and that there would be times when the only thing I could do was walk away. He said, *Meez, you might as well do it in style.*

His wisdom stung my eyes, even now.

Ivy was stuck with Super-dad, whose concern went only so far as was convenient. I had always had Jack Sutton—my champion from the day I was born...not to mention a closet full of great shoes.

My ringing cellphone yanked me from my reverie, and I scrambled to find it. When the number displayed was a mile long, I squealed. *Syria.* "Hey, you!" I nearly screamed into the phone.

"Hey, baby," I barely heard through the thick static.

"Hey!" Static. "Derek?" More static.

Then halfway clear, glorious laughter, then, "Mia! I can't believe I got you."

"Are you okay?" I said loudly.

"I'm great. I just miss you. I miss everything about you, baby."

"I miss you, too! Are you safe? What's happening?"

"I'm safe. Staying put, as far as I know. I just called...I just had to hear your voice and tell you...tell you I love you. I love you!"

"What?" Static. "What? Derek?"

"I love you, Mia!" he shouted.

"What did you say?" I shouted back even though I had absolutely heard him and had gone completely numb. "Derek...Derek!" But he didn't hear me because the line had filled with impenetrable static and then gone dead. "Derek!" I shouted. "Don't go... Please don't go!" I blew out a breath and stared through tears at my phone. My heart was hammering. Did that just happen? Did my guy who was a world away really say he loved me for the first time? I started to giggle and cry uncontrollably. Yes. Yes he did!

Thirty-Five—Bo

"Ivy, I'm not leaving, so you might as well let me in," I yelled. Then I knocked again—for the fourth time. Then again. When she finally opened the door, relief like I couldn't believe washed through me even if she was wearing defeat inside a wicked scowl.

"What do you want, Bo?" she snapped.

"I...I made you some lunch." Stiff grin.

"I'm not hungry. But thanks." Sheer annoyance.

"Can I come in anyway?" I asked, handing her the plate I'd covered with a clean dish towel. "It's just some fruit and cheese and a baguette. You might want it later."

She let go of a sigh and slumped a little. "That's very sweet, Bo," she said. "*You're* very sweet." She stepped aside. "I'm sorry. Of course, you can come in."

Inside, we looked at each other for a long, silent moment until she walked over and set the plate on the bedside table. Now that I was staring, I could see that she did not look good. She looked thinner and in pain. She squinted and rubbed her forehead, which confirmed my assessment.

"Mia told me about Tim," I said.

She shrugged. "Lovely, right?"

"I'm sorry."

She shrugged again.

"I don't know Tim," I said. "But I know he never deserved you, Ivy. And you...you obviously deserve better."

"That's such a nice thing to say, Bo," she said wearily. "But...No, I don't. Look at me."

"Look at what?"

"This," she said, her arms outstretched. "This."

"What?"

Her eyes filled with tears then, and I felt bad because the last thing I wanted was to make her cry. "Bo," she said with effort. "This is me. If *this* can't even hold onto the affections of a poorly educated underachieving tire salesman who'd rather be with a fickle stripper who's broken his heart a hundred times, then there is no hope for me. None. And don't look at me that way! I absolutely know how pathetic that sounds. But I'm feeling pathetic at the moment because the other side of my great worth, according to my mama, is keeping my parents' love life rocking." She slumped down onto the bed and rubbed her temples. "And on top of that, I'm almost certain there is a nest of pit vipers slithering around in my head."

I swallowed, suddenly overwhelmed by the sight of this girl so hurt and hurting, so battered by her own low opinion of herself, that my heart started to pound and my palms got sweaty. But this was a different kind of panic than I was used to. This panic was like seeing someone drowning and being too terrified of the water to jump in and help her. I sort of gasped. "Ivy! You're scaring me."

"Don't be scared, Bo," she sighed, still rubbing. "I may have exaggerated a bit about the snakes in my head."

I groaned a little. "Not that—but I am sorry about your headache. I'm talking about Tim. And I have to know...Would you...Are you really telling me that if he crawled back today—after everything he's done, knowing everything he is...Would you really take him back?"

She stared up at me, and a sob tore from her throat.

"Answer me."

"Stop it, Bo. Just leave me alone. Please!" She coughed. But then the floodgates opened, and she was crying again. Without really thinking, I sat down next to her and took her hands. "Would you?

Ivy in Stills - 173

Would you take him back if he asked you?" I probed with an insistence that surprised me.

She was trembling, almost deflating as she hung her head. "No," she finally whimpered. "No. No, I couldn't."

I'd been holding my breath, I realized. But as I blew it out, I pulled her close, and she fell against me and sobbed. It took a few seconds to realize that she was actually in my personal space where absolutely no one was allowed. She seemed to sense that at the same time I did and tried to pull back, but I didn't let go of her, and somehow it was okay. "Well, now you know," I said into her ear. "Now you know."

She looked up at me with her beautiful, agony-filled eyes. "Thank you, Bo. I'm sorry you have to see me like this."

"Like what?"

"You, know...all unraveled and *tragic*. Pathetic."

"That's not what I see, Ivy. I see a nice girl going through something brutal. That's all. You're not any of those things."

"Bo Sutton, you are sweeter than sugar on honey, but...but what if I am? That stuff?"

"Ivy, if you could see yourself through..." I sighed, desperate to make her understand. "Ivy, do you know who Prue Sarn is yet? Prudence Sarn?" I asked.

"No."

"Kester Woodseaves?"

She shook her head.

"You really need to read *Precious Bane*. Prue, the amazing Prue, sees only her flaws. She can't believe when the weaver falls completely and utterly in love with her despite them."

Ivy narrowed her eyes at me, and I suddenly felt overly exposed. What was I doing? I cleared my throat, desperate for escape. Any escape.

"I'm intrigued," she said. "I'll start it tonight. *If* I can ever get rid of this headache."

And there it was. "Oh, well...that's actually the real reason I came by."

"What?"

"You were in my medicine cabinet."

She palmed her temple. "Mia said it was okay. I took some of your Ibuprofen. And I almost borrowed a couple of your Xanax, but I didn't think you could spare them." She tried to smile. "How come you have so much of that? I think I counted nine bottles."

I felt myself redden and chuckled to cover it. "Uh, it's prescribed for me, with a refill every month. I try not to take it very often, but because I'm me, I refill it, so I won't run out."

Ivy nodded, then grimaced at the pain in her head. "Not much chance of that," she squinted.

"Are you okay?"

"I'm fine. I just have a Tim-and-Angela-and-baby-sized headache wrapped in a mom's-mean-letter migraine. That's all."

I swallowed. "I'm sorry, Ivy. I'm sorry to barge in here when you're just trying to rest. I was just...I don't know what I'd do if anything happened to you," I said, not planning to say it.

"Bo, why? Why should you care?"

For a moment I didn't respond, I just stared at her. "Because...you are my friend, Ivy," I finally said. "And I don't have too many of those. That's why."

Ivy's face filled with emotion, and for a long time she just looked at me. "You are so sweet, Bo Sutton," she said at length. "Brace yourself, because I'm gonna kiss you now. But just on the cheek, so you don't need to freak out."

"You don't have to...do..."

"Shhh," she scolded. "This is what people like me do when they're found digging their own grave and sweet people like you come along and pry the shovel away. We thank 'em. So, thank you, Bo. Thank you for being my friend."

She kissed me then, softly, on the cheek, and lingered there a bit longer than necessary. It was nice, and though it made me anxious, it was a good anxious, if there is such a thing, and I didn't freak out.

I definitely did not freak out.

Thirty-Six—Ivy

I didn't know what time it was when I woke up; I just knew my headache was gone. And as I lay there reveling in that little miracle, thoughts of Bo gently descended on me, and I relived—this time pain-free—what had happened between us. The way he'd held me and let me bawl against his surely disinfected shirt, his raw concern, the kindest words I'd ever heard. I almost couldn't believe it. Bo Sutton.

I ate most of the lunch he'd left me, even though the cheese was a little room-temperature-slimy, then splashed some cold water on my face and spritzed and scrunched my new hair. It helped a little. Then I took the plate Bo had left me back over to the kitchen.

Mia was at the counter shuffling photographs that had apparently migrated from the living room floor. "Hey," she said, then proceeded to scrutinize me. "You look like you could use some chocolate."

"I do?"

"Absolutely," she said, pushing a Symphony bar in my direction.

"No, thanks," I said. "I just ate warm cheese. I don't want to tempt fate. What are you doing?"

Mia eyed me, then sighed. "Another round of elimination, and it's not going well. My portfolio has to be no more than twenty images, and I've got close to six hundred—weeded down to these ninety-two." She shook her head in frustration and put down the photo she'd been staring at. "How are you, Ivy? Honestly."

"My headache's gone. So that's happy. And Bo helped."

"Really?"

I nodded, not sharing the details, and Mia didn't ask. But I stared at her, again recalling my conversation with him. That man was a mystery wrapped in a really good but oddball guy who'd seen me at my worst. And I'd let him—that was the mystery. And he hadn't died at the sight of me falling apart, and I hadn't died trying to pretend I wasn't falling apart. It was all a little unexpected, and it made me wonder if the Universe had maybe sent me Bo instead of Mia, because surely she couldn't have sent me both. I should maybe discuss it with Geneva.

"What?" Mia said.

"Nothing...You've just been really good friends to me, and I'm not sure that was the plan when I came here."

"Let's just call it a bonus," Mia smiled. "I really am sorry about Tim and...and your mom...and your dad..."

I shrugged but refused to cry. "I did hit the jackpot there, didn't I?"

"Are you sure about the chocolate?" she said. "There's really nothing better than chocolate and freshly shaved legs to pull your mood out of the toilet. It's my no-fail recipe."

I tried to laugh. "Good to know. Rain check."

"Okay," Mia said. "How about for now you save me and pick out the most interesting faces?" She handed me a stack of photos. "Keep in mind that imperfection is my platform."

"I'll try," I said. For the next few minutes, I studied the images Mia had captured, and I was blown away by her gift. There was a shot of a soot-blackened fire-fighter, his expression frozen in a desperate shout you could almost hear; the note on the back said *Pinnacles National Monument—the day we almost died.* There was a shot of a woman, slumped and end-of-the-day rumpled. She was a professional of some sort, but it had taken its toll. She'd been crying, and her blouse was missing a button. Another was of a very dirty woman, old, deeply-lined, and toothless. She was smiling and holding a rusty soup can with a daisy in it. Each photo told its own story and depicted a slice of humanity so visceral that it was its own definition of lovely. The last one in the stack was of a big woman eating ice cream. There was some on her chin, and she was laughing so hard that her eyes had almost disappeared behind her ample cheeks. She was beautiful. The caption on the back said, *Lullaby— wedding #5.*

"This is your aunt?" I said.

Mia looked over at the photo. "Yep. That's Lully." She took it from me. "I like this picture." She sighed dramatically. "I *like* them all. I just don't love them. What am I going to do?"

"I don't know, but you have to use this one," I said, taking the photo back. "She's so...*alive*. Why have I not seen her? Why are there no pictures of her anywhere?"

"Lully prefers rare art," Mia said absently. "Except in her office." She looked up at me then. "Those walls are covered with her life."

"Can I see them?" I asked.

She bit off a chunk of chocolate, which I'm sure was not Bo-approved. Then with her mouth full, said, "Of course. Come with me."

I followed Mia through the living room now cleared of her photographs, down the hall past Bo's room, to a set of double doors. Her aunt's 'office' was enormous, and the only part that was even remotely office-*like* was the massive antique desk. There was a wall of bookshelves, a fireplace and double French doors that lead out to a private garden. Two overstuffed red sofas took center stage and flanked a huge round ottoman rimmed with colorful tassels. And there were pictures everywhere—on the walls, on the mantle, on the desk and side tables. It was an amazing room, and I couldn't remember ever being in a space that felt so *lived in*. Lullaby Sutton was a large woman, and if the pictures were any indication, she was a happy woman who had about a million friends—many of them men.

"She's really been married five times?" I said taking in the images.

"Yep. But only divorced once," Mia said. "The other three died. And, of course her new one is very much alive." She laughed.

"Really?"

Mia nodded. "Her first husband was before I was born—but he was a bad guy. Apparently. She never talks about him, and neither does my dad. So, whatever happened must have been, you know...There's a picture of him—Anthony. It's over there," Mia pointed. "The one with the dart in his forehead."

I laughed, but sure enough, on the wall just left of the door we'd just walked through hung a headshot of a good-looking man who could have been the dad in Modern Family. And he did indeed have a big ol' dart sticking right between his eyes. I looked at Mia. "Wow."

"I know," she said. "That's Lully, for you. But I was just thinking...If you've got any pictures of Tim, I know where Lully keeps her darts."

I laughed. "I like your aunt."

"You would *love* my aunt."

"Tell me about the rest of her men," I said, taking in the big room.

"Well, that's Roland," Mia said, pointing to a picture of a bald man laughing with Lullaby—both of them were wearing mirrored shades and were dressed like clowns. "Here's a good one of just him—he was the editor of a newspaper. I was just a little girl when he died. He got cancer," she said. "I don't remember too much about him, except he always gave me quarters." Mia pointed to another photo. "That's Toby. He was my favorite. Always told funny knock-knock jokes. He had a seizure while he was driving and crashed into the library. That was awful. Lully was with him, and she broke her wrist and some ribs. He owned The Restaurant Tobias, which Lully now owns. Here's a picture of their New Year's Eve party. See, that's Lully on the bar, singing with the Mayor."

I smiled. Lullaby Sutton looked like a big disco ball wearing a laugh that looked like it could take her breath away. She was clearly having fun. And so was everyone around her.

Mia walked over to the end of the bookshelf, and I followed her. "And here's Alfred," she said picking up a rustic framed 8x10. "He was the oldest, and oh my gosh, he adored my aunt. He had a heart attack." Mia pulled a funny face. "In bed. Lully said he went out happy, though. That's probably TMI."

I grimaced. "How old was he?"

"He was nineteen years older than her, and he died when she was 56. I remember because it was the day after her birthday—two...no, three years ago." Mia said all this while walking over to the desk, and I was thinking, my goodness, this woman gets around.

"And this is Matisse," Mia said. "He's seven years younger than Lully and seems like a pretty good guy. We don't know him very well yet. He owns vineyards and a little mansion in Dijon, which is somewhere in France."

"Where did she meet him?" I said studying the short and portly Frenchman with the crooked smile.

"At a charity wine tasting over in Carmel. She was raising money for refugees, or to get cats neutered. Or it might have been international adoptions—she's on *lots* of boards. Anyway, he was there with his wine, and he fell fast and hard for Lullaby."

"Wow. What's her secret?" I asked, gazing around at the evidence of her busy life and the many people she knew.

"Oh, it's probably her...*everything*." Mia chuckled. "Lully is just..." She shrugged. "*Lully*. She's generous and funny and kind and a little sarcastic. She's so nice. Unless she's mad. Then she just yells you to death." Mia shook her head. "She just lives her life...very *out loud*."

"What does that mean?"

"It means you *know* when Lullaby Sutton is in the house. She doesn't hide—she's like everybody's mom, or best friend. She talks to you like you're the only one who matters. She laughs easy, and she's very huggy—and it doesn't matter if you've known her for years, or you're meeting her for the first time. She's just got a knack with people. My dad says Lully could make friends with a cobra. He thinks I got some of that from her."

"I would agree with that," I said.

Mia smiled. "And she looks people right in the eye—she says that changes everything. Peter the Great doesn't like her—no surprise there. He can't stand to be looked at too closely."

"Who?"

"Pete—my demon brother-in-law."

"Oh, right—looking people in the eye is Geneva's superpower too."

Mia nodded. "Yep—and we saw how much he loved that?" She sighed. "He's such an ass. Lully knew there were issues, but Camille..." Mia shook her head. "Camille told my aunt to stay out of it. I don't know what exactly happened—Camille doesn't talk about it. And Lully never would—it's between them—but I can tell you that Peter avoids my aunt like the plague, so he probably knows Lully could crush him—literally and figuratively."

"Yay, her," I said. "I want to meet her."

"I hope you get to. She's so interesting. She almost died a couple of years ago and she got really introspective for a while. Here's a picture of her in the hospital."

"She's still smiling. What happened?"

"It was right after Alfred died—she had her knees replaced. She was doing fine, but then blood clots from her legs somehow made their way to her lungs. It was very scary. She got super serious after that; started looking at caskets, planning her own funeral. Oh, she even had me take her portrait."

Mia then walked across the room and got down on her knees. She slid her hand under the sofa and pulled out a huge, framed photograph. "I took this last year in studio," she said, gently peeling the butcher paper from a large canvas. She stood up and held it at arm's length. "Even though black and white is my trademark, Lully insisted on color, and I have to say, I'm pretty pleased."

"Oh, my..." was all I could say of the full-length portrait of Mia's much-ballyhooed aunt. Lullaby Sutton had short dark hair streaked with gleaming silver. She was wearing a long red dress—custom designed, per Mia—with elbow-length black gloves, which had been her mother's, and a necklace made of huge pearls strung on black ribbon—Bo's handiwork.

"She's...she's beautiful," I said, mesmerized by Lullaby's smile, which was wide and genuine, and there was authentic joy in her blue eyes—nothing staged. She was enormous, but either no one had told her, or she simply didn't give a damn. And that was perhaps the prettiest thing about her. "Just beautiful," I murmured again.

"Even though she's like three of you?" Mia elbowed me in the ribs.

I ignored her but shamefully got her point. In fact, my first thought was that the woman's loveliness had everything to do with how proud she seemed being exactly who she was. I wanted some of that in the worst way. I elbowed Mia back but didn't look at her. "So...have you always been close with her?"

"Very. Lully couldn't have children. She had two brothers, but my uncle Giff—I never knew him; he died in Vietnam before I was born—never had kids, and my dad has us. So, Camille, Bo, and I are seriously adored. And don't even get me started on my nieces."

"Oh, I can imagine."

 "About six months after she got home from the hospital, she said, 'Mia—I don't want to leave anything to chance.' She showed me the dress and asked me to take her picture. So, I did." Mia sighed. "She told me about her will that day, too—which was a little weird. Almost everything goes to us—me, Bo, and Cam—but we have to promise to be generous in charitable giving, take care of our parents, and never spend a dime on cosmetic surgery." Mia grimaced at me. "Lully is a little miffed that I wear hair extensions."

I laughed. "What's this?"

Ivy in Stills - 183

"I don't know," Mia said of the folded sheet of paper taped to the back of the portrait. She gently worked the tape loose and unfolded it, and I read over her shoulder. The first line said:

Whoever finds this, please read at my funeral service...

A note to my Beloveds—and if you are in attendance here today on the solemn occasion of my untimely death, you are absolutely my beloved, and you know how I must always have the last words, so here they are:
I have had the good fortune to be loved by outstanding men (not counting that one), I've been befriended by outstanding people, taught by outstanding parents, protected by an outstanding brother who shared with me his outstanding children, Camille Dawn, Benjamin Oliver, and my Mia Lullaby. And in a category all her own, Eileen Sutton is my truest sister. I adore you all, and I don't know what made me worthy of such blessings, or the accidental wisdom that came with those blessings. But I thank you! I thank you with all my heart.

I heard Mia sniff.

Today, as you gather to remember my delicious life, let there be no tears. Life is too short for such nonsense. Obviously!
My very wise new husband, Matisse, said the day he begged me to marry him, "Lullaby, whenever possible choose happiness because the alternative is simply unthinkable." He was so right!
So, my friends, on this occasion of goodbye, let us raise a glass to choosing happiness and loving with abandon and breathing joy and believing in us. And let us gulp it all down with deepest gratitude, every single day! Because the alternative truly is simply unthinkable!

Always and forever,
Your Lullaby.

"Oh...my goodness. This woman," I said, resting my chin on the back of Mia's shoulder.

She sighed. "Oh, Lully. Only you."

We were quiet for a moment as we each read her words a second time. Then Mia turned to me. "She could have addressed this little note: 'Dear Ivy...'"

I met her gaze without flinching. "Well, I think your fascinating aunt could have addressed it: 'Dear Absolutely Anyone With a Beating Heart'...So, there!"

Thirty-Seven—Bo

I called my sister. Or that was the intent. She'd been gone over a week, and she had a new phone number, which I had misplaced, so I had no choice but to call Geneva Talbot. I'm not very good at small talk with people I don't know well. But Geneva had somehow infiltrated my comfort zone with amazing ease, and speaking with her came as natural as a conversation with my mom.

"Bo! How lovely to hear your voice! I've been thinking about you, sug. How are you?"

"Pretty good," I said, smiling but not believing her for a minute.

"What have you been up to?"

"I'm busy. I'm always busy. I need to hire a fulltime IT guy, but other than that..."

"So, your business is growing! That's wonderful. Wonderful! Hop on a plane to Savannah so I can hug you! Come right now!"

I coughed. "I don't fly, Geneva. Ever. All that uncirculated, recycled, microbial-laden air—it would absolutely kill me."

"Oh, my." Geneva laughed, deep and gravelly. "I guess I'm lucky to be alive."

"Anyone who flies is lucky to be alive, Geneva." I informed her with complete solemnity.

Again, she laughed. "Well, maybe someday you'll risk it—when you're properly motivated. But for now, you just consider yourself thoroughly hugged."

"Okay," I said. "I will. I actually called to check on my sister, but I lost her new number."

"Well, I can get that for you, but she's taken the girls swimming, so I'm not sure she'll answer."

"Oh. Well, I can call her later. How is she?"

"Bo, she's finer than frog hair split four ways."

"Ummm, is that good?"

Geneva laughed. "It's very good. Your sister's only been here eight days, but I tell you, the difference in her is night and day. I brought a beautiful but dying girl to Savannah, and she has simply blossomed. And those little ones—oh, my gracious, but they have become my heart. And Olivia's little arm is healing up nicely. All is well, Bo. All is well."

I was truly relieved—and surprised. "It's been a long time since Camille—or her girls—have fit that description," I said. "Do you know...has she talked about her plans? Her marriage? Peter?"

"Well, I'm not sure about him, but I think your sister is planning to stay in Savannah for a while. Which I think is grand."

"Really?"

"I think so. She enrolled her girls in Montessori Summer Preschool—they start next week. And my Bree has talked her into helping out at her shop in the afternoons while the girls are gone."

"That...that sounds great," I said, again surprised and not sure what I'd expected. "You've really worked your magic, Geneva. How can we ever thank you?"

The old woman chuckled. "I'd love to take the credit, Bo, but the simple truth is Camille was suffocating with that man—and so were those angels. Now they can simply breathe," she said. "Everyone breathes better in Savannah."

"That's...good to know."

"And what about Peter?" said Geneva. "Has he been a bother?"

"Oh, that's all he knows how to be," I said. "He's been here looking for Camille a few times. And he's been stalking my parents, but there hasn't been any ugliness. I think he's too worried about his heart exploding."

Geneva laughed. "Well, we can hope, sug," she said. "Now, how is my Ivy?"

I swallowed.

"Bo?"

I swallowed again.

"Bo, what's happened?"

"Geneva...did you know about Tim?"

"Did I know what about Tim?"

"That he married the...*dancer*?"

"What?"

"And they had a baby? Did you know, and you didn't tell Ivy?"

"I'm sure I do not know what you are talking about, Benjamin. Tim Marsh is married?"

"Apparently so. And when Ivy found out, well, she pretty much crashed and burned."

"Well of course she would. My poor girl. That little toad—how could he? Of course, I didn't know. Did he call her?"

"No. It was her mom. It was Bree."

"Bree? What are you talking about?"

"She gave Ivy a note just before you left to go home. It wasn't very nice; in fact, parts of it were pretty mean. I guess they had an argument in Carmel... and...Anyway, the news messed Ivy up pretty good for a few days. She's still having a hard time, and we're—"

"A note? A *note!* What is wrong with that daughter of mine? That kind of news should come with hugs and hankies. Lordy, now she'll never come home. Is my sweet girl all right? You be honest with me, Benjamin."

"She's had a rough week," I said. "But you should call her. She was afraid that you knew and didn't tell her."

"I would never do that!"

"That's good. I'm so happy to hear that, Geneva."

She groaned. "Has her father...has Daniel been any help at all?"

"No," I said. "He seems mostly annoyed by the whole thing."

"Sounds just like him. Useless little pissant!" she spat. "Oh, I wish Ivy would come home. She feels humiliated, but she shouldn't. Timothy Marsh is despised for what he did to her. And now this? He won't be able to show his face around here. But my girl is simply beloved. She'd know that in the first five minutes, if she'd just come home."

I don't know why this caught me. To hear Ivy tell it, she was nothing and no one without Tim. Now Tim was married and had a family, and Ivy was hopeless. "Geneva, is she going to be okay?" I asked, sounding ridiculous.

"Of course she is! She's my granddaughter."

"I wish I knew her better," I said stupidly. "Um...then maybe I could help her..."

"Sug, you already know everything you need to."

"I...I don't..."

"Oh, I think you do, Benjamin."

I swallowed. *Benjamin*. She meant business, and I was letting her mean business.

"I..."

"Dear man, you know she's hurting—what else is there? You've probably figured out she's been bruised and not just by that boy. But I'll tell you this, she's a survivor and she'll survive Tim—course it would help mightily if he would just die—or tragically break a hip or two," Geneva said. "But right now, Ivy's confidence has taken a blow, she's in mourning. But that is not her regular self, Bo. Far from it. She's just smack in the middle of a very bad year—we call it a *year of ashes* around here."

"What is that?"

"Her life blew up, Bo. All that's left of her dreams and hopes and wishes—or what she thought they were—is a big fat pile of ashes and no wind. It's a refining process. There's no hurrying it, but my Ivy will get through it. She will. You don't come out of a year of ashes weaker. Only stronger and more formidable. I surely hope you're still around to see it, Benjamin, because it will be a beautiful sight."

"I...I do, too," I said.

"Now, you tell my darling girl to call me so I can set her straight on this Tim situation. You hear?"

"I will, Geneva."

"And I will tell Camille that her sweet brother called."

"Okay."

"You take care."

"I will. Thank you, Geneva."

"For what, hon?"

"Uhhh..." I panicked and hung up, because I'm insane.

Thirty-Eight—Ivy

I didn't always feel this bad. There was a time, a long time, when my chin was pretty darn level with the rest of humanity, when eye contact came natural and I used to laugh. There was a time when I slept easy, and my soul didn't ache and I felt like a relatively normal girl. How I let this...this *implosion* happen in me...to me, is one of the biggest shame storms of my life. I almost can't remember who I used to be.

It takes an extraordinary person to ruin someone's life. Mia had said that the day I moved in here.

Tim was not extraordinary. He was barely even special. I think I'd always known that. I wanted him to be. I built him up to be something fine and wonderful in my mind. But he was just Tim.

When he left me standing stupidly alone in the gazebo, just before the enormity of what was happening had sunk in, what he did was just one more time when he'd left me for Angela—a girl he didn't love but couldn't stay away from. And in that same microsecond, I figured he'd come back—because he always had before. That wasn't me in denial. That was me knowing another person inside out. I was Tim's safe place. That was my job. Angela was his live-for-the-moment place. His exciting place. But she was like fireworks, a short burst of exhilaration that quickly fizzled itself out and always left the smell of scorched air behind. That's when he came back to me. Sorry and clear-eyed and desperate. And I let him. I always let him. I'd been doing it for so long, I didn't know how not to.

People back home, Mama, Gran, my friends, they all thought the reason I would never come back to Savannah was because the humiliation of my botched wedding was too great. I was fine perpetuating that line of thinking because I knew the truth was even more disgraceful: I was afraid I still loved Tim. And that was a whole new level of pitiful that I would prefer to deal with from three thousand miles away.

When Bo asked me, actually said the words and made me answer him: Would I take Tim back if he asked me? I said no even though I wasn't sure. But then saying it out loud felt true—it was even a profound relief. But Bo didn't ask me the bigger question—did I still love Tim? I didn't know that answer. I didn't even know if my weird little heart would ever know, because all it did was ache.

I groaned and pulled the covers over my head. I was exhausted, but I couldn't sleep. Again. It was a quarter to four in the morning.

After walking through Lullaby Sutton's world, reading her funeral letter and then hearing Mia tell me she could have written it for me, I broke down a little. I didn't mean to, it just all started to leak out of me. Mia had simply held my hand and said, "Cry if you need to. Cry all night if you want. But then be done. You've given Tim Marsh more than enough of you. Maybe it's time to be finished."

I told her she sounded like Mama but nicer. At any rate, I knew she was right.

She also informed me that after our laps tomorrow morning, she was taking me shoe shopping. I like shoes. But that was tomorrow—well just a few hours—which didn't leave me much time to work on being done. I wasn't making much progress.

I picked up my phone. It was a quarter to seven in Georgia, and I knew my grandmother was up. She'd left me a message late last night. No greeting, no: "Hello my darling," just: "*I did not know about Tim. You call me so we can talk.*" I dialed and she answered already speaking. "Oh, my sweet girl! I am so sorry."

"Is the Universe trying to tell me something?" I whimpered.

"Always, my love. Why?"

"Nothing. I just...I'm having a very bad life right now."

There was a long silence, and I didn't expound. Finally, my grandmother said, "I'm sorry your mama told you about Tim in a note."

"I think I hate her a little, Gran."

"No, you do not, Ivy Lee. She's your mother. She was wrong in her approach, and I'm very disappointed in her, but she is your mama, and she loves you. You should call her."

"No. I don't have anything to say to her. It doesn't matter that she was mad at me at the time; this was always bigger than her little fit. She *wanted* to hurt me, Gran. She wanted to get back at me because she was wrong, and I called her on it. Did you know she was meeting up with my dad in Carmel two or three times a year? Did you know that, Gran? She never brought me. Not once. We couldn't have that, right? Who brings a kid on a tryst? What kinda mama lets her kid tag along on a booty call?"

"Don't be like that, Ivy."

"Why did she get to decide that I didn't need a dad—a decent dad? A real dad?" I was almost howling now. "I can't believe how mad I am at her. And I can't understand why it's taken me so long to get this mad at her. Oh, wait, yes I can, I'm finally far enough away to *see* her. Now that I can, I hate what I see."

"Hush now!" Geneva said. "I mean it. There is not one ounce of hate in you, Ivy, and you know it. I wouldn't have chosen your dad to be the love of her life, but it wasn't my call. It wasn't yours either, so just stop all the snippiness. It's fruitless and unbecoming."

"I know that, Gran," I sighed, coming down from my high horse. "I'm just spewing."

"I know, darling."

"I should go."

After a long moment of neither of us hanging up, Geneva said, "To answer your question, sug, yes, absolutely, the Universe is indeed trying to tell you something. But you'll have to figure out what it is on your own."

I blew out a big and dramatic breath. "Of course," I said, my voice dripping with sarcasm. Then I hung up because the tears were back.

After a few minutes, my phone buzzed. I thought she was calling back to lecture me with more nonsense, but it was a text from Bo.

Are u awake?

Yes. Sleep hates me.

Lol. Sorry. Left u some organic nectarines.

Why? When?

Thought you'd like them—they're good for you. Just now. Sleep hates me, too.

I do like them. Thanks. I feel your pain.

LOL. Well...enjoy...

I peeked outside to be sure he wasn't lurking in the shadows, then I opened the door and found a small bag of nectarines and some pita chips—homemade, I'm sure—sitting there.

That Bo Sutton...sweeter than sugar on honey.

Thirty-Nine—Mia

After yesterday, I wasn't sure Ivy would show up for laps, and I had no intention of bugging her into it. A girl needs space and privacy when the ceiling crashes in. But in the meantime, I wanted to kill Tim the Tire King and both of her parents. Honestly, how *was* Ivy supposed to get over all the crap in her life?

I stopped in the kitchen for a bottle of water. From the window, I could see there was no activity going on in the pool house—the blinds were shut and so was the door. I sighed and headed to the pool, and when I rounded the corner, there was Ivy doing laps. "Hey!" I shouted, surprised.

"You're late!" she panted, not breaking stride. "It's almost 7:30!"

I jumped in and caught up. "Slow down! Where's the fire?" I yelled.

She ignored me and kept swimming.

I didn't know how many laps she'd done before I got there, but together we did our full twenty, and it was a little bit of work keeping up with her. But she looked great, and I told her so as we walked the perimeter of the pool to cool down.

"I don't know how that's possible," she said, out of breath. "Seeing as how I have had exactly no sleep all night long."

"Why?"

"My brain refused to shut down with trying to be done—as in *done* with Tim—and being mad at my mom and scolded by my Gran for being mad at my mom, and just generally being sick to death of myself."

"Oh...*that*. Girl, you so need new shoes. Today."

"I do?"

We walked over to the steps, and I followed Ivy out of the pool and had to do a double take. When she turned around, I said, "You've lost weight."

"It's just this suit, I think," she said, squeezing the water out of her hair. "The chlorine has stretched it out."

"Oh, I guess that's possible. Not!" I yelped. "Face it, Ivy, you're shrinking."

She looked down at herself.

"You're looking good," I said. "Deal with it."

"Really?"

"You've been to hell and back, Ivy. And then back to hell, and somewhere along the way you decided to look kind of great."

Ivy looked down at herself again. "Maybe a couple more pounds since Carmel. I guess being out of sorts burns calories."

"See," I said, tossing her a robe. "I don't make the news. I just report it. Now let's eat."

Bo was at the sink cutting organic strawberries. He was wearing an apron and rubber gloves and looked more suited for surgery. I grabbed a strawberry and popped it in my mouth. "You're cutting us some, right?"

"Hey," he snapped. "Those haven't had their final rinse."

I laughed. "Ivy," I said, "If I don't make it through breakfast, make sure my obit states clearly my cause of death: consumption of rinsed, but not final rinsed, fruit."

"Very funny, Mia," my brother said. "Hi, Ivy."

"Hey, Bo," she said, pulling her robe tighter around herself.

"How did you sleep?" he asked.

"Not great," Ivy said. "But I did nod off for a bit after I ate a couple of nectarines the good fairy left on my doorstep."

I saw my brother smile at his sink full of strawberries. It was a little weird, and I wondered what that was about, but I didn't ask.

"So, what's the plan today?" he said, not really addressing anyone.

"Here's what I think," I said. "Ivy, let's head out about ten, and we will shop for shoes until we find the perfect—and I do mean perfect—goodbye Mr. Tim shoes. We'll have some lunch. Then you can come over to the campus with me and hang out for about 20 minutes while I take a quick quiz. Are you cool with that?"

She looked at me with no expression. "As it happens my engagement calendar is woefully wide open. So...ten it is."

I smiled—relieved that she hadn't taken much convincing. I thought we might be looking at another day in bed. "Great! Hopefully by the time we get home my head will be sufficiently cleared to tackle my sim cards and make a freaking decision about my freaking project. Maybe you could help me."

"I'd be happy to," Ivy said. "I'll take a shower and check in with my many fading job opportunities." She pulled a face, then gave a fake laugh. "Be back later."

"Take these with you," Bo said, handing Ivy a bowl of strawberries. "I know how much you like them."

"Why thank you, sir," she smiled. "I do, indeed."

Forty—Ivy

Maybe I should call Bree. I probably should. But it was that *should* word that stopped me. I didn't want to talk to my mother. I still had nothing kind or understanding to say to her. I knew she was waiting. She'd left me two messages, not warm, not pre-apologetic for her part in what happened. They were more, *I'm here, when you're ready to grovel for my affection* type messages. Or that was my interpretation. And I wasn't, so I hadn't called. Maybe tomorrow I'd be ready to hold my own with her.

But I kept thinking it wasn't all Mama. It was me being stupid with my life, too. If things hadn't happened exactly as they had, I'd be married right now to a man who I knew was living a double life—kinda like my father. And I'd probably choose to be completely blind to it—kinda like my mother. I would still be in Savannah living pretend-contented in the bubble of my faulty perceptions. *My* faulty perceptions. AP was right, I had to own that.

I should call Mama. It had been more than a week.

No. I'd call her tomorrow. I'd be stronger tomorrow.

Instead, I took a shower and shaved my legs, and Mia was right: the smooth made me feel fantastic. I then filled my hands with mousse and pushed my hair around until I liked it. I lifted my chin and tried on a variety of expressions. I looked very different. I'd always thought girls with short hair were so brave and daring, and now I looked brave myself. Maybe feeling brave was on my horizon. My skin had never been a problem, but with some California sun I looked healthier than I felt. My blue eyes, though a little tired, looked bigger because of my bangs and bluer because of my tan. I decided to go for broke and put on some makeup. I hadn't worn any since I came to California, and I was amazed at what a little mascara, a little shadow and blush and lip-gloss, could do. As I scrutinized myself, I decided I had news for Mia: It wasn't chocolate and shaved legs that brought a girl back from the brink of death—it was new hair and wedding makeup.

 Still naked, I stepped back from the mirror to take in more of my form. Maybe Mia was right about that, too. It wasn't that I was thin, I would never be thin, and it wasn't just that I was a little smaller, which I was; it was that I seemed *firmer*. When you're not stick thin and never will be, you sort of measure success of the girth battle by the loss of land mass around your middle, your thighs, and under your chin. I was definitely missing some land mass. I guess I could thank my heartaches for something, just like Mia said. My eyes filled with tears, and it made me mad because the last thing I wanted was to ruin my makeup. I took a deep breath and willed some of the brave I craved and stepped on the scales I'd not been on since I arrived. What? Down nine pounds That couldn't be right. I stepped on them again. What? For a third time, I stepped onto the fancy digital scale. It must be broken. But assuming I'd lost *something,* I tried on all my clothes. My pants *were* looser, my bra had to be cinched, and my tee shirts fell nicely from shoulder to hips with only a slight detour over surprisingly shrinking muffinage. My neck had even shown up. Wow. I knew I'd crashed after I'd read Mom's letter, and I'd spent a lot of time in the dark, not eating much. But this was the result?

 Surely some of it had to be real, didn't it? The walking, swimming, occasional downward-facing-dog, and all of the repeatedly rinsed raw foods had surely had an impact. I pulled on my newly acquired skirt and a black tee and gave myself a once over in the full-length mirror. I looked better than I felt, but that made me feel better than I had in days. And with that booster shot of confidence, I grabbed my book and walked over to the main house.

When I couldn't find anyone, I headed down the stairs to Bo's workroom.

He was bent over a project at his little desk, inspecting his work through a headband magnifier. I cleared my throat, and he looked up.

"Sorry," I said.

His mouth dropped open as he slipped off his headgear. "H...hey. Hey, Ivy."

"I just wanted to thank you...again," I said.

Bo stood up, and his gaze traveled the length of me. When he got to my face, there was a look in his eyes that could have meant I'd gone too far or just far enough. He swallowed. "For what?"

"I guess...everything. Yesterday. Letting me cry all over you. The nectarines in the middle of the night. The strawberries this morning. Pretty much this whole week."

Finally, he smiled. Sort of. "You're welcome. Is that *Precious Bane*?"

"Yeah," I said, holding up the book. "I thought I'd work on it while Mia is taking her test."

"Are you liking it?"

"I just started it. But if you want to know the truth, so far it's kind of breaking my heart."

He nodded. "Keep reading."

"I will." I nodded back. "Okay, well..." I shrugged. "I guess I'm off to do some shoe shopping."

"It's about time, Ivy."

"What do you mean?"

"Nothing...It's just that today might be less about buying shoes than you think." He took me in again. "You look ready. You look good."

I had no idea what he was talking about, and for a long moment, we just stared at each other. Then I said, "I think maybe you noticed, I did myself up. Is it too much?"

He smiled. "No, Ivy. It's perfect. You're beautiful. I've always thought so."

I shook my head, felt myself get hot. "Bo Sutton. You stop that! You stop that right now."

He laughed, and I got hotter.

"Ivy?" Mia shouted. "You down there?"

"I'm coming!" I yelled back. And I couldn't get up those stairs fast enough.

Forty-One—Bo

Successfully living with anxiety takes extreme planning, maintaining routine, limiting human interaction, creating order. And, of course, avoiding known triggers. I try to plan for contingencies so that when something unexpected shows up on my road I won't forget where I'm going. Even so, contingencies can be very disruptive. There's therapy, but I don't really like therapy. It just takes too long to grow a therapeutic alliance into helpfulness, and it seems a waste of my highly inflexible time, especially when a new clinician is seldom interested in anything but stamping a diagnosis on me and reinventing the wheel. They hate to admit it, but at the end of the day, all that's really left for me to do is exactly what I'm already doing, so I don't see the point. I do keep my semi-annual appointment with Dr. Delveccio whether I need to or not. He refills my prescription for the only medication that has ever helped—the Xanax I try not to take but refill every month so I won't run out.

The short of it is that as long as I adhere to the things that work for me, I function just fine. It's when something new is introduced that I get thrown. Ivy Talbot is a good example of something new, but I think I've adjusted to her quite admirably—until now. She's taking up space in my head formerly devoted to issues of organization, ritual, and the peace that comes with freshly vacuumed carpet and a glistening toilet. I'm not stupid; the highly evolved portion of my brain knows how vulnerable she is. But the less evolved portion of me simply can't stop thinking about her. And what on earth was she doing looking so good today. What is happening? What is wrong with me? Stop it, Bo! "Just freaking stop it!" I said out loud.

I groaned. I was painfully behind schedule trying to finish the bead-braided arm clasp I'd been commissioned to create for a layout in *Modern Bride*—another excellent opportunity for me. But I could not concentrate. How could a girl going through so much garbage look so good?

Again, Bo. *Stop it!*

For the next hour, I battled my belligerent focus, but I could not bring it into submission, and I was getting nowhere with my project. I decided to take a break and go for a run, which was not ideal since it would require a re-shower, followed by a thorough cleaning of the shower, a change of clothes, and laundering the ones I'd had on. But it would be worth it to clear my head. I'd be two-and-a-half hours behind if I hurried, but I'd complete the clasp if it took me all night. So, I ran. I ran at a punishing speed that made my heart an anvil in my chest. It was cleansing and exhilarating and like a vacation from myself. And I probably would have kept going for ten miles, except my phone rang. Again. I'd ignored it the first time and again a few minutes later. But by the third time, it seemed clear someone seriously wanted my attention.

"Hello!" I panted. I'd stopped and leaned over, trying to catch my breath.

"Benjamin?"

"Hello."

"Benjamin, its Geneva Talbot."

"Geneva? Hey," I said, gasping.

"Benjamin," her voice broke. "I have some very bad news."

My pounding heart tripped over itself. "What? Is it Camille? The girls? What's wrong?"

"No, no. It's Bree. It's my Bree." Geneva's voice faltered, and then there was a moment of silence.

"Geneva! Did I lose you?"

"There's been an accident, Bo," she said in a trembly voice. "A terrible accident and she's..."

"What? Is...is she okay?" I coughed.

It took her a long time to answer, and then she rather squeaked. "I don't think so, no."

I swallowed as I sank onto the curb. "What happened? Tell me what happened."

"I don't...all they've told me is she was coming back from lunch, and there was a robbery—not at her place but a few shops down—and the police had roped off access. They made her wait on the sidewalk, I don't know, they wanted to make sure it was safe, is what they told me. She was just standing there, Bo. Just standing there, and out of nowhere a car came speeding down the walkway trying to get away from the police. They ran her down, Bo. They just ran right over my daughter. And now..."

"Good Lord, Geneva. I'm so sorry. Have you seen her?"

The old woman's voice quavered. "She's...she's in surgery, but..."

"What can I do? Geneva, what do you need?"

Ivy's grandmother reined in her emotion. "The doctor just came out and...Bo, Ivy needs to come home. I need you to tell her what's happened, and then you need to get her on a plane. Today. As soon as you can. Can you do that for me, sug? I don't know how much time there is, and I can't tell her that over the phone, Benjamin. I just can't. So, I'm depending on you."

"Oh...O...Okay, okay, Geneva. I...I can do...I'll call the airline right now," I said, shaking.

"Thank you, Benjamin. And when you tell her...hugs and hankies, sug. Hugs and hankies."

"Right. Right." I hung up feeling like the earth was giving way beneath me. My heart was racing, but it was no longer because of my run. How could this happen? How could I tell Ivy what her own grandmother couldn't? My cell rang again. "Bo," Camille said when I answered.

"Cam!"

"Have you talked to Geneva?" she asked breathlessly.

"I just hung up. How bad is it? How bad really?"

"It's bad, Bo," my sister said. "Bree has a crushed pelvis and collapsed lungs, massive internal injuries. The doctor said they are doing what they can to stop the bleeding, but...it's not good."

"Good Lord. Are you okay?" I said.

"I was right there, Bo," Camille said softly. "I was right next to her. She'd asked me to help her unload a shipment this afternoon, so I left the girls with Geneva. But when I got there, it was a crime scene. The police were everywhere, and then all of a sudden this car..." Camille let out a shaky breath. "I still can't believe it. I'm not hurt, but I'm not okay either."

"Cam..."

My sister started to weep. "I'll be fine! But Bree... It's so awful. And poor Geneva. Bo, that woman is the kindest woman I've ever known. I can't believe this is happening."

Forty-Two—Ivy

I couldn't believe Mia made me try on the Pradas. I couldn't believe how I fell in love with them. And Gucci. And Manolo Blahnik. And Pedro Garcia. And Jimmy Choo. Of course, she had to capture me strutting in each pair with her fancy camera. I'm pretty sure I tried on the equivalent of the cost of a small condo, but it felt out of this world to walk around Giselle's Designer Shoes in $1200 sandals. They took my breath away. But I was still a hard sell since I couldn't believe my father had actually authorized this insanity. Mia just shook her head and insisted that she had given him the heads up and that we had his blessing. And when I still couldn't bring myself to choose between the Gucci 'Lelias' and the Manolo mules, she said I should get both. But I couldn't do it. So, I walked out of the store, but I heard Mia tell the salesgirl not to put anything away—*we'll be right back*. She caught up with me just outside the entrance and took my hand. "Have I ever told you about Kyle Crandell?"

"Who?"

"He was the love of my life when I was thirteen. But he didn't love me back—can you even imagine?" She checked her watch and said, "It's a story to be savored over lunch. So, pizza or Chinese?"

"I vote lettuce wraps," I said, suddenly starved.

"Girl after my own heart!" she said and tugged me down the sidewalk.

An hour-and-a-half later, I was wearing the Guccis and carrying the Manolos. And every step was more liberating than I could possibly have imagined. Walking away shoes—who knew! Leaving behind what I could not change and doing it to the tune of $1,457.22. But, I'm sorry, in the harsh light of *Tim* it didn't seem indulgent, it seemed lifesaving. Symbolically walking away—*far and fast, with my head held high*, to quote Lullaby Sutton via her niece—felt a little amazing. I felt a little amazing. And of course, Mia captured it by taking my picture when I wasn't looking. But I didn't care; I was having a surprisingly great day. And all the way to the campus, I couldn't stop looking at my feet.

But then Bo called demanding to know where I was, and he did not sound good.

He was waiting for me when I came out of the library, where I'd been immersed in *Precious Bane*. He looked awful.

"Wh...what are you doing here?" I said, taking in his running gear and the sweatband holding back his wavy hair.

He didn't say anything. He just took my hand and pulled me toward a bench.

"Bo...What are you doing?"

He looked hard at me, like he was trying to remember exactly what he came to say. Suddenly we were standing so close that if not for the pain in his face, it might have seemed a romantic gesture, which I suddenly realized I would not have been totally opposed to. But it wasn't that. *Terrible* was radiating off him. "Bo...You're scaring me. What's happened?"

"C'mere," he said, pulling me into his arms. "I want to hold onto you while I tell you this." And then into my ear he said something completely unbelievable about my mother and a car and broken things and doctors and that I was booked on the 10:10 to Savannah that night.

I went limp as he eased me onto the bench, where I asked him to tell me again. And when I started to tremble, he held me tighter. I looked around me, trying to understand. Everywhere, people moved and spoke and laughed, and I thought how was that even possible when my world had just skidded to an absolute standstill? It was like I'd hit a wall. For a moment, nothing made sense, and my face had gone a little numb, and I wondered what had just happened. I looked at Bo. "Tell me again."

So, he did. And this time his words took root in me. *My mother. Very bad accident. Hospital. Booked on the red eye out of San Jose.* I let out the breath I'd been holding and then dug through my purse for my phone. Geneva answered on the first ring. "Gran," I blurted. "How is she?"

"Oh, my sweet girl," my grandmother coughed. "She's out of surgery, but..."

"Gran?"

"Ivy...the doctor is...not optimistic, sweetheart. But he says if she can get through the next twenty-four hours, she might..."

"Might what, Gran?"

"Survive for the next twenty-four..."

I swallowed a sob. "Gran, tell me...What do you really think? What is the Universe telling you?"

Geneva took a hard swallow to answer. "It's telling me you need to come home, sug."

I nodded but couldn't speak. It felt like if my voice came out of me, everything else would spill out of me with it. I dropped my suddenly weighty phone into my lap and Bo picked it up.

"Geneva," he said. "Yes. Her flight gets in at 8:35 in the morning. Can you arrange for someone to meet her?" Then he nodded. "Okay. I'll let you know."

For a moment, I just stared into what pretended to be an ordinary afternoon. *Was my mother dying?* These were words thought in a foreign language. *Was she? Could she?* The deceptive scene before me blurred with my tears, and I felt Bo take my hand. He didn't say anything. He just waited for me to catch up with this horror. Finally, I looked over at him, desperate to not do this by myself. "Will you come with me? Please, Bo? Please?"

Agony and shame filled his eyes, and I watched panic bloom there. "Ivy..."

"Please, Bo. I need you. I can't do this by myself."

"I...Ivy. I can't. I...I can't fly..." he said, suddenly trying to catch his breath. "I can't get on a plane. I'm so...I'm so sorry."

I looked at him in disbelief, then let out a stupid sob as Bo's Bo-*ness* slapped me. "Of course not...it's okay. I shouldn't..."

"Ivy..."

I checked my watch, cutting him off. 3:20. "I have to tell my dad. I have to tell him what's happened."

"Ivy... I'm...*sss so* sorry. I..."

His ragged breath scared me, and I could see anxiety escalating in his eyes. "No. Bo! I was dumb. I was kidding, I'm sorry. Forget what I said." I breathed deep, reconstituted a bit, hoping he would, too. "I'll be fine," I lied. "I wasn't thinking. But I have to go. I have to tell my dad. And I have to hold his hand when I do."

"Ivy...please. Don't...don't hate me."

"Bo, it's fine. Just breathe. Slow down, slow down," I said as I rubbed his back with one hand and dialed Mia with the other. I was supposed to meet her at the track at 3:40. She might not even be out of class yet, but she answered.

"Hey...I'm just walking out, be there in ten—"

"Mia, Bo's here, and he's in trouble. We're on a bench on the Common between the Fine Arts building and the library."

"What? Why?"

"Please hurry!"

Four excruciating minutes later, I saw Mia running toward us, her long skirt and long blond hair flying behind her. She was holding her sandals. When she reached us, panting, I stood up. "I need to borrow your car. Bo can explain."

She looked from me to her brother, trying to land on something that made sense, but she didn't dawdle. She handed me her keys. "Are you all right? What's happened?"

"It's Bree," I said. "There was an accident...I have to tell my dad..."

"Oh, my Lord..." She looked at Bo, who was bent over and looking at the ground.

I couldn't hold back my tears. "I have to go, Mia..."
"Go. Go!" she said. "I've got this."

Forty-Three—Ivy

My dad's firm was about ten minutes away in Pacific Grove, and for the life of me I do not know how I got there. I know I was shaking. Shaking like I was freezing to death, and I couldn't stop, and I might have cried the whole way, but it wasn't so much the business of crying as much as my face just leaking—a steady stream running from both eyes and my nose. It was all too unbelievable, what was happening. I couldn't actually be driving to my dad's office to tell him this awful news about my mama. It didn't make sense. None of it made sense.

I played Bo's and Geneva's words over and over and was so preoccupied that I was frankly stunned that I'd made it to the right location. I'd never been inside my dad's building, but I knew it well because it was a short bus ride from the place where I'd stayed when I first got to California. His firm owned a studio apartment, which made it convenient for out-of-town clients and daughters best kept out of sight, I suppose. I pulled into the parking lot of Willis, Proctor and Holmes and killed the engine. Daniel had asked me—told me—never to drop by unannounced, and I never had. He'd told me I could call his cellphone day or night, and he'd meet me as soon as he had the time to give me his undivided attention. That naturally sounded like nothing but the ultimate declaration of his concern for me—his emotionally mangled daughter who'd been dumped. Now, walking through his fancy marbled foyer, I knew he'd simply preferred I stayed out of sight.

But these were extraordinary circumstances. He'd understand. Surely.

There was a reception desk, but it was unmanned at the moment, so I ducked into the restroom to pull myself together. I dabbed a wet paper towel under my eyes, which cleaned up the mascara but did nothing for the puffiness. I looked as upset as I felt, and there would be no hiding that from my dad. I took some deep, shaky breaths and sipped some water from my palm and tried to calm myself. Then I walked out.

There was still no one to point me in the right direction, so I headed down the hall where I saw a directory. As I scanned it, I heard, "Can I help you?"

I looked at the girl, and she looked at me. "Are you all right?" she said, taking me in with sudden concern. She was pretty, about my age and somehow familiar. I wondered if we'd met.

"I'm looking for Daniel Proctor," I said.

"Oh. Is he expecting you?"

"No. But it's very important." My voice tripped over *important,* and my eyes welled up. It alarmed the girl.

She didn't press me. "Come with me," she said. "He just got back from court, and he's in a short meeting, but I'll round him up." She walked me down the hall and around the corner, sort of eying me like I might ignite without warning.

The hall opened up into a large common area where there were sofas and a credenza laid out with snacks and cans of soda on ice. Directly across were two glassed-in offices side by side. One had the blinds drawn for privacy, and the other shone with afternoon sunlight. The gold lettering on that door said Daniel Proctor, Esquire, Senior Partner. The girl pushed open the door, and I walked in behind her.

My father's office was thickly carpeted, library quiet, and very modern. There were four leather chairs around a glass table and a desk that seemed overly neat. In striking contrast, there was a Persian Prayer rug hanging on the wall behind more glass. It was distinctly my mother's taste. Behind my father's desk was an enormous family portrait.

"Can I get you a bottle of water? Coffee? A Coke?"

I tore my gaze from the portrait and looked at the girl. "Uh, water. Thank you."

"You got it. Have a seat, and I'll go find him. Who should I say is waiting to see him?"

"Ivy." It came out on a little sob.

"Ivy...?"

I sniffed. "Just Ivy. He'll know who I am."

The girl looked at me through kind but narrowed eyes. She was polished up nice. Blond bobbed hair. Sleeveless white blouse, orange pencil skirt. Long legs and shoes that could have come from Giselle's. She also had enhanced green eyes, where I again saw something oddly familiar.

"Okay, then..." she said. "Make yourself comfortable, and I'll be right back."

I nodded, and she left. I meant to sit down, then; I was pretty shaky. But instead, I walked over to the portrait behind my dad's desk. My father's family. As I stood there, a new ache bloomed in the bottom of my stomach. His family. *His* family. They were on vacation somewhere—somewhere fresh and beachy. My dad was deeply tanned, but in this context, it looked right, natural. His wife was his same height, thin, with dark blond hair. Mrs. Proctor was model-pretty, and there was contentment in her eyes, oblivious joy. A very good-looking young man stood next to her; he was tall and had dark hair like Daniel used to have and was wearing his smile.

And then...I swallowed hard when, tucked in next to Daniel, I found the familiar face that in this arrangement made complete sense: blond hair, green eyes, the perfect mix of her parents. She looked like her dad...my dad. I swallowed and suddenly wished I hadn't come. Staring at her standing so close to my dad felt like a bullet to my heart. She had her arm around another boy, younger, maybe ten or eleven. He had longish hair and a sunburned nose and a great smile—an absolutely carefree smile. I stared, remembering the summer Daniel stayed with me and Mama—the summer we'd felt like a family. I'd turned eleven that summer, and Mama had talked non-stop about weddings. Then one day Daniel left, he just disappeared, and Mama cried for a month. That was ten years ago. Daniel's youngest son—this boy with the sunburned nose and the mile-wide smile looked...about the right age. Tired tears filled my eyes until they ran down my face, and I couldn't believe how much I hurt. Everywhere hurt. I knew my father had a family, I'd always known, but suddenly the most amazing pain ballooned inside of my already amazing pain, and I couldn't breathe.

This portrait was truth—absolute and undeniable truth—and staring into it was agonizingly clarifying. I felt completely false and every inch the illegitimate. The man I was staring at surrounded by his adoring family certainly did not seem like he intended to change a thing. Not one thing. Not this life he was living. And not the arrangement he'd had with my mother for twenty-two years. And now my mother was...

"Ivy?" The girl with the green eyes sidled up to me and handed me a bottle of chilled water.

"This is you," I croaked, trying not to.

"Uh, yes," she said, taking in my emotional imbalance. "Not the greatest pic of me, but it's my dad's fave of all of us. So...are you alright?"

I sniffed, tried to cover my emotion. "Where...where was it taken?"

"The Cayman Islands—last Easter. We have a condo there."

I suddenly wondered if my mother had ever been to the Cayman Islands—I knew I hadn't. "So...I guess you work for your dad?" I managed.

"I do. I'm in law school," she offered, still preoccupied with my tears. "But right now, I work as a paralegal-slash-receptionist-slash gofer," she said, half-smiling, "for him and my grandpa mostly—Lloyd Willis—he's the other partner."

"Wow." I nodded, avoiding her eyes. *Willis. Not* my *grandfather. Daniel's father-in-law.* "All in the family, I guess."

"I guess so," the girl shrugged. "My mom used to practice, now she teaches. My brother just started here, and I have three more years."

I looked at her. "You look awful young to have all that under your belt."

"Not really. I'll be twenty-two next month. Pretty on schedule. I'm Liz, by-the-way—Elizabeth—Proctor."

Seven months older than me. More tears. "You look like your dad," I rasped.

She smiled uncomfortably. "That's what they say. How do *you* know my dad?"

I opened my mouth not having a clue what was about to come out. But fortunately, behind us, the door opened with a rush of cool air. Liz and I turned at the same time, and the look on our father's face was priceless—suddenly slackened jaw, blanched skin, alarm-rimmed eyes.

"Dad." I almost said it, but the word came out of Liz Proctor. "Good," she said. "You're here. This is Ivy. She needs to talk to you about an urgent matter. Dad? Are you...are you okay?"

Daniel pulled his eyes from me and looked at his other daughter. "Wh...what? No. I...I'm fine. It's just a headache. Rough afternoon."

"I'll bring you some Advil." Liz Proctor patted her father on the chest as she left—a familial gesture, rife with belonging. As she walked out, I watched Daniel swallow, hard, his adam's apple riding up his neck. He looked suddenly small to me, frightened, like I could destroy him with the sound of my voice.

"Wh...what are you..." he looked over his shoulder, made sure his door was shut, moved closer to me. "I've asked you not to, *never*...to...What are you *doing* here?"

I stared at him, not appreciating his tone, and at the same time overwhelmed by it. "There's...there's been an accident."

"You were in an accident?"

"No. No, it's Mama...She was hit by a car," I said, my voice cracking.

"What?" he said, more blood draining from his face. "What are you talking about?"

"Mama was hit by a car today. It's bad. It's very bad. I'm going home, and I think you should come with me. You have to come..."

"I don't...Slow down!" he said with an edge. "Start at the beginning."

I looked around, feeling cold and very out of place, especially when my gaze again landed on the happy portrait of his happy family.

"Ivy? Focus! What exactly happened?"

I squeezed my eyes shut. "All I know is that there was a robbery and she...she got in the way..."

"Oh, good Lord. But she'll be okay, right?"

"I don't know. Geneva doesn't think so. There's a flight to Savannah tonight out of San Jose. You need to come with me. Mama needs you."

"Ivy..." My father slowly shook his head. "I'm afraid that's impossible."

I looked at him. "Then make it possible! She *needs* you."

"I'm in the middle of a trial. I have to be in court all week."

"I don't care. Make some calls. You have to come," I said, again sounding like petulance personified.

"I can't do that...I'm sorry."

As I met my father's eyes, the waves of my reality nearly knocked me over. Again. I looked past him to his vacation portrait where he so...*fit,* right there in middle of that family he'd built. I looked back at him and fought more tears. "If your wife had been run over and was lying broken in a hospital three thousand miles away, would you go to her?"

His shoulders slumped and a deep, pained furrow appeared between his brows. "Ivy... it's not the same thing."

My breath and tears gushed at the same time. "If your daughter—your other daughter—if her mother was three thousand miles away hurt and broken...Would you go then?"

My father looked hard at me, sighed, then dropped his gaze in something that looked like shame. I saw it, and he knew I saw it, and in that moment, I also saw the pitiable tableau of my makeshift family: my beautiful, deluded mother lying broken somewhere in Georgia, this man who'd strung her along my whole life with false promises, and the inconvenient daughter they'd made now begging him to care. It all smacked of bad reality TV. When Daniel again met my eyes, they were filled with twenty-two years of something that wasn't actually love at all, and it turned my stomach. It seemed to surprise him as well, because, I swear, he fell inward, just slightly, buckling a bit under the weight of his duplicity. It might have been me seeing it, or it might have been him letting it be seen. Either way, my father had shown himself to me.

Liz Proctor came back then with a bottle of medication and a glass of water. When she saw us, she was immediately wary, and I wondered if she could possibly imagine what she'd walked into.

"Is...is everything all right?" she said, looking from me to her father.

I studied her, a dozen knives poised on the end of my tongue. But all I said was, "No. Nothing was ever all right, was it Daniel?" I looked back at my father, her father, the love of my mama's life. I stared at him for a good long minute, watched him try to regain his footing for the sake of his other daughter. He lifted his chin, found his lawyer voice. "I'm so sorry I can't help you, Miss Talbot."

From somewhere not usually accessed, I found my glare and I laid it on him. "I doubt that," I said. "But I'll be sure to pass it along to my mama." I turned to leave, and Liz Proctor hurried to the door.

"I'll show you out."

"I don't think that's necessary, Liz," Daniel said quickly—too quickly. "I'm sure Ivy can find her own way."

His daughter looked at him through questioning eyes, then she looked at me.

"It's fine," I said. "I've been finding my own way for quite a long time, now." Not trusting myself to say more, I opened the door and walked out.

Forty-Four—Mia

My brother was a total mess, close to a full-on panic attack, but as I rubbed his back, he rallied enough to eke out his story. It was awful, and I couldn't believe that I'd let Ivy leave here alone. I almost couldn't fully grasp what had happened to Bree Talbot. And I definitely couldn't believe what Bo had done. My brother had gotten himself to the campus, half-clad and sweaty, to tell our friend—while holding her—that something terrible had happened to her mother. As he told me all it had taken for him to tell Ivy, he seemed to relive his delivery of this devastation and, in so doing, began hyperventilating. He tormented himself over all the ways he could have been gentler and how much of a disappointment he had been in her time of need. His self-loathing was heartbreaking, and I didn't fully understand what had provoked it.

I had a Xanax in my wallet and an unopened bottle of water in my backpack. I handed them to him, but he just stared at me.

"C'mon, Bo. You need this," I said. "You'll feel better."

He bent over his knees and filled his lungs a few times. When he sat back up, he placed the little pill in his shirt pocket. "I'm worried about Ivy," he said. "She shouldn't be alone."

He stood and paced in front of me for a moment, took a few more deep breaths, then headed toward the library parking lot. Of course, I followed him, wondering when he would realize that he was run-sweaty and wearing shorts—something he never did in public aside from running the hills behind Lullaby's neighborhood. His hair was pushed back with a sweatband, and his sunglasses were smudged—two additional sources of shame that, for the moment, had apparently escaped his awareness as well.

When we got to his car, he asked—more like ordered—me to google Ivy's dad's address. I mapped it on my phone and gave him directions as we pulled out of the parking lot. "What are we doing?" I said. "She has my car."

"I have a bad feeling, Mia. I don't think she should be by herself right now."

Bo drove in cold silence, his face a brick of agitation. He looked like hell. "Bo, settle down. You did good," I said, gently, still trying to sooth him.

He didn't respond, but his breathing had slowed a bit, even if his incessant tapping on the steering wheel still advertised his anxiousness.

"She'll be all right," I said feebly. "She's got to be..."

"She won't be all right, Mia!" Bo barked. "Don't be ridiculous!"

"Hey! No snapping at the sister!"

Bo pulled up to Daniel Proctor's building and told me he wasn't going to wait with me. "I'm the last person she wants to see, Mia. I'm going home to take a shower."

"What? Wait! Why would you be the last person she wants to see? What did you do?"

"Nothing. Just go. Go find her."

"Bo!"

"I'm fine!" he snapped.

"I'm not getting out of this car until you take the bloody Xanax," I snapped back. "And I have all day!"

He glared at me but wasn't hyperventilating, which I considered a good sign.

I glared back.

"Fine!" He made a production of pulling the little pill from his pocket and swallowing it with no water. "Happy? Now get out and go find Ivy."

It was weird, the way he was acting—even for the king of weird. I watched as he drove away thinking something did not add up.

Now I was leaning against my car trying to decide if I should go in and look for Ivy or just wait out here for her. What an amazingly horrible afternoon. Two hours ago, we had been having so much fun spending Super-dad's money. Ivy had smiled for the first time in days. Now her mom had been hurt...maybe worse than we could imagine, which was tragic enough, but telling Daniel? Bo was right; one of us should have been with her. I should go find her.

As I made my way across the parking lot, Ivy walked out, or rather she stumbled out, of the entrance. She looked a little unsteady, and when she saw me, her shoulders sagged. My heart ached for her, and all I could think to do was fold her in a hug, and she clung to me like I could save her life. "What happened? Are you okay?"

"Oh, Mia. I didn't know how bad I needed to see a friendly face."

We got in my car, where I cranked up the air and then we proceeded to sit in silence for a moment. When Ivy did not offer anything, I finally asked, "Did you see your dad?"

"He's an ass."

"Big ass? Little ass?"

"He can't be bothered with Mama. That kind of ass."

"Ouch," I grimaced. "I'm so sorry, Ivy."

She looked over at me, tired and overwhelmed. "I met my sister," she said softly.

I felt my eyes widen. "Ummmm. What?"

Ivy nodded. "She's my age, Mia. My age. Do you know what that means?"

"No?"

"It means my dad had two little kids by two women—or even better, one little kid and a pregnant wife, when he and Mama made me." She shook her head. "I always knew he had a family, but I didn't truly know it—down where it counts—until just now."

"Ivy..."

Ivy in Stills - 221

She ran a hand under her nose. "It was all lies. He was never intending to leave them for us, no matter what pretty promises my mama fell for. He was never leaving his family. He was growing it. He has a little boy that I don't even know if Mama knows about. And the kicker is the *Willis* in Willis, Proctor and Holmes is his wife's family." She shook her head. "Who lives that way?"

"Ivy...I'm...I've got nothing," I said, completely helpless.

She sniffed. "I asked him to come to Savannah with me," she said flatly. "I told him Mama needed him."

"And?"

A tear fell down her cheek. "He said no."

I looked out my window and hated Daniel Proctor. I also had no idea what to say to his daughter.

Ivy shut down after that. I didn't blame her—what was there to say? Having met her dad, seen him in action, I could only imagine what she was going through. But it wasn't just Daniel. I was also—despite everything—having terrible feelings about Bree Talbot. But she was not in any shape for me to think badly about, so I kept all that to myself.

When we got home, Bo wasn't there, but he'd left the flight information on the counter. He made me so mad. He'd said he was worried about Ivy, and that had been beyond obvious—so where was he? I'd thought it would be nice if we both took her to dinner on the way to the airport, which was more than an hour away. But he wasn't answering his phone, and he was ignoring my texts.

I was so upset that while Ivy folded her laundry, I ducked into my bedroom and called my mom—my voice of reason and clarity. I told her everything that had happened, along with Bo's weird ownership of Ivy's heartbreak. It was so him, but somehow extra *out there*, which also made me mad since this was Ivy's crisis, not his. But somehow my brother had managed to usurp her personal disaster and turn it into his own. Mom let me rant but said she understood.

"Have you tried to reach Bo?" she asked.

"Messages and texts! And I'm swearing at him telepathically right now. I'm just so mad at him!"

Mom sighed. "It doesn't sound like him, does it? How is Ivy?"

"Bad, Mom. I'm worried about her."

"That darling girl. You give her my love. Stop worrying about Bo. It sounds like he got busy...which is code, dear daughter, for him just not knowing how to say goodbye."

"You think?"

"Yes, that's what I think. Now you get Ivy where she needs to be. I'll try and get a hold of your brother. You're a good girl, Meez."

"Yes, I am."

"Hug that Ivy. Tell her to call us."

"I will," I promised. "I love you, Mom."

"I love you, too."

As I watched Ivy finish packing, it hit me that I didn't know when I'd see her again. Or if. And the thought hurt. She filled one suitcase and a small duffle with her things, and in mere moments, it was like she'd never been there at all. I looked around. "Wow. It will seem so strange to not have you here."

"It will seem strange not bein' here," she said. Then she looked at me. "Thank you, Mia, for all that you've done for me. I don't know what would have become of me if you hadn't met with my dad that day."

"I'd have one less friend," I said, getting emotional.

"Me, too."

I tried Bo one more time to let him know we were hitting the Bread Bowl for dinner if he wanted to join us. But I never heard from him. It was kind of a bust anyway. Ivy barely touched the salad she ordered, and our stilted attempt at conversation was derailed by a lengthy phone call from Geneva. Apparently, Bree had been taken back into surgery, and Ivy's grandmother had nearly been admitted to the hospital herself for heart palpitations. She called just to hear Ivy's voice—so Ivy talked to her through dinner and almost the entire way to San Jose International.

At the curb, I pulled Ivy's things out of my trunk and my eyes filled with tears.

"Don't start," she said. "Or I'll have to start, and I can't cry anymore."

I pulled her into my arms. "I'm going to miss you! I so wish I could go with you, but..."

"Stop—you've been wonderful enough."

"Maybe this weekend," I said, not sure what I even meant.

"Shhhh. Don't. It's okay. Hopefully Bree will be on the mend, and then...who knows? I'll probably get that call from one of the hundred jobs I've applied for, and I'll have to come back."

"Promise?"

"Of course. Probably. Maybe—it's a possibility."

I swallowed. "Call me when you land. And then call me when you see your mom."

"I will," she said. "I will."

Just before she went through the doors, Ivy turned to me and shouted. "Please tell Bo goodbye. And tell him I'm so, so sorry."

"What? Sorry for what?"

But Ivy just waved and disappeared into the airport.

Forty-Five—Bo

I knew I was being unfair, unforgivably unfair. That wasn't my intention, but there was only so much I could manage at the moment, and seeing Ivy was not on the list. Neither was talking to my sister. She'd called, she'd texted, and she'd called again. Several times. One of her messages was particularly brutal, excoriating me for not saying goodbye to Ivy. Did my fool sister really imagine I hadn't been excoriating myself for hours over that same thing? Her last message was a hair softer. She was worried about me. And now Mom had called, and the whole family was in turmoil because I hadn't been seen or heard from in 4 ½ hours.

One would never guess I was an adult male. Challenged but not totally debilitated, quite possibly worthy of a formal, latest-edition DSM diagnosis, but not gravely disabled. Not insane. Not completely. However...I *was* sitting in a parking lot just outside of Bakersfield, nearly four hours from my home. Perhaps there was something amiss.

I rolled the window down, but the air was heavy, moist, and probably crawling with pollutants, so I rolled it back up. It was just dark. I pulled out my phone and texted my mother. *Hey, Mom. All's well...had a crap day. Sorry Mia worried you. I'm fine. I'll call you tomorrow.* My thumb hovered over the send button while I worried that my words didn't sound convincing enough. I added an *I love you, thanks for checking on me* and pushed send, immediately wanting to recall the message, wanting to add to it, mad that Mia had put me in a position to have to write it in the first place.

My phone almost instantly dinged. Mom sent me a smiley face with *Thanks for letting me know. Take care!*

I blew out a relieved breath, hoping she'd let Mia know.

I actually felt a little bad for my sister. Mia had taken on the unofficial responsibility of keeping me tethered. She was also the one who kept my parents informed and reassured of my wellbeing. I loved her for it. But I did not want to talk to her right now. I didn't want to talk to any of them.

I'd had one plan this afternoon: to *get as far away as possible.* I'd grabbed three bottles of Xanax and drove away. I'd grabbed the Xanax so I'd have options, but I'd spat the one Mia had insisted I take in Daniel Proctor's parking lot out the window. What Mia doesn't understand, what no one understands, is that sometimes just having the medication within reach calms me. It calms me just knowing it's there. So, after I'd cleaned up, I grabbed the pills and took off. And I'd just kept driving, until now I was in Bakersfield. *Bakersfield!*

I wish I were normal. I wish I could step outside of my weird reality and do normal things, be a normal guy, laugh and let anxious things roll off my back. I so envied the ease of most of the human race, the way they simply adapted to the nuances of their existence without tension creating a gravel carpet under their skin. Me? I had to know what was coming, and when. If not, I got apprehensive, which was the precursor to anxiety, which led to panic, which ended in crisis. Or *could.* I kept it all in check by confining my life to a metaphorical prison cell, into which I walked every day of my own volition because *that* I could usually control. Mine was a clearly defined world filled with only what I could predict. And all so I could feel safe. Safe? Please! My life filled me with self-loathing.

I could take this tiny pill as prescribed. I should. It helped, but it made me a little dull. So, I didn't take it, unless I had no choice. It was a ridiculous game I played called *Can Bo Get Through the Day Without a Pill?* It was a bad way to live, and I couldn't really explain it except to say that somehow, I felt more like a man when I finally shut down for the night having won that small battle. And if I ever needed proof of my particular insanity, there it was. But I was managing; everything had been manageable until Ivy moved in. And I did not understand how I had allowed that girl to so *disrupt* my formerly manageable status quo. And I didn't know what to do with my constant thoughts of her; I just knew she'd utterly ruined my predictable little life.

And I wanted to thank her for it and hate her for it and make her stop doing it and hope she never stopped doing it and show me what she saw in me that didn't scare or disgust her, what she saw that would make her say the words *I need you, Bo. She* needed *me?*

But what did it matter now, she'd never say them again. I'd let her down.

Ivy needed me, and I was so *me* that I failed her. A breath shuddered out of my throat.

In a lifetime spent falling short, Ivy Talbot seeing my unforgiveable smallness was a singular low. I dropped my head to the steering wheel and grimaced in pain.

How many pills would it take to erase this pain?

She'd left me one message that I'd listened to twenty times. "I'm so sorry, Bo. I should never have asked such a thing of you. I hurt you, and I would never, never hurt you. I was only thinkin' of myself. Please, please forgive me."

Me forgive *her.*

How many pills...

Forty-Six—Ivy

I boarded the mostly full flight and prayed for an empty seat beside me. Thankfully God was listening. My nose was pressed to the window when the lovely older man a seat away said, "I guess we got lucky. Do you mind if I put my briefcase here?" He indicated the empty space between us.

"Not at all." I tried to smile.

He looked at me with kind eyes. "Are you okay?"

I don't know what it is about kindness that makes my eyes water, but that's exactly what happened as I took in the Black man's gentle concern. I imagined myself saying I'm *here*, and *Okay* is somewhere on another continent, but thanks for asking. Instead, I said, "I'm fine. Allergies."

He didn't buy it, I could tell, but he smiled—not big, but understanding. "I'm sorry," he said. "Allergies can be very upsetting."

I nodded and turned back to the window. Bless Bo for getting me a window seat, where I could hide my misery. I closed my eyes and tried not to cry, tried not to imagine what was happening with my mama, Geneva. Bo. I squeezed my eyes shut. How was I ever going to make it through the next eight hours?

The last thing I'd packed was the book Bo had given me, and now I took *Precious Bane* out of the bag I had shoved under the seat in front of me. Just in case. I knew I was too preoccupied, too worried to read, but maybe there would be a lull in my overflowing angst and I could speed the time along by getting into this story.

He'd left me a note in the book that said, *Ivy, this is my favorite novel. It's about what is truly beautiful and worthy of love...*

What did that even mean?

I felt so bad about how things had ended with Bo. I should never have put him on the spot like that. What had I been thinking? What *had* I been thinking? I'd been thinking...how much I needed him. *Needed?* Him? Him or just someone? Did I really need Bo Sutton? Or was it want? *Wanted? Him?* Could that be it? Yes. I wanted Bo to just be here and take my hand—which he didn't really do because of the germ thing, so I don't know what I was thinking. I just knew that right now, wondering if Mama would be alive when I got to Savannah, it would be so nice to just look over and see Bo holding back the world.

He knew that the last thing I'd done was fight with Bree over her rendezvous in Carmel. He knew how hurtful her letter had been. He knew hers was the last mean voice in my head. He knew I hadn't called her back. And now...now it might be too late. And not suffocating under all that guilt only seemed possible if Bo was sitting close enough to remind me to breathe.

Maybe if he was just sitting there close enough to touch, my thoughts of Liz Proctor and her place in my dad's magazine-cover family wouldn't make my chest ache like it did. Honestly, I didn't know a person could hurt this much. And I had no idea how to tell my mother that the love of her life was too tied up to make it to her deathbed. I just knew it would all be easier if Bo was with me. But he wasn't. And he hadn't wanted to see me before I left, and now I had to fit that sharp piece of pain in with all the rest.

Lord, what if I never saw him again?

As more tears filled my eyes, I listened to the flight attendant give her instructions.

Eight hours. A connecting flight. And a head full of terrible.

I opened the book and began to read.

* * *

I was exhausted when I landed in Savannah the next morning, exhausted to the point of dizziness. It was everything, I'm sure. No sleep, worry on steroids, deep sadness, and unrelenting heaviness. I'd been stuck on a plane with a running commentary on my life, my mother's life, pick-axing through my gray matter, each pick determined cruelly to explain and clarify my existence, and hers. When it got too painful, too overwhelming, the state of our affairs, I read about Prudence Sarn—a girl also heavy with circumstances outside of her control, living a life she would not have chosen had she been in charge. She had a harelip—a heroine with a harelip— unspeakably homely and incapable of beauty, if you ask her. But clearly, she was an unreliable narrator—just like Bo said.

While I waited to disembark, I made a quick call to Mia because I'd promised, then I gathered my things and trudged off the plane. In the restroom, when I finally faced the mirror, I wanted to cry. I looked like I'd been slapped, a lot. The makeup was long gone, so there was no camouflaging the pain in my red eyes. I brushed my teeth and doused my face with tepid airport water, but I still looked like a girl something bad had happened to.

I made my way to baggage claim, expecting Geneva to materialize and tell me something miraculous—Mama was awake and doing amazing, she'd made it through the worst of it—but I didn't see her, and I knew I was fantasizing. I was just digging for my nearly dead phone to call my grandmother when I heard, "Ivy?"

I turned and perused the faces of strangers, thinking I was hearing things.

"Ivy. Hi. Sorry, have you been waiting long? I don't know your freeways well enough yet to get anywhere on time."

"Camille?"

"Hi, sweetie," said Mia's and Bo's beautiful sister, giving me a quick hug. "How was your flight?"

"I...I was expecting...Hi. It was all right. Long. Is my grandmother here?"

Camille Diamond made a sad face. "No. She won't leave Bree's side, so I volunteered to come get you. We should go." When her eyes made clear the gravity of the situation, adrenaline found its way through my veins. I picked up my bag. "Where's your car?"

On the way to short term parking, Camille brought me up to speed, and I appreciated her dispassionate delivery. My mama had been crushed by the front and rear wheel of a stolen Escalade. She had a shattered pelvis, broken back, collapsed lung, and several broken ribs. She'd been pinned and taped and splinted back together, and now she had a very high fever and her kidneys had shut down. "Ivy," Camille said, taking my hand. "I need to warn you. The doctors are not hopeful."

"How not hopeful?"

She sighed. "Geneva has simply been demanding that Bree stay alive until you get here."

Forty-Seven—Mia

My ringing phone woke me out of a dead sleep, and I immediately thought I was late for something. Coming quickly alive, I grabbed my cell off its charger. The screen said, Ivy. "Hey..." I said, sitting up.

"Mia, did I wake you?"

"No. No. Are you in Savannah? Did you make it? How was your flight?"

"Long. But we just landed, now I'm waiting to disembark, and I thought I'd...you know."

"I'm so glad you called. Are you going right to the hospital?"

"We are."

"Well...how are you?"

"I'm bad, Mia. I'm having bad dreams and haven't even been asleep."

"Oh, Ivy..."

She sniffed. "I'd better go. I just wanted you to know I got here."

"Good luck, Ivy. Give your mom our best. And...you know... stay in touch."

"I will, Mia. Thank you. For everything."

I disconnected and could only imagine the day she was facing. I honestly wished there was something—anything—I could do for her. I'd known Ivy Talbot for just a few weeks, but she'd become a dear friend, and I ached for her. And I missed her. As I lay there, coming awake, I pulled up the photos on my phone looking for one I remembered taking of the two us in Carmel. It was pre-haircut, and we'd been to an art gallery. We'd stopped at a bakery and were noshing in the sun and laughing with her mom and grandma, and I'd just snapped a selfie of us—mouths full, pulling faces. I found the pic and sent it to my email so I could print it out. Then I proceeded to scroll. I'd taken a few more shots of her and her family that afternoon—I'd promised to send them to Bree but hadn't done it. As I was scrolling, I found a shot I'd snuck of Ivy without her knowledge, face to the sky, hair blown back, eyes closed, her skin reflecting light a thousand ways. I remembered Geneva saying, "Looks like she's just waiting for a kiss from God, doesn't it?"

I pulled the picture wide between my fingers. My iPhone camera was good, and for a change, my lens had been clean. Still, I could have kicked myself for not pulling out my Nikon. This was a great photo of Ivy.

7:40. I groaned. I was already behind for the day, but I pulled on my swimming suit anyway. Looks like I was back to doing laps by myself.

By nine I was showered and made up, with my damp hair wound through a gigantic scarf. For added drama, I was wearing hoop earrings the size of bangles that I'd stolen from Bo. Sadly, the rest of me was pretty boring: white tee and gray leggings—but no biggie, I only had one class today, and I might blow it off. I might be too busy fighting with my brother, I thought when I walked into the kitchen and found that he was still avoiding me. He had not left me any breakfast.

He hadn't been here when I got home from the airport last night, and I hadn't waited up to give him a hard time about not making it. I guess Mom could have been right—maybe goodbyes were just not his thing. He was Bo, after all. I tossed two pieces of nine-grain bread into the toaster and was about to pour myself some juice when the doorbell rang. I ignored it, thinking Bo would surely get it. When it rang again, I wondered where he was.

I opened the door to find a woman with big hair and big sunglasses wearing a red pantsuit that looked two sizes too small for her. She had an enormous chest. She looked at me and did not smile. So, I didn't either.

I cocked my head and offered a look that said, *What can I do for you?*

"Is Benjamin Sutton here?" she said with a slight edge. "We have an appointment. I'm Katrina Gearhart."

"I'll get him. Would you like to come in?"

She eyed me like I'd asked *the* dumbest question, which I guess I had. "Yes."

I opened the door wider and told her to make herself comfortable, all the time planning how I was going to yell at my brother.

There was no way he was still in his room, but I checked anyway—not there. Bed Military crisp, absolutely nothing out of place, a particle of dust would not dare exist within these walls; he'd obviously been up for hours. So, I slipped downstairs to give him hell. But as I opened the door to his makeshift studio, I found it empty—and dark. "Bo?" I stepped in and turned on the lights. "Bo? Bo!" I didn't know what was happening. Where was my brother? A tingle started at the base of my spine and spread up to my neck. Where was he?

I took the stairs two at a time, and when I'd reached the back door, I had convinced myself that he'd gone for a run and would be back any minute. But then I opened the door leading to the garage to find his car was missing. *No, no, no, no.*

I stopped. Breathed. Fought a rising panic.

There was no way to know if he'd come home last night and left again this morning, but I was suddenly, instinctively, certain that he hadn't been home at all. "Boooo!" I screamed, slamming the door. "Where are you?" I hurried through the kitchen yelling his name as I grabbed my phone. I was just dialing my brother when the red-breasted pantsuit appeared in the doorway. She looked irritated. I had completely forgotten about her.

"Is he not here?" she said daring me to say no.

I swallowed. "No. Apparently not."

She pushed out an irritated breath. "But we had an appointment. I drove in from San Francisco to meet with him." She glared at me like it was my fault.

I narrowed my eyes at her, not caring at all where she'd come from. "What exactly are you here for? Maybe I can help you," I said, trying to keep my tone in check.

She gathered herself, took me in, and with dramatic patience stated, "Somehow I doubt that."

"Oh, cut the crap, sister!" I snarked, losing it. "I'm in a bit of crisis right now, and I'm not in the mood. Now you are welcome to come downstairs and look around for whatever it is Bo's been working on for you. I'll even help you if you can be nice about it. Or you can leave. It makes absolutely no difference to me."

She looked at me like I'd thrown scalding oil in her face. I just stared at her. If I couldn't yell at Bo, this helped. A bit. "Are you the snake lady, by chance?"

"I beg your pardon?"

"Is he making a snake for you. A choker...a necklace?"

"Yes. Yes." A modicum of relief colored her features.

"I think it's downstairs. Come with me."

She followed me, slowly. Big women in tight clothes wearing open-toed stilettos apparently use extreme caution when descending stairs—sideways. But that gave me time to get down there and look around a little before she arrived. The gleaming snake choker with the emerald eyes was coiled on Bo's workbench. It was arranged on a piece of red velvet because I had taken some shots of it the other day for his website.

When Ms. Gearhart finally made it all the way into his workroom, she seemed honestly impressed with Bo's setup and stopped to admire a set of earrings made of coral and sapphires.

"What an unusual combination—lovely. Oh! Is that...That's it!" she said of the choker I was holding. She touched her ample chest. "Look at that! It's stunning." She took it from me and studied it from all angles. I want to see it on. May I?"

I thought she was going to put it on herself, but she placed the snake around my neck. Then she stood back and oooed and awwwed. "That is *exactly* what I wanted. His sketches did not do this justice."

"He does good work," I agreed. *For a man M.I.A.*

She looked at me. "He's a bit eccentric, your brother."

"Ya think?"

She eyed me. "But...absolutely worth it."

"Are you taking this with you today?"

"Yes. It's paid for."

"Okay." I looked around for a box. I had no idea how Bo wanted this baby packaged up, but I knew that was a major part of his brand—the packaging. I opened a few drawers, checked a couple of shelves, and finally located a gray padded case, hinged, and lined with fanciness. It was inside a box that was embossed with the gold letters of Bo's insignia—*Sutton*. It looked the right size, but when I turned to arrange the snake inside, I found that Katrina Gearhart had placed it around her neck. "I'll take the box, but I'm wearing this." She grinned and posed, and evidently, we were now friends.

She made her way back up the stairs, again slowly, again sideways, and left not exactly expressing appreciation but thanking me all the same.

I shut the door and grabbed my phone. When Bo didn't pick up, I nearly screamed. Where are you?

"You've reached Benjamin Sutton. Sorry I missed you. Please call back. Or leave a message if you absolutely have to. I'll get back to you within 24 hours."

"Bo! This isn't funny anymore. I need to know you're okay. I don't have to know where you are if you don't want me to, but I have to know you're okay. I'm not kidding. I haven't seen you since yesterday at, what? 4:30? It's a quarter to ten—the next day! If you don't call me, I'm calling the police. You don't do this. You never do this! You don't blow off appointments. What was I supposed to do with your snake lady? Yeah! She just showed up, and we had to plow through your workroom for her choker. I hope it was okay that she took it. Bo! Call me!"

I ended the call and threw my phone onto the couch. Then I screamed. I did not know what else to do. Should I call Mom? The last thing she knew was that he was fine—according to the text she shared with me. What was that about? He must have been okay last night. *Was* he okay last night? Why would he text Mom and not me? Was he over at Mom's? Had he ended up over there? Did I dare call and find out? If he wasn't, then they'd freak out...like I was freaking out. I bent over and groaned. "Bo...what are you doing?"

My phone rang, and I dove onto the couch for it.

Finally! I wanted to cry. "Bo! Bo, are you there?"

"Mia!"

"Bo! Where are you? I've been so, so worried. Are you okay?"

He didn't answer, and I thought I'd lost him. "Bo!"

"Mia! I don't know what I'm doing!"

"What does that mean? What have you done? Tell me where you are." Was he crying? "Bo? Talk to me. Where are you?"

Shakily he pushed out, "I'm sitting in a parking lot in Flagstaff, Arizona."

I blinked. Then I blinked again. "No, you're not."

"Yes. I am, and I need your help."

"Is this a joke? Because it's not funny. What are you doing? Do you know what you've put me through? This isn't funny! I can't believe—"

"Mia! Listen to me," he panted. "Shut up! I need your help! Stop talking!"

I heard the panic—the panic beyond his regular panic—and my heart stopped. "Bo, what's happened? Are you in trouble?"

"Yes! I need...I need to pee!" he said in a shaky voice. "And I need your help...And I'm in hell about needing your help."

I swallowed. He wasn't kidding. "What? What do you need?"

"Mia..." he cried.

"Okay. Okay," I said gently. "Take a breath, Bo. Where are you, exactly? What do you need me to do?"

He blew into the phone, shakily. "I...I...I'm sitting in the parking lot of a 7-Eleven wannabe that, I kid you not, looks like it has never seen a fresh coat of paint, let alone a health inspector."

"And.... You can't go in?"

"I've tried. A dozen times. I'm shaking...You should see this place..."

I shook my head, clearing it. "Okay. Okay. Get out of the car."

"I can't. I've been trying to for almost an hour."

"Bo. Yes, you can. Get out of the car. Just open the door, get out the car, and walk in the store."

"I can't."

"Yes, you can. Just open the door."

"Don't hang up, Mia."

"I won't. Just get out of the car." I heard the car door open and not close for a full minute—then nothing but hyperventilating in my ear. "Bo, deep, slow breaths."

"Right. Right. Okay, I'm out."

"Okay. Now walk into the store." An eternity later, he informed me he was inside. "It's a convenience store, right?" I said.

"Yes."

"Find the hand sanitizer, or Clorox wipes, something like that."

"Yeah. Good. Okay," he breathed. "This place is disgusting, Mia," he squeaked as if in pain. "Okay, okay...I think...Okay, I found them."

"How's your bladder?"

"I can literally *taste* my pee."

"Okay. Well, thanks for that. Is there a line to pay?"

"Yes. And I'm dying. Three people. One has kids trying to decide what they want. I'll be here all day! I'll die here...in a pool of pee."

"Find the restroom, Bo. Pay for the wipes later."

"Really?"

"Yes, really. Go!"

"I don't know—"

"Go."

A few deep breaths later, I heard him groan.

"What?"

"The door is painted green and says *Amigos* in magic marker.... Kill me now."

"Oh, dear..."

"And the doorknob—is *alive* with..." He groaned again, this time louder. "I just know it's been handled by the entire western hemisphere."

"I'm sure it has," I said, with phenomenal patience. "Open it with a wipe."

"Really?" his voice was an eyeroll. "You think that's going to protect me?"

"No. The wipes are for when you pee down your leg! Open it with three wipes if you need to. Just get yourself into the bathroom."

"Right, right. Sorry. I'm putting the phone in my pocket."

I heard a series of machinations and more groans, a squeaky door opening and closing, then locking. Then I heard a whimper and what sounded like a prayer, then the line went dead.

I sighed. I guess although there was an outside chance that my brother had met with malice behind the dirty green door of the public restroom at the 7-Eleven wannabe a state away, it seemed more likely that he'd simply opted for privacy. Bo did guard his dignity when he could, and I was actually grateful. I walked to the other side of the living room and back, twice. Then I went into the kitchen and grabbed a bottle of water. I gave him almost three minutes, then I called him again. No answer.

I paced some more and Googled Flagstaff, Arizona. It was 700 miles from Monterey. I nearly dropped the phone. What was he doing? Had my brother had a stroke? I mapped it on Google maps. Bo had driven 700 miles. Had he even slept? What was he thinking? I pushed redial. No answer.

Should I call Mom? I should call my parents. I couldn't keep this from them, could I?

Finally, my phone rang, and my lunatic brother was calling me back. "Bo! What the—"

"Mia! You let Katrina Gearhart downstairs?"

"What?"

"You let that woman into my workspace? What were you thinking?"

"What are you...? Ugh, shut up!"

"Don't deny it! I listened to your message!" he shouted. "I can't believe you!"

"You. Can't believe *me*?" My blood was suddenly boiling as he ranted about his perceived ruination and my unbelievable lack of regard for his rules and boundaries and that the final polish had not been done on the snake—none of which was my fault. "You. Can't believe me?" I bellowed again. "That's rich coming from you, Bo, considering that without me, your bladder would have exploded all over the ceiling of your car!"

I hung up on him and didn't even feel bad. And I didn't answer when he called me back two seconds later. Or the next ten times in three minutes.

Forty-Eight—Ivy

Before she started the car, Camille turned to me. "I have to ask, Ivy. Is your father coming?"

"No." I looked down, ashamed of Daniel and wanting to call him terrible names.

Camille took my hand, and when I looked up, her eyes were warm and kind. "Your mom is heavily medicated, but she's been asking about him. Your grandmother and I think you should lie," she said softly.

I stared at her. "How...How much do you know about my parents?" I asked.

"I know...*some*," Camille said. "I know Bree adores him."

"She does. She always has."

"And you?"

"To be honest, I never had too much of a relationship with Daniel. I mean, he came around, of course, but I was pretty much supplemental to him seeing my mama, if that makes sense."

"Bree didn't tell me that part," Camille said with sad eyes.

"I'm not surprised," I told her. "She's pretty blind where my dad is concerned."

Camille scrunched up her pretty face. "I'm sorry."

"Me, too. And now he's too busy to come be with her. That's not love."

"No." Mia's sister shook her head as she turned the key. "But that your mom loved so deeply and believed she was loved so deeply in return..." she shrugged. "When you get to the end, does anything else really matter?"

"I guess not," I said. I thought of my father and his family—his *real* family—his tidy little life in Monterey. His *other* life. And I thought of the almost-shame, the almost-regret that had found its way through his arrogance when I'd begged him to come home with me. That looked a little like something Mama could be fooled by and pretend was love.

"Bree told me that like any smarter-than-smart nineteen-year-old, she'd loved your dad from the moment she saw him." Camille said this as she navigated the traffic merging onto the freeway.

I shrugged. "That's what she says. He was in town for something, and he wandered into where she was working, and apparently the heavens shone on him," I said with sarcasm.

"Well, if you believe her, he fell in love with her that fast, too. And he wanted to be with her," Camille said.

"Yep," I said. "That's what he told her. And told her and told her."

Camille frowned. "Sometimes, love makes us stupid, Ivy."

Tim flashed through my psyche. "Yes, it does." How could I begrudge my mother when love had made me just as stupid? Or, was that exactly why I should begrudge her? I sighed. Liz Proctor was almost twenty-two. I was twenty-one and change. Seemed my dad had been a busy little procreator the year of our conceptions. "Why did she tell you all of this?" I asked, feeling slightly betrayed; these were our darkest family shames, after all.

Camille glanced over at me. "On the night I got here—I was such a mess, Ivy. We were drinking Merlot and lamenting love and men and husbands and almost-husbands. I told her my very sad and ridiculous story, and she told me hers."

I looked at Mia's sister and smiled—of course, that made sense. She was so pretty, and she looked a hundred times better than when I'd seen her last. She looked a lot like Bo, and it made me miss him.

As Camille drove, she told me she and Mama had talked all night. "I actually think she saved me." Camille said. "She made me look at my life, really look at it. And I think she looked at hers, too. Ivy, she knew things had not turned out the way she'd planned, the way she'd hoped. But in the end, it didn't matter as much as she thought it would because of *you*. You were the prize."

I tried to laugh. "I was *one* of the prizes."

Camille smiled. "Ivy, sometimes we let men completely torture our lives. It's stupid, unforgiveable, sometimes even indictable, and we're idiots because we let them. But one day, you're sitting on a big porch in Savannah, Georgia—the last place in the world you think you'll ever find yourself—and you look around at the mess you think you are and you're watching your angels run around—laughing—and you suddenly realize that a stinking dog of a man gave you everything that matters." She looked over at me with sad eyes. "Everything. Your mom said that. About you...and your dad. I just borrowed it because I needed it."

I tried to smile. "My mom called Daniel a stinking dog?"

"Oh, heavens no. That's all me. But you get my drift."

* * *

It was just after ten when Camille dropped me at the entrance of Memorial Hospital with directions to my mother's room. She had to get back to her girls, so she didn't come in with me. I took the elevator to the ICU and steeled myself, but when I got to room 216, I realized the sight before me had nothing whatsoever to do with me. It couldn't. My mama did not even resemble herself. She was a supine arrangement of stillness, the broken parts of her propped by pillows and held together with gauze and tape and splints and compression bandages. She slept and was attached to things that beeped.

Geneva was at her side, and my grandmother had never looked so small and unequal to a task in her life. She was bent over, kissing Mama's hand. As I watched this awful, gentle scene, something happened to me, something sudden and distinct: I felt myself shed who I'd been yesterday and become someone altered. It was an inescapable shift into certain adulthood, and it happened in a blink.

Everything before that moment fell away diluted in significance. Tim. Not marrying Tim. My fight—my many fights—with Mama. Even Daniel. It all paled compared to the sight of my mother and her mother and what I knew was inevitable.

I walked over to my grandmother and touched her lightly on the shoulder. When her eyes met mine, I was shocked at how she had aged. Her little face crumpled.

"There's my Ivy girl. C'mere, sug." She stood up and pulled me into a long, weak hug and said, "You made it," into my ear. "You made it." Over her shoulder, I stared at my mama. Bree didn't stir, but her eyes flittered open a slit. She tried to smile, and I saw her finger lift.

Geneva let go and looked hard into my eyes, then cupped my face in her gnarled hands. "You look exhausted, sweet pea. Have you had anything to eat?"

"I'm not hungry, Gran."

She nodded knowingly, then bent to gently caress Mama's head. "I told you she was coming," she said softly, but falsely upbeat. "I told you, Bree." Then she turned to me. "She just had a pain shot, so she's kind of sleepy, but you sit down here. You sit with your mama now. I'm just going to grab a cracker from the nurse. I need to take my pills. You sit. I'll be right back."

I did as I was told and pulled the chair closer to the bed. As Geneva walked out, she turned and met my eyes with a telling sadness that took my breath away.

I sucked back my tears and reached over to touch my mother. But I pulled back—I didn't want to hurt her. She was so terribly broken, looked so terribly fragile. She opened her eyes again, and as she stared at me, tears seeped and spilled into her hair.

"Mama..."

"You came," she rasped.

"Of course I came."

"I...baby..." she said haltingly. "Sssooo s...sorry 'bout thele...tter."

"Mama, it doesn't matter."

"Wwwas h...h...horrible."

"Shhh," I noised. Was that letter really the biggest worry of the moment? "That was my fault. Mama. I'm sorry I didn't call you back."

She tried to reach up, but the effort was too great, so I took her hand and placed it on my face. Her palm was unbelievably hot. "Sss...sweetheart..." she whispered.

"I love you, too, Mama."

She started to cough then, and I could see it was killing her. "What do you need?" I asked, alarmed. "Should I get the nurse?"

"No," she gasped. "N...nooo..." she coughed again, and I ached watching her. When she calmed, her voice was a wet whisper. "Baby, c'mere..."

I leaned closer.

"I n...need...to ... are you o...over Tim?"

"What? Mama..." I sighed, surprised at how truly small he felt in light of what was happening.

More tears seeped from her eyes. "You...re...too...good," she said, painstakingly. "For...him..."

I kissed her warm cheek. "I love you, for thinkin' so, Mama."

She squeezed my fingers lightly and shut her eyes, and for a moment I thought she'd fallen asleep.

"He's n...not here?" she pushed out.

I knew she was referring to Daniel. "Not yet, Mama," I lied. "But he's coming..."

Bree looked at me through slits, smiled wanly, then started to cough again as her machinery pealed her distress. For a moment, she held on to my hand like she was falling, and I was about to run for the nurse when a blue-clad woman walked in with a vial of something she quickly shot into Bree's IV. The nurse looked at me with naked pity that said *I'm so sorry your mama is dying*. "Can I get you anything, hon?" she asked.

I shook my head. All I wanted was to crawl in beside Bree and *love her better*. She used to say that to me when I was little and had

had a bad dream, or the flu, or a bruised ego. She'd say I'm just gonna have to scoop you up and love you better, Ivy Lee. Or had that been Geneva?

Just before the medication pulled her under, my mother opened her eyes and slurred, "D...don't hate him, baby girl. Hhhhe loves us."

* * *

Bree's fever continued to rage, and her lungs filled with fluid. I never left her side. The shift changed, and new people wandered in and out, tapping notations on the bedside computer. But she held on, which surprised everyone. More than once, Geneva wondered out loud what God was doing putting her baby through this. The doctor assured us that Mom was in no pain thanks to the morphine, but she was restless, and it was hard to watch. I was very worried about my grandmother, who aside from the crackers she'd had when I first arrived, had not left this room. At about a quarter to four that afternoon, like an answered prayer, Everett Moss showed up to take her home. His backyard butted up against Geneva's on Isle of Hope, and ever since my grandfather died, he'd watched over her—going on thirty-five years. He was tall and thin like her, but with a pot belly, and he was unmoved by Geneva's blustered objections. He simply took her hand. "C'mon, old gal," he said. "You could use a nap and a change of clothes. Probably some eggs."

It broke my heart when Geneva started to cry, defeated. For the moment.

Forty-Nine—Bo

I thought of turning around. I was going to turn around. Mia had certainly brought to my attention the folly of my impulsivity—I had a business to run; I was a responsible business owner. In theory. But at the freeway, instead of heading south back to California, I took the north ramp. Hands sweating, heart pounding, two showers behind and setting a record for time spent in the same clothes, I merged behind a semi, then passed him. Then I set the cruise control for seventy-five.

Did I know what I was doing?

Not yet.

I just knew I'd survived so far—public restroom panic attack notwithstanding—and it felt strangely liberating. Even if I had needed my sister to get through it, it still felt liberating to be so far from home and on my own and a little bit afraid but not paralyzed by it.

I cranked up the air conditioner.

Did I know what I was doing?

Still no.

319 miles to Albuquerque. I'd decide what I was doing when I got to Albuquerque.

I started to shake a little. I shouldn't have yelled at Mia.

And now she wouldn't answer her phone.

Fifty—Ivy

My mother hung on through the night. Gran and I never left her side. Earlier Everett did get my grandmother to take a short nap and eat something, but she turned right around and drove herself back to the hospital and was sitting with me by evening rounds. Truth be told, I was glad she was there; I did not want to be alone with Mama if something happened. *When* it happened.

I was exhausted though, but I didn't dare sleep. There was too much quiet inevitability in the room. I think Bree was just waiting for Daniel. Part of me too, hoped my dad would actually show up. Then maybe Mama could just let go.

I thought of Daniel's face when he saw me standing in his office with Liz Proctor, my sister. It seemed like the sum-total expression of his worlds colliding, and for just an instant, he seemed undone by his secrets. But surely, he'd gotten his priorities straight by now and was on his way. Surely, he loved Mama enough to do that. I sighed.

"What is it, my sweet girl?" my grandmother said, taking my hand.

I looked at her and shook my head, tears threatening to overtake me.

"I know, sweetheart."

We were quiet for a few moments as we got back to watching the rise and fall of Mama's little chest and the green line on her heartbeat machine—both reassuring evidences that she was still with us. But studying them both so closely was nerve-racking. She'd been in a lot of pain and was finally sleeping with a hefty dose of something that was keeping her comfortable, but her breathing was shallow. They said it was a catch twenty-two at this point, but I wasn't sure what that really meant.

"Talk to me, sugar plum," Gran said, tugging on my hand. "Tell me something. Anything. I need to hear your voice."

"I met my sister," I said to the air in front of my face.

Geneva didn't respond, but she squeezed my fingers.

"Yep. When I went to tell Daniel what had happened, she was there," I said. "She works for him. Did you know she's the same age as me?"

"I did. I'm so sorry, dear girl."

I looked over at her. "When did you know, Gran? When did you know he had another family?"

"I found out before you were born."

"No. So you've always known?"

Emotion filled Geneva's tired eyes, and she looked over at my mother with brimming tenderness. "It's true. Did you know your mama was just nineteen when she met him?"

"I did."

"Do you know how *young* nineteen is, Ivy Lee?" She shook her head. "Of course you do. Your dad was a grown man, seasoned and away from his regular life, and your mama was untamed and adventurous and naïve. Of course, she fancied herself smart and worldly, but she was no match for him. And he knew it. And I'm sure it didn't hurt that they were both movie-star pretty and wanting the same thing from each other. So, they started something they shouldn't have. And when he went home, she was in love. And you know that has never dimmed. Never."

"I know," I said.

"But for what it's worth, I think he was in love, too. He came back a few weeks later. And a few weeks after that. And then one day, my not-yet-twenty-year-old daughter—who had not talked to me for the better part of a year—showed up in tears and told me I was going to be a grandmother. I did not know this man, and I was not thrilled—which is absolutely no reflection on you, my love," she said with a sad smile. "But I just figured we'd whip together a hurry-up wedding and get things on track." Geneva shook her head. "But of course, they had different ideas—well, Daniel did. Your mama would have married him in a blink and a grin. He said he loved her, but he wasn't ready to get married. He said he wanted to, but he had things to wrap up on the west coast before he could. That's what he said. *Things to wrap up.* So, I decided to go see what *things*, and I took a little trip to California." She looked at me with a raised-up eyebrow. "That's when I found out, sug. Little boy and a very pregnant wife, a dog and a mortgage, and a thriving law practice in a firm his wife's daddy owned. If your grandpa had been with me, he'd have shot him. First between the legs and then between the eyes."

I chuckled.

"You think I'm kidding," she said. "I'm not."

"What did Daniel say?"

"He cried." She shook her head and looked over at my sleeping mother. "Big, important lawyer man cried like a baby. Broke my heart a little," she said looking back at me. "I thought what a mess he'd made of things, but God help me, after we talked, I believed he loved my daughter. Now, I think I just *needed* to believe that—it was easier that way. But it didn't matter. I knew then that he'd never leave them. And when I told Bree that, it damn near ruined her and me. And we were already pretty ruined."

"Mom didn't know?"

Geneva shook her head. "And I don't think he was ever going to tell her. It just would have taken too much courage for your father to tell the truth in the middle of him living that big old lie. But when everything blew up, he still promised her they'd be together one day, and she believed him. I think telling themselves that was how they lived with what they were doing." She sighed. "And here we are all these years later, sug. Twenty-two years of him paying your mama's bills, twenty-two years of her listening to his woes and lies and mopping up his dissatisfaction with life. Twenty-two years of those two meeting up in exotic places whenever he had the notion and the freedom."

I didn't want to hear any of this. I'd known it forever; it was our life.

Geneva started to weep. "I despise that man for what he's done, and her too, sometimes. But I've had to keep quiet about all that—the best I could, anyway—because my relationship with your mama—and you—has always depended on it." She wiped her dripping nose with a balled-up hanky. "Y'all deserved so much better. So much better." She looked over at my mother again and took a shaky breath. "And now...Ivy Lee, I don't know what I'll do without her. I simply can't imagine..."

I squeezed her hand because her heart was breaking, and I would have done anything to alleviate my grandmother's pain. This struck me as a little shameful because I realized the pain I felt on this tragic occasion paled in comparison.

* * *

At about 7:30 the next morning, something changed, a feeling in my mother's room, a portent. I'd dozed off I guess but had wakened inexplicably to find Geneva had done the same thing. We looked at each other. Bree was still and her machines were quiet, but a slow heartbeat continued to register on the tiny screen above her head. My grandmother took my hand but said nothing. As we sat there considering the omen we both felt, a man walked in. He was crisply dressed in dark slacks and a blue dress shirt, pretty tie. He had white hair.

"Good morning," he said quietly, so as not to disturb. "I'm Robert Flynn. I'm covering for Doctor Blumenthal. How is Aubrey doing?"

Upon hearing his voice, Bree opened her eyes a slit, and he moved closer to address her. "You are quite the fighter, Aubrey, despite that fever. I'm just going to listen to your lungs."

"Yooouu caame," she moaned, in a drug-weakened voice, and Geneva gripped my hand.

The doctor smiled, but I'm not sure he heard due to the stethoscope in his ears. He went about his business, apparently oblivious to the adoring look on my mother's face, unfocussed eyes wider than they had been since I got there, her futile attempt to smile. She thought he was Daniel. When he stepped back, she reached for his hand. "I...I knew...you...come," she pushed out.

Dr. Flynn looked over at us.

"She thinks you're my father," I said, softly through a tear-soaked voice. "Who isn't going to make it."

He nodded and seemed to consider this. Then he did the kindest thing imaginable. Robert Flynn took my mother's hand and leaned down very close to her. "Of course, I came. I had to see that beautiful face."

"D...Dan...I..." she rasped, tears spilling from her eyes. "I...I...love..."

He touched her face gently. "You rest now. I'll be right here."

My mother tried to say more, but her eyes fell shut.

They never opened again.

Fifty-One—Bo

It would not require an advanced degree in psychology to determine that the last 48 hours of my life might reflect poorly on my sanity. I had driven away two days ago without a fully formed plan in my head—something very not like me. But at the time, I was obsessed with a single objective, and my capacity to obsess is quite legendary. My objective, of course, was to avoid Ivy. She'd asked something of me that had shamed me in my inability to deliver. I could not face her. So, I got in my car and drove. I pulled onto the freeway and didn't get off until my fuel light was flashing.

I'd driven 226 miles. But at that time, Ivy had not yet caught her flight. So, with my predictably faulty rationale, I gassed up and kept driving. Much, much later, when I pulled into the forlorn parking lot of the Bee-Line Mart in Flagstaff, I was pretty sure I'd lost my mind—I'd been gone for almost fourteen hours. Fourteen hours. It was just after seven the next morning. I was hungry, I was exhausted, and I had to pee, but I could not get myself out of the car. And as a true testament to my weirdness, I actually tried to sleep off my full bladder—for almost two hours, I tried. Then I called Mia. I called *my sister* to talk me out of the car and into a public restroom—which she did. Now for the record, panic doesn't always accompany chores of this nature, but this time it did, and I could not have done it without her talking me through it. And with that achieved, I would have cried had I been able to withstand one more ounce of self-imposed indignity.

Instead, I kept driving, inordinately pleased with the triumph of growing mileage between me and all that was safe and predictable. I was so pleased, in fact, that I was a little pumped, maybe a bit manic. No sleep. Nothing but caffeinated beverages consumed through individually wrapped straws changed hourly—I happen to keep a stash in my glove compartment—two granola bars and a banana.

By late afternoon, I was in Albuquerque—as in New Mexico—which was surreal and inexplicably liberating. I'd made a deal with myself that I'd decide what I was doing when I got here—which meant I'd probably turn around and head home. But by the time I rolled in, I desperately needed a shower and to sleep, which entailed checking into a hotel, which entailed purchasing a change of clothes and a set of sheets, which would then entail time spent at a premium laundromat preparing said sheets and clothes. It was almost eight o'clock when I actually checked into the Marriott. I ordered room service, but only because I was starving and only because it was the Marriott. I put my own triple-washed sheets on the bed and by nine had fallen into a coma and slept the sleep of the dead until twenty minutes ago.

Twenty minutes ago, my phone pinged—7:36 AM in Albuquerque—and it rattled me to the core because only one number was allowed past the gates of my smartphone's silent mode: Ivy's. My heart had become a hammer as I sat up. I couldn't answer it. Nothing had changed. There was nothing I could do to atone for what I'd done—what I *hadn't* done. I'd reached for my phone anyway, and sure enough, the caller ID had said Ivy. I wasn't even sure why I'd programmed her number to ring through when I didn't want to be bothered by anyone else. I couldn't talk to her, though. I couldn't! I'd rammed my free hand roughly through my hair, then over my face, waiting for the call to go to voicemail—the whole time hating myself for failing her yet again—*I couldn't even answer my freaking phone.* Finally…Another ping, a different ping: I had a message, which bizarrely, I could not listen to fast enough.

Twenty minutes later, I'd now lost count of how many times I'd listened to it.

"H...Hey, Bo..." Ivy's voice was soft, tear-clogged. *"I'm...I'm so sorry I missed you. I think it's early there, you might still be sleepin'. But I just actually kinda wanted to hear your voice..."* I heard her sniffle, and it took her a second to speak again. *"My...my mama died...'bout an hour ago...and I...I just wanted you to know."* When she started to cry, I felt my shoulders give way—again. *"That's all,"* she continued softly. *"You don't have to call me back, it just...It just feels better, you knowing. Is that weird?"* She took a breath. *"Bo...I... I also really need to know that we're okay. I never meant to upset you. I wouldn't do that on purpose in a million years. I hope you know that."* Another shaky breath. *"Well, I'd better go, I think I'm heading into a very rough day. Anyway, I just wanted to thank you again, for being such a good...friend. Have a good day, Bo."*

I stared at the ceiling and let the phone drop from my hand onto the floor. For a moment, there was barely enough strength in me to breathe. That girl. In twenty-seven years on this planet, no one, *no one*, aside from myself, had ever scared, distracted, confused, or overwhelmed me more.

I didn't like it. But whatever *it* was, somehow fed me in a way that I'd never been fed before. And it hurt me that she was hurting, and I had never hurt this way before. I'd never cared like this before. I didn't like it. But I didn't want it to stop. This was insanity—and I knew insanity—but this was insanity on a different level. This was borne of having disappointed someone... someone I cared about. This was some kind of rogue humanity in me that recognized I was simply not man enough to...to be there for her. I squeezed my eyes shut. *Not man enough...Not man enough to be there for her...To be...there...*

There. There?

My eyes opened, then my mouth, as realization slowly bloomed awake in me.

One of the side effects of being me is that I've developed a finely tuned *executive function*—in other words, I seem to be able to effectively succeed in my life, despite my massive preoccupations with minutia. This is only possible because somewhere in the upper twigs of my rat's nest of a brain, there is a master controller that has the ability to circumvent the rest of my bizarre fixations. At times—like now—my insight expands, and it becomes obvious to me that my executive function has been working all along—despite the circus.

I was shaking when I leaned down to pick up my phone from the towel I'd placed on the floor by my bed—there were three lying end-to-end, making a clean trail from me to the bathroom. It *was* the Marriott, but still. And I was shaking when I pulled up a road map of the United States.

No way.

I sat up, a chill crawling up my spine. I-40 E, on which I'd been driving since I left home, was a straight shot from Monterey to Savannah. "No... No freaking way."

I stared at my phone, stared so hard I could have burned a hole in it. According to this map—and my demon EF—two days ago when I'd driven away, even though it had felt like it, I had not actually been driving away from Ivy at all. Instead, it seemed, I had been driving steadily toward her.

And not only that, it looked like I was almost halfway there.

Fifty-Two—Ivy

Numb, empty, disoriented. I felt like a small earthquake had shaken me apart. My mother was gone. How could that be? Was it really just two weeks ago that she'd come to Monterey and we'd all been together? Dinner on Lullaby's patio? Carmel-by-the-Sea? Life did not change that quickly. It couldn't. There was supposed to be more warning, more time between living and dying to plan, to steel, to get ready to let go. That I'd been sitting here waiting for this didn't seem to count.

I needed to surface here. I needed to be strong for my grandmother, but I couldn't seem to stand up straight. I wasn't ready for the green line on Bree's monitor to be flat, or the tortured one-note finale ringing out from that same place. This wasn't happening.

She couldn't be gone.

***

It probably wasn't very long, but it felt like a long time before the room filled up with people and attention. Somehow my grandmother was able to rally. She did all the paper-signing when the doctors came in to do their declaration. She did all the instructing when the mortuary people came. She's the one who called Everett and told him it had happened. She's the one who said it was time for us to go. I seemed to be standing outside of it all—watching. Watching the details of death go on around me, a mere witness to someone else's tragedy.

But it was mine. My mother had died, and I kept watching her, willing her to change her mind and breathe. But she didn't. This was my tragedy, and everything should have stopped. But nothing stopped, and it seemed mocking of the Universe, even cruel for everything to go on when my mother was dead.

"Breathe, Ivy girl," Geneva said. "Just breathe."

So, I breathed.

For some reason, a social worker had given me some orange juice. She was lovely, kind, worried that I might not be all right. I wasn't, but I said I was. I just didn't know how exactly to act—I didn't know how to *be* in this 'dead-mama' place, and I was shaking a little. I drank the juice and excused myself to find a restroom. That's when I called Bo. That's all I could think to do. I don't even know why, really—I just wanted to hear his voice. I thought I might not feel so undone if he could just help me *know* this terrible *unknowable* thing that had happened. But he didn't answer. Neither did Mia.

So, I splashed some water on my pale, smudged-up face and swished some around in my mouth. Then I fiddled with my hair and stood back from the mirror. I was on my own—truly—and I needed to get strong fast.

If not for me, then for my grandmother.

Fifty-Three—Mia

The hardest thing I've done for a very long time is keep Bo's secret from my parents. And I hated my brother a little for putting me in this position. And I was a little cranky at them for the same reason. But Mom had just left me another message that Bo was ghosting her, and I had no choice but to come clean because he obviously wasn't going to. *Damn him!*

Now I readily admit that I got most of the good moxie in my family—which should come in handy at times like this. Camille had plenty at one time—not as much as me, but plenty—but she let a creep suck it out of her, so she was no help at the moment. And Bo—a major contributor to my current pissiness—had a kind of warped moxie that was obviously a problem. I'm not complaining, not really—I wouldn't trade places with either one of them. I just get a little peeved that my particular gift comes with so much responsibility. I'm too busy trying to graduate to be this preoccupied with my brother's disappearing act and protecting my parents from it. He makes me so mad!

But then, admittedly, I was already mad—about everything. My pathetic unimpressive, final project, Mom's early morning worried text because of my insane brother who was in New Mexico which was a secret I was keeping from her. Another snarky message from Peter demanding to know where Camille was and day eight without a word from Derek. Would it kill that boyfriend of mine to let me know he was alive? Eight days. I hadn't heard from him for *eight days*. No text. No email. No letter. No call. Was he mad at me?

Hurt that I hadn't said I love you back? And why hadn't I? I'm *such* an idiot.

I hated waking up in a bad mood—feeling like I was outrunning an avalanche of crap before I was even out of bed.

I sat up with a pit in my stomach. Then I fell back into the covers and groan-yelled at the ceiling. It was at that moment that my phone buzzed. I grabbed it, not realizing it had been on silent mode. *Please be Derek!*

But it wasn't Derek. It was Bo. At ten after seven in the morning, it was pretty early for another crisis. But it was Bo, so I steeled myself and answered with: "Are you okay?"

"I think so. No, *I am*."

"Are you on your way home?"

"Ummmm...."

"What?" I said, balancing on my last nerve.

"I'm not coming home, Mia. I was. I thought I was—"

"No! No, no, no. You can't do this. What are you doing?"

"I need you to tell Mom and—"

"No! No way! I'm not covering for you one more day! You call them! You call them right now. Mom's been texting me. What are you doing?"

"It's...it's Ivy," he said. "Her mom died, and I'm going to Savannah."

I swallowed my tirade. "What?"

"Bree died," he said. "This morning. Ivy left me a message a little while ago..."

"Oh, no. No."

"I'm almost halfway there, Mia. I can't quite believe it, but I have to do this. And I need you not to freak out. I'm not, so you can't."

I breathed out. "You're going to Savannah? You? Alone? Are...are you sure you're okay?"

"Yeah...yeah. Shockingly. I slept and ate and I'm good. She doesn't know I'm coming, and I don't want her to, just in case I...I, you know, turn into the debilitated flake we all know so well. But it's weird, Mia. I thought I was running away from her—it started out that way, anyway. But it kind of seems like I was always headed straight *to* her. That's crazy, right?"

I pulled my phone from my ear and stared at it, briefly wondering if I was dreaming this conversation. Then, once more into the phone, I said, "Who is this? This is not my brother! My brother does not do this. My brother does not *not* plan things out. He does not drive to Albuquerque, *sleep* in Albuquerque—then have an epiphany," I said, trying not to scream-cry. "You...you slept in Albuquerque, Bo."

"I did."

"What's happening to you?"

"I don't know. I'm not sure," he said. "But I kind of like it."

I suddenly could not speak for tears and a boulder in my throat.

"Mia, did I lose you? Mia?"

"I'm here."

"Are you okay?"

I bit my lip, rallied. "Yeah. Just trying to wrap my head—."

"I know. I'm sorry I've been so...*weird.*"

"You *have* been weird. But..." I swallowed. "You can do this, Bo," I said, meaning it—surprised that I meant it. "You can."

"Yeah? Really? I think so, too," he said. "I really, really want to, Mia. I want to for Ivy."

I sniffed. "And for *you*...This is huge."

"Which is why I... I might not make it," he said. "I am *me*, remember."

"Yes, you will. I'll help you. What do you need?"

"I need you to tell Mom and Dad what I'm doing. I love them, you know I do, but I don't want to deal with them right now...their worry. Mom will probably be on the next plane, and I can't, I just can't. So please do this for me, Mia. Tell them I'm okay—I'm fine. And don't tell Ivy. Promise me! Or Camille. And tell Mom not to either. I'm serious. Just let me get there and I'll figure it out."

"Are you sure? Okay. Okay," I agreed. "On one condition."

"Nooooooo. No conditions," he whined.

"Yes, and here it is: You check in with me every few hours—and you answer your damn phone when I call. If you do that, I promise I won't let you flake out."

He seemed to think about this. "I'll check in with you. I promise. And if I need your help, I'll ask. But Mia, I have to do this on my own. I have to. But thanks. You're a good sister."

I let Bo hang up first, then stared at my phone for a long time. *Wow. Just wow.* The whole conversation had left me a bit awestruck. It also inspired me. Bo might not be admitting it to himself yet, but he had real feelings for Ivy. And the manifestation of those feelings left me questioning who in our family actually possessed the most moxie after all. It rather pinched to realize it might not be me at the moment—lying here in my puddle of whiny self-absorption and talent-doubt, love-doubt.

In the eight days I had not heard how missed and adored I was by the man who'd become a permanent resident in my head, heart, and fantasies, that same man had also not heard those things from me. My brother shamed me. Truly. Why had I not reached out to Derek? Because I'd written last? Because it was his turn? Because I was scared of my own feelings for him? Scared I might send him the wrong message? I groaned. There was no wrong message. I was an idiot.

I pulled my laptop onto the bed and opened my email. Still nothing from him. I hit compose and made it short and unmistakable.

Hey.

You're scaring me. Eight days without hearing that you're okay is agony. Eight days of imagining the worst is making it hard to breathe. But worse than that is eight days of you not knowing how much you mean to me. I love you, D. I do. I'm sorry it took so long to tell you. I'm sorry it took imagining my life without you to know how completely, utterly, totally, and absolutely in love I am with you. But it did, and I am. So please, please be safe and come home to me.

I love you. I love you. I love you. Oh, and I love you!
M

I knew I meant it when peace and relief—and not an ounce of regret—washed through me as I pressed send. But I ached. I ached not knowing what was happening with him. I ached hoping he hadn't changed his mind about me. I sighed and screamed a little at the ceiling as tears filled my eyes and leaked down my temples.

To say that I forced myself into the pool fifteen minutes later to do twenty laps would be a massive understatement. It was a lackluster workout at best, and my phone ringing at just past eight was what ended it. I missed the call, but it was from Ivy. She didn't leave a message, but I could have kicked myself when I noticed that I had an earlier voicemail from her that had come in at just past 6:30 this morning. I listened and wept as she informed me of what Bo had already let me know: her mother had died.

Ivy didn't answer when I tried to call her back, but I told her how sorry I was and that I would call later. I so wished I was there to hug her.

As I sat there, on the edge of the pool, I looked again for photos of us on my phone. I wanted to send her one of the two of us, to remind her that she had a friend across the country who was thinking of her—maybe the one from Carmel with our mouths full that I hadn't sent the other day. But when I started scrolling, I couldn't stop.

I was looking for a pic I'd taken the night I met Ivy at my exhibition. I'd gotten the shot of her just before I walked up and introduced myself—but I couldn't find it now. I remembered that she'd been a bit folded in on herself, trailing her weird dad, no hint of life in her lovely features—almost like she wished she could disappear. But again, that pic was not on my phone. Nor were the ones I'd taken of her later that week when she'd met me at the track. I suddenly remembered how timid, unsure, *burdened* she'd seemed. Deeply wounded. But I had gotten a tiny grin out of her after we'd shared pieces of ourselves with each other and declared we were meant to be roomies for the summer.

No, all those had been taken with my Nikon. I take pics anytime inspiration hits. Sometimes I use my phone, but more often I use one of my three cameras. Now, I wanted to find the one from the track because I remembered it was nearly perfect in composition: full sun illuminating her delicious skin, lots of slightly sweaty curls as I recall, sad eyes, but the beginning of a friendship.

On my phone, I found a selfie I'd taken of Ivy and me right after she'd argued with her mom in Carmel. We were in that little restaurant killing a plate of onion rings. It was a good picture of us. But I was pretty sure Ivy would remember the occasion and her mother's part in it, so I decided not to send it.

But staring at that picture gave me an idea.

So far, this semester had been one long class arguing technique with guest experts. Kyle Donohue, whose work regularly graced the best photog magazines, had been the latest. He was good, but not great in my opinion. But that might have been his arrogance and not his actual talent. Still, trying to appreciate and incorporate his expertise into my work had been frustrating and left me doubting my abilities. I kind of hated him for that. I was being tutored by one of the premier black and white photographers of all time. Why not use it instead of just keep whining about it? I blew out a grumbly breath. Because I could do better, that's why. Kyle Donohue was Kyle Donohue, and he had his own unique style—brilliant by industry standards, magnificent by his own. But the truth was he was no Mia Sutton.

He didn't have my eye. And he didn't have the perfect subject. Ivy.

Since the day I'd met her, I had been taking her picture—I'm a freak that way—I take everyone's picture. My camera loved her face—her skin reflected light with the raw purity of a child's gaze.

Her expressions hid nothing, and my camera missed nothing, and between the two, Ivy was a canvas where subtlety told entire stories. Ivy—guileless Ivy—somehow managed to own the emotion of the moment completely unfiltered.

Imperfection was my trademark, but it wasn't to be found in her face. Her skin was immaculate, her features gentle and proportionate, blue-gray eyes, fullish lips, generous brows, no-nonsense nose. Completely, perfectly, Ivy. The imperfection came from the shadows and contours caused by what she was feeling, the emotion inhabiting that landscape—the pain, the unworthiness, the self-doubt, the emergence of a long-lost laugh, concern, regret. I'd seen entire wars fought on that face—but how much had I actually captured?

I got up and pulled a towel around me then headed back to my bedroom to get myself organized. Then for the rest of the morning I studied every picture I'd taken of Ivy Talbot. And as I did, I knew, absolutely, why I'd become a photographer. Ivy didn't know how lovely she was—inside or out—so she wasn't in the habit of trying to convince the camera of anything. It was hard to believe what she'd been through in just the time that I'd known her. But I'd taken so many pictures of her that you could see it, you could see the evolution. And I ached when I saw what I had accumulated. Lovely. Tragic. Raw. Redemptive. Healing. But would she give me permission to use these images as my final project?

It was early afternoon when I drove over to my parents' house. Mom had called again, and I could not ignore her another moment. When I pulled up, she was watering the lupine near the front door. She looked nervous when she saw me, like I was there to deliver bad news—and I guess I was: I needed airfare to Georgia, and because of the short timing, it was a substantial amount. She turned off the hose and sat down on the front step as I got out of the car.

"Bo's fine, Mom," I said as I made my way across the lawn. "He's a butthead, but he's fine,"

She visibly relaxed. "So, you've talked to him?"

I nodded as I sat down next to her.

"Where is he? What's he doing?"

"Well...the short answer is he's on his way to Savannah. Bree died. The longer answer is, I think he's on his way to falling in love with Ivy."

Mom's features slackened, but I'm not sure which of those three declarations caused it. "What? Bo and Ivy?" she stared at me, processing this. "Bree died? No...Oh, no...Poor Ivy. Bo didn't fly? Did he?"

"No. He's driving."

Her eyes widened.

"He's about halfway. Apparently." I took her hand. "He sounds good. He wanted to tell you himself, but he thought you would talk him out of it...or, you know, be worried."

Mom eyed me, still processing but did not dispute what I'd said.

After she stared a bruise between my eyes, I cleared my throat. "I want to go to the funeral, Mom. Is there any way you can lend me the airfare to get there? I'll pay you back. It's just one-way. Then, I'll drive home with Bo." I did not tell her that Bree's funeral was only part of my motivation.

Of course, she said yes. Of course, she did. My mother is completely stellar that way.

Fifty-Four—Ivy

It was after noon when we drove past Wormsloe and headed into Isle of Hope. I was driving—even though Gran said she was fine, it was time I took a turn, and I surprised myself by being up to the task. The live oaks were in their mid-day splendor, and the street I'd traveled a million times seemed like it had been waiting to welcome me home, to tell me it was all going to be okay. It must have been that sensation of sameness, the comfort and safety of home that brought feeling back into my limbs.

My disastrous wedding had branded a terrible moment on my soul and overshadowed everything in my life for a time, but it hadn't altered this place one bit. This stately island of history and old ways that I had loved forever was warm and familiar and soft against my aches. It seemed amazing, but I couldn't believe I'd actually considered never coming back here, because as we rounded LaRoche, I couldn't imagine being anywhere else. This was my home. Savannah was my heart. Here—right here—was the salve on my skinned-up bloodiness. And it always had been.

By the time I pulled up to 40 Bluff, the numbness in me had lifted, and I was overwhelmed with sadness. I was suddenly weak with the reason I was here. Camille was waiting at the front of the house, and when she helped Geneva out of the car, my grandmother thanked her for being a godsend.

"The girls are at preschool for two hours, so I'm all yours," she said. "What can I do for you? Are you hungry?" Mia's sister eyed me, then Geneva, then me again.

"Oh goodness, I doubt we'll be hungry for a week. I'm pretty sure that by later this afternoon, we will have run out of space for what will arrive in my kitchen." Gran sighed and patted Camille's face. "Get ready to see what happens in this community when tragedy strikes. But, how 'bout you come in and be our official door-answerer? That would be wonderful."

Camille smiled. "I can do that."

We made our way across Geneva's lawn to the big porch, all three of us trying to be in charge, none of us quite making it. At one point, I asked my grandmother if she was okay.

"Heavens, no, sweet girl," she said. "I suspect I'm going to have to reinvent *okay.*" She squeezed my hand as new tears filled her old eyes. "But I'll get through it, sug. We both will. Together. One foot in front of the other." She offered a sad wink, and suddenly looked very, very old to me. I couldn't have loved her more. Or needed her more. On our way up the front steps, she linked arms with me. "Like I said, within an hour or two, there will be a parlor full of big-hearted folks heavy with food and love, so if you were thinking you wanted to shower—or better yet—take a soak in my big tub, you have a small window of opportunity."

I tried to smile. "Sounds glorious."

My grandmother took my hands. "You know they're pure in their intent, these folks, that's all they know. But I also think some will just plain be curious about you."

"I know, Gran."

And they were. Neighbors and lifelong friends, who'd last seen me in barrels of lace and utterly devastated, arrived throughout the afternoon and early evening and approached me like I was blown glass, beyond fragile. Not only had my life been upended by Tim Marsh, but now my mother was dead. There could be no possible hope for my recovery. It was in their faces, and I loved them for it. All of them. The Warrens, the Broadheads, the Parkers. Everett Moss, the Marshes. Tim's parents were as kind as they had ever been. Their house was two streets behind Geneva's, and I knew it as well as I knew hers, from years of having dinner there, playing night games, doing homework, and hiding away in their treehouse. I hadn't realized how much I had missed them—my would-be parents. Paula touched my face, then kissed my cheek. "I just can't believe this has happened, Ivy. I am so sorry about your mama." She kept looking sideways at me, and I heard her say to my grandmother that I'd gotten too pretty for her knuckleheaded son. It made me remember that I'd cut my hair.

Bryce Marsh nodded, also taking me in. He seemed genuinely lost for words. "I don't know what to say, Ivy. We just love you."

"I know. And I love you back." I hugged my almost father-in-law, meaning it, and found it hard to swallow over the massive lump in my throat. Their words bespoke their sympathy for my loss even as their eyes probed me for signs of lingering damage done by their son. My current sorrowfulness, however, was so palpable, they could not see beyond it to suspect that most things *Tim* had receded. But they had. As I looked at them through soft eyes, I had the same sensation I did upon seeing my mother for the first time yesterday, a feeling of distinctly being thrust into adulthood and past what would never matter as much as it once had. I hugged them both. I would love them forever, but right now I had to get away from them—from all of them.

Isle of Hope was a tight place—a very tight place—and the support for my grandmother here was real if not a bit cloying. My grandfather's great-grandfather had helped establish the community. He'd been a milliner who'd come from London in the early 1800s. He'd built this house and much of it, thanks to Geneva, had retained its historical character. Especially the parlor, which was still full of sad-eyed cheek-kissers in no hurry to leave. I loved these people, I truly did, but I craved the quiet of someplace else. I found my grandmother and said into her ear, "I have to get out of here; can I borrow your car?"

She eyed me with knowing and a little concern. "You're not going to your mama's?"

"I'll be fine, Gran," I promised. Then I hugged her and didn't wait for her to say more.

* * *

Savannah's historic district was a twenty-minute drive from Isle of Hope, and for a Friday evening, traffic was predictable. But I was pretty lost in myself, so it didn't bother me much. Neither did the relative bustle of Chippewa Square, which was sporting its share of tourists at the moment. When I pulled up to the shop at the corner of Perry and Bull, of course I found Mama's store closed, but I wasn't prepared for the crime scene tape cordoning off the curved sidewalk in front of it. I parked and realized I was shaking. Images of Mama splayed at wrong angles on that sidewalk filled my mind. I imagined sirens. Screaming. Paramedics doing CPR. Onlookers. Police shooing them away. And all that was left, literally, was this crime tape, most of which had come loose and was blowing listlessly into the street. It looked unforgivably forgotten and anticlimactic—an overlooked crime scene, the victim long removed and now deceased, no longer an issue. It looked shoddy and uninspiring, and it broke my heart and made me mad at the same time.

I got out of my car, and with no concern about whether I needed permission, I gathered the yellow tape—rolled it into a big, obscene ball and stuffed it into the communal trashcan on the corner. No reminder of what had happened here was far better than a faded, blowing-in-the-wind afterthought—that was my thinking.

There was a little wilting pile of flowers stacked up by the double front doors to our shop. It was touching, and for a moment I just stared at them. I could probably name the deliverer of each stem—Mama had lovely, lovely friends. She would be missed. She would.

I gathered the flowers and used my key to let myself in. The lights were off, of course, and the blinds had been shut like at the close of any other day of business at *Bree T. Creations.* I disabled the alarm before it went crazy and flipped the light switch, which activated not overhead fluorescents, but three huge Victorian lamps. Soft light and the fragrance of citrus and sandalwood imbued the space with familiarity. I looked around. My mother's personality was everywhere, the walls, the shelves, her artwork adorning her many antique display tables. Her specialty was handmade frames, small, ranging from ornate and beaded to misshapen hardwoods, to cracked plaster, to distressed pine. Very unique, each made with a little attitude and each containing an original watercolor done on homemade paper—something Savannah: A fountain from Forsythe Park, a bed shaped mausoleum from Colonial Park Cemetery, Oglethorpe's saber, an iconic pied-a-terre.

My mother had an amazing eye, and she'd made quite a name for herself. About eight years ago, maybe ten, she'd caught the attention of someone on the board of trustees at the Savannah College of Art and Design—SCAD—and had been recruited to teach a Design Management course. Now she allowed her top student per quarter to sell their wares in her shop, and it looked like hand-painted silk scarves had made the cut this time. The wrought-iron hall tree in the corner was covered with beautiful one-of-a-kind designs. They fluttered in the soft breeze of the ceiling fan.

A note had been slid under the front door that I did not notice when I first walked in, I picked it up. It was addressed to me. *So sorry to hear about your mama, dear girl. Prayers and wishes pouring forth. Delia.*

Delia Gwinnett made me cry. She lived across the square on the other side of Chippewa in a walk-up she'd been restoring for years. Her walls were crowded with Mama's handiwork, and she had been a great friend to us. On Fridays, when I was little, she used to bring me homemade gingersnaps and cream to kick off the weekend. I went to school in Isle of Hope and stayed with Geneva during the week. Friday 'til Sunday, I stayed with Mama and helped out in the shop. Mostly I helped her make paper. I could make paper in my sleep.

I took a final look around and turned off the light. Then I walked up the back staircase to our apartment. Again, the soft familiarity that greeted me was like an embrace: Mama's ratty paint shirt hanging on the laundry room door, the silk-lined throw sitting in a puddle by the sofa, a diet Pepsi—probably half-full—by the lamp. So *her*. I loved this room, with its rose-colored walls, sporting a chronology of me throughout the years, and the bay window Mama left perpetually open a crack to let in the sound of horses clopping along on the street below—part of the soundtrack of Savannah.

I pushed out a shaky breath and sank down onto the overstuffed sofa. The cushions folded in on me like a hug and suddenly everything felt so terribly undone. How could she not be here? How could my mother not be here when—good, bad, or messy—she was the ever-present hook on which my life hung? Right here was where we'd laughed and argued and teased and yelled. Right here in this room, over lasagna and pizza and tears and nail-polish and *American Idol* and *The Bachelor*, where we'd talked and listened and not listened at all. Where we'd annoyed each other and hurt each other and even switched places in the hierarchy of smart and dumb a few times, but at the end of the day, where we'd belonged to each other with that kind of vicious stickiness known so well to mothers and daughters who were each other's *only*.

I looked around and ached. I didn't know how to be me without her.

I must have fallen asleep in the warm stew of my musings because I woke with a start when a pebble bounced against the bay window. Then another. Then another. It was just after 10:30. Maybe the police had noticed the crime scene tape had been cleaned up, or maybe Delia had seen the lights on and brought me cookies. But as I came fully awake, I knew it was neither of those. Only one person ever threw rocks at my window. I sighed, bone tired and not at all ready, but I stumbled downstairs and opened the door anyway.

"Hey, Ivy," he said, sheepishly.

"Hey, Tim."

He swallowed. "Mom said you'd be here. I...don't be mad. I had to see you. I hope it's okay." He shook his head, and tears filled his eyes. "Ivy, I'm so sorry. I'm so, so sorry."

I stared at him for a few beats. "What for, Tim? Mama? Angela? The wedding?"

He looked truly pained. "All of it. I'm sorry for all of it. Can...can we talk? Please?"

I breathed deep, knowing pretty much everything he would say to me because I'd heard it all before—aside from the few forthcoming particulars having to do with our current circumstances, of course.

"Please, Ivy," Tim pleaded, his eyes full of emotion.

This, too, was familiar. His sorry was always genuine—and genuinely sad. But I must have been truly exhausted because for some reason, I was surprisingly...*unmoved* by him.

"We could go for a walk," he suggested hopefully.

As I considered this, I took him in. My almost-husband seemed older to me, somehow, and saddled with heavy things. And strangely, he felt like he'd been *missing* from my life much longer than the mere weeks it had been since I'd last seen him. He was wearing a dirty white tee shirt and had muscles on his arms that didn't used to be there. Then I remembered his new job and that tires must be heavy. The dark shadow on his jaw made him look serious and, I thought, better looking than I remembered. He was taller than me by a head, and as I looked up at him, I felt...*Nothing*. Well, not nothing, exactly. But nothing that hurt.

Maybe I was just too tired or too filled with my mother being dead to have room for anything else. But whatever it was, feeling nothing at this moment was not what I'd expected. And somehow that made me stronger than I realized. "I guess we could talk for a minute," I said.

"Really?" he breathed. "Thank you, Ivy."

I grabbed the key from the cash register and locked the door, and we headed down Bull Street. I didn't say anything because I didn't want to make this easy for Tim, plus I didn't really have much to say anyway. But I did sort of admire him for taking me on right now. I knew Tim—he wasn't good at this kind of stuff—so it was no surprise that we were well past Liberty Street before he finally spoke.

"Do you hate me?" he said on what might have been a tiny sob.

"I wanted to," I said, my gaze on the sidewalk. "I thought I did for a while. But turns out I'm not really very good at it. Hating."

He made a laugh noise that wasn't a laugh at all. "Well, if it helps, I hate me."

I looked over at him. "That's good. I think it actually does help, a smidge."

He tried for a smile, and I did, too. And then I missed him.

Tim and I had been friends our whole lives. He'd hit Felix Dunn for calling me fat in the fourth grade. When we were thirteen, he waited six hours in the hospital lobby while I got my tonsils out. He threw me a surprise party when I was sixteen, and it wasn't even my birthday. I knew his faults and his secret fears, and he knew mine. So, he knew how deeply he'd wounded me. And I knew how hard he'd tried not to. I also knew he'd had no choice when he'd finally realized how much he wanted to be with Angela, which I now realized had everything to do with her being pregnant. Of course, his timing—at the time—had sucked. But I knew now, with certainty, that if he'd been five minutes stronger and said 'I do,' we'd be married like I'd dreamed. The rub would be I'd be competing with the girl he really wanted, not to mention their child. And we'd be miserable. All of us. As it stood, because the Universe actually rolled the dice in my favor, Angela would always compete with me, at least with the idea of me. Every time she hurt him, every time they fought, every time he was disappointed with life, he'd think of me because that's what he did; I was his safe place. I knew it, he knew it, and she knew it. It was twisted and sickish and very sad.

But because Angela had swooped in to save herself at the eleventh hour of my wedding, by the grace of God, this ridiculous cycle had spat me out for good.

Silver linings, I thought. Who knew it would take the hardest day of my life—which turns out *not* to have been my failed wedding day—to recognize them?

I looked over at him. "Are you happy?" I said softly.

He considered me. "Some days, yeah. Some days for sure—but marriage is a lot of work," he informed me, sounding like a dime-store philosopher. "You know I have a son."

"I do. Congratulations."

He smiled. "He's pretty awesome."

"He's your son. What choice does he have?"

Tim looked down at me with an expression of gentle surprise. "How do you do that, Ivy? How do you not despise me?"

I ignored his question. "Do you have pictures?"

"Of him? Umm, yeah. 'Course." He stopped and pulled his phone from his back pocket. "He's just starting to smile," Tim said, punching apps on the small screen. Then we huddled under a streetlight near Monterey Square, and Tim showed me his baby boy—seven weeks old tomorrow. Timothy Jack, TJ, was beautiful. He had his dad's dark hair but looked just like Angela—which I thought was unfortunate. I sniffled. He seemed so small and safe and adored, nestled in the crook of Tim's arm. And the expression on Tim's face...That pinched.

"He's perfect," I rasped.

Tim caught my emotion and quickly put his phone away. Then it was awkward for a moment because it couldn't be anything else. "I'm so sorry," he said again.

We crossed the street at Forsyth Park and headed back down Drayton in silence. A horse-drawn carriage passed us, and the driver tipped his hat. Tim jutted his chin. After a minute, he said, shyly, "You look great, by the way. I really, *really,* like your hair."

"Oh, thanks," I said, touching it. "I'm getting used to it."

"So where did you go...after...?"

"Oh...California. I left the day after, with my dad. I was actually never planning to come back here."

"Never? Because of me? Ivy—"

"But then my mom..."

Tim studied me, renewed pain on his face. He shook his head. "I'm so sorry about Bree," he said. "I...I couldn't believe it. I heard what happened on the radio, but I didn't know she died until Mom called tonight. I was working. I tried to get off early, but..."

I looked at him. "It's...it's...it feels *sooo* weird. So completely wrong."

We stopped, and Tim looked at me with tears shining in his eyes, and of course that got me crying, too. When he held his arms out to me, I almost walked into them. Almost. Heaven knows I needed a strong place to fall apart, a safe place. Unfortunately, my dear Tim was neither one of those things, and we both knew it.

I looked at him, then stepped back from his invitation and brushed my tears away trying not to see the sting of my rejection in his eyes. "I'm okay," I said, sniffing. "I'll be okay. Eventually..."

"You *do* hate me," he said in a raspy voice.

I shook my head. "No. No, I don't. I just don't think I trust you with my hurt right now. It's probably because I don't love you anymore...so I'm...you know..."

The saddest tear filled his eye, then rolled down his cheek. It was a little heartbreaking. And after a few beats of neither of us saying anything, I looped my arm through his and we walked the rest of the way back in silence, because what else was there to talk about really? At his car, I gave Tim a little hug because he seemed to need one. He cried into my neck and truth be told, I cried, too. It was all very sad and felt very final. But a little bit good, too, freeing. Which was quite surprising.

After Tim drove away, I did not know what to do with myself. I wasn't ready to go back to Geneva's, but I wasn't sure I wanted to spend the night here. So, I walked across the street to Chippewa

Square and sat down on the bench facing my home—Mama's home. Bree used to tell me how lucky I was to have two addresses, two phone numbers, two bedrooms—two lives, really. And I guess I was. It's what happens, I suppose, when you're raised by two generations.

There were still a few tourists roaming the streets at almost 11:30, which I found comforting. The shops were closed, of course, and the restaurants, but the bars on the river front would be open for hours. Of course, the ghost tours were still doing their creepy business. Savannah was known for being a city of extreme paranormal activity. I'd never experienced any, but I wouldn't have minded a little tonight. I gazed up at the statue of James Oglethorpe—Savannah's founder and guardian of Chippewa Square. "Where were you when Mama needed you?" I whispered, fresh tears filling my eyes, blurring everything into a buttery glow.

It was the fireflies. I hadn't even noticed them. They were everywhere, glimmering up the shrubs at Oglethorpe's feet, the trees, the bushes.

When I was a little girl, Mama and I used to come out here, sit on this very bench and watch them. Make wishes. She'd make up outlandish stories about their magical powers and where they went when they left for the season—some secret location where they weaved your dreams true.

She used to tell me they were very, very busy conjuring up the perfect someone worthy of my heart.

Ivy in Stills - 277

Fifty-Five—Bo

The day had been long and not easy. But I'd made it with no pill, so I felt a bit triumphant. I'd come close to taking one somewhere in Oklahoma, but I'd powered through and I was pretty proud of myself. The truth was I'd never ventured this far alone before, and it was hard. Probably more significantly, I'd never ventured this far *into* alone before, and that was harder. The view from here was overwhelming with its reflections and questions. *What was I doing out here by myself* was still at the forefront of my thoughts. But I wasn't really alone. A therapist would say I'd taken care of business when I asked Mia to inform my parents of what was happening. Of course, the predictable result was that Mom had blown up my phone. But that was okay. That kept me tethered.

I actually ended up having a fairly long conversation with the amazing Eileen: friend, support, confidant, and worried mama. It was just outside of Oklahoma City when panic was creeping up on me. And not so surprisingly, Mom said all the right things. She's good that way. She even seemed to grasp my reasoning for crossing the country as well as getting the liberating side dish of challenging myself. She said she was proud of me, which sounded a little too mothery and obligatory, but she echoed my sister in her certainty that I could do this. So, whether she meant it or not, Mom's words were just what I needed to hear.

But that had been hours ago. Now it was dark and very late, and I was hungry and battling myself in this parking lot in Carlisle, Arkansas where my critical reverie flowed unfiltered. It was disturbing and a little frightening. I looked around feeling vulnerable and very isolated. I didn't even know for sure where I was, but I did know I was someplace I'd never been, nor dreamed of being, motivated by circumstances I would never have imagined for myself. A girl and a favor I could not live up to and a burning need to prove something to her. Why?

Was it love? This was another question that had plagued me for hours. Did I love Ivy Talbot? And was that even possible for someone like me? And how would I even know since I had virtually no experience in this realm, no tool of measurement. I didn't know the protocol, and the whole question of worthiness confused me—mine, not hers. And what about timing? Wasn't it supposed to take months, if not years, to determine something this life-changing? So, with all that in the mix, how was I supposed to decipher what was real? And if it was love, was I supposed to be this utterly riddled with conflict?

Clearly, if this was *it*, I was doing it wrong.

I blew out a noisy breath. I was starving, and I had been for long enough that it was making me a little weak, perhaps even a little nuttier than usual. I also had a pretty good headache, but that might have been the thought war going on in my brain, and of course I had to pee. I sighed, truly dreading my only choice, and got out of the car. The sign flashing in the window of the Pancake Pavilion said "Open 24 Hours." I grimaced as I walked through the door. I'd passed better options. Dozens. But I was quite discriminating when it came to restaurants and made it a rule, when possible, to familiarize myself with the latest results of their health inspection. But since I'd not reached this critical point of deprivation before a quarter to three in the morning—of I didn't even know what day—I'd glibly driven through Little Rock and undoubtedly much more palatable alternatives.

A small chalkboard at the entrance read 'Please Seat Yourself,' and it took me several minutes of intense table scrutiny to finally decide on a remote booth near the window. But as I sat, the faux leather upholstery of my seat felt as nauseatingly sticky as all the other options. If there'd been anything in my stomach at all, I think I may have vomited.

A gray-haired waitress who seemed to have been enjoying my weirdness approached my booth with a smile. "We here to stay?" she said. "Or would you like to check out our conference room down the hall?"

I offered her no reaction. "I'm a little picky, but I guess this will do."

"Whatever floats your boat, hon." She winked and handed me a menu.

I was sitting on a biohazard with only a thin layer of denim as protection between me and it, and I refused to further tempt fate by handling the plastic-coated germ farm she was proffering. I looked at her without accepting it. "Do you have anything...packaged? Unopened? Anything at all?"

"Like cereal?" she said. "I have little boxes of cereal. Oh, and chips. I have chips. And we have candy bars up front."

"What about bottled water?"

She nodded.

"What brand?"

"Whatever Costco sells. And I have bottled green tea, too."

I sighed. "Okay. I'll take that."

"What?"

"The tea. The cereal. Can you bring me four or five? Unopened."

"Do you want an assortment?"

"Sure."

"Chips?"

"Ummmm, maybe not the chips. But bring me a couple of bottles of water, I guess. Do you have any canned Coke?"

"Pepsi."

"Bring me three, please."

"Okay then," she grinned. "I won't even have to wake my cook. He's going to love you."

I lifted a brow, which was the best I could do. "Could you tell me where your restroom is?"

She pointed and walked away.

As restaurant restrooms go, this one wasn't bad. But I still used an entire travel package of wet-wipes to get in and out of it. Thank you, Mia.

I sat back down in my chosen booth—this time on the other side, it didn't help—feeling infinitely more comfortable. Bladder-wise, at least. From the window I stared into utter desolation. Dark, no foreseeable landmarks. No signs of life. A night full of silence with only the choir of critics pummeling my gray matter for company. But that was okay; I knew them. They were in check. If it wasn't so late—or early—I would have called Mia. She would love another opportunity to define all of this for me and listening to her would be a nice change from listening to myself. Besides, I wanted to know if she'd heard from Derek. But that would inevitably lead to a definition of her own experiences, which would be sort of useless to me. No, this, *this* was *my* quest—figuratively and literally—and though I really craved the sound of a familiar voice, I knew I was just tired. Unless...Maybe Lullaby, again. What time was it in France?

The waitress returned and blew up my reverie with a tray full of packaged cereal. Little boxes of Cheerios, Fruit Loops, and Corn Flakes. Two of each. And three small cartons of milk with straws. She winked. "You seem like a straw guy."

I nodded, appreciating her. There was also water, tea, Pepsi, and a handful of candy bars.

"Thought I'd give you some choices," she said, with a smile.

She may as well have presented me with a gourmet dinner of stuffed Cuckoo Marans, it all looked *that* good. "Thank you," I said. "Do you have some plastic utensils, by chance?"

She reached into her apron and pulled out a handful of packaged spoons. And I went to town on a box of Cheerios—breaking it open at the perforated markings, tearing into the wax enclosure to the

Ivy in Stills - 281

cereal—all very hygienic by General Mills standards, I'm sure. I poured the milk right into the box and tried not to obsess about where the spoon had come from. I wolfed down both boxes of Cheerios and both boxes of Corn Flakes in record time. I'm not particularly proud of that since I'm not really a wolfer, but I could feel the microbes teeming beneath me, imagined them infiltrating the thin fiber of my jeans. I also sucked all three cartons of milk dry and asked for everything else to go when the waitress wandered back to check on me.

She put it all in a paper bag and I handed her my credit card as I stood up.

She looked at her watch. "Eleven minutes flat. You must be in a hurry, hon."

"You could say that." I tipped her ten dollars because she didn't make me feel as stupid as she could have.

Fifty-Six—Ivy

I woke up on Mama's bed, wondering momentarily how I got there. Momentarily, I was back in Monterey. That's where I wanted to be, waking up in a pool house, talking myself into a swim. But then my new reality descended on me like a bucket of warm tears, and I couldn't believe I had abandoned my grandmother for an entire night. How could I have done that?

After Tim had left, I'd fully intended to leave, too. But I wanted something of Mama's, I didn't even know what, her perfume, her pillow, her ratty slippers? I don't know, just something. So, I'd come back up here and apparently fallen asleep on her bed crying into her pillow...which smelled like her perfume.

I'm terrible. I am an awful, awful granddaughter and that's what I spilled forth when Geneva finally answered her phone. "I am so sorry, Gran. I fell asleep, which is shocking to me because I fully intended to come back to your house."

"Darling girl. Darling, darling girl. I did the same thing. It's been a hell of a few days, and they've taken their toll. We deserved it. Worry not about this old gal. How are you?"

I sighed. "I think I'm okay. Maybe I feel a little...*amputated*. But I think I'm okay."

Oh, Ivy girl, that is exactly how I feel. Amputated." Her voice wobbled, and then she started to cry. And then my grandmother let go of a gush of emotion that pierced my heart. Her pain crawled through the phone line and made it impossible not to hurt with her. We cried together for good long minute, and in the middle of it, I told her I was coming home. "I'm leaving now Gran. I'll be there in twenty minutes."

Fifty-Seven—Mia

What a difference a day can make. Well, actually almost two. Yesterday morning, I woke up miserable, no viable final project, the love of my life ignoring me, and my brother...*my brother*. This afternoon, at the end of a grueling week, I have a final project, accepted by my committee of professors and even better, blessed by one Kyle Donohue. More importantly, I heard from Derek's commanding officer that my D had been in the infirmary being treated for a shoulder injury. Infuriatingly, the man had left no details other than Derek's insistence that he make contact with me to let me know that he was fine and would be in touch soon. My first thought was he must have gotten my email. My second thought was that I'd meant every word—no regrets. My third was: Shoulder injury? Did that mean bullet wound? Snake bite? Shattered bones from falling out of a plane? I blinked back tears. If I didn't have ninety-nine other things to distract me, I knew I would have curled up in a corner and obsessively chewed on my hair.

My phone rang, and I was never so grateful for the interruption. Even if it was Bo.

"Hey. Did you get to Savannah?" I said.

My brother barked out a cryptic laugh. "No. And at this rate, who knows."

"What's going on? What does that mean?"

Heavy sigh. "My car broke down in Crab Orchard, Tennessee. I was lucky to limp off the freeway. Triple A took two hours to get to me, and then I sat in a plastic waiting room watching Dr. Phil reruns for four-and-a-half hours until they told me it couldn't be fixed until tomorrow."

"What?"

"Kill me, now. I mean it, Mia. Kill me now."

"What's wrong with your car?"

Heavier sigh. "Radiator pump. Supposedly easy fix, except they had to order the part from Nashville, which is two-and-a-half hours away but might as well be Tibet. Four-and-a-half hours, Mia. On a plastic chair in a plastic room. I offered to Uber to Nashville and pick it up for them, but no. Against company policy. Apparently."

"Where are you now?"

"I'm in hell. And by hell, I mean a place called The Roll Inn in Crossville—about twenty minutes from my car. Nice woman, terrible room. The best I could do was beg her for as many towels as she would allow me and spread them over the sheets. I'm lying here, fully dressed, on a layer of threadbare terrycloth staring at a stained ceiling."

I bit my lip to keep from audibly groaning. I didn't care, which makes me an awful sister. "I'm sorry..." I managed. "What about your car?"

"They'll bring it to me in the morning, is what they said. I'll believe it when I see it."

"Well...slight setback. You just have to get through tonight. Right? You can do that. You probably need the sleep anyway."

"I do!" he bit. "But that's not going to happen here!"

"Oh, stop. Is there a convenience store you can walk to?"

"I don't know!"

"Hey! Tone. Find out. Get something to eat, grab some Excedrin PM—or better yet, take a Xanax because I know you haven't. Go to sleep. It's not the end of the world."

"I hate it when you're glib, Mia."

"I hate it when *nothing* is more important than you. Get over yourself!"

"Well, thank you very much," he said with more tone. "This isn't hard for me or anything."

I shook my head, wearily. "Bo, life is supposed to be hard—builds character, remember? But the good news is by this time tomorrow you'll probably be there, so buck up." I hung up on him, frustrated and bothered. I knew it was because of Derek…and perspective…and my annoying brother who had none. He must have figured it out because he immediately called back. I didn't pick up because I was feeling snotty. I just texted what had happened to Derek and that I didn't have anything else to say right now. Bo texted back that he was sorry he was a jerk.

I let him be sorry for a minute. Then I texted back, "Me, too."

After that, I tried to call Ivy. Again. We'd missed each other twice, and as her phone rang and rang, it looked like it was going to be three times. When she said to leave a message, I left the same one as last time: "Your turn, girl. I hope you're okay. I'm here. Call when you get a chance."

I hung up wanting to cry. I definitely wanted to check on her and everything she was going through. But if I'm being completely honest, I also really needed a friend.

Derek, Bo, Camille, Ivy, Lullaby, my globe-trotting besties—all M.I.A. at the moment, and I was feeling it. It's not like I didn't have any other friends I could call tonight, but somehow that seemed like too much work. I sighed. It looked like it was going to be a mope and movie night with plenty of cookie dough on the side. And if I got ambitious, I would try and whittle down my collection of Ivy photos to the twenty I would use for my capstone project.

I wasn't optimistic.

Fifty-Eight—Mia

The next morning, I was just finishing laps—I'd done an extra ten to atone for the tube of chocolate chunk cookie dough I'd nearly polished off watching *Me and Earl and The Dying Girl*—when my phone rang. It was Ivy.

"Hey! Is this really you?" I panted.

"Hey. I know, we keep missing each other. But it's Sunday, and I figured you'd either still be sleeping or doing laps, and I might catch you."

"Just getting out of the pool. What about you? What are you doing?"

"I'm making Gran a peach smoothie, then I'm headed out. I have to go to the mortuary."

I swallowed. "How are you, Ivy? Dumbest question on the planet, but...how are you? Really?"

She sniffed. "Hug your mom, Mia. That's how I am."

"I'm so sorry."

"Me, too," she said, her voice soft.

"So...the funeral," I said. "When is it?"

"Tuesday. One o'clock. Yesterday we spent all day making arrangements and planning the service. Letting people know. I went shopping and bought Mama a dress that turns out I knew she would surely hate for all of eternity."

Despite myself, I laughed. "I doubt that."

"No, it's true. I can't believe I went to five stores searching for the perfect dress for my very particular dead mother. I thought I hit paydirt, but when I took it over to the mortuary and laid it on top of her, it was sooo wrong. Before I go back there, I'm headed over to rake through Mama's closet. I'm hoping I'll be inspired to make the right choice." Ivy sniffed. "It doesn't seem real, Mia. None of this can be real, but it is."

"It doesn't seem real," I echoed.

She cleared her throat and rallied. "Anyway...and then sometime today, I have to get over to the cemetery to clean up our family lot. Gran said she'd get Everett—her neighbor—over there to do some tidying but he's like a-hundred-and-ten, and that just doesn't seem right."

"Do you mind if I come?" I blurted.

"To the cemetery?"

"To your mom's funeral?"

"What? *What?* Are you kidding? I would love that! But...but you don't have to do that, Mia."

"I want to. I really do. I just don't want to impose..."

"Please impose! We have so much room! Yes, yes! Please, please come. Can you bring Bo?" Ivy caught herself then tried to cover with a chuckle. "I'm sorry, that was stupid. I'm so stupid, of course you can't. He doesn't fly."

"Right...he doesn't fly—how...how do you know that?"

"Oh, Mia. I did something so awful. I asked him to come home with me. He'd just told me about my mama and that he'd booked me on that late flight, and I just desperately didn't want to be alone. I wasn't thinking, and I begged him to come with me. I put him in a terrible position, and he was so embarrassed..."

"Oh, Ivy..." I said, realization washing over me.

"He told me he absolutely could not fly. But I didn't believe him, and I pressed him, and I think...I think I've ruined everything. I think I drove a spike through our friendship and now he won't answer my calls or text me back. I think he hates me."

"Oh...Oh Ivy, that's ridiculous, I'm sure he's just been busy," I said lamely because of course I couldn't tell her what I knew. I couldn't tell her Bo was probably within hours of Savannah as we spoke. "If it makes you feel any better," I said. "No one has seen or heard much of him for the last few days," I fibbed.

"Is he okay?"

Trust Ivy to be concerned about someone else—anyone else—at a time like this. I didn't want her to say anything else I might have to lie about so I blurted, "Ivy, my battery is nearly dead. But I'll get on the same flight tomorrow night that you took, which gets in, what at 8:30ish the next morning?"

"I think so. 8:35."

"Great. I'll have Camille pick me up."

Ivy blew a breath of shaky emotion into the phone. "Thank you, Mia. Again, this is so totally not necessary. But I can't wait to hug you," she said in her drawl.

"Oh, we'll hug! I'll see you Tuesday."

"Remember what I said," she said.

"What?"

"Call your mama," Ivy said. "Tell her you love her."

"I will." When the line went dead, emotion was stinging my eyes. It was Bo, it was Ivy and Bree, it was Mom.

I pressed the #2 on my screen—speed dial for my mother. I knew she was running, so I wasn't surprised to get her voicemail. "Mom," I said after her greeting. "Just thinking about you, and I wanted to tell you thanks again for the airfare. And...I just love you! I don't think I tell you that enough, but I do." My voice cracked, and for a moment I couldn't say anything else. Then I rallied...a bit. "I'm leaving for Savannah tomorrow night, and I could use a ride to the airport. I'll buy you dinner. Let me know if you can help me out, Mom. Did I say I love you? Have a good run. Hug Dad."

Fifty-Nine—Ivy

Bonaventure Cemetery is famous thanks to John Berendt and his novel *Midnight in the Garden of Good and Evil*. And because of that, the massive graveyard is annoyingly high on the list of tourist attractions in Savannah. It has been dubbed as hauntingly beautiful, quintessentially Southern gothic, inspiring, and other pretty words—and parts of it are. It sits on an old plantation and is now a hundred acres of dead bones buried beneath live oaks that drip with Spanish moss. I'd always thought it was a very creepy place, and though I hadn't been here for months, it hadn't changed. It was still creepy. I parked at the turnabout and headed on foot down aisle K5 to our family lot, a bucket of supplies slung over my shoulder. It was quiet this afternoon, except for the cemetery birds, and it was a pretty end-of-July day, so the creepiness factor wasn't terrible. In truth, I didn't mind being here right now; things were a little too *deliberate* at Geneva's.

I followed the dirt road until the angel came into view. Like a monarch, she stood regally atop the Talbot Family Arch, six feet tall with carved wings, braided hair, and holding a basket of flowers. She was exquisite and had been commissioned by my great-great-grandparents when their two-year-old daughter, Charlotte, died of yellow fever in 1907. Her brother, Simon, was one of four siblings interred here along with their parents and two spouses. Simon was my great grandfather. Titus Legrand Talbot, TL, was my grandfather and the love of Geneva's life. They were all buried here on this 12-space plot. My mother would take space number 11, then Geneva. I would have to find other accommodations, which left me both bereft and relieved.

I stepped through the gate onto our designation, which was cordoned off by concrete slabs, and walked to the arch. The angel still had a beautiful face despite being over a century old. She was nestled in an enormous bouquet of Palmetto fronds, and the rich green against the glistening white marble made you forget about the dry and dead things everywhere else. The angel had always seemed a gentle emissary, and I felt certain comfort now standing at her feet.

I looked around. It was shaded in this corner of the cemetery, which Bree would appreciate since she hated the heat. Her marker would resemble the rest of those arranged on this parcel—stark white stone with just her name, dates, and who she belonged to carved in a classic font. It would be undoubtedly lovely, but so...*insufficient*. The history buried beneath my feet, my mother to be added to it on Tuesday, this space, these simple markers, it all seemed a sadly inadequate honor for the lives lived and the impact made by these people. My people. I looked up at the angel again. Thank goodness Bree—and all of them—would be sheltered by this beautiful effigy. That was something special, anyway.

I had about an hour before the diggers were supposed to be here, so I got to work manicuring around the stone markers and sweeping off the bird droppings. We were fortunate at the top of Aisle K to be in close proximity to a spigot, so I filled my bucket and rinsed off the headstones. Then I got on my knees and started wiping them down with a rag. I was pretty lost in this task, so I was startled to hear my name. And even more so when I turned to see who had spoken it.

He stood there like an apparition, a little rumpled, badly in need of a shave, his untamed hair held back with his sunglasses. He didn't smile, and his eyes searched me, seemingly looking for open wounds. "Bo?"

He walked toward me, and I was overcome by where I was and his presence in the same place. "What...?" I got to my feet. "What's happened? How...what are you doing here?"

"Your grandmother said you'd be here. She gave me directions."

I stared at him, open-mouthed, and started to cry. "What?"

He stepped close to me. "Ivy...I...I..."

I couldn't help myself. I wrapped my arms around him and pulled him close, and when he didn't resist, when his arms came around me, too, I pulled him closer. I had never been so happy to see anybody in my life, and I prayed I wasn't dreaming. We fit together perfectly, my wet cheek pressed against his neck, my arms up under his, my hands clinging to his shoulders. I shut my eyes and breathed him in, unable to fathom how empty I had felt without him. And for his part, Bo Sutton held me like he could drown if he loosened his grip. "Are you really here?" I said on a little sob.

"I'm really here."

I did not want to let go, and it seemed he didn't either, so we just held tight to one another, our only audience the marble angel.

"Bo..." I whispered into his neck. "How did you get here? Here? To Georgia?"

"I drove."

I swallowed and pulled back to look at him in surprise. "You drove? Across the country? Why would you do that?"

He shook his head and his eyes got watery. "I let you down, Ivy," he said with shame. "When you asked me to come with you, I let you down and...and I just couldn't live with myself until I made that right. So, I'm here...to make it right. If I can. I'm sorry, Ivy. I'm sorry I'm a freak. I should have faced my demons and just gotten on that plane and..."

Tears were rolling and breathing was hard, and I couldn't really grasp what I was hearing. But then I did, and everything stopped.

"You love me," I said, surprising both of us. "It sounds like you might love me, Bo Sutton."

He didn't flinch. He just looked at me with sure and unapologetic eyes. He was a little rugged at the moment—nicely rugged—and with such intensity in his expression that I was frankly alarmed.

"Ivy," he said. "I'm standing here in desperate need of a shower. I've peed in public restrooms in six states, I've eaten gas station nachos—well, one, and I spit it out, but still. I've slept in my car. I've slept on towels of dubious cleanliness in the worst motel on the planet. I've had these clothes on for so many hours that they need to be burned."

I stifled a smile.

"I didn't know I was headed here when I left, but somewhere along the way I realized I had to find you. I *had* to. Nothing else mattered. I don't have much experience with love—none, actually—but I don't think what's going on with me could be anything else."

I looked at him, weak in my heart. Was I dreaming? I had to be dreaming! Two minutes ago, I had been cleaning bird poop off my ancestors' headstones. And two minutes later, this? I studied Bo's beautiful face without breathing, trying to catch up to what was happening. And then it hit me.

"I've been reading the book you gave me about the girl with the harelip. You think I'm her, don't you? I'm Prudence Sarn."

He shook his head. "No. I think that *you* think you're Prudence Sarn. I see you, Ivy. I see the *you* that you can't see yourself. And that girl is impossible not to love." He pulled back farther and took hold of my hands. Then, very calmly, he said, "But you don't have to love me back. That's not what this is. Not only because I'm *me* and I can't even imagine it, but because your life is so... *wounded* right now and I would never...I would *not* take advantage of that. Never. I'm just sorry, I'm so, so sorry, that when you needed me, I couldn't...I just want to make that right, if I can."

"Bo, you're doing it. My mama's dead, and you're here..." I whispered tearfully.

"I am...."

"Can you just hold me?"

"I can do that," he said. And then he pulled me back into his arms.

I laid my head on his shoulder like I'd found its true home, and for a long time, we were quiet, except for the noise in my head. *I don't need to love him back?* Who was this man?

"When?" I said at length. "When did you see the *me* I can't see myself?"

"Oh, Ivy..." he breathed. "I hadn't known you five minutes, and you were helping me clean the lawn furniture in the middle of the night without thinking I was a fool. The day you talked me through my panic attack. When you brought me tea and tried to make me feel better by comparing my humiliation to your *backyard*. When my family was in crisis and my nieces were scared and you just...rescued them. When you told me to *suck it up, buttercup* and dry the dishes..." He chuckled. "I probably knew right then. And when you told me about your parents without any bitterness. And Tim...without any hatred. And you saved my sister from her insane husband. Do you need more? I have more."

I sniffled. "I think that answers my question. Thank you."

He hugged me tighter. "You see an imperfect package," he said softly. "Which is in no way imperfect, Ivy. I see every beautiful, honest thing about you."

"Oh, goodness, Bo. I don't know what to say."

"You don't have to say anything."

"I think I do...I'm not sure if you realize this, Bo, but I am not the only Prudence in our story. I see you, too. And you are really quite somethin'."

He didn't say anything, but I felt him shudder. So, for a long minute I just held onto him and this feeling of complete and utter peace.

Finally, I said into his neck, "You really peed in a public restroom?"

"Several, actually," he said into mine. "And it was absolutely disgusting. But strangely liberating."

Ivy in Stills - 295

I laughed, but then I cried because I suddenly realized that where this man—*this man*—was concerned, there really could not be more powerful proof of his feelings for me.

"You must really love me," I said softly.

"Oh, Ivy. You have no idea."

Sixty—Mia

I hadn't been to too many funerals in my life, and in truth I wasn't looking forward to Bree Talbot's. But I was finally in Savannah, late—as in mechanical problems causing a two-hour delay in take-off—sleep-deprived, starving, but here. And I couldn't wait to see Ivy. I'd brushed my teeth in the airport bathroom, changed into a long black sleeveless dress, wound my hair into a loose mess behind one ear and donned some dangly earrings that didn't seem terribly inappropriate for the occasion. I looked pretty good, and a little lip-gloss helped.

As we'd agreed, Camille picked me up at the curb, and I thought I would die when I saw the girls. I climbed in the back and slobbered all over them, careful of Livvy's cast. But when the airport security van honked for us to move on, I jumped back in the front and hugged Camille. "Hey," I said.

Camille smiled. "Hey, yourself."

I eyed my sister—my beautiful sister—with surprise. "You look *great!*"

"Thanks. I feel good. This place, Geneva...Bree..." she shrugged, got tearful. "It's all been very healing...and a lot *clarifying.*"

I reached over and squeezed her hand, and she squeezed back.

"Did you know Bo's here?" she said.

"He made it," I said, relieved.

"You knew he was coming?"

"Not at first. And even he had his doubts that he'd make it—he made me promise not to tell. How is he?"

"He's...*good*. Better than I've seen him in a while," she said, pulling into traffic. "It's a little strange."

I looked over at my sister. "But he's okay?"

"I think so."

"You know, he drove all the way here because he was convinced that he'd let Ivy down," I said. "I think he loves her."

Camille nodded. "I think so, too. I have never seen him like this."

"Like what?"

"Like...kind of at ease. And focused outside of himself. If that makes sense."

"Really?"

Camille glanced over at me. "He hasn't really said much. I kind of get the impression that he's been through something huge. He's a little reflective, but somehow...like I said, he's very okay. Very concerned about Geneva. And, of course, Ivy."

"Hmmm. I still might have to strangle him," I breathed. "How are they? Ivy? How's Geneva?"

Camille sighed as she eased onto the freeway. "They're so injured, Mia. And both of them just want to take care of the other one. At first Geneva was doing the best, but now Ivy seems to be handling things a bit better. Maybe that has something to do with Bo being here."

"That could be," I agreed.

Because we were behind schedule, Camille drove straight to Our Lady of Good Hope Chapel near Geneva's home. The historic church was swarming with people, and for some reason it surprised me to see such a turnout. It also forced me to see Bree Talbot as a real person. Not just a mom who had hurt my friend or a shallow cliché who'd fallen for Daniel Proctor's wholly unoriginal lies, but as the architect of a real life, someone who'd accomplished real things and left her mark on the world. If funeral attendance was any indicator of respect and popularity, Bree Talbot seemed to have scored on both counts. We parked down the street and followed a small parade through a tunnel of live oaks to the church. The day was hot but breezy and absolutely lovely. I couldn't help myself. I set Olivia down—she'd hitched a ride on my hip—and unzipped my small camera from its case.

To silence her disapproval, I took a few shots of my sister. Through my lens, Camille looked amazing, like she hadn't looked in months. I had to stop and take her in to fully appreciate the change. She had gained back some badly needed weight and appeared to have a chest again, but better than that was the absence of worry that had furrowed her forehead for so long. She'd been here two weeks, but she looked like a new woman. Her plum-colored dress hugged her thin frame, and nude heels showcased her great legs. "I have to say, Camille, you look completely cured of the venereal disease that is your husband."

"Mia!"

I laughed and brought her shocked face into focus and snapped. "Only speaking the truth, my dear. I can't help it if Georgia looks really, *really* good on you."

She smiled despite herself. "I actually love it here. And the girls are absolutely thriving," she said as we crossed the street.

I spied Ivy on the steps of the church, chatting with a tall guy and a middle-aged couple. She was wearing a pink blouse and a grey pencil skirt that showed off her curves. She'd combed her new short hair off her face, and she was wearing sunglasses. I zoomed in on her and took several photos, then I stowed my camera. I didn't see Bo or Geneva anywhere. When Ivy saw me, her lip quivered, and she tried to smile, then she met me on the stairs where we had a little hug fest, with tears. "You really came," she said.

"I told you I would."

"I'm so glad you're here."

"Me, too."

She took my hand, "C'mere."

We walked back up the stairs, where Ivy said, "Mia, I want you to meet the Marshes. This is Bryce and Paula—dear, dear friends. This is Mia. I've been staying with her in Monterey."

I shook hands with them both. "Nice to meet you."

"And this is Tim," Ivy said, and for a second it did not click. But when I looked up into dark eyes that seemed distinctly uncomfortable, it did. I decided not to say *As in flakey, jerk-bob, almost-husband Tim?* but I knew that's exactly who he was. Instead, I shook his hand and said, not smiling, "I've heard a lot about you, Tim."

He nodded, a bit shamed. "I bet you have."

It occurred to me then that it had probably taken some courage for him to show up here today. Ivy had spoken of her profound humiliation in front of this community, and now that same community had shown up in droves to support her. I suddenly felt a little bad for Tim Marsh.

Inside the church, Camille found us seats, and I went in search of my brother. I found him in a receiving room chatting with Geneva, who was holding court near Bree's open casket. When Bo saw me, he seemed to relax, sort of like he'd been holding his breath and could now stop. It was a familiar reaction. But to Bo's credit, I doubted his anxiety was apparent to anyone but me. I waved and he nodded, still chatting. Geneva followed his gaze, and as I approached, she gave me a huge hug. "You sweet girl! Ivy told me you were coming. It means the world that you're here. I believe I now have a complete set of Sutton siblings, and I could not be happier." She steered me closer to the casket, which was arrayed with funeral sprays on every side. It was the centerpiece of the small room, completely unavoidable. I breathed deep. It seemed a strange tradition to gawk at the dead, but I walked over and gawked at the dead.

Ivy's mother was stunning, lying there fully made up, the platinum waves of her hair softening her arranged expression. There was absolutely no hint of the brokenness that was underneath the beautiful blue dress Ivy had chosen; someone had done a very good job. The dress was tight—or just tucked tight—around Bree Talbot, and she was wearing an enormous pendent that rested between her breasts. A matching set of bangles encircled one thin wrist, and her nails were freshly manicured. *Good choice, Ivy,* I thought, and again admired Bree Talbot's sense of style.

After Geneva's attention was claimed elsewhere, Bo sidled up next to me. "Can you believe where we're standing right now?"

"Weird, isn't it?" I said.

"It's a little disorienting," he said. "I can't believe how different the world seems here."

I slipped my arm through his. "You look nice. New suit?"

He looked down and nodded. "Not bad for off-the-rack. I didn't exactly pack anything before I left."

"Bo. What were you thinking?"

He sighed. "At first? So many things. Some you probably don't want to know, Mia."

His words suddenly froze in my brain, and I tugged on him to force eye contact. But he would not look at me. "Bo."

"Do you know that I've lived my whole life in a hamster wheel?" he said, his eyes fixed on Bree Talbot. "I'm almost twenty-eight years old, and I have never been out of my own head."

I couldn't argue that. "How does it feel?" I asked.

"It's a little terrifying. But I'm kind of managing, which sort of shocks me."

I took him in and saw a little of what Camille had described. "Are you okay? I've been worried about you."

He nodded, still not looking at me. "I am okay."

"Why wouldn't you talk to me?"

"I talked to you."

"I mean, why didn't you tell me why you left?"

"I couldn't. I was ashamed. I didn't know what I was doing—you wanted answers. I had none. Until I did." Finally, he looked over at me and offered a weak smile.

"Bo..."

"I'm okay, Mia. Actually, I think I might be more okay than I've ever been."

"Care to elaborate...on any of that?" I said, sort of pleading.

Bo shook his head and looked back at Ivy's mother. Then he reached in the casket and lightly touched the pendent lying on her chest. "Impressive work, don't you think?"

Sixty-One—Ivy

That night, we were sitting on Geneva's front porch swing, just her and me. Mia was in the parlor looking through a stack of my grandmother's old photo albums, and Bo had gone with Camille to pick up some ice cream. Ice cream seemed a bit of a sacrilege, somehow, after the day we'd had, but Geneva said it was just what we needed. Of course, the fridge and the freezer were stuffed full of neighbor offerings, and Sylvia Turner from over on Parkersburg had just dropped off bread fresh from her oven. Geneva took my hand. "Nothing says you're well thought of better than hot bread baked on a hot night. That's saying something."

I smiled and laid my head on her shoulder. "They love you."

"They love *us*," she corrected.

"Yes, they do." I thought of the pure kindness and worry that had been extended to me over these past few days. Love in its cleanest form. I don't know what I'd thought would happen when I came back here, because of course I had never planned to come back and find out. But I certainly had not expected that the collective embrace of these wonderful people would so fully cure my hurt and humiliation. The truth was, all that had happened at my wedding didn't matter as much as I thought it would in light of everything that had happened since. I guess it's true that the best painkiller is a worse pain.

"How are you holding up, sweetie?" my grandmother said.

"I'm...I don't know... Depends on the minute," I said. "How 'bout you?"

She sighed. "Well, I'm tired enough to sleep. And I haven't cried since the cemetery. That feels like progress."

"Yes, it does."

She turned to me and smiled sadly. "I want to say something to you, sug, before too much more time passes."

"Okay," I said, looking up at her.

"I do not want you to be mad at your mama. I've been worried since we talked about her in the hospital, and the last thing I want is for you to harbor ill feelings toward her. Lord knows you have every right, but I don't want you wasting time on that. Won't hurt her a lick, but the same cannot be said for you."

"I'm not mad at her."

"And I'm not old." Geneva nudged me with her shoulder.

"I don't think I'm mad at her," I said again. "I mean, I will never understand her exactly, but it was her life. That she seemed to waste so much of it on Daniel...who has a whole other family..." I felt suddenly gut-punched all over again. "Maybe I am a little mad."

Geneva patted my hand. "We just get one heart, sug. If we're smart, we guard it, make sure we give it to someone worthy of it. But our Bree was not careful, and to make her feel better about not being careful, I think she told herself pretty lies until they sounded like truth."

"I know." I swallowed hard, thinking of Liz Proctor. I thought of my father professing his love to two women at the same time, making two daughters. Pretty lies... But hadn't I fallen for the same exact lies with Tim as my mother had with Daniel? I couldn't even imagine the shape I'd be in if my storybook day had actually panned out. I shuddered. "I'm not so different, Gran," I said.

"Are you talking about Timothy?"

"I thought that was love," I said.

"No, you didn't. Not in your heart of hearts."

That pinched. "He's sorry, you know," I said softly.

"Of course he is. Most fools have regrets."

I tried to laugh. "Mom said I dodged a bullet."

Geneva nodded. "You did. But let's not forget the Universe shot the gun. And She did it for a reason. Tim's a nice enough boy—an idiot, but a nice one. And I think you can thank him for showing you your life."

"What do you mean?"

"I mean, thanks to Tim Marsh, you know things now that you didn't know before. Important things about what love is and what it isn't. Your route to that realization was painful, and I'm sorry about that. But I think your destiny might be coming into view."

"Oh, Gran..." I said, wondering if she'd been talking to Bo, wondering if all this was a just a ruse to get me chatting about him.

"What I mean, dear girl," she said, "Is that your life's possibilities are spread before you as far as your eyes can see. Happiness is out there, Ivy. So is love. And you are not your mama."

"Thanks, Gran."

She reached over and patted my face.

"Bo says he loves me," I said after a long silence.

"I think that's lovely."

"But he says I don't have to love him back. He came all this way to tell me he loved me, never expecting to hear me say it back to him. What kind of man does that?"

"It would seem one without pretense. Or agenda," Geneva said.

No pretense. Yes, that described Bo perfectly. He was a man who lived *in the raw*, I thought, borrowing a term I'd heard from Adam Pembroke. It meant his focus was mostly inward on his creativity, controlling his world, being productive, meeting his raw needs, which sometimes meant simply surviving the day. He was complex and fascinating, and he certainly had his challenges. But the Bo Sutton I'd come to know over these past weeks did not strike me as a man capable of telling pretty lies for any reason. And in that light, what he'd said to me suddenly overwhelmed me. Thankfully, just when I thought I would cry, the screen door opened, and Mia walked onto the porch.

"Am I interrupting?"

"Not at all," my grandmother said, oblivious to my musings. "Come sit with us; enjoy the breeze off the river."

I nodded because that was all I could muster at the moment.

Mia smiled. "Can I get you anything? A drink? Slice of hot bread?"

"Thank you, no, sweet girl," said Geneva.

I shook my head and managed to say, "I'm never eating again."

Mia laughed. She was still wearing her black flowy dress, but she'd let her hair down, and she wasn't wearing any shoes. In her arms was a thick photo album, her index finger keeping her place.

"Did you find something?" I said.

She sat down next to me and opened the book. "Tell me about this picture of you."

Geneva and I both leaned over. "Oh, that was taken right down there on the pier," my grandmother said, pointing across the street. "But I can't recall what made you so sad, Ivy girl."

For me, the memory was instantaneous. It was my sixth birthday, and my mother was going away for the weekend. She was going with my father, and I wasn't invited, so I'd been dropped off with Geneva, who was throwing me a cupcake party to make it all better. But I'd thrown a little fit and marched myself down to the pier to avoid the all-out rejection of my parents' leaving. Daniel had followed me. He had his camera and kept trying to make me smile, promising he'd come back with a big old birthday present. He even promised that he'd teach me to swim before he flew back home. I didn't believe him, and I wouldn't smile, and he took the picture anyway. This picture. Taken at dusk, a little forlorn me, my hair blowing across my face, the sunset reflected in my sad eyes.

I made a laugh sound. "Oh, that was just me wanting to go on a trip with my parents," I told Mia. "But I wasn't invited. Daniel took it."

"Really?" Mia looked at the photo again. "That explains the heartbreak on that little face."

I nodded. "Well, at least he promised to teach me to swim. He never did, but...he promised."

"Another stellar reason to wish an incurable rash in unreachable places on your dad."

Geneva laughed. I did too.

Mia went back to the picture again. "It's amazing because all the elements are perfect, the lighting, the angle, the movement, the subject. And I'm betting your dorky dad had no idea what he was doing."

"Oh, I don't think he ever knew what he was doing," I said, being snarky.

"Unintentional brilliance from Daniel Proctor," Mia said shaking her head. "Can I borrow this?"

I shrugged. "Take whatever you want."

"Really?" She eyed Geneva for confirmation. "There are a few I'd love to steal—but just for a couple of weeks. I'll guard them with my life and send them back unscathed. I promise."

"Then they're yours," I smiled.

Geneva arched a brow. "Unscathed."

"I promise."

Sixty-Two—Bo

The difference between being able to sleep on sheets whose history is unknown to me and not being able to sleep on them is Xanax. The difference between being able to shower in a bathroom whose history is unknown to me and not being able to shower in it is also usually Xanax. It had likewise been a major factor in my being able to drive across the country wearing dirty clothes. Of course, none of that had been on my mind when I left California with three bottles from my medicine cabinet—and nothing else. At the time, I had simply been overwhelmed and wanted to disappear. I had been thinking I had nowhere to go and plenty of time to get there, and no one would miss me because what good was I?

I've never been suicidal in the strictest sense. But there were many miles of obsessive solitude when I knew the reason I'd grabbed three bottles of Xanax had little to do with controlling my anxiety. I drove in this state of mind for quite a while. Blew off Mia's calls. Blew off Mom's calls. Blew off Ivy's calls. But for some reason, I eventually called Lullaby. And finally, when the impulse to escape my self-loathing began to dissipate, I was simply grateful. I was grateful because, strangely, even in my self-destructive state, I did not take a single pill. I simply took comfort in the fact that I had the tiny benzos in my possession; they were there if I *needed* them.

Xanax had been prescribed for me for years, and for years I had filled the prescription. But I only took it in what I considered to be emergency situations. Certainly, full blown panic was an emergency, and the aura of a panic attack coming on usually gave me time to consider medicating myself. Unless it didn't. I always carried one. So did Mia and Camille and each of my parents. Everyone knew how effective Xanax was for my condition. Even me.

And yet...Part of my particular weirdness is my need to control what I can control. When I'm successful, when my day goes as predetermined, when I limit my distractions, when my world is clean and organized, I don't get anxious, and therefore I don't need the pill. But when new things enter the picture, things outside of my control, I balance precariously on the blade of my two choices—debilitation or drugs. I often choose to be debilitated because I hate needing drugs. The needing somehow shames me. The needing makes me feel *less than*. I also have an irrational fear of becoming a drug addict, which I've been told for years is patently ridiculous. Four milligrams of Xanax per day is the high therapeutic threshold. I can get by on a half a milligram, repeated in an hour if I'm not back in control. And I take great pride in only succumbing on occasion. Like in extreme circumstances that necessitate sleeping in sheets whose history is unknown to me. Oh, and the turmoil of being in love with Ivy Talbot.

I'd explained all of this to Camille—well, not all of it—and she was nodding because she'd heard most of it before. We were driving in search of ice cream. Now she reached over and squeezed my elbow. "I know how much you hate taking them," she said maternally. "But can I just say—you seem more comfortable in your skin than I've seen you in a while. That's got to feel amazing for a change."

"It does...but I will have reached the pinnacle of feeling amazed when I feel amazed without pharmaceutical assistance."

"There is no shame..."

"I know...it's just a personal goal. But thanks for the props. I could say the same thing to you," I said.

"What?"

"You look pretty okay in your own skin. I haven't seen you this stress-free since...*forever*."

She looked over at me and smiled. "Being here has given me some badly needed perspective."

"What are you going to do?" I asked.

She blew out a sigh. "I'm not sure, but I know I'm not going back to him. Can you believe I have choices, Benjamin?" She looked over at me again, this time with a film of tears.

"I have a confession," I said.

"What did you do now?" she groaned.

"I told Lullaby about you. I called her the day after you left because...well, she needed to know where you were."

Camille laughed. "I know. She called me, and we talked for a long time. I told her all about Peter. And I told her about Geneva and Bree and Ivy and that I was in Savannah saving my life. She told me you had called. That was sweet of you."

"Did she lecture you?"

"No. She just said it was about time."

"Signature Lully," I mused.

She was our touchstone, our aunt—mine, Camille's, certainly Mia's. We adored our parents and were adored in return, but Lullaby was our cheerleader, our advocate, a bit of a warrior on our behalf. It's why she'd insisted I set up shop in her basement until I could decide about a loft—she knew I wasn't functioning under that blade. She was my confidant and my base coach, and she cheered me on until I made it to Georgia. I did not tell my sister that Lully was the one who kept the thoughts of me snacking on my Xanax at bay. I didn't tell her that Lully was the one who had talked me off the cliff before I was even out of California. And I never would because then I'd have to admit that for a while, there actually *had been* a cliff.

But because Lullaby was so far away, so far removed, and so willing to listen, I was able to spill, and she was able to scold in a language that I heard. I ended up telling her how I'd completely ruined my friendship with Ivy over my weakness, and I also admitted how I thought I felt about Ivy. Lullaby wept. So did I. She said the girl must be incredible, and I agreed. Lully also said that if there was a cure for my life, it would be found in loving someone else—the unsaid portion, I already knew: it did not lie in being loved *by* someone else in return. It was when I was leaving Albuquerque that she told me Ivy had a right to know what she'd done to me—that she had awakened an ability in me I had not known I possessed, a need and a gift all at once. Her words were lifelines. They made it possible for me to open myself up to the unknown with no expectation. "Risk your heart," she'd said. "There are no guarantees, but that's what makes life so interesting."

And Lully was right. Somewhere just past Mississippi, I realized that loving Ivy was its own peace—and I desperately needed peace. But the best part was that I did not spend any hope on the possibility of reciprocal feelings. Ivy was my friend. And that was its own gift.

Camille and I had been gone about a half-hour, and all these thoughts of Ivy made me anxious to get back to her. She'd told me once that she was Tim's safe place. I suddenly understood that. Not in the same context, certainly, as the loser who'd left her at the altar. But Ivy had a way of posing no threat, which made her the softest, indeed, the safest person to trust with one's foibles. I'm sure that quality is what made it possible for Tim to even approach her after what he'd done. I know it's what had made it possible for me to bare my soul to her.

All day today, I had watched her navigate her neighbors, her friends, her grandmother, me, with unimaginable grace, despite her emotionally fragile state. She was generous with everyone—even Tim, who was plainly just trying to assuage his guilt—anyone could see that. I sighed, recalling the way he filled out his suit. Clearly there were benefits that came from continually hefting heavy tires. Still, it was a little hard to hate the man when his idiocy had placed Ivy squarely in my path. I still managed. He was too tall for my taste, too good looking, and a bit too humbled to inspire anything but annoyance. But worse, surely—he was waking up to what he'd done to the beautiful woman he'd walked away from.

Surely, he would want her back. How could he not?

Sixty-Three—Mia

There are some moments that grab you by the throat with their perfection, and this was one of them. I was sitting on Geneva Talbot's massive front porch on a wicker sofa eating ice cream surrounded by people I cared about. My brother and sister, Ivy, her grandmother, my adorable nieces crammed against either side of me. And I'd just gotten an *I love you*, from Derek. A three-word text from somewhere in in the Middle East that made me ache with joy and missing and wishing he was right here with the rest of us. My relief after days of worrying he'd changed his mind—or worse, regretted what he'd said—left me breathless.

I leaned back and let the soft breeze pushing around the perfect temperature of night play over my face and breathed deep the contentment. I decided right then that Isle of Hope, Georgia, was a healing place. It had to be considering all that had happened in the last week and the feeling of subdued tranquility that permeated the end of this day.

Geneva caught my eye, "You look thoughtful, Mia. Are you well, sug?"

I licked my spoon and nodded. "It's just so lovely here. Do you ever get tired of it?"

The old woman chuckled. Geneva Talbot looked completely regal in her dark blue tunic and long coral skirt, the soft folds of her face framed by long white hair that puddled on her chest. Her eyes were sad and tired, but she smiled when she drew in a deep breath. "This place is like my skin," she said. "Sagging, old, bruised, completely familiar. And I love it. I grew up here, and I'll die here."

She said looking a bit pinched by the thought. "My husband grew up in this very house, and I think he still wanders around in there from time to time."

I smiled.

Geneva looked at us. "He would surely have loved you Suttons. TL was a sucker for families. If he'd had his way, we would've had ten kids." She laughed. "And I would be very, very tired."

Ivy had said something similar about loving the whole idea of families. I looked at her now and thought of Daniel's family and what that had put her through. She reached over and took her grandmother's hand, and Geneva brought Ivy's wrist to her lips.

"I think you'll just have to adopt us," said Camille.

"Consider it done, sug," Geneva said. "And I want y'all to know you're welcome to stay as long as you want. All y'all. It is lovely to have you here. Just lovely." She took in each of us, and I for one felt her gaze like a blessing. She nodded at Camille with warm reassurance, and my sister teared up. "Thank you," she mouthed. When Geneva got to Bo, she said, "Oh, that reminds me, Benjamin: Ivy and I have been talking, and we want you to have Bree's jewelry—share it with Mia, of course. It's a substantial collection, and most of it is one of a kind, which I know you can appreciate. I would have no idea what to do with it, but I figure you could use it or repurpose it or find a good home for it."

I swallowed a happy gasp. "Really?"

"Ivy, don't you want it?" Bo said, surprised.

She shook her head. "There are a couple of things I want, but Mama had her own style, which you can probably tell is not my style. So, no. Gran and I want you to have it. I'll take you over to Bree's tomorrow, and we'll gather it up." Ivy smiled at my brother, and I wanted to cry at her tenderness. And at his in return.

"I don't know what to say," Bo said.

"You could say *thank you*," I chided.

"Thank you!" he said with feeling. "I'm honored, Geneva. Truly."

"You are completely welcome, dear boy."

Bo looked at Ivy, then stood up and walked over to where I was sitting. "It looks like this little one is done," he said scooping a sleeping Olivia into his arms, careful to not dangle her cast. "Ivy, how about you help me, and we put them to bed? That okay with you, Camille?"

My sister looked at Bo being so smooth and obvious. "Absolutely, Benjamin," she said, smiling. "Pajamas are in the top drawer. Thanks."

If Bo's request made Ivy uncomfortable, she didn't show it. In fact, she looked a little complicit as she gathered up Scout and followed Bo off the porch and around the side of the house.

When they were out of earshot, I leaned back and smiled. "Geneva, what does the Universe think about my brother?"

She lifted her brow thoughtfully. "That he's got a very pure heart and he's in the process of giving it away." She winked at me then spooned the last of her Rocky Road into her mouth.

I would love Bo forever if he brought Ivy into my life on a permanent basis, I thought. I sighed at the possibility, and it struck me as almost otherworldly that we were all here together in Savannah, Georgia, on this porch talking about my brother's pure but disabled heart...and Bree's jewelry. Geneva put her empty ice cream carton down and folded her arms. "What about you, Miss Mia? Who has your heart?"

I smiled, but for some reason tears pricked in my eyes. "A soldier," I said, wistfully. "A gorgeous, kind Marine named Derek. Derek Lehman."

"You love him."

"I do. I love him so much. I didn't mean to, but I am one hundred percent smitten." I pulled up the photos on my phone and found my favorite of the two of us together, then handed my phone to Geneva. It was a shot of Derek hugging me from behind, his cheek resting against mine. We had matching smiles.

"Oh my," she said, taking the phone. "He *is* impressive, and clearly he belongs to you."

"Really?"

"Oh, yes."

"So...does the Universe think we'll to end up together?"

Geneva laughed and handed me back my phone. "I certainly hope so, Mia, because I'm pretty sure I just caught a glimpse of your children in that photo."

I gasped. "What? Really?"

"Hundred percent, sug. Hundred percent."

Sixty-Four—Ivy

My grandmother's property spanned about an acre and a half, and the guesthouse sat on the north corner facing Rose Avenue. Bo and I were quiet for the short walk so as not to wake the little girls we were holding. Coming up on the backside was a small patio off the kitchen, and Camille had left the French doors unlocked. Inside, I flipped the light switch with my elbow and headed down the hall, Scout limp in my arms.

I'd forgotten how cozy this little house was, where two bedrooms, a bath, a kitchen, and a tiny sitting room all fit in less than 900 square feet. And Camille had cozied it up even more with little girls' paraphernalia. The space looked happily inhabited. In the bedroom, we worked in silence and got Bo's nieces out of their sundresses and into their nighties and tucked in bed without waking them. I couldn't help it. They were so adorable that I had to kiss both of their little heads. When I straightened, Bo was studying me. I let him. In fact, I studied him back, sort of amazed at the easiness of our sustained eye contact.

Finally, I walked toward him, and on my way out of the room, I took his hand and led him back down the hall. We stopped in the kitchen, where Bo washed his hands, and to make him more comfortable, I did too. Then we went out on the patio and held hands some more. We were quiet, but it wasn't awkward.

"Quite a day you've had," he finally said. "You doing okay?"

"I think so. It just hits me every few minutes that she's really gone, and I can't catch my breath. But then I do, and I'm okay." I looked over at him. "Thank you so much for being here. You don't know what that means to me."

He squeezed my hand. "I'm sorry again...for..."

"Stop it! I'm just happy that you're here," I said. He smiled, and it emboldened me. I looked at him, then down at our joined hands. "I've been thinking about, you know, everything you said...at the cemetery."

"And?"

"I was wondering—is there anything you wish you hadn't said?"

"No, Ivy. I said exactly what I wanted to."

I nodded. "It's just that you seem so different. I like it, but it's different."

"What do you mean?"

I lifted our clasped hands. "For one thing, *this*. Bo, how can you do this? Hold my hand and not be...*nervous* that you're touching me?"

He took a deep breath and contemplated me. "I guess I'm...I guess it's the medication."

"So...What?"

"Remember all the Xanax in my medicine cabinet?"

I nodded.

He shrugged. "There's a reason it's prescribed for me. It helps me."

"But you don't take pills," I said.

"I don't. Except when I need them," he countered.

"So, you needed them to say those things to me? You need them to hold my hand?"

"What?" He looked suddenly uncomfortable. "Ivy...some Xanax might have helped me tell you how I felt, but I felt it—feel it—all by myself."

I smiled up at him. "That's good to know."

"But it bothers you," he said.

"No. Well...I don't know. I like this version of you, Bo. I just...I just don't know it very well."

"It's still the same me, Ivy. Just less tense."

I looked at him. "So, your pills, what? Take the edge off?"

"Kind of. Does *that* bother you?"

I turned fully and faced him. "Bo, are you planning to kiss me anytime in the near future?" I let my inquiry hang there, knowing I'd surprised him. He grinned and leaned in, and I knew he would taste delicious, but I had the awful feeling that sharing wet germs with me would do him in, utterly. I leaned back.

"What?" he said.

"Bo, you said such pretty things to me yesterday at the cemetery. Do you think you could say them again?"

"Of course."

"Unmedicated?" We were so close, with just the moon glow lighting our faces, but I could see I'd upset him. "I'm sorry, Bo. I like *this* you so much. I like that you're holding my hand, and I think I'm really gonna like kissing you, but for some reason I need to know that you can do that—that you want to do that—all on your own."

He stared at me, and I could see the pulse beating at his temple. He looked so uncomfortable that I almost never-minded everything I'd just said. But I couldn't. This was my life, and it seemed to me that making way for this eccentric man to worm his way into it required a real time adjustment to the would-be fantasy.

"Bo," I said softly. "I have lived my whole life in the shadow of the truth, which is no truth at all. In case you didn't notice, my very existence is based on a lie. A pretty lie. And my only experience with loving was Tim, and that was a lie he told me—and I told myself—so clearly I'm not very good at this."

"I'm not lying," Bo said.

"You might be," I said. "You know, under the influence, things might feel different—maybe they're just medicated fibs. Maybe they're not, but don't you think we should find out? Mostly you, I mean. Don't you think you should be sure?"

He looked at me pained, like I was dressing him down.

Ivy in Stills - 319

"Don't get me wrong, buttercup," I said. "I don't ever want you to stop taking your pills. I like this calm and relaxed you. You deserve to be calm and relaxed, and I definitely want to spend more time with that guy. But..." I breathed. "But this is too big, too important, and I need both of us to know the truth, unfiltered." I looked into his eyes, past them and into him, and couldn't imagine the conversation we were having. But it was a game-changer for me, and it didn't have to make sense to anyone else.

I leaned over and kissed his cheek, then I stood up. He held onto my hand for a moment as I stared down at him. Then he let go, and I walked away.

Sixty-Five—Bo

I didn't sleep well, even with the Xanax, but without it I would not have slept at all. I really tried not to need one when I went to bed. I did. I'd washed my sheets and let them soak in a Clorox rinse while we were at the funeral, so I knew that wasn't the issue. The issue—the relentless anxiety-producing issue—was the conversation I'd had with Ivy on the back patio. That was a loop that I was destined to relive all night. But taking her concerns to heart, I was hoping to power through medication-free, even if I had to stare at the ceiling all night and hyperventilate. Which is what I was doing when Mia showed up with disturbing news: We had to go home. I looked at her. "What?"

"I have to get back," she said. "So, let's leave early in the morning."

"No," I said.

"Yes," she said.

"No! I need one more day, Mia. Fly back if you need to," I told her, already dreading the solitary drive. "Besides, didn't you book a round-trip?"

"No. One way," Mia said. "And I have strict instructions from Mom to drive home with you and get you back to her in one piece. Not to mention I have a mountain of photo editing waiting for me. So we have to go."

I stared at my sister for a long moment. I wasn't ready to leave Ivy, and I wasn't ready to face that drive again. But admittedly, I had to get home, too; I was an entire week behind schedule. I groaned, desperately in need of a Xanax. "I need tomorrow," I told my sister. "We'll leave the next morning and drive straight through and be home by Sunday afternoon, but I need tomorrow."

"No, Bo," she said.

"Yes, Mia," I said back.

"Fine," she sighed with resignation. "I guess tomorrow we can see the sights of Savannah. Maybe Ivy can show me the best places to take pictures," she said. "Who knows? I might find a southern gem to add to my portfolio."

I glared at her. "Whatever, Mia. But go with Camille. Ivy will be with me."

My sister looked ready to argue, but instead she narrowed her eyes and shut her mouth. "Goodnight Mia," I said ending the discussion..

So, not only was I contending with the loop in my head, I had to actually imagine leaving here without Ivy. I imagined that until my hands started to sweat and I could hear my heart pound. I gave up and took a Xanax. It was 1:37.

But it still took me a while to stop thinking about her.

When Ivy had walked away from me on the patio, she had left me a mess of knotted emotion. She'd called me out on something I hadn't even considered, and in so doing my feelings for her had redoubled, which frankly amazed me. Or maybe it was just her that frankly amazed me.

Her very gentle confrontation was a fair point that I could not begrudge. Confidence, lost inhibition, even medicated fibbing, as she put it, could, in theory, come easy when fueled by pharmaceuticals. It's what made the production of mood altering *everything* such a lucrative enterprise. In basic parlance, it's why drunks could fall in love so easily, and how stimulants could transform the timid introvert into an obnoxious clown. It's why benzodiazepines so enticed the ill-at-ease. I got that. I'd just never associated that mindset with my particular situation, *my* benzodiazepines. Not until Ivy had so eloquently pointed it out.

So, yes, it made sense.

But, no, I hadn't lied to her when I'd said everything I'd said.

When I went downstairs the next morning, I was surprised to find no one in the kitchen, so I grabbed an apple of dubious origin from a basket on the counter and washed it three times—and then once more. It was 8:30. Where was everyone? The apple tasted organic, so I took another bite and breathed in the brilliance of my setting. Bright, unfiltered sunlight poured through the huge picture window in Geneva's kitchen; it was beautiful. For a moment I just reveled, thinking how amazingly peaceful I felt right here, right now—which was a little surprising given the fact that I'm *me*.

As I stood there, I became aware of the sound of laughter coming from outside, and I walked onto the porch to check it out. Everyone was across the street on Geneva's private pier, and Scout was screaming. Apparently, she'd caught a fish. Bluff Street faced the Skidaway River, which fed the Wilmington, according to Geneva. She'd told me that land ownership on Bluff included a private pier, which was located across the road and directly in front of each home on the street. Geneva was sitting in a lawn chair on hers, sipping coffee from a mug. Camille was holding Olivia, who was rather freaking out at the sight of the tiny fish on the end of Scout's pole. Ivy was in the middle of it all, helping Scout reel in her prize. Mia was still in her pajamas and playing the part of cheerleader. I walked over and stepped onto the lengthy pier. "Benjamin," Geneva shouted. "Come join us. Your niece has caught us some lunch."

Naturally, I stayed a fair distance from the festivities, but it didn't keep me from enjoying the scene. Especially when Ivy noticed me there and smiled. I waved.

She finished reeling in Scout's trophy and disconnected it from the line. Then she walked over to me. She was wearing a denim dress, and her short humidity-infused curls were pulled back with a red scarf. She looked tired—and who wouldn't?—but great. Really great. "Hey," she said.

"Hey," I said.

"Mia said you're leaving tomorrow."

I nodded. "I guess we have to get back."

Ivy sucked in a breath that I hoped was disappointment. "Well," she said. "We've got today. How 'bout I show you my Savannah?"

"I think I'd like that."

She smiled.

"You two headed out?" Geneva shouted.

"Yep," Ivy said, taking my hand. "We're off to explore the big city."

"Have fun," Mia shouted, nodding at me. "I mean it: Have *fun*!"

As we turned to walk off the pier, I suddenly stiffened, acutely aware of the hand in mine. "Ivy," I said. "You touched that fish."

She grinned and squeezed my fingers, making it impossible to disengage. "I did indeed, with both hands," she said. "But I promise you, Bo, that we will live long enough to get across this street and back into Gran's kitchen where there is Borax under the sink." She squeezed tighter. "So, suck it up, sweet pea," she teased. "Because I'm not letting go of you."

Sixty-Six—Ivy

Savannah is the oldest city in Georgia, built by the sweat of indentured servants brought here from Europe by Captain James Oglethorpe. He had a distinctive vision for the land, which today still comprises the original twenty-four public squares. He dreamed of a pedestrian city in 1733, and his dream came true and stays true on this two-square-mile bluff overlooking the river. So said our guide.

I'd dragged Bo onto the trolley tour for a three-hour overview of Savannah's landmarks and her history. And though he was reluctant about sitting on a bench that had been sat on by four gazillion other tourists before him, he was a pretty good sport. He didn't touch anything but my hand, and he didn't lean his elbow on the rail, but he seemed attentive to our guide, and he smiled a lot. And even more so afterwards when we strolled the entire city, square by square—just the two of us. It took most of the day, and we didn't hurry, and I have to say I saw a side of Bo Sutton that surprised me. He was like a kid in a candy shop—or in Bo's case—an organic farmers market—genuinely fascinated by it all and not wanting to miss one iota.

When he told me he'd read *Midnight in the Garden of Good and Evil*, I dragged him through the Mercer House. When he told me how unsettling were the short stories of Flannery O'Conner, I showed him where she'd lived on Monterey Square. Bo was particularly interested in SCAD—Savannah College of Art and Design—which had taken over a good chunk of the city with its museums and galleries and student housing complexes. "Bree taught a design class for them," I'd told him as we walked through Forsythe Park. "And my silly dad even offered to pay for me to go there for four years."

"But you didn't go?"

"Bo, it's an Art school—I admire art, I don't *do* art." I shook my head, thinking of yet another example of how little my dad knew me. "No, Bree was the artist," I said, reminded suddenly of why we were here in my hometown.

"You doing okay?"

We sat down on a bench near the fountains, and I looked over at him. "I'm fine. My world feels weird, for sure, knowing Mama is not in it anymore. But you are a lovely distraction, Bo Sutton."

He nodded. "I wish I could stay longer."

"That makes two of us."

We had dinner at the Olde Pink House Restaurant, a Savannah icon, which had a Zagat's rating of exemplary and no current citations by the health department. Bo called them. Whatever they said reassured him enough that we were able to enjoy a lovely—and very expensive—dinner on reportedly sterile china. And there was candlelight. It was very romantic, and I didn't want it to end.

As we strolled back to Chippewa Square, I said, "So, how do you like my city?"

Bo looked around and smiled. "I could get used to your city," he said. "It's not like anywhere I've ever been. Course, I'm not much of a traveler, so I haven't been many places."

"Well, you could be," I said. "I'd love to travel."

Bo squeezed my hand but didn't say anything.

When we reached the corner of Perry and Bull, I stopped. The crime scene tape was gone, of course, and the 'Closed' sign in the window was just as I'd left it. I looked around still amazed that the wide sidewalk gave no hint of who had bled there; in fact, there was no evidence, anywhere, of the terribleness that had happened. It made me sad. Life and business and happy people on vacation went on like nothing had changed...

"Ivy?"

"This is my mama's shop. This is where I live--lived."

He turned and took in the gold calligraphy on the glass—Bree T. Creations.

"Ivy..."

I unlocked the front door and turned on the Victorian lamps. A stack of mail lay puddled on the floor under the slot, and I skimmed through it while Bo looked around.

"I had no idea," he said. "She did all this?"

"Yes. She was very talented."

"All handmade?"

"Even the paper," I said. "That was my job."

"Really? I know a paper-maker?"

"You do."

He moved close to the wall to decipher a small watercolor set in a hammered copper frame, and another one set in gold and silver twigs. "These are amazing, Ivy."

"I know. She was good." I put the mail on the counter. "Her studio is in back. C'mon, I'll show you." I led Bo down the back hall and through a set of swinging doors to a big space that boasted two large tables, an assortment of small saws, and shelves and shelves of the materials Bree had used in her projects. On the far wall, there were two deep sinks, stacks of molds, a portable drying machine, sieves, and presses. "That's everything you need to make paper," I said. "Oh, and paper—you need paper," I added, pointing to two barrels. One brimmed with mostly white scraps, store receipts, bills, packaging, and the other was filled with scraps of every color known to man.

The space was a little messy, but Bo seemed to appreciate it, and he didn't touch anything. Of course.

"Impressive," he said, looking around. "What will happen to it?"

"I don't know. Geneva owns the building. So, I guess she'll rent it, which is fine. But I think it will be weird having someone else live upstairs. That's our home."

"You lived *here*?"

"Upstairs. I lived here with Mama, and with Geneva. Two homes." I smiled.

"Can I see it?" Bo said.

"Of course."

Upstairs, we took the grand tour. The living room with the *me* parade on the wall, the kitchen, my room with the lumpy bed, the tiny bathroom one person could barely turn around in, the bigger one in Bree's bedroom. I made a point of showing him the tallboy in the corner of that bedroom, which was filled with Mama's jewelry. "We should probably take a look at this," I said, pulling out a drawer and bringing it to the bed. It was full of chunky necklaces—all unique, many gaudy. Another was filled with nothing but bracelets and rings. A carved box that could hold a ream of paper was filled with more delicate pieces made with precious stones. I found an ancient, bejeweled locket Bree had worn sometimes. In one frame was an eight-year-old me, toothless, laughing. In the other was a picture of my mother at the same age, albeit much prettier, also toothless, also laughing.

Without warning, the faces blurred with my tears, and it took me a minute to reconstitute. Bo must have seen this, because he stood up and wrapped his arms around me. He didn't try to fix anything; he just let me weep.

"I don't want to leave you," he said.

"I don't want to be left," I said back.

For a moment, Bo Sutton looked at me the same way he'd looked at me at the cemetery. Finally, he shook his head. "Ivy, I want to explain something to you. For three thousand miles, I imagined I was falling in love with you, worried that I wasn't capable of that—worried to the edge of hating myself for *not* being capable of that, and then worried about *that* to the point that I stowed my medication in the trunk so I wouldn't eat it like candy." He held my gaze for a beat, punctuating his meaning.

I swallowed.

"I had stowed it long before I ever reached Tennessee," he continued. "And the bacterial crisis that was waiting there—it had to do with a plastic chair, and trust me, without my meds, it was a crisis that turned into the worst night of my life. But my pills were in the trunk of my car, and my car was out of reach until the next morning. When they brought it to me at ten to nine—almost an hour late—I hit the road and drove straight to the cemetery where I found you." He blew out another breath and looked pained. "And when I finally saw you, Ivy, every question was answered, every doubt...*gone*, just gone, and I knew. I knew I loved you. I knew it, and I knew it with Xanax-free clarity. Do you get what I'm telling you? Everything I said was pure yours truly; I had not taken a pill for more than a day."

"Bo..."

"And this may sound strange to you, Ivy, but I didn't know it would mean just as much to me as it does to you to know the absolute—the unfiltered—truth of how I feel. Not until you asked me. And now I know. I meant it when I said I loved you."

"What about now?"

Bo didn't answer me. He just slowly leaned in and ever so softly kissed my lips. It was so soft that I hardly felt it, but I felt it completely. Everywhere. And then his eyes closed, and my eyes closed, and we were lost in something that was part hunger and part promise and part pain and like nothing I'd ever felt before.

When it was over, Bo shuddered in my ear. "It's almost 10:00, Ivy and I have not had a pill since 1:30 this morning, more than twenty hours. And I still love you. I still love you," he breathed. Then softly, "And you still don't have to love me back."

I lifted my head from his shoulder and looked at him. Hard. Then I gently put my hands on his face and pulled him the inch that separated us. "But what if I do?" I whispered. "What if I do love you? What then?"

Sixty-Seven—Bo

Mia and I had been on the road for about forty-five minutes, and she seemed to know I was not in the mood for conversation. Not that she'd tried to engage me. I think her tearful, future-unknown, goodbye to Ivy had left her unsettled, much like mine had.

I thought again of the sweetest question in the English language: *But what if I do? What if I do love you, Bo? What then?*

Ivy's words fed me, fed my deepest hunger, but I'd shut her down before she could say anything else. As wonderful as those words were, they weren't true, and they couldn't be trusted—and not just because of my obsessiveness. I knew that Ivy was in no shape to declare such a thing—even if she made me believe it. I clenched my hands around the steering wheel. I didn't want to analyze it all again—I'd been doing that all night long—so I told myself what felt the safest: We'd only known each other for a couple of months—which was way too soon for something as big as love. At least for her.

"What?" Mia said.

I looked over at her, not realizing I'd said anything. "Nothing. Please get your feet off my dash."

"No. Your dash will live," she proclaimed, ignoring my request. But she was looking at me. "Are you okay, Bo?"

"I'm fine."

"Bo?"

"Not really. No."

Mia turned toward me. "Did you fight with Ivy? What happened between you two?"

"No. We didn't fight." I shook my head and blew out a breath, not sure I wanted to get into this, and Mia didn't push. Then we were quiet for a moment while a question burned in me. "You love Derek, right?" I blurted.

My sister looked at me. "I do..."

"What are you going to do about that? Loving him?"

"What do you mean?" she said.

"You love him, he loves you. What happens next?"

My sister eyed me with sudden knowing, and I felt entirely exposed, which made me mad because my fantasy could not be measured against Mia's reality. But Mia is a good sister when she has to be, and she didn't press me. "I don't know, Bo," she said answering my question. "We're not exactly together at the moment. But...well, Geneva said she saw our children, so apparently, we're going to be."

I arched a brow.

Mia grinned. "She asked me the other night who had my heart, and I showed her some pictures of us on my phone. She said two very cool things. She said Derek clearly belonged to me—which I loved—and that she had caught a glimpse of our kids, which I also loved. I know she was just being funny, but..."

"But?"

"But then I saw them...I mean, I started imagining them and...and it's not freaking me out, Bo. Falling for Derek—falling for a sniper who has a target on his back—is not what I planned, believe me. He's a Marine—things could happen, bad things, awful things—he is fighting in hell, you know."

"So. Why love him?"

She seriously scoffed. "I know you know that by the time love happens, it's way too late to question it. Or deny it. Don't pretend you don't know that, brother dearest."

I didn't look at her, but we both knew she'd nailed my quandary.

"You can decide what to do about it, I guess, but you can't decide not to love who you love. It's imprinted and out of our hands."

"You really believe that?"

"I do."

"So...back to my question," I said. "What are you going to do about loving Derek?"

My sister's gaze slid past me and out my window, and for a long time she didn't speak. Finally, she sighed. "I might just have to call that boy and tell him to marry me."

She wasn't kidding. I could see it in the set of her jaw, the tears that had filled her eyes.

We were quiet for a few minutes, then Mia turned back to me. "What are *you* going to do, Benjamin? About loving Ivy?"

"Nothing. There's nothing for me to do. Just love her."

"Did you tell her?"

I nodded.

"Did she tell you?"

"She tried, but..."

"But what?"

I shook my head. "She can't love me. I'm...*too much*. Besides, she's still recovering from her life. It's not even possible."

"Bo!"

I turned on the radio. "I don't want to talk about this anymore."

Mia turned it off. "Not an option! Where do things stand?" she said. "I mean, when will you see her again?"

"I don't know! But like I said, she'll come to her senses, and her life will take over, and...I don't know. She did say she had to come back to Monterey to talk to her dad face to face. But I don't know when. She has to get some of her mom's business taken care of, and there's Geneva...so, you know..."

"Then what?" Mia said.

"Exactly, Mia. Then what?"

My sister sighed dramatically, then stared over at me until I met her eyes. "Did you kiss her?"

I ignored her.

"Oh, my gosh, you did. Tell me!"

I looked straight ahead at the road and willed Mia to shut up.

"I'm not going anywhere, Benjamin," she said. "And I will keep hounding you, so you might as well dish."

"Yes, Mia," I sighed. "I kissed her. Are you happy?"

Her mouth dropped open. "And... and...was it fabulous?"

"Yes. Actually, it *was* fabulous."

"Did it bother you? I mean, I'm assuming it was skin on skin, lip on lip, maybe some tongue with no sterile shield between you..."

"Mia! Shut up."

"Sorry. But I'm serious. How did you do?"

"I don't think Ivy had any complaints," I said, stifling a grin at the horizon.

"You know what I mean, Casanova."

I groaned. "Is there no pride, no dignity left in this world for me? Am I really driving through Alabama dissecting the most personal moment of my life with my sister? My *sister*?"

"Yes, and you're doing a piss-poor job of it. Now spill!" Mia insisted.

I sighed and glanced over at her. "It was...not a problem. I'm sure it must be because of my feelings for her. Or maybe I've just been worried over nothing. I mean, I was a little... *afraid*, I'll be honest. I didn't know what to expect. But...it's almost like Ivy was an extension of me, if that makes sense. Like part of me, not something from the outside of me that I had to contend with. It was very...cool, surprisingly natural. Awesome, if you want to know the truth." I nodded, reliving it. Probably I smiled.

"You really love her."

"I do."

My sister put her hand on her heart and grinned dorkily. "I'm so proud of you, Benjamin, You manned up and claimed your woman!"

I rolled my eyes. "Down, girl. I kissed her. And I told her I loved her. But that is as far as it will ever go, so nobody was *claimed*."

"What are you talking about?"

"Nothing. I'm talking about nothing. Ivy's a beautiful, broken girl who lives in Georgia and will soon figure herself out and be just fine. I, on the other hand, will always be the nut case who lives in California. See? Nothing is going to happen."

"It's not nothing. You'll see her again."

"Maybe. But when? For how long? That's not a life, Mia. She lives in Georgia."

"You could live in Georgia."

I didn't dare look at my sister for fear she would see my desperation. All I wanted was to be close to Ivy. I could move. I had the ideal job for relocating—I could create a suitable space anywhere, which I would do if it were just up to me, because the truth was I wanted Ivy as deep in my life as possible. I hadn't known her ten days before I realized my life was so much more manageable when illuminated by her. And that was all fine and good and great for me, but what could I possibly offer that girl in return? Nothing but stress which would turn to pity which would turn to resentment. I drove myself crazy, and as much as I ached to be with Ivy, I couldn't imagine imposing *my life* on her.

"That would be a lot to ask of her, Mia," I finally responded. "Why would she want that?"

"Because she loves you, Bo; if she said it, she does. She loves you despite your myriad drawbacks—*myriad*. And if she loves you, it means she chooses you. *You*, Bo—the apron-wearing germaphobic, laundry-doing, shower-taking, bead-counting, floor-board-dusting, compulsive that you are. That's you. That's who you are. But that's not *all* you are. You're also a very good man. A kind man. You're creative, a great cook, well-read. Brilliant. Not half bad looking—for a brother. You're so much more than your weirdness, Benjamin, just accept it."

"Stop it, Mia!"

Ivy in Stills - 335

"Look, Bo, love is a leap—that's what Lullaby tells me all the time. That's the beauty and the terror of giving yourself to someone—letting go of all the pieces of you and grabbing onto all the pieces of them. Then making something brand new out the whole mess. That's what love is. And I'm sorry, but if you want it, Benjamin, a little faith in you and in Ivy will be required."

"You think you're so smart, Mia."

"Yes, I do."

"You really believe that?"

"Yes, I do."

Sixty-Eight—Ivy

I was feeling very disconnected—free-floating, definitely untethered. I wasn't sleeping, and I wasn't eating much either, which was a bit of a benefit, I guess. I now hovered at my lowest weight since junior high, so that should have been a nice bonus in the midst of my unrest. But I didn't care.

I just couldn't land. Ever since last week when Bo had left, I could not find my footing.

If my mother were here, she would probably take my hands and say *Talk to me, Ivy Lee, before you burst.* Bree could read me. I didn't always open up to her because the conversation invariably turned to Daniel. But at least she always knew when I was bothered. That was something. It would have been nice to talk to her, but the truth was she wouldn't have been any help to me right now. No, where Bo was concerned, I was on my own.

I blew out a tired breath. Maybe he was right—it probably was too soon for us. But it was confusing, his assurances that he loved me—the medication-free assurance I had so yearned for—because when I tried to say it back to him, he shut me down. He'd said I needed to let the dust settle in my life before I decided I was in love with anyone. And then with the most earnest look in his eyes, he'd said, "Ivy, it's easy to fall in love when everything else hurts. But it doesn't make it real. Sometimes it's just a distraction from the pain."

That made some sense to me—there had been a lot of recent pain in my life. But I was still pretty sure my feelings were real. But what if they weren't? What if I couldn't trust myself? It was all very overwhelming, and it would have made for a good long conversation with...*someone*. Instead, I felt alone and very lost and like I was circling the drain.

But at least I was staying busy, and I was sweaty and bone-tired to prove it. My job this week had been to box up my mother's shop. Her inventory would go on sale next month, her equipment, materials, and unfinished projects would go to auction the week after. It was a huge undertaking, but I was making good progress, and it felt good to work this hard. Gran showed up every day with the best intentions, but being in Mama's world was very hard on her. So, she usually didn't stay long, which was kind of fine with me: I was not great company, and without her here I didn't have to pretend. Camille had apologized up and down for not being here to help, but she'd planned a surprise trip to Disney World for Scout's fifth birthday. So, for now, it was just me and my ghosts— and some occasional tears.

I was in the back workroom, slapping a label on a box of frame parts when I heard the door chimes. There was a 'Closed' sign in the window, but I'd left the door unlocked for a potential renter who wanted to take a look at the space. I was a mess and didn't want to meet with him, but Gran had not yet come in today, so I had no choice. I ran my hands through my hair and made my way up the hall.

The woman was very large and very well-dressed, and she was fingering a silk scarf when I walked through and startled her. "Sorry to keep you waiting," I said taking in her palazzo pants, long tunic and diamonds. "I was in the back. Are you here to see the space?"

She turned and smiled. "No. But it is a lovely space. Is it for rent?"

Now I was confused. "Uh, yes. Sorry. I was expecting a gentleman, actually. He didn't really have an appointment...But you're obviously not him." I shook my head, mad at my rambling, but did I *know* her? I cleared my throat. "Ummm, we're actually not open right now..."

"I see." She cocked her head. "By any chance are you Ivy Talbot?"

"Uhhh, yes. I'm Ivy."

Her smile widened and it made her beautiful. "Well, my goodness," she said. "It is lovely to finally meet you. I'm Lullaby Sutton."

My mouth dropped open; I *did* know her. From the portrait Mia had taken. "H...hi," I said, dumbfounded. "It's...it's nice to meet you. What...What on earth are you doing here?"

"I'm so sorry to just pop in like this," she said, stepping closer. Then she took both of my hands. "But I simply had to meet the girl my family cannot stop talking about."

"What? I don't..."

She kept smiling. "I feel like I know you, Ivy. And from three perspectives, I bet I do."

I blushed, a little alarmed to learn I'd been such a topic of discussion. I didn't know what to say, so I pulled one hand free and ran it over my face. "I'm sorry I'm so messy, I've been cleaning my mama's studio. I must look a fright."

In a distinctly maternal gesture, Lullaby Sutton squeezed the hand she still held. "You are absolutely lovely, my dear. *And one never apologizes for being lovely,*" she arched a brow to drill her point.

"Oh, goodness. That's such a nice thing to say when I haven't even showered today. Thank you."

She laughed and let go. "You are as cute as my Mia said you were."

I chuckled, embarrassed. "I love Mia," I said. "I love all the Suttons."

"Well, the feeling is completely mutual," she smiled. "And you need to know that there is not much I would not do for Mia—which is why I'm here. She asked me to check on you on my way home."

I swallowed. "Really? Why? I mean why do I need checking on?"

The big woman contemplated me. "My niece told me about your mother. I am so sorry."

"Oh, thank you. It was very sudden."

"That's what Mia said." For a moment she studied me with such soft regard that it almost brought tears to my eyes. Then she glanced around the room. "So, this is her shop?"

"It is. I was just boxing up some of her things. My grandmother needs to rent the space, so we're trying to get it cleared out."

Lullaby nodded, still perusing. "I absolutely love her sense of style. She was obviously very talented."

"I think so, too," I said.

"Would it be terrible to ask..." Lullaby ventured. "Could you show me around? I've always been fascinated by artists."

"Sure," I said.

And for the next half hour I introduced Lullaby Sutton to my mama's world. I think she fingered every little thing Mama had on display, and she talked non-stop about...*everything*. She especially loved Bree's studio. It was kind of a warzone of boxes and equipment back there, but Lullaby Sutton didn't seem to mind at all. She even begged me to show her how I made paper. So, I did. She asked a lot of questions and seemed genuinely interested, which I sort of ate up. Mia's aunt was a lot like Mia: open-hearted, confident, kind, with that uncanny ability to make you feel interesting and worthy of her time. We laughed a lot, and she told me about her honeymoon, which she didn't want to be over.

"I'm trying to talk that little man of mine into taking a cruise before we go home," she said. "He's never been on one."

"How's it going?" I asked.

"I think I've just about convinced him," she told me. "But I have had to promise him some rather unspeakable things, if you know what I mean." She winked, and I barked out a laugh. I liked Lullaby Sutton very much.

When we'd seen every inch of Mama's shop, Lullaby thanked me profusely. "You are just delightful," she told me. "I'm so glad that my family has gotten to know you. You've grown quite important to them."

Her words made me choke up a little. "Thank you," I said. "They've become very important to me, too. And thank you so much for letting me stay in your pool house. I think it saved my life."

She smiled. "Could we talk, Ivy? I know you're busy, and I've already taken up too much of your time. But could you spare me a few more minutes?"

"Of course," I locked the front door, then I said, "Why don't we talk upstairs in my living room? I think I have some sweet tea in the fridge."

"Oh, that would be lovely."

Upstairs, I poured Mia's aunt a tall glass of Geneva's brew—she'd brought me a thermos yesterday, worried that I was getting dehydrated. I poured one for myself, then I joined Lullaby on the lumpy sofa. She was laughing.

"I think this couch is making a pass at me," she said. "And I *like* it."

I laughed too and handed her the tea. "I know. Mama restuffed it about ten times, but it was never right. I'm gonna miss it, though."

"Where will you go, sweetheart?" Lullaby asked.

I looked around. "I wish I could stay here. But this apartment is part of the rental agreement."

"So...Isle of Hope?" she said.

"Probably. For a while anyway. Do you know it?"

"I do now," she said. "I spent the morning with your charming grandmother—a decidedly unexpected blessing." She smiled. "Camille sent me the address—and, of course, you weren't there, so I had the most delightful visit with Geneva. I liked her immediately. But I knew I would, from everything Camille has told me. I believe—speaking of saving lives—that your grandmother has saved my sweet niece."

"You might be right. Gran has a gift. But I'm so sorry Camille's at Disney World."

Lullaby shook her head. "Don't be. I didn't really come here to see her. I came to see you, Ivy." Lullaby set down her glass. "I understand that you've had quite a year."

I pushed out a weary sigh. "That's true, I...I have. My grandmother calls it my year of ashes. It's supposed to be a refining process. Jury's still out on that."

"Year of ashes. I like that," she said. "I've had a few of those, I think."

"Really?"

"Oh, of course. You don't live as long as I have and not know some pain and humiliation. So, yes. Really. But I had lots of support, so that helped."

I shrugged. "I have my grandmother."

Mia's aunt studied me for a moment. "And you're so very lucky to have her. Especially at a time like this. You must miss your mother terribly."

"I do miss her."

"What about your father?"

"Um... We're not close."

She smiled with sad eyes. "I know your dad. I'm not surprised, Ivy. And I'm sorry."

"Thank you," I said, suddenly remembering that she knew Daniel. "It just is what it is, I guess. Do you know his family?"

"I've met his wife...Her dad is the Willis in Willis, Proctor and Holmes. And I've met Daniel's daughter."

I sucked in my bottom lip and fought the sting of tears. "She's pretty," I said. "Did you know she's my age?"

Lullaby nodded. "She looks about your age."

We were quiet then, for a moment, sipping and avoiding eye contact. "I'd been kinda' fighting with my mama," I finally offered, looking into my tea. "Just before her accident—a few days before. It was over Daniel, and I...I wasn't really... We weren't really speaking. And when I heard what happened, I went to tell my dad—I didn't know what else to do—and...and that's when I met her. His other daughter..." I shrugged, my eyes filling.

"I'm so sorry, Ivy. Mia told me about your parents, about your situation," Lullaby said. "Then Bo did. And then Camille did."

I looked up at her, not sure how to feel about being on the tip of so many tongues. "Kind of pathetic, isn't it?"

"Ivy...I'm just going to say this: Honey, it's okay to be upset about other people's choices—even if they're the people you love. Especially when those choices impact *your* life."

I sniffed. "But I hate being upset. It gives me such a headache."

Lullaby chuckled, then reached over and patted my hand.

"It just seems to go from bad to worse, my *situation*," I said.

The woman smiled warmly. "Are we still talking about your parents? Or...it was a wedding that didn't work out, right?"

I squeezed my eyes shut for a second. "There's just nothing quite like your honey knocking up his ex and her showing up at your wedding to tell the world." I shook my head, feeling once again small and tired. "I was so mortified that I swore I was never coming back here. And if Mama hadn't..."

Lullaby reached over and lifted my chin. "I know. I wanted to hide, too. I was mortally wounded by a man I thought I loved, and who I thought was supposed to love me back. I got hurt and tired and ashamed and angry, and I swam in that swill for a long, long time. Which, translated, means I wasted a lot of time trying to find out where I fit. And the truth was, I didn't fit *there* anymore."

"That is exactly how it's been for me."

"Then you know. You have no choice but to hurt for a while—but not let it destroy you. That's what I figured out about myself."

I thought about this profundity for a long moment. "Fitting someplace new...I almost can't imagine it. And now...now I just don't know if I can even trust myself."

"Because of this young man?"

"Because of him, and because of Bree—my mama. Because of my dad." I sighed. "Tim's gone—married and happy *most days,* according to him. My mother's...gone. My dad...was never..." I swallowed. "I think I've trusted all the wrong people my whole life, and now I'm afraid I just don't know how to do it. And when I think I can trust myself, someone else says I can't." I did not tell Mia's aunt that the *someone else* was Bo.

Lullaby nodded. "My first husband turned out to be a horrible man. He was never physical, but he was very, very cruel. One day, I looked at myself in the mirror and I could not see a shred of the girl I'd been before I met him. He had all the power. I'd given it to him—I didn't even trust myself with my own opinion—so...I get that, Ivy."

"What did you do?"

"Well, it took me a while to figure out that I was the only one who could save me. So, I did." She looked hard at me. "One day I just walked away—from him, of course, but also from the *me* that I'd been with him. And it took some time, but I finally found myself again."

I stared at her, drinking in her wisdom. "I think I've believed lies and liars my whole life. And I don't understand how I can be that stupid."

"Oh, Ivy, sometimes stupid is stupid. But sometimes it's just us doing our best to survive other people's stupid. It sounds like you chose someone unworthy of you—you'll never do that again."

"No, I will not," I said.

"You're a survivor. You've survived your parents—which is huge. You'll survive this. You will move past your wedding. None of that makes you stupid. I think that makes you rather extraordinary."

"I don't feel extraordinary."

"Oh, my dear girl, if you ask me, you deserve a medal."

I didn't want to cry, so I dropped my gaze. "Why are you saying these things to me, Ms. Sutton? Why do you care what I'm going through?"

She took a deep breath. "Well, according to your grandmother, it's because the Universe placed me in your path. But, I actually prefer to think it's because we're kindred spirits. And with every conversation I've had with Mia and Camille...and especially Bo, that has been confirmed."

"Bo?"

"He loves you, you know. And that is a wonderful thing because we are never truly alive until we love. It's life-changing, and I've always known it would take a remarkable woman to inspire such a phenom in my strange but precious nephew." Lullaby smiled. "Bo's very interesting," she said. "A bit tortured, as you know. Eccentric. Exhausting. Some would say mentally ill. But he certainly recognizes goodness and beauty."

"He's so good," I said, softly. "I've never met anyone as *real* as he is. I've decided—kinda' late in the game, I know—that I don't really care for people who pretend. And I don't think Bo even knows how." I swallowed back a threat of new tears. "But you don't have to sell me on Bo, Ms. Sutton. He sort of sells himself."

She looked suddenly sad. "Oh, sweet girl, I'm not here to sell you on Bo. I'm here to sell you on *you* regardless of Bo."

"What?"

"Ivy, sweetheart, it strikes me that you've been pushed down a lot. But you keep getting back up. That makes you strong and very capable of creating exactly what you want. I'm only here to tell you that you're worthy of it. So, whatever you want; go get it!"

I stared at Lullaby Sutton, feeling very *intervened* upon, in a good way. "I don't know what to say," I finally managed.

"I do tend to have that effect on people," she chuckled. "My apologies, if I've crossed a line."

"Absolutely not—apparently the Universe knew I needed a talking-to. I don't know how to thank you for taking the time."

"Well, if you ever want to, please call me. Anytime. *Any. Time.*"

"Really?"

She nodded. "Really. You know I don't have any children—I've been blessed with a few wonderful men in my life, but no children of my own. And suddenly, sadly, you don't have a mother. I think we should be friends."

My lip quivered, and then I was crying. I felt so raw in this woman's presence and so inexplicably safe with her at the same time. "I'd like that," I wept. "I'd really like that."

"Then, why these tears?"

"I don't know. I just don't understand what's happening to me."

She smiled. "Life does like to dangle us from high branches."

"It does," I sniffed.

"You are stronger than you think, Ivy. And you can take that to the bank because I am an excellent judge of character."

"Thank you, Ms. Sutton."

She laughed. "Technically, I am now Mrs. Matisse La Quint. Isn't that lovely? And the man is even better than the name. Oh, my, my, my, my how I love my little Frenchman!" She narrowed her eyes at me. "Despite your unfortunate wedding, don't be afraid to love, Ivy. It keeps us alive and smiling."

I chuckled through my tears struck by her big, bold, unquestionable sincerity. "I love Bo," I blurted. "I'm sure I do. He says I can't know that in the middle of my messy life, and I almost believed him. But he's wrong. I love him. I do."

"Sweetheart, you don't have to convince me."

"But he left here absolutely positive I wasn't capable of those feelings. How do I fix that?"

Lullaby shrugged. "Well, I guess first you need to be sure that's what you really want—it's Bo, and loving him comes with some stuff," she said pointedly.

I nodded. "I know."

"But if he's what you want...Then go get him, Ivy."

I looked at her. "How do I do that?"

"I don't know," she chuckled. "But I'm pretty sure you can't do it from Georgia."

Sixty-Nine—Mia

I picked up the three copies of my portfolio at noon and then drove to Pacific Grove, not sure of my next move. When I got there, I sat in the parking lot contemplating my work. I was pleased, for the most part. Actually, I was excited, anxious, and also filled with second-guessing dread over my final project, wondering if I could have done more. But then I went page-by-page again, and again, I knew I had nailed it.

Since we'd gotten home from Savannah, I'd worked non-stop, including obsessing over every minute detail of this collection. It was due by five, and I was sort of reveling in being done with it, the exclamation point on the end of this quarter, the permission I could now give myself to obsess about other things—tall, amazingly good-looking marine type things. The second-guessing, the dread, was because I'm a bit of a perfectionist with my work, but honestly compared to my original lackluster idea, I knew I'd blown this out of the park.

It was the pure gold I'd found in Geneva's albums. That's what saved me—and my final grade. And my enthusism for the composition had grown with each passing mile that Bo and I had driven home—Ivy, the topic of conversation from Alabama to Nevada feeding my creative bone.

It wasn't just her face, which was its own definition of interesting. It was her life, her turmoil, the deep well of her eyes, the emotion that could transform her. As soon as I'd gotten home, I'd printed out every single photo I'd taken of her and couldn't believe how I'd captured the progression. I could actually see Ivy changing, growing. They were all random shots, many of which had to be cropped to include just her. But now every image was perfectly imbued with the purity of human imperfection. Take that, Kyle Donahue!

Two nights ago, I had lined up my chosen images for final inspection and been admiring my work when Bo walked in. He'd taken one look at Ivy spread over the kitchen table and couldn't seem to find his voice.

"What do you think?" I'd said. "They're good, right? I'm calling the collection *Ivy in Stills: A Tribute to Ashes.* What's the matter?"

He'd leaned over, silently taking in the photos, and after a long moment, all he could say was, "Good Lord, Mia... these are amazing,"—high praise from his critical eye, or maybe it was simply the subject matter. Of course, they weren't all mine. Twenty percent of my final project could be enhanced treatment of existing photographs. I'd brought back several images from Savannah. The rest I'd been snapping from day one because, well, that's what I do. Bo had picked up the picture I'd taken of Ivy at my exhibition the day I'd met her. "Look how sad she seemed, Mia," he'd said.

It was true. The Ivy I'd met that day had been beaten up pretty good, and I'd been hesitant to use the image, with its poor lighting and everything going on in the foreground. But all of that had actually added to the overall mood of the picture—shadows borne of commercial illumination, picture noise, and her utter aloneness in the midst of it. The competing elements poignantly enhanced the message of a gutted girl putting one foot in front of the other. It was tragic and lovely at the same time. I remembered that Daniel had made Ivy look that way. He'd been impatient with her, barky, and I had sort of hated him from that moment on.

Daniel Proctor was an ass. But he was an ass with good taste in black and white photography, so he'd appreciate this collection. On so many levels. He might even recognize his own work since I'd set the tone of my project with an image of the deeply human vulnerability he'd captured in his little girl that day on the pier. I'd made a copy of Geneva's original so I could edit it, then digitally saturated the image with muted color. Then, I'd reworked it in gray scale. I'd cropped the image to include only that forlorn little face against the deepening sunset, her eyes filled with disappointment. Because I knew the story behind it, I'd named the image *Abandoned*. Daniel would love that.

During this process, my inner photographer had matured beyond what I'd thought possible. I now consciously applied the core takeaway of this final advanced placement semester: *Don't bother capturing what doesn't hold a secret.* What a concept—and totally worth the summer I'd missed abroad with my friends. That simple directive, I knew, would inform my work for years to come.

Every photog understands instinct. It's huge. We take pictures when the urge quickens our pulse—but something has to translate, a subtle mix of curiosity and fascination—a secret that must be present in the final image to draw the eye, engage the brain, and inspire a visceral response. Beauty was everywhere, and photographers everywhere were capturing it, exploiting it, claiming it for their own and splashing their name on it. But it wasn't theirs. And this wasn't mine. I'd simply shone a light on this girl and offered her images up as a gift to anyone smart enough to identify them as such.

Twenty 8x10s of Ivy. All done in black and white—actually grayscale. Each one infused with a secret.

I'd brought back a photo from Savannah that had been taken when Ivy was about sixteen or seventeen—it was one of my favorites. She was sitting at a kitchen table, a bowl and a box of cereal in the foreground. An oversized tee shirt hung off one shoulder, her long curls wild, a crushed note in her hand. She hadn't been awake too long when the picture was taken, and she was not amused by whatever she'd read, but she was beautiful—barefaced with sleep-plumped features. She was facing the morning sun, so aside from her dark hair, she was just a bit washed out. I'd treated the image so that her lips and eyes were more defined against the fairness of her skin.

In these borrowed images, I included a 2x3 of the original with the breakdown of my edits to each one. It always impressed instructors when you could make someone else's photo your own, and I was very into impressing my instructors. The last one I'd borrowed was a close- up of Ivy's flawless face in the mirror the day she was supposed to get married. She was putting on mascara while someone behind her arranged her veil. I'd chosen it because her large eyes were filled with laughter and excitement, animated and hopeful. Three minutes from when this photo had been taken, it was probably over, and in all the pictures I'd studied of Ivy since, there was not one shot so saturated with optimism and joy.

That image especially had affected Bo, who'd commented, *She really has no idea how beautiful she is.*

It was true. When I'd called her to ask if I could use her as my senior project, Ivy had laughed. But when I'd told her what I was doing, what I had captured, she'd gotten very humble, simply stunned that I would find her project-worthy. Ultimately, she'd given me her reluctant permission; I have no idea what I would have done had she'd said no. After that, we'd spent the next fifteen minutes talking about Bo. I'd informed him later that Ivy missed him very much.

"I know that," he'd said.

"And you miss her," I'd said.

He'd been quiet for a moment. "Of course I do. But that doesn't change anything, Mia. She's still there. And I'm still here."

"Doesn't have to be that way..." I'd told him.

Bo had looked at me, sadness softening his glare, then he'd walked away. My sulky brother had been a bit hard to live with since we got home. And Ivy had asked me not to tell him that she was flying in this week, so I could offer nothing to lift his spirits.

Now I closed the album and looked up at the imposing building in front of me. Willis, Proctor and Holmes. I blew out a deep breath and got out of the car. From the back seat, I retrieved the photo Daniel had so admired at my campus exhibition—*Battu at Sunset*. Then I grabbed one of the boxed leather-bound albums and walked into his building.

A pretty girl with blond hair was sitting at the reception desk. She reminded me of Daniel, and I narrowed my eyes. "Are you Liz?"

She smiled. "I am."

Daniel's daughter. "I, um...I called earlier. You said I might be able to catch Daniel Proctor if I was here by one."

Still smiling, she said, "Yes. And you're in luck; he is here, but he has to be in court at 1:30, so you'll have to make it fast."

"I can be fast."

She gave me directions, and I left her in happy oblivion as I walked down the hall.

Daniel's office was behind a wall of glass, and when he saw me, he got up from his desk and waved me in. He too was all smiles, a family trait apparently. I didn't return it as I walked toward him. "Hello," I said. All business.

"Mia. Has something happened?"

"What?"

He hurried past me and shut his door. When he got back behind his desk he said, "I was just surprised by your call."

"Oh, no need," I said, taking in the portrait that hung on the wall behind him. "Nice family."

He turned to look at it, then back to me. Clearing his throat, he said, "What can I do for you, Mia?"

"Well, there's this," I said, handing him back his credit card and the receipts for the purchases made for Ivy. "I won't be needing that anymore."

"Thank you for being so thorough," he said. "Of course, you know I got an alert each time something was charged."

"Of course you did," I said, sounding a bit snarky. "But just in case, I saved all the receipts." I rather held my breath then, thinking some scolding was forthcoming for the shoes we'd bought at

Ivy in Stills - 351

Giselle's, but Daniel didn't say anything. "And then I wanted you to have something else," I said. "Well, two somethings." I handed him the framed photo of the tattered ballet slippers on the pier. It was wrapped in butcher paper, and I waited for him to pull it off.

"Oh, I do love this, Mia," he said, holding the 16x20 at arms' length. "You are a rare talent. But I can't accept this as a gift. Let me pay for it."

"That would be great," I said. "Because it's not a gift."

He laughed at me, and when I didn't laugh back, he pulled his checkbook from a drawer. He didn't even ask me my price; he just wrote with a flourish and handed me a check for five hundred dollars, which was three hundred more than I'd been hoping for. I put it in my back pocket and told him thanks. Then I handed him the album. "This actually *is* a gift," I said.

"For me?" he said with surprise. "What is it?"

"It's my senior project. I thought you'd like a copy."

He opened the box. "*Ivy in Stills*...What is this?" he said, a crimp appearing in his forehead. I didn't answer him, and after an awkward beat, he lifted the book out and turned the page to the photo he'd taken of Ivy as a little girl—the one I'd edited to perfection—and I'll be damned if he didn't deflate, just a hair. It made me happy because I actually wanted to hurt Daniel Proctor. I wanted to do it on Ivy's behalf, and maybe that made me a horrible person, but I could live with that. *Always stand up to put downs.* If there was a theme to my existence, *that* was it, and as far as I could tell, Daniel had been putting Ivy down her whole life.

I didn't say a word as he slowly perused my photographs. Ivy sitting on the patio bundled in a blanket, sadness flattening her features. Another at our dinner with her family, frustration bending her brow because she was being talked over instead of listened to. Daniel lingered on each page, and I wondered what he was thinking. The pictures were beautiful because the subject was beautiful, and Ivy's father could not deny it. The last shot was one I'd snapped of Ivy alone at her mother's graveside, her expression one of disbelief morphing into reluctant acceptance. He studied that page the longest.

When he finally looked up at me, there were no tears—I'm not sure Daniel Proctor was capable of tears—but there was sadness, and the idea of tears in his eyes. "As I said, Mia, you are a rare talent."

"Thank you." I stood up. "I also have to thank you for reaching out to my aunt, which led to you renting her pool house," I said. "I would not have met your daughter otherwise, and she has become my good friend."

He eyed me as though he didn't believe me. "Have you talked to her?"

"I talk to her all the time."

"Really? She won't return my calls."

"Did you really expect her to?"

He tried for a glare, but it fell flat. "How is she?" he finally said.

"How do you think she is?"

He shrunk a bit at that, and I let him squirm for a second.

"She's coming back next week," I told him. "I don't know how long she'll be here, but..." I shrugged. "I thought you'd like to know."

"When?"

"Wednesday."

He nodded but didn't say anything else.

I stood up. "I guess that's everything. Oh, and if you decide not to keep that," I indicated the book he was holding. "I mean I guess having it could prove awkward—your daughter works here, right? Anyway, if you decide not to keep it, I'd like—"

"I'm keeping it, Mia," he said coolly, shutting me down.

"Okay, then," I said after a beat. "I guess we're done here. Goodbye, Daniel."

"Goodbye, Mia. And...thank you."

I looked hard at him but said nothing else. Then I turned to walk out. In so doing, I met the curious gaze of Liz Proctor, who was standing on the other side of the glass. She opened the door to let me pass by, offered a weak smile, then walked into her father's office.

Seventy—Ivy

Sixteen days after Bree died, I flew back to Monterey with Camille. We'd been talking—well, mostly she'd been talking—but we decided together that it was time. Camille had filed for divorce in absentia through a friend of Peter's, and Peter had been served. She'd chosen to gamble and use someone who knew her husband, but it appeared to be paying off. According to Ryan Bliss, Peter, when faced with the allegations of abuse sited in the summons, of course denied it all, but agreed that his marriage had been a monumental waste of time. He'd informed his friend, Camille's lawyer, that his wife had actually saved him the bother of filing himself. Right. And the true test of Camille's resolve was her decision to now meet with him face to face. I hadn't known Mia's sister before all her awfulness, but clearly in the time I *had* known her, she'd gained enough confidence that she was no longer afraid of the man she'd married. She was even a bit steely.

Camille had informed Peter that until he proved his willingness to cooperate and conditions were agreed upon and common decency had been achieved between them, she would not allow him to see his daughters or know where they were. Scout and Olivia were staying with Geneva, which was a gift to them all, and Peter was not expecting to see them.

The girls had fallen in love with Savannah, the laid back safety of Isle of Hope, the relaxed wellbeing of their mama. It would be hard for them to leave, but Camille was trying not to think about that. She knew Peter might threaten to sue for custody, but she had the ER report of Olivia's broken arm and pictures of her own black eye, not to mention the police report. She knew that allegations of abusing his wife could cost Peter his job, where he was fast-tracking to upper management. He would never jeopardize that. It seemed she had covered her bases, and I was proud of her. So were her parents. Certainly, Lullaby would be doing a happy dance.

Lullaby Sutton might do a happy dance on my behalf, as well, because thanks to her, I was going back to Monterey for just one reason. Well, actually two.

We landed at the Monterey Peninsula Airport just before five in the evening after a long and uneventful flight, each of us tense for different reasons. Camille squeezed my hand. "We made it. Mom's meeting us at baggage claim," she said with forced cheer.

"Are you okay?" I asked.

Her nod was unconvincing. "I'm just so glad I didn't bring the girls," she sighed. "They'd know I was nervous and try to mother me. Can you imagine? My babies trying like crazy to love away my nerves. That's what I did to them, Ivy. How could I have done that to them?"

"Peter did that to them," I corrected, and it made her eyes mist.

"Thank you, Ivy. Thank you for coming back here with me. That was a lot to ask, and I appreciate it."

I smiled. I had not discussed Bo or my motives for making the trip. I had simply agreed because I was coming anyway. I hadn't even planned to tell Mia, but then she'd called to ask if she could use some of the pictures she'd taken of me for her final project. I couldn't think why she'd want to, but I didn't care if she used them. We ended up talking for over an hour, mostly about Derek, who she was loving more every day. Of course, I was happy for her. And intrigued. "How did you get there?" I asked.

"Oh, Ivy—it's very tenth grade," she'd laughed. "But the truth is he's the first thing I think of when I wake up and the last thing I think of when I'm falling asleep, and when I look down the road at my future, he's right there. He's the center of everything...and I love him. I love him, awful—did you ever see *Moonstruck*?"

"I laughed. "Can I use that?" I said. "Because, if you replace Derek with...I don't know, someone else...it's kind of a big ditto."

Mia had giggled. Actually, she'd cackled. "Only if that someone is my mopey brother. *Please* come back and do something with him."

"Well, as a matter of fact," I'd told her. "I'm coming back next week with Camille, but please don't tell Bo," I'd said. "For some reason, I need him completely unprepared for me."

"Well, that sounds deliciously intriguing."

"Please, Mia."

"All right, I won't tell him," she'd promised.

And now, here I was. Was I ready? I hadn't realized the depth of my musings, or that we had nearly reached baggage claim, until I heard my name shouted. I surfaced and looked around and thought I was mistaken, but then a familiar face emerged from the crowd.

"Who's that?" Camille said as he hurried toward us.

I stifled a groan. "It's my dad," I said. Then to him, "Daniel, what are you doing here?"

His smile was big and forced and false. "I...I knew you were coming in, and I...I wanted to surprise you. Surprise, sweetheart."

"How did you..."

He cut me off as he introduced himself to Camille. Then he nodded. "So, do you need a ride?"

"Camille's mom is picking us up. What are you doing here?" I said again.

My father looked from me to Camille and back to me. "Ivy, can I give *you* a lift? I'd really like to talk to you. It's been a while."

I swallowed my annoyance. "Go meet your mom, Camille," I said. "I'll, um...I'll catch up with you later."

"You sure?"

"Yeah. It's fine."

She gave me a little hug and offered Daniel a tepid smile with her "Nice to meet you." Then she walked away, leaving me in the middle of the concourse with the last person on earth I wanted to be with right now.

"What's this really about, Daniel?" I said. "What are you doing?"

"Can't a father just—"

"No! No. What are you doing?"

He moved close and put his hands on my shoulders and looked as solemn as I had ever seen him. "I want to talk to you, Ivy. I want to explain myself. Can I buy you dinner? A drink?"

"No. I can't. I have to be someplace."

"I'll drive you, then."

"No." I blew out a breath. "We can talk here if you want. I guess you can buy me a Coke."

"That's ridiculous. Let me take you…wherever you're going." He took my arm and tugged, but I stayed put. "No, Daniel. I'm not going anywhere with you. If you want to talk to me, you can talk to me here. Then we can go our separate ways."

He eyed me with disapproval. Especially when I lifted my elbow out of his grasp. I didn't care.

"Ivy…"

"It's the best I can do, Daniel."

We walked in silence to the McDonald's at the end of the concourse. It was mostly deserted, so I found a table while my father ordered us some soft drinks. I'd been dreading this moment—even though *this moment* was supposed to take place at his office later, sometime before I went home, his office where I could leave when I'd said what I had to say, his office at a time of my choosing, when I was prepared. Every day since Bree had died, I'd thought of this conversation. I'd even thought to avoid it all together and just put my thoughts in a letter. But what I needed to tell him seemed to require something more adult. I ran my hands over my face and took a deep breath as Daniel set down our drinks.

After a moment of watching me, he placed his hand on mine and said, "How are you, Ivy?"

"I'm...I'm *fine*," I said, slipping my hand away.

"Good. I've been worried about you."

"I'm not sure I believe *that*, Daniel."

"Ivy, that's not fair. Are you still mad at me? Can't you understand the position I'm in?"

"I don't care. Look, Daniel, I don't want to fight. I...I was planning to talk to you later this week anyway."

"Then it looks like I've saved you a trip." He half-smiled. "What did you want to talk about?"

I took a breath and avoided his eyes. "I wanted to thank you for bringing me to Monterey. I know Bree pressured you to do that, and it was only supposed to be for a few days. But...you actually saved my life." I looked up at him. "Because of you, I met Mia. Do you remember that day—the day I met her? It was at the college; you walked a few steps ahead of me the whole time because you could not risk anyone seeing us together." Now I was locked on him.

"Ivy, it wasn't that—"

"It was exactly that, Daniel. It's why you're here now. Somehow, you heard I was coming to town, and you could not risk another surprise visit from me at your office. Not with your real daughter there walking around, taking such good care of you."

Now he was the one to drop his gaze. "I'm sorry about that, Ivy. I really am."

"Well, that might be. But if you are, I'm sure it has more to do with her than me." I shook my head. "It doesn't matter now. I just have to be finished with this; this *us* without Mama. That's what I wanted to tell you."

He looked up.

"Daniel, I know Bree was incidental to your life. I get that, even if she never did. I know that being with her involved careful planning, getting your lies straight, and covering your tracks. I know she was an escape from your regular life. I get all of that. But what you don't seem to get is...is...she was my *mom*, and she should have meant more to you. She should have been at least as important as you told her she was. But you lied to her, Daniel. You lied to her my entire life..."

"How dare you, Ivy," he said grappling for authority with his tone. "I will ask you to remember who you're talking to."

"I know exactly who I'm talking to. I'm talking to the man who lied and used my mama for almost twenty-three years. I'm talking to the man who has been lying to his real family for all that time, too. I'm talking to the man I'm saying goodbye to. Officially." I took a breath while that sunk in, and it felt strangely freeing. "I was planning to come to your office to say all this in a final, more formal way. But I guess this will have to do."

"Ivy, what are talking about?"

"I think you know." I stared at him for a long minute. "It's not my intention to be mean here, Daniel. I just need us to stop pretending there's anything between us when we both know there isn't.

"Ivy...you don't mean that."

Emotion filled my throat, but I swallowed it down. "I do. I need this to be over and done. The simple truth is my mother is dead, and I have no interest in a relationship with her married sometimes boyfriend who just happens to be my father."

Injury filled his eyes as he processed the apparent incredibleness of my words, never releasing my gaze. I didn't blink.

At length he cleared his throat. "Do you have any idea how hard this has been for me, Ivy?"

"I don't care how hard this has or has not been for you."

He seemed to shrink a little. "Whatever you may think," he said. "You need to know your mother was very important to me."

"No, she wasn't."

"That's *not* fair," he insisted, raising his voice a notch.

"Well, none of it was ever fair, Daniel."

My father stared at me, irritation creeping in around the edges of his eyes. "Are you trying to hurt me? Is that what this is about? Do you think I'm not hurt enough already? That I don't live with that hurt every single day?"

"I don't care," I said, again. "This isn't about you. This is about me—my life. And Mama."

"Ivy, that is not fair."

I stared at him. "Again, Daniel: It was *never* fair. Not to Mama, certainly not to me, and definitely not to your nice family. But none of that mattered to you."

His jaw hardened. "How dare you judge me? Or your mother? Our relationship was... special, albeit very complicated. And frankly, it was none of your business."

I lifted a brow, as I glared. "And yet, here I am. The poison fruit of that special...albeit so very *complicated* relationship. Well, I have news for you, *Dad*: That makes me the perfect judge. And I said the same thing to Mama."

He closed his mouth.

After a few beats of silence, I said, "She waited for you."

"What?"

"She did. Mama simply refused to die until you came. And she knew you would—she *knew* you loved her at least enough to be there. So, she hung on. In all that misery, she hung on. Her bones were shattered, she was bleedin' inside herself, she was delusional. At the end, she wasn't even Bree anymore," I said. "She was so broken and fevered. But she knew you'd come because your lies were so real to her. She knew you loved her. She waited to die until you came, and you finally did." I nodded and sniffed back emotion. "The doctor had white hair, and she thought he was you. He was kind enough to play along so Bree could let go knowing you hadn't let her down. But it was just another lie. A lie my mother clung to until the moment she died."

Daniel had long dropped his gaze, and I let him squirm. When he finally met my eyes again, his shame was so bare that I almost felt sorry for him. Almost.

"*You* are a lie, Dad," I said softly. "You and my mama were a lie. And that sort of makes me a lie. And some days that is exactly what I feel like. I'm working on that, but just so you know, that is a terrible...a wicked thing to do to a daughter."

"I...I'm sorry."

"Maybe you are, maybe you're not. I don't care, it doesn't matter anymore. It's over now. I think it just took Bree dying for me to figure out that sometimes you just land in the wrong life. And you have to somehow claw your way out before you can find the right one." I looked hard at him. "This is me clawing my way out, Daniel," I said. Then I pushed my chair back and stood up.

"Ivy..." he said with pleading in his eyes.

I shook my head. "We were always just strangers, anyway. Connected by someone I loved and you didn't. And now she's gone." I held his gaze for a beat. "I have to go now. I need to be somewhere. Goodbye, Daniel," I said.

Then I picked up my things and walked away.

Seventy-One—Bo

Christmas orders were starting to come in. Not many, as it was still just August, but most of my regulars knew that I tended to ignore any personalized requests that came in after September. I was just a one-man show, after all, so it was a good thing they were planning ahead—for them and me. These days, I needed plenty of lead time; I wasn't concentrating well at all.

It was Ivy. I couldn't stop thinking about her. And I'd made the mistake of sharing that with my aunt, who'd told me to quit obsessing and do something about it. Lullaby had called from her world-tour honeymoon last week to tell me Matisse had never seen Alaska, so they were taking a detour before they headed home. They were jumping on a nineteen-day cruise, she'd said. Jumping. On a cruise. So very Lullaby. But she'd taken the opportunity of our phone call to let me know she was thinking of investing in some retail property in Savannah, and that she would need someone she could trust to develop it. She said I immediately came to mind. Again, so very Lullaby. I didn't bite, though her suggestion made my pulse race. To get her off the phone, I'd told her I'd think about it without the slightest intention of thinking about it. Nothing had changed. I was still me, and Ivy was still three time zones away figuring that out—probably beyond grateful that I'd stopped her from saying something she couldn't mean but would feel compelled to stand by. And yet...here I was thinking the hell out of it, thinking, thinking, and more thinking about my thinking.

I groaned, loudly. It blows to be this neurotic.

My phone buzzed, and I glanced over at it, knowing Katrina Gearhart was texting me. Again. The soap opera producer had asked me to *consider* duplicating the custom designed snake choker I'd done for her earlier. She wanted one for each of the female leads for Christmas. Eight snake chokers. We were negotiating a price, and she was nickel and diming me to death, but I refused to go lower than $800 each, and that was already with simulated emeralds. I picked up my phone and read the text—*Bo, I'm having a hard time clearing this with the purse strings. Any chance you can do all 8 for 5000.00??*

I replied—According to my math 5000.00 will get you 6 and a couple of emeralds. I could almost hear her cursing me.

When my phone buzzed again almost immediately, I wanted to throw it and Katrina Gearhart against the wall. The text said *Do you still love me?* Which I thought was an odd question from the producer. I checked my cell to make sure it was working properly, and then I read the message again. It wasn't from the producer. I swallowed and typed. *Ivy...what???*

It's a simple question, Bo. Yes or no will do.

What r u doing?

Waiting for your answer.

I swallowed again, and it was harder this time—then I typed. *I love you so freaking much that I can't stop thinking about you, and you have no way of knowing this, but you keep me awake at night and ruin my concentration during the day. So, yes Ivy. Nothing has changed. I still love you.* What was wrong with me? Delete. Delete. Delete. *Yes. Yes, I do.*

I want to see u, Bo. R u busy?

What do you mean? Do you want me to come back to Georgia?

Would you do that?

Are you serious?

Yes, Bo. I have to see you. I have to tell you something important, and it has to be face-to-face.

My heart was pounding. What was she saying? My thumbs moved at warp speed. *Still a freak and can't fly, but if I leave tonight, I can make it by Sunday early.* I'd pushed send before the daunting task of driving across the country again hit me fully.

Really?

Yes! Daunting but doable.

How 'bout I meet you part way?

Was I hyperventilating? *That would be great, Ivy. Where?*

On your porch...

??? Yes. I was hyperventilating.

Bo. I'm on your porch.

I stood up from my worktable so fast that I knocked over a container of seed pearls, and the cloud of beads bounced in a clatter of tiny pings against the wood floor. They were everywhere, and I nearly tore myself in half trying to respond to these two urgencies. I immediately got down on my knees and scooped a shaking handful back into the dish but hardly made a dent in the bouncing puddle. Then I got up. What was I thinking? Ivy was at the door. *Ivy was at the door!* But then I was again on my knees, scooping, impotently. I groaned as more beads scattered with my efforts, fighting the need to see this through against knowing Ivy was waiting. I gave up on the mess and took the stairs two at a time, desperately compelled to turn back.

Upstairs I pulled open the front door, afraid I'd imagined the whole conversation, definitely not expecting she would actually be standing there. But she was, and she looked amazing. Ivy's thick hair was a little longer than that last time I'd seen her, and her eyes seemed bigger, more wizened somehow, maybe just open wider. She didn't smile; she just studied me with those eyes as my heart pounded against my ribs. She was wearing a long navy-blue dress, and it made her look taller, and I couldn't help but appreciate the way she wore it. "You're... beautiful." I finally managed, sounding stiffly polite.

"Am I? Thank you," she said back, also polite.

"Always."

"You're so sweet, Bo. How are you?"

My breath caught a little. "Honestly, I haven't been great since I came back."

"Why's that?"

"I think it's because...because I left Savannah when all I really wanted to do was stay."

She nodded and tears misted her eyes. "I've missed you, too, Bo."

"You have? Really?"

She nodded, and we moved closer, our eyes sort of diving into each other.

"Thanks for meeting me." She finally smiled.

I smiled, too. "Do you want to come in?"

"I need to say this first." She took my hands in hers, and as our fingers wove themselves together, I suddenly realized how much I'd ached for her touch—me, who would have recoiled had she been anyone else. She looked at me with her wide, clear, certain eyes and cleared her throat. "I love you, Bo," she said. "I do. And don't you be arguing with me about it. You are not allowed to doubt my feelings."

When her eyes filled with more tears, I knew she meant it, and I almost couldn't breathe.

"When you left," she continued, "you said I was dealing with too much, and I couldn't possibly love you. And it's true there is a lot of garbage in my life. Complicated grief. Humiliation. Disappointment—all that and probably more—so yes, I am dealing with a lot of nonsense. But I am not confused about the way I feel, and I'm a little mad that you almost made me doubt myself. You were wrong, Bo. I still know what love feels like. So, I'll just say it again. I love you, Bo Sutton."

Ivy probably thought I was having a stroke because I couldn't speak and I couldn't move, but I did squeeze her hand—hard, so she couldn't change her mind and let go.

She didn't. "It's gonna take me a bit to get used to Mama being gone," she said, stepping closer still. "But the other stuff, the Tim stuff, I'm kinda done with."

She was very in my personal space. And it was okay. It was so very okay.

"I divorced my dad," she said. "At the airport, just now."

I narrowed my gaze at her. "Are you all right?"

She nodded. "I'm an orphan. But I'm surprisingly all right."

"You know, neither one of them—Tim or your dad—deserved you," I whispered. And then my intelligence flooded back and caught up with my emotion. "I don't deserve you either, Ivy."

"What are you talking about?"

I sighed, wanting to stay right here in this awesome bubble, but it was impossible. "Ivy," I said. "I...I *appreciate* you loving me. I do. But nothing has changed. I'm still me, and loving me...well, that's just a lot to ask."

"Who's askin'? Nobody's askin'!" She shouted in her beautiful southern drawl. She yanked her hands free, and the look in her eye made my heart lurch. "And you *appreciate* me loving you? I don't want your appreciation, Bo. You said you loved me. I want to know that I'm safe inside that love, and I want you to know that you're safe inside mine. That's how this works. Now please tell me I haven't fallen for an idiot."

"I'm sorry! I just meant...Ivy, you deserve a man who doesn't drive himself—and everyone around him—crazy. You deserve someone intact, not someone who..." I groaned. "Someone who even now is preoccupied with one thousand seed pearls I spilled downstairs and the pressing need to clean them up. *That's* my world, Ivy. That's the world I live in. Why would anyone volunteer for that?"

She folded her arms, and I watched her agitation dissipate.

"It's a good question," she said, calmly. "And you might be right— I probably deserve that kind of man. He sounds perfect. But what would I do with perfect? I want honest, I want a man blind to my

Ivy in Stills - 367

backyard. I want a creative man, someone loyal. Someone who sees me in a book would be nice. I want a man who will make room for just me—not a bunch of other girls to compare me to, just me. I want a man who sees me and accepts me with all my junk and will even drive across the country to say he's sorry when he absolutely has nothing to be sorry for."

She took a breath and narrowed her eyes at me.

"I want a man who doesn't pretend to love me, doesn't feel obligated to love me, just loves me. I don't much care about his quirks as long as he's that guy. He can even be a little stupid. Like you. You're a little stupid if you think because you triple wash your strawberries, or vacuum at midnight, or line up your pills and socks like they're little soldiers, that you're somehow not worthy. I don't care about that stuff right now, Bo. But if it gets to me one day, I'll go shopping for an hour or a week and leave you to your desperate need to clean or count or organize. But I will always come back. That's what love is—deep breaths and little breaks from each other."

She sighed and looked hard at me.

I could not find my voice. And that only got harder when she put her hands on my chest.

"Bo, I just want someone who's real, someone I don't have to figure out. If I found that guy, I would definitely volunteer to move into his world because it would be a good world. Not perfect, but sort of excellent anyway because we'd make it that way. Now I'm going to ask you one more time, Bo Sutton—and I just want a one-word answer: Do you love me?"

I swallowed and almost couldn't push the words out. "God help you Ivy, I do," I rasped. "I adore you." A tear was running down her beautiful face, and without thinking, I rubbed it away with my thumb.

"I love you too, Bo," she said. "Now please tell me that will not be a problem."

As I looked at her, I couldn't fathom what was happening to me. I just knew I'd never imagined a moment like this, and all I could do was pull her roughly to me. "It will not be a problem," I said. Then I kissed Ivy Talbot like she belonged to me, like she had always belonged to me. And I knew I would kiss her for the rest of my life because in that kiss was everything: promise, patience, hope, every dream I'd ever dared to dream. We kissed like we were starving for each other, and when our breath took on the sound of marathon runners, Ivy pulled away to catch hers. She looked at me, a little surprised, then sort of panted, "Just so you know, Mister. I think I could get used to *that*."

I kissed her neck. "Well, good, because I think you're going to have to."

She sort of melted into me again. "Maybe we *should* go inside."

"Maybe we should," I agreed.

But we didn't move. We just held each other as close as was humanly possible while the night deepened around us.

"Sooooo..." Ivy said after a long silence. "You spilled some seed pearls, huh?"

I groaned, suddenly remembering. "When you said you were on my porch, I jumped up so fast, I knocked them over. They're everywhere, Ivy. Literally everywhere."

She lifted her head and brought my face close to hers. Then she kissed me softly and said, "Well, we'd better go clean 'em up, then, so we can get on with more important things. Like dinner...and stuff."

I looked at her and wanted to cry. "Good lord, woman. Do you have any idea what that means to me?"

She grinned. "I think I do, sweet pea."

Seventy-Two—Ivy

I wasn't one bit nervous because my custom designed dress fit perfectly over my custom designed pre-Tim body. The makeover I'd gotten with the bridesmaids had left me with a movie star glow, and my shoes—which were to die for, thanks to Mia and Gisselle's—brought me to a statuesque 5 foot 5. All in all, I'd cleaned up good, as Geneva would say, and I wasn't nervous at all. Nope, I was giddy on this New Year's Eve because if anyone was ready to bury the last year, it was me. When the organist finally started to play the intro to the wedding march, I squared my shoulders and waited for my cue—which was delayed because Olivia got a good look at the packed chapel. Camille had no choice but to sweep her little one up and take hold of Scout's hand. Then the adorable flower girls made their way slowly down the aisle accompanied by the striking matron of honor, their mama.

Up ahead, the groom was magazine-cover gorgeous, tall and chiseled and boyishly anxious, which seemed incongruent with his recent history and the medals he currently wore on his chest. I'd met Derek Lehman last night at the rehearsal dinner for the first time, and I was an instant fan. He was humble and kind and clearly adored my friend. And when Mia had introduced us, he'd picked me up like I was a child and dang near squeezed the life out of me. "I hear you and me belong to the same club: in love with Suttons." He'd said this into my ear, and I laughed and cried at the same time. "It's a good club!" I told him. Now he caught my eye, and I could not keep the grin off my face. He may have appeared imposing in his dress blues, but at the moment, he was like any other groom, excitedly anticipating the biggest moment of his life.

I took my place on the podium and turned to face the congregants. Everyone was standing as Mia and her father made their way up the aisle. Mia was exquisite in her form-fitting cap-sleeve gown covered in antique lace. Her hair was beautifully gathered at the base of her neck, and she wore a bejeweled headband fashioned, of course, by her brother. Diamonds were at her ears and her throat. She smiled as she took in her wedding party: her best friends, who'd brought her a vintage garter they'd found in Lisbon—reportedly once worn by a princess; her sister, who had continued to bloom back into herself since her uncontested divorce had been finalized; and me. Mia's smile was tender as our eyes met. It seemed a lifetime ago that she'd rescued me. Because of her, my life had been transformed, and she had a friend in me for life.

When Mia got to Derek's side, she broke tradition and stood on tip toes to peck his cheek. Mia was tall, but Derek was taller, and the gesture brought tears to his eyes. Mine, too.

It was impossible to stand here and not relive my own wedding—but the sting of that memory was long gone. In its place was relief and gratitude because if not for Timothy's fickle heart and fickler nether regions, I wouldn't be here. I wouldn't be in love with Bo Sutton and Bo wouldn't be in love with me. And I definitely wouldn't be wearing this Victorian poison ring on my finger. Now I fought the urge to let go of my flowers and glance down at it. Instead I ran my thumb over it. It wasn't exactly an engagement ring because our relationship was so new. Instead, we called it a promise, a place-keeper, but we knew what it was. We knew exactly what it was.

When Bo had given it to me on Christmas night, he'd explained that a poison ring opens up to reveal a secret compartment under the stone. Historically it held poison that could surreptitiously be poured into the drink of someone unsuspecting but undoubtedly deserving. He had pressed the tiny button on mine that lifted the Lapis Lazuli—the stone of truth, which he had chosen for its deeper meaning. In the hidden well was a single seed pearl. He'd kissed me then and said the tiny bead represented the truth of who he was, and my wearing the ring would represent the truth of who I was. He then said the meaning of his very deliberate design represented the truth of who we were together. He didn't know it yet, but this *was* my engagement ring because I was never taking it off.

Now I caught Bo's eye and winked. His dark wavy hair was pushed back off his handsome face, and there was a two-day shadow over his jaw that I particularly loved. He was so cute I almost wanted to jump down and give him a big wet kiss. But of course, I didn't. Bo was still Bo, and I didn't think he'd appreciate my spontaneous display of slobbery affection. But then again, judging from the way he was looking at me, he might. I'd missed him so much. We'd been playing back and forth across the country for the last four months because it was Bo's busy season, and a move to Georgia would have disrupted his productivity. But next week, we were going back together driving a U-Haul packed to the gills with his life.

Lullaby and Geneva had come to an agreement about my mother's shop on the corner of Perry and Bull. Bo's aunt had written my grandmother a check for twelve months rent—after which I would inherit the property, along with its exorbitant tax bill. But by then *Sutton.* would be established in Savannah—and surely solvent, given Bo's ever-expanding clientele. I had spent the last two months readying the property for him. You could now officially eat off every surface of the studio, the renovated upstairs apartment, and the store front, which of course only meant it was clean enough now for Bo to don a HazMat suit and completely disinfect it once again with a toothbrush. I loved him, but Lullaby was right; he came with some stuff.

Bo's aunt was sitting next to Mia's mother, and I couldn't imagine my good fortune at having these two women in my life. Lullaby had saved me from drowning in self-pity, and Eileen Sutton had just quietly, without any fanfare whatsoever, put on the mantel of a mother. Her second-nature affection toward me had felt more maternal than anything I had ever known. And when I mistakenly thought I had earned that regard by simply loving her son, she'd scolded me. She said the fact that I loved Bo was the cherry on top of the blessing that I was in her life. Of course, I ate that up like a starving mongrel.

And then there was Jack Sutton who had sat me down on Christmas Eve and told me he'd always wanted another daughter and that if he was very lucky, he would get his wish the easy way. He then explained how much he loved his son—as if I didn't already know. He told me that when you're a serious parent, all you really want for your kids is their happiness. And your deepest fearful heartache is that they may never achieve it. He'd cried then and called me sweetheart and laughingly said, through his tears, "No pressure, Ivy—marry him or don't. I will still love you." I'd hugged him and said, "Me too." He must have felt my stare now because he met my eyes and smiled with such warmth, it made me cry.

Next to him was my sweet grandmother snuggling Olivia. Geneva, looking every inch the grand dame in deep maroon, winked at me. The Suttons had extended their open family border to her, and she had graciously accepted their loving invitation. Even better, she and Lullaby were certain they'd been sisters in another realm. It made me smile.

Suddenly there was some serious kissing going on in front of the lectern, and I couldn't believe that in my reverie, I had missed the vows. But in watching the happy, tearful, giggling Mia devour her Marine, I got the gist. It was a joyful moment—one that would last ten days until Derek had to leave again for parts unknown. But nobody was thinking about that right now.

Soon the wedding party bled off the dais, and the chapel began to empty. Next stop, Carmel, and a reception dinner for two hundred. Limos and town cars were lined up at the curb and the evening promised to be spectacular. In a moment, I was swallowed up by my Bo. *My Bo.* He pulled me into his arms, and it felt like home. Over his shoulder, Lullaby gave me the thumbs up with a laughing smile, and I gave her one back. I would love that woman forever. I was pretty sure I would love them all forever.

"So, what do you think?" Bo said. "Next time, us?"

"Maybe. But not here," I said. "I was thinking on a beach somewhere."

"With sand?" he said aghast.

"Yes. And barefoot. Maybe Bermuda...or Maui, the breeze blowing through my dress."

"Barefoot, as in no barrier between the sand that birds have used as a toilet and nearly naked humanity has...you know—*that* sand and *my* feet?"

We were nose to chin because of my heels, and I stared up at him and didn't crack a smile. Until I did. "I'm kiddin', butterbean," I grinned. "I know how important your footwear is."

"I knew that."

"Of course, you did."

"I love you," he said.

"I love you back," I said. "And if we get married, I want to do it in Geneva's parlor."

"If?" Bo said pointedly.

I smiled coyly. "When."

He smiled too. "Geneva's parlor. That would be nice."

"What about my parlor?" Geneva said, walking up to us.

"Nothing," I told her. "Just talking about weddings."

She eyed us shrewdly. "Do tell, my little sugar plums."

Bo and I just smiled.

"Hey, are you two riding with us, or are you walking to Carmel?" Bo's dad shouted, and we were saved.

"We're coming," Bo shouted back. Then he kissed me quick and took my hand.

As I walked out of the church on that glorious New Years' Eve, holding the hand I was pretty sure I was destined to hold for the rest of my life, I couldn't help but laugh. I laughed because I suddenly realized I had survived the worst year of my life—*my year of ashes*. And I also knew with certainty that for the chance to be right here, right now, living this moment, I'd go through it all again.

Oh, yes, I absolutely would.

THE END

Acknowledgements

Thank you to my Mark. I love him. I love him. After all these years, I love him.

To the best beta readers on the planet: Hilary Bawden, Whitney Thompson, Abby Graham, Carol Warburton, LouAnn Anderson, Dorothy Keddington. Amy Hoggard, Allie Bingham, Samatha Palmer, Joyce Lloyd, Misty Perry, Heather Brooks, Stephanie Bott.

And of course, to Emily Poole, editor extraordinaire.

To my small but essential writing group—sisters, critics, cheerleaders and expert wordsmiths each! Dorothy, LouAnn and Carol—Thank you simply does not cover it! You are my heart.

Also by Ka Hancock

Dancing on Broken Glass

The Duzy House of Mourning

Reader's Discussion Guide

IVY IN STILLS

1—In the beginning scenes of the book, Ivy Talbot is minutes from 'settling' for Tim Marsh. Given what we know of her life, upbringing, and personality, why might she feel this is a viable life choice for her?

2—Bree Talbot is a beautiful, talented, successful artist, she owns a thriving business, she teaches, she has style. What would possess a woman like this to carry on with a married man—believe his promises—for over two decades? Discuss Bree's influence on Ivy. As a mother. As a woman. As an example of worth.

3—What are your thoughts about Daniel Proctor? Describe the way he sees his relationship with Bree. How does Bree see it? Now describe it as experienced through Ivy's eyes.

4—Geneva is a woman of sorrows and eccentricities. What life lessons do you think Ivy learned from her about love?

5—Meanwhile in Monterey: During the initial interchange between Mia Sutton and Daniel Proctor, who had the most power, and how was it established? Why was Mia not intimidated by him?

6—Why do you think Mia and Ivy became such fast friends?

'

7—Bo Sutton is a highly anxious man. Order and routine keep his world manageable. So when he is informed that Mia has offered up the pool house and a stranger will be roaming among them for the summer, he reacts poorly. How is Ivy able to ease past those barriers, how do they establish a friendship?

8—Discuss what Ivy learns about Bree and Daniel on the girl's trip to Carmel. Describe the dynamic between mother and daughter. Would you consider Bree emotionally abusive? Petty? Defensive? What was her intent in writing Ivy the letter?

9—Meanwhile back in Monterey: When it's decided that Camille and her children will accompany Geneva and Bree back to Savannah the Suttons and the Talbots become families intertwined. Why do we trust Geneva's sincere offer to protect Camille?

10—When Ivy comes face to face with Daniel's other daughter, and the happy portrait of his *real* family, the truth of her own life becomes suddenly, painfully clear. When he refuses to come back to Savannah with her to see Bree, it breaks her heart—for her deluded mother. She holds all his secrets on the tip of her tongue. But Ivy walks out without saying anything to her 'sister'. Would you have done the same?

11—Describe Bo's cross-country liberation. What was the purpose of 3 bottles of Xanax. Where and how did he gain the strength and determination to keep driving?

12—Describe Lullaby Sutton. How did this character have such a profound effect on Ivy? On Mia and Bo? On Camille?

13—Geneva calls this painful time: a *Year of Ashes*. For Ivy, it was a year of loss and discovery, change and new beginnings. One profound decision Ivy makes by the end of the book is to sever ties with her father. If you were in Ivy's shoes, would you have regrets about that? Or would you find it liberating? Or would it simply be facing the truth of never really having a father in the first place?

14—What was your favorite scene?

15—Bonus question: Have you read Precious Bane yet?